I FELL
IN LOVE
WITH
AN
ALEUTIAN
VAMPIRE

I Fell in Love with an Aleutian Vampire

The World War II in Adak Commemorative Edition

Quinn Robert Haber

Based on the War Report of Lieutenant Jake Harper

For Asia Blossom and Ocean Blue

Taatax̂ loves you
Eternally

[*taatax̂ —Aleut for "father"]

Adak Memorial marking the site of the island's cemetery. All the bodies were eventually transferred to the lower 48 states. (Photo by the author)

Send danger from the east unto the west, so
honor cross it from the north to south.

—William Shakespeare, *King Henry IV*

Contents

(AP Wirephoto map, 1965)

Foreword

THE WAR in the Aleutians was bloody and bloody cold. Before World War II, the US Navy tried to maintain a modicum of surveillance offshore of Alaska, daring to venture further west into the tempestuous waterways that bedevil the far North Pacific. After the United States had purchased Alaska from the Russian Empire in 1867 for $7.2 million dollars, the U.S. Navy formally moved into the Aleutian Island chain in 1888, deploying several gunships to monitor the movements of Canadian and Japanese sealing vessels active around Unalaska Island. The United States regarded these foreign fishing fleets as threats to its domestic sealing zone—an area that extends sixty miles outward from land and which was guaranteed in the Alaska Purchase. In those days, the British Imperial Government was still in charge of Canada's foreign affairs, and it wasn't until 1891 that an accord was reached between the United States and Great Britain regarding the fishing dominion further beyond "the zone," allowing the British (and, by extension, the Canadians) to continue sealing in the North Pacific and Bering Sea beyond America's offshore jurisdiction. In order to enforce the new deal, numerous American and British Naval vessels remained in Unalaska to protect their mutual interests.

Dutch Harbor, Unalaska in the early 1900s (Exclusive photo)

Back in Washington, military pundits were increasingly theorizing how an ever-more aggressive Japan might launch an attack on the United States, with a 1911 report from the Naval War Board considering a Japanese assault on the Aleutian island chain as one possible scenario. But further analysis of the area's highly prohibitive weather prompted the board to discard that as an unlikely if not impossible outcome. After all, the U.S. Army had long since passed the duty of patrolling that bleak storm corridor onto the U.S. Navy, who remained there only minimally, showing no interest in exploring further west along the chain because of the perilous seas and weather. As for air bases, a plethora of U.S. government committees decided in the 1930s that these too would be impractical on account of the area's ultraviolent atmospheric conditions. Thus by all pre-Pentagon accounts, the Aleutian Islands existed within their own wall of natural armor, barely penetrable by either side militarily due to thunderously blinding storms and gunmetal grey fogs. Then the first bombs fell.

TWO JAP AIR RAIDS ON ALASKA IN SIX HOURS!

San Francisco Examiner 6AM—EXTRA

Monarch of the Dailies

VOL. CLXXVI. NO. 155 — CCCC ★ ● SAN FRANCISCO, THURSDAY, JUNE 4, 1942 DAILY 5 CENTS. SUNDAY 12 CENTS

Bremen Raided by RAF; 4th Night Of Mass Attacks

Plan Blitz by 2,000 Planes At a Time

STRATEGIC OUTPOST WHERE ENEMY BOMBS FELL

Planes Bomb DutchHarbor Naval Base

Entire Pacific Coast on Alert; Further Thrusts by Nippon Awaited

By EDWIN STOUT

Axis Supply Line Periled

KeepEyesOpen for Japs in Uniform!

4 Gallon Weekly Gas Ration for Nation Hinted

Brief Alert in S.F.; Radio Silenced

First Blow Made at 6 A. M.

Permanent Control Plan in East; Unlimited 'X' Cards Banned

Jap Subs Sink Ship East of Australia

French Coast Raided By British Commandos

L. A. Civil Defenses On Emergency Alert

Planes Believed From Carrier

Important Notice

The Imperial Japanese started the horrid engagement on June 3, 1942, by bombing Dutch Harbor, taking out the town's radio station and some oil storage tanks, and making a direct hit on barracks 864 and 866 of Fort Mears, killing twenty-six enlisted servicemen. The squadron of deadly aircraft, their

xiii

fuselages and wings emblazoned with the dreaded red dots, returned the very next day to target an aircraft hangar, some grounded planes, the military base's hospital, several merchant ships, and a barracks ship anchored at bay, killing sixteen more servicemen and a civilian, and wounding a total of sixty-four Americans in the two-day blitz.

Dutch Harbor bombed, 1942 (Repro-photo from Lt. Harper's file)

The Japanese summarily occupied Attu Island—the United States' westernmost territory, just 2,000 miles from Tokyo—and several other U.S. islands along the far western Aleutian chain. There they built airstrips and submarine bases, amassed ground forces, and dug in behind a continuous curtain of east-ward moving sleet, the "williwaws," laying plans to leapfrog with it over the Aleutians and into America proper. This would be Phase 4, the final phase of *The Tanaka Memorial*, formulated in

1927 by then Japanese foreign minister Baron Tanaka. Phase 4 was no less than "the Conquest of the United States." So the war for the Aleutians began.

Baron Tanaka, 26th Prime Minister of Japan and author of The Tanaka Memorial, *is seated at left of photo. At center is Cabinet Minister Takejiro Tokonami, while at right is Premier Reijiro Wakatsuki. (AP photo, 1927)*

The yearlong battle for this northern corridor separating Japan from the United States would claim 4,350 Japanese lives and 1,481 Allies, with many more returning home with deep physical and psychological wounds begot from waging war in one of the most hostile environments on the planet. Foot soldiers commonly lost their feet to frostbite, while more pilots died due to the foul weather than they did to enemy fire. Planes frequently became lost in the pea-soup fog, crashing blindly into lofty volcano walls or disappearing forever into the chilling frost. A total of 225 Allied aircraft were confirmed destroyed, sixty-three due to bad weather alone, while 640 planes went missing.

The Aleutian Campaign would be waged here, in one of the most hostile environments on the planet. US troops resemble a line of marching ants amid the monstrous peaks and ice floes of Attu, where they would be forced to do battle against the Imperial Japanese, who had gained a formidable foothold there on American soil. (US Army Archives photo, May 1943)

Yet, for one serviceman, Lieutenant Jake Harper, fate had an entirely different plan in store, presenting him with a trial that would turn the very tide of the "Forgotten War." This account stems from his diary, presenting us with an icy, hostile, remote, yet beautiful frontier at the furthest reaches of the North Pacific. In the throes of his own survival, Lieutenant Harper's desire for victory would find true clarity and this, coupled with a powerful indigenous force, would bring upon the enemy its own order of ferocious storm.

*Additional exclusive photos of the bombing of Fort Mears and the
bayfront of Dutch Harbor (From Lt. Harper's file, 1942)*

In commemoration of Adak Island's central and pivotal role in the Aleutian Campaign, and in honor of the military personnel and those who made the ultimate sacrifice defending it and the United States from foreign annexation, I am proud to present this beautifully graphic edition of a gripping wartime chronicle.

Quinn Robert Haber, Chief Editor and Photographs Archivist*
Adak Island, 2020

[*Editor's notes, including most language translations and conversions of weights and measures, shall appear in square brackets [. . .] throughout the book, while rounded brackets (. . .) and the information therein are directly from Lieutenant Harper's original text, and also shall be used in referencing the illustrations.]

CHAPTER I
INTO THE WILLIWAW

DWELLING ON ICE

COLD, DARK, the Aleutians are. Winter nights last for twenty hours, while the common weather, even in summer, is storm and fog. It was in this blighted place that, in 1942, I served alongside the 807th Aviation Engineering Battalion of the US Army. Adak Island was my post, 1,200 miles southwest of Anchorage, or about halfway out along the Aleutian chain.

Wintry winds hamper Seabees work only a little at a base in the Aleutian Islands, where a bulldozer levels the final section of a two mile spur road joining a main road. (AP photo and caption, 1942)

To help build Adak's airbase, I assisted in the construction of a runway composed of two million snap-together steel girders called Marsden matting. Under the command of Colonel Benjamin Talley, 260 of us worked on that hell project; hell because of the ridiculous weather, and hell because every large earth-moving vehicle would sink into the mud like bricks in quicksand.

Seabees fight Aleutian mud. When it is not snowing and freezing, soldiers and sailors in the Aleutians have mud conditions such as this to contend with. (AP photo and caption, 1943)

The airfield was built on a lagoon, which first had to be drained by the battalion, leaving a soggy bed of muck almost like a peat bog. Resorting to the lifting of 1,500,000 square feet of steel girders by hand, we trudged out onto the bog bed, sinking up to our knees in our muck boots. But, in working around the clock, we managed to finish the runway in an impressive thirty-six hours flat. Given the Japanese occupation of U.S. islands further west, and periodic harassment by their bombers, we knew that timeliness was critical in our counteroffensive. The entire airfield from start to finish, including draining the lagoon, took just ten days and eleven nights, reaching its completion on September 30, 1942.

They build the road to Tokyo—tractors and grading machines grind out intricate patterns in the stubborn, icy soil of Adak as Seabee units construct bases on Alaskan strongpoints. From the frozen islands of the North Pacific to the torrid land "Down Under," the talented, tireless Seabees of the US Navy are building the road to Tokyo. Stubbornly fighting heat and jungle pestilence in the tropics, and severe cold in the Aleutians, the men of the Construction Battalions will celebrate the second anniversary of their founding—and their second year of war work—on Tuesday, December 28, 1943. (Dept. of US Navy photo and caption, December 26, 1943)

The airstrip was codenamed A-2, or "Longview." The 807th was the same battalion that had constructed the Panama Canal and here, in the outermost reaches of Alaska, their ingenuity—and airstrip—proved sound. The Marsden matting held up surprisingly well in the sodden conditions, with hundreds of flights a day taking off or touching down, flying bombing sorties to nearby Kiska, 220 miles to the west, or delivering supplies from as far south as San Francisco. Heavy B17 and B24 bombers made up the bulk of air traffic, along with their fighter escorts, Curtiss P40D Warhawks.

US Navy Construction Battalion—Seabees—work through a mile-a-minute gale at this Aleutian base, laying down strips of Marsden matting that will eventually compose a runway capable of heavy bomber operations. (Navy photo from ACME, 1944)

When the heavy bombers landed on the steel apron, which was usually pooling with rainwater, at military speed of 165 miles per hour, it was like watching seaplanes landing. Wakes shot up from the landing gear like sprung fire hydrants, striking the undersides of the wings and abruptly slowing the planes down. But this was a blessing not long in disguise, for on the handful of dry days we experienced that first October, several planes overshot the runway and crashed into the deep muskeg beyond.

Muskeg! Never have I seen such a plant. A mass of intertwining vines three feet in depth, the tenacious, surface-hugging roots stretched across the rocks, gullies, streams, and bogs like a King Kong's weed. There were sinkholes in the muskeg that could swallow an entire jeep. If a man were to fall into one and nobody saw it happen, his voice would be drowned out by the dense ceiling of vines, while the slippery, convex way in which those caverns were shaped precluded any chance of his escape by hand. Death by exposure would likely come before death by starvation, for in the Aleutians, cold and dampness prevailed. I soon learned to carry a rope and grappling iron whenever I ventured out alone, which happened with increasing frequency once the runway was completed.

Those goddamned Aleutians! If it's not the weather or the sinkholes, it's the sodden muck! In this exclusive photo captured by Lieutenant Harper during the Aleutian campaign, several tractors are seen attempting to pull a heavy cannon up through a thick bed of sodden topsoil that characterizes much of the archipelago's lower elevations. (Lt. Harper exclusive, Adak Island, 1942)

As mentioned previously, I worked *alongside* the 807th Aviation Engineering Battalion, helping them build the airstrip. This had been my first assignment, but afterward I volunteered for the Army Service Forces (ASF) on Rommel spike reconnaissance.

Rommel spikes were sharpened rods, straight or spiraled, driven into the ground to halt the advance of foot soldiers. They were developed at the onset of World War II by General Erwin Rommel, a decorated German field marshal. These anti-personnel stakes weren't much different than sinkholes in their ability to kill a man slowly, only they killed far more painfully: jutting up out of the muskeg anywhere from a few inches to several feet, a Rommel spike, if stepped on, could pierce clean through a man's foot or corkscrew up through his leg. That's why they were also called screw pickets. The pain of such an occurrence would often cause the victim to fall onto other spikes typically surrounding the area, reducing his chances of survival even more.

The Japanese had visited Adak on a covert airfield reconnaissance mission and, as they departed, they planted Rommel spikes by the thousands, the exact placement of which was not always predictable. Trying to find the life-threatening stakes before they found me proved extremely stressful. While walking off the base, I'd gotten into the habit of keeping one eye a few paces preceding me while carefully surveying each step before me with the other eye. It was the lowest spike heads, the ones that rose but a few inches above the muskeg, that I was most cautious of, given the difficulty in spotting them. A four inch Rommel spike could puncture clean through my gummies [tundra boots], including my foot. Removing the spikes from the ground proved easy in comparison to actually finding them, storm force winds notwithstanding.

Almost three months into my Rommel stake extraction mission, I'd logged a personally impressive but overall insignificant 324 successes, finding and removing an average of three to four spikes per day.

As winter set in, my task became much more difficult but, ironically, far less stressful. With a thick groundcover of snow, the smaller, more insidious spikes were well-covered over by the ice pack and out of harm's way, while the larger ones, rising a few feet above the surface, became easier to spot against the white backdrop (as opposed to blending into the high grasses of autumn). The difficulty was in trying to remove them from the solid icepack, and also, because more were covered by snow than not, my recons took me increasingly deeper into the wilderness to find them. While bears were not a worry on Adak (because bears are nonexistent in the western Aleutians), the weather proved a most formidable foe on almost a daily basis.

Captain Heizer on way to supper. He is standing still and leaning against the wind. We have had worse winds. This one was estimated at 40–45 mph. (Exclusive photo and caption by Lt. Harper, Adak Island, 1943)

WHITEOUT

IT WAS on the blighted afternoon of December 7, 1942, that I found myself trudging through falling snow approximately eight miles out from Kuluk Bay (native Aleut spelling: *Kuhluk*), where the airstrip and the bulk of my unit, the ASF, were garrisoned. My terminus would be Boot Bay, located on the Pacific side of Adak Island about twenty miles south-southeast from Kuluk through open wilderness. A crack unit of Allied combat intelligence scouts who'd made the initial August 28 landing on Adak in conjunction with soldiers from the Alaska Defense Command reported to Commander Buckner that the Boot Bay route was one of the corridors used by the Japs in their retreat from the island. Thus I was tasked by the commander's underlings to investigate further, for the Japs had ostensibly booby trapped the area with an abundance of Rommel spikes and screw pickets, which would prove as further evidence and also would need to be removed for the safety of our own troops amassing on-island. High brass was still trying to gauge the full extent of the Jap contention in the Aleutians: their bases, numbers, equipment, hideouts, and supply routes. Significantly, Allied scouts had also discovered numerous test holes along the southern Adak stretch, on plains where the Japanese had explored possible sites to build an airfield of their own.

The weather had been crystal-clear the morning I set out into the interior. But if there was one thing about the Aleutians, the weather never held up for long, and soon I found myself ankle-deep in snow and thinking of turning back. While I had the gear and provisions necessary to proceed through passing snow-storms, I was wary of the williwaw—a terrible downdraft, which could occur unexpectedly, making for whiteout conditions. I'd spent a few nights out in such a blizzard before, and suffice it to say, it would put a major damper on my search for Rommel spikes. Had I not had a radiophone with me at all times, connecting me to the base at Kuluk Bay, I wouldn't have ventured out alone in winter at all—the volatile climate made it too risky.

Lieutenant Jake Harper with full camping pack checks his radiophone at Longview before heading out on foot into the tundra. (Exclusive image from Lt. Harper's private collection of his tour of duty at Adak Island and the Aleutian theater, dating 1942–1943)

Being temporarily stranded was only operational with my radiophone lifeline, should the setback prove too difficult to overcome on my own. I'd been retrieved by a rescue party once before, who came with cramp-box assist [a small-scale snow tank]. It'd become common for guys on wilderness missions such as mine to call for outside help from time to time, but was not something to be particularly boastful of.

I was seconds away from an about-face back to Longview when a large antipersonnel stake appeared on my periphery. I'd almost missed it because of its spiraling shape, which in the falling snow made it less obvious to distinguish. I was under no obligation by duty to get it, but it seemed like an easy extraction, and would serve as quite a visual: my Boot Bay trophy to showcase at base.

Lieutenant Jake Harper, far left, with fellow enlisted servicemen of the 807th Engineering Battalion on Adak, pose behind a giant whalebone they discovered high up on a beach there. (Exclusive photo, 1942–1943)

I set my gear beside the rusting screw picket and began digging a hole around it in the snow. I would need to get at least down to the muskeg in order to cut it short beneath the viny surface so that its remnant spike wouldn't be a future hazard (I rarely pulled an entire stake of this size and shape up from the ground, due to the difficulty in extracting it and unwieldiness in transporting it by shoulder pack).

This particular picket took a bit of additional effort to extract, because with the snow falling on my back, I had to keep shoveling the powder back out of the hole. Finally, I attained to the muskeg undergrowth, but when I reached for my steel saw, I felt only a bed of snow.

Alas, I stood to find myself being blasted by whiteout conditions and shin-deep in fresh powder. Realizing I'd have to take shelter until the blizzard blew over, I hurriedly began shoveling out a footprint [a secure demarcation] for my tent. I gained almost two feet of depth before I felt the tent could sensibly withstand the wind. I dug four more holes adjacent to each corner, tying the tent's anchor ropes to the muskeg beneath, then climbed in beneath the canopy and propped up the center post.

The wind was now screaming outside, literally screaming like a banshee, and while the tent wobbled something fierce, it always pushed back from collapsing.

I made quick work of my propane stove and soon had a can of beans bubbling in a pan before me, warning my hands all the while. The boys back at Kuluk would be a trifle worried about me, but would know I was sufficiently equipped for the weather and that I would establish radio contact should I run into any real trouble, which this was not.

It wasn't long until I was snuggled up in my sleeping bag, my three layers of long johns helping to keep me warm. Falling asleep by the howl of the williwaw as it ripped at my tent was something I'd grown used to, unfortunately.

What wakes a man up in the Aleutians is not the sound of storm, but an absence of wind—that's how much of a rarity it is. But then suddenly, my ears smarted on a noise and my eyes opened wide in curiosity. It would've been preferable to brush it off as an arctic fox foraging around for food, because they rarely grew more than knee high and were generally skittish creatures. But the sound of rustling through fresh snow was too heavy and measured to be wild, which meant it could only be a man, because aside from reindeer, the western Aleutians were as yet devoid of large animals.

The all-important question that my life depended on was whether the person or persons outside were American, Canadian, or Japanese. If an Allied rescue party had been sent for me, that would mean a fresh cigar for breakfast, but if those were Japs on the prowl, I'd likely eat a sword instead.

The sun was just rising, imbuing the canvas of my tent with a greyish olivine glow. I trained my pistol on the tent flaps before me, acutely aware of every shadow and sound.

The report of footsteps scrunching through the snow drew nigh. It sounded like one person only. My suspicion of Japs was heightened, however, because if a search party had been sent for me, there would've been more soldiers or the grind of a cramp-box. I was due south of Scabbard Bay, which was some distance away from the Allied base at Longview, and so my rescue so swiftly—and at my own lack of signaling—was extremely unlikely.

The intruder approached the side of my tent, his shadow in the gaining light now becoming discernable. I aimed my pistol at the figure, preparing to blast him, but in leaning back, I pushed into the tent's center post, causing the shelter to list. The intruder took off running.

"Damned Jap," I uttered under my breath. I quickly dressed, holstered my pistol and untied the tent flaps. An enemy spy on the island—an island that the US forces had ostensibly cleared—would be a major risk to our operations at Kuluk Bay, from where we ran daily bombing sorties against Jap positions holed up on neighboring islands.

As I sprung from my tent, my knees pushed into two feet of fresh powder; but I just caught sight of the enemy as he retreated over a misty berm. I surmised he must've been wearing snowshoes that allowed him to flee so quickly, but then I saw his footsteps: he was of such slight bearing that he'd scarcely sunk into the snowdrift. It could only have been a sprightly and furtive spy, one who could navigate the terrain quickly.

Upon attaining to the berm's crest, I glimpsed the imposter again, this time descending into a ravine, the beige color of his impermeable khakis evincing the uniform of the Japs. Had I only skis or a sled, I could've swooped down on him in an instant, but, as it were, my pursuit was greatly slowed by the deep snow, while additional precaution was required in tracking him through the narrow ravine.

Tracking the enemy. "Winds that have a velocity of 100-miles-per hour, squalls, and fog as thick as clam-chowder are a few natural enemies combated by American soldiers based on the island chain." (Navy photo and caption from Adak, passed by censors, ACME ref#4-3043)

With all the blind spots the narrow canyon held, rushing ahead could've invited my easy ambush. But the tactical terrain proved a double-edged sword whose advantage could just as easily be made mine: if my target didn't know I was tracking him, I could shadow him back to his base. Should I find a greater retinue of enemy combatants there, I could radio their location back to Longview for an airstrike and then hightail it out of there before the big buzzards roared in to drop their eggs.

The fresh snowpack made the enemy easy to track. However, the sun was becoming more intermittent, denoting another band of bad weather already on the advance. I picked up my pace through the ravine, tracking directly over the footsteps of my predecessor.

The ravine continued to meander downhill for hundreds of yards and at times grew so narrow that I couldn't see beyond its extending corners; yet the Jap's footsteps were sure, inspiring me forward. Soon I heard the recurrent trilling of Aleutian sparrows, which, I knew from experience, meant I was nearing the ocean.

At last, emerging from the ravine, I beheld the south coast spreading out before me, and sure enough, the spy could be seen making his way toward a Quonset hut tucked into a finger bay. As he drew near the partially snowed-in shelter, two soldiers came out and communicated with him before they all proceeded back inside together.

With my target now determined, I procured my radiophone to call in an airstrike over Boot Bay, where the enemy's Quonset hut was situated. But when I went to call out, I got only static.

Fresh snowflakes began to fall, their crystalline forms peppering my face with a cold, ticklish sensation. I made haste to the nearest ridge. My radio signal still failed under heavy atmospherics, but now the reason was abundantly in evidence: my entire purview north, which encompassed Kuluk Bay, was a wall of storm. If this was to be anything like the cyclone that'd hit the night before, I knew I needed to find shelter fast. I memorized the position of the enemy Quonset and then diligently marched back through my footsteps toward my itinerant campsite. The tender snowflakes turned to a driving hail as the wind ratcheted up to thirty, forty, and then fifty knots per hour. Time was ever so coldly of the essence.

My trek northward slowed to a slog, hindered as I was by the onslaught of the williwaw. With each step, I sank knee deep into new snow, and the old footsteps I'd been using as a guide quickly disappeared before me. Then disaster struck.

A sharp pain ripped through the side of my leg. When I tried to get away from the afflicting source, it twisted and bit into the back of my calf like a venomous cobra.

I fell over and issued an uncontrollable scream, then bit my lip, fighting hard to shield my presence from the enemy cantonment. A screw picket, buried beneath the snow, had sliced into the side of my limb before piercing the upper back of my calf.

Pile of screw pickets as photographed behind Constantine Harbor on Amchitka Island (Photo by Battle of Britain International Ltd., London, undated)

I rolled to and fro, trying to weather the pain through my own silent hell as the snow continued to pile up over me. But this may've been my saving grace, because the ice slightly benumbed the injury. Finally I was able to tie off the wound with one of my undershirts, which I could get at only by removing my snow parka first.

I struggled to my feet. It was difficult to stand, let alone walk, and while I'd put my parka back on and buttoned it up to my chin, having had to remove it in the chill of the storm had sent a shiver into my bones that I was unable to relinquish. With my tent still a way off through the whiteout in an uncertain direction, the full severity of my predicament became apparent: I had neither shelter nor provisions to hunker down with, while surrendering to the enemy at Boot Bay was not an option.

In desperation, I tried my radiophone again, but was answered with the same slush of white noise—a cold, unintelligible static that fused with the screeching wind like a million steel shovels scraping at an icy grave.

I patted my pockets for anything of use, finding only my pistol. My expression grew cross and critical: I had to come to terms with my predicament. While I imagined I was far from giving up, the fact was, I was in a blizzard in the middle of nowhere, injured badly, and hypothermia was probably not too far off. If it came right down to it—I knew without giving it too much focus—a quick bullet to the head would be my final option.

The paper! The map! I urged myself, realizing I'd patted more than just an instrument of my pending suicide. Indeed, within my chest pocket I still carried a map of the local topography, which included the locations of several survival barrels scattered across the tundra. In studying one that mustn't have been more than a few hundred meters from my present position, I knew that I had a fighting chance. If I could only make it through the blinding snowfall, I could ride out the storm in a survival barrel and then radio for help in clearer weather, or otherwise hobble back to my tent later, from where I might fortify myself with a fire, first aid kit, and provisions. But getting to the alternate shelter *now* was critical, and by keeping on moving I could keep my body temperature safely elevated. Based upon the direction I'd come, I made my best guesstimate—west-by-southwest—where the survival barrel was indicated, then forced myself through the ever-thickening powder.

The hope that the survival barrel might be equipped with a fire source and provisions drove me well beyond the point of common human endurance. Established not long after the onset of the Aleutian engagement, these steel barrel sections had been strategically placed throughout the archipelago to increase the chances of survival for downed US pilots, shipwrecked navy sailors, or foot soldiers such as I who might fall victim to sudden storm or battlefront defeat.

The williwaw ratcheted up to a blinding sixty knots plus. It would've pushed me over each of my agonizing steps had not the thick powder been propping me up at the knees. It was all I could do to keep moving forward in the direction in which I believed the survival barrel was located. My experience in the Aleutians on Rommel spike repossession had taught me two things above all else: stamina and resolve. On the most basic level, inner fortitude and force of will was all a man really had to go on, while prayer could go a long way as well. Hysteria and loss of vigor, on the other hand, were always readily available for the weak in spirit, and invited quick disaster.

I thought I perceived, on my periphery, a change in hue from the whiteout around me, so I set course in that direction. Would I come upon some beige rock face, coldly denying my last hope of survival?

Nay, the good Lord had been watching o'er me that day, for as I approached the object, its color solidified into a steady orange and its shape took on the form of a large cylinder lying in the snow.

"The barrel!" I exclaimed, struggling to hasten my pace before my lower extremities became numb with frostbite.

The cylinder's door was missing, allowing easy access. I pulled myself inside and lay down on the cold concrete floor. There were no boards within the concavity, no tarps—nothing from which to seal the door against the bone-chilling wind. I thought of building a wall of snow before it, but with my hands already numb with frostbite, I decided against it.

I pressed my shirt pocket and felt my lighter nudging against my chest. I looked around for something to burn, but the barrel was as barren as an empty tomb. The implications were heart-wrenching: while I'd made it to the bolt-hole, I had neither food nor fire, and without a door it could hardly be called a shelter. I began to shiver.

I burned my map in desperation, but the flames were short-lived, and as I held the last burning corner, I thought about removing another of my undershirts and torching it, as well; but, as with the map, I quickly realized such an action would only be a futile stopgap, leaving me even colder in the end.

In an attempt to offset hypothermia, I crawled to the rear of the barrel and sat up against the wall, then drew my hands within the cuffs of my parka and began to vigorously exercise my arms.

Hours later, with the blizzard still blasting away outside, my energy was utterly depleted. I lay slumped up against the cylinder wall, delirious and defeated.

I never fully appreciated what it meant to die. Intellectually I'd known, but to actually be dying was something entirely different. To be dying felt so lonely. I considered shooting myself to get it over with quickly, but as hypothermia set in, even this idea soon became muddy, my thinking process eventually slowing to a standstill. I could do naught but sit there, numb, immobile, devoid of all reason. At the mercy of the elements and succumbing to some abstract notion of God's will, I closed my eyes and awaited final peace.

ADRIFT

THE WIND was a cold whistle of death, as I drifted in a strange delirium . . . floating over deep snow banks, my fingers raked the powder as I passed.

I was being carried by a dark, shadowy figure. Had I been captured by the Japs? What man had such stature to hoist another over his shoulders and trudge through a monstrous blizzard thus? The enemy was not known for his brawn.

(Exclusive art by Ovidiu Kloska)

Perhaps a fellow GI had pulled me from the bolt-hole, only to carry me someplace else to die. My limbs were frozen stiff, and, as my forehead plowed into the ridge of another icy footstep left by my unknown pallbearer, the whiteout around me went black.

A smoky smell of burning seaweed and musk slowly seeped into my half-consciousness, rousing me from my delirium. The raw scents of sea, earth, and hearth evinced that I still belonged to the world of the living and not the dead. With a warm sensation upon my forehead, I opened my eyes to behold a khaki-skinned, dark-haired woman cleaning my face with a wet cloth. Her age appeared to be twenty-something; she had prominent, upturned lips and a tattooed chin. Her irises were black as coal, and when they caught the gleam of a nearby lantern, they shone gold in color in a way that seemed almost otherworldly. I tried to speak, but could barely move my frost-bitten lips.

Reading my prevarications, the mysterious young woman indicated for me to remain quiet as she continued administering her care. I was now certain that I'd been captured and was being revived by a nurse of the enemy forces before they meted out a final interrogation.

I reached for my pistol, but she got to it before me and tossed it into a darkened corner. My thought had been to shoot myself, ending what was sure to be a prolonged trial of tortures.

I tried to sit up, but was so weak that I could only lift my head. In observing the rest of my body, I discovered that I'd been stripped down to my underjohns, my leg bound in a makeshift cast. The splint appeared to be made of the bones of a sea mammal, while holding fast within it appeared to be a mossy poultice of sorts that pressed against my leg on all sides. Whatever the specifics of this apparatus, it seemed to be doing a decent enough job of stabilizing my leg, which I could now feel throbbing—a pain I considered a good thing, for it meant that sensation was returning to my badly afflicted limb. As for the rest of my body, I was wet but warm on account of a nearby iron stove, numerous stone lanterns, and the hot water the Japanese nurse was rubbing over me.

As she swabbed around my afflicted leg, her rag became red with blood. She appeared curious, even conflicted by the sight of it. On two separate occasions, she drew the bloodied cloth close to her eyes as if in wonderment, and then smelled it before extending it far off to the side, turning her face away as she squeezed it dry. I could only assume she was both fascinated and disgusted by the sight of an enemy combatant's blood; I knew how much the Japs had been brainwashed by their leaders into believing all sorts of superstitions about themselves and their enemies. Just as the rising sun represented their supposed status as heaven-sent conquerors of the world, to the Japanese, American soldiers were deemed as little more than soulless, materialistic, overindulgent monstrosities that would stop at nothing to torture them, their Imperial Forces and innocent civilians alike. No wonder, then, that my blood drew so much curiosity from the field nurse. Perhaps I was the first American she'd ever had direct contact with, outside of her state-sanctioned myths.

My initial assumption was that I'd been taken into the enemy's Quonset hut, the one that I'd observed earlier, nestled at the foot of Boot Bay. But in studying the ceiling and surrounds by lantern light, I became less sure. While the structure partook of a great bow arching over me like a Quonset hut, its walls appeared to be formed of muskeg, almost like the inside cavity of a giant sinkhole.

Of even greater curiosity, in addition to the nurse's tattooed chin, was a piercing beneath her lower lip fitted with a small bead labret, while numerous other piercings lined the edges of her ears. Another strange thing I noticed about her, besides her inordinately long thumbnails, was a hole driven through the septum of her nose at the columella—the fleshy wall that divides the nostrils.

Suddenly, a trapdoor in the rooftop flung open and chunks of snow fell in, breaking apart over a notched log ladder descending from the portal. The nurse regarded the door with a start, and shortly the dark figures of gear-laden men began climbing down through the hole.

I struggled to move, but the nurse held my hands fast to my chest while shaking her head, *no, no,* as if urging me to play dead. Unfortunately, due to my utter infirmity, I had little choice but to do just that. As the enemy combatants approached the woven reed cot upon which I lay, I closed my eyes and tried to conceal my breath.

The men exchanged terse words with the nurse in a strange sounding language that was not Japanese. And then she screamed.

I opened my eyes to discover they'd pushed her aside and were coming at me with primitive-looking spears, the tips of which appeared to be made of sharpened bone.

What transpired next in my half-conscious state I could not so clearly ascertain, but as I lay helplessly before these men about to execute me, the nurse darted up from behind them and threw them aside like a bird of prey tossing threats away from her nest. The next thing I knew, she was standing with her back to me while pointing two spears into the faces of the men she'd just seized them from, as they struggled to get up off the ground. They backed off and soon departed. This individual, who now seemed my savior, I suddenly recognized as the one who'd rescued me from the survival barrel. In that long walk through the icy tundra, I'd gotten to know every detail of her snow boots as she carried me over her shoulder. *But how could she have mustered such strength?*

"*Wha . . . what's your—*" I wanted to ask her name, but she covered my mouth with her hand, her roughhewn mitten smelling of leather and salt.

"Conserve thine energy," she said in archaic English. "Thou art still weak."

"*But . . .?*"

"Silence!" she admonished. "If thou wish to walk again, if thou wish to live, thou shalt remain quiet under my command."

This woman wasn't Japanese and couldn't have been from the lower forty-eight, for nobody in their right mind would move to Adak, especially during wartime—and nobody aside from play actors talked that way. Her dialect was old English and anachronistic. By her looks and primitive habits, however, I was now assuming her to be an Aleutian native who'd somehow evaded relocation to Sitka after the Japanese bombed Unalaska Island. At the onset of the Aleutian campaign, for their own safety, 881 Aleuts were forcefully moved from their island villages to former mining camps in southeastern Alaska. Thus, at risk of their being discovered and relocated should I try to escape, the tribe that had captured me would undoubtedly hold me prisoner, or worse. The regaining of my strength and faculties thus became my clear priority if I had any chance of making it back to Kuluk alive.

The "Aleut" woman, if I may, continued to tend to my leg with a poultice of warm, wet grass. For the time being, my fate was indeed in her hands. She procured a roughhewn bowl filled with crackling, smoldering weeds, and as she gently blew the smoke into my face, I at length fell asleep.

No safe place to bed down. Trouble was never far from Lieutenant Harper. The above two photos he took in 1942 show the SS Northwestern *docked at Dutch Harbor. Once an illustrious transport ship, it had been converted into barracks to house 280 civilians of Unalaska. The vessel was bombed by the Japanese on their June 4, 1942 raid, its forward port side struck and catching on fire. Miraculously, at the time of the bombing it was unoccupied, and only an infestation of rats was killed onboard in the subsequent three-day blaze. The Japanese reported in their state media, however, that they'd scored a "major hit" on a "US warship." (Exclusive photos by Lt. Harper, 1942)*

THE MEN DRESSED IN SEAL-GUT COATS

AT THE sound of gruff men arguing, I came again to myself. A man approached from a darkened corner and stood over me. He wore a rubbery parka that stunk of fish and his face was half shadowed over by a bentwood hat. His lips, framed by a scant white beard, held a stern expression. He extended several dirty fingers before my eyes, stretching my eyelids far back. "You, GI?" he asked.

I endeavored to speak, but my body was in a sort of stasis.

"Answer me!"

"He's mine!" riposted the Aleut woman, still standing on my other side. "I captured him!"

"You drugged him!" admonished the hale old man. "Why? You know the rules. He must die!"

Others gathered in the darkened corner rumbled in agreement.

"Don't touch the mortal!" my strange captor shot back, thrusting a pointed finger at the lot of them.

The mortal!? Who on earth were these people?

"Why do you protect this wight, Aniqdux̂six̂?" replied the bewhiskered inquisitor. "He was hunting us, planting Rommel spikes."

"You lie!" she hissed, bearing her teeth. *Her canines were fanged!* "It's his blood you seek!"

Another figure approached from the shadows and dropped a bundle of Rommel spikes onto my legs, crushing them painfully. I cringed in agony. "These are his!" he accused.

"He was removing them from the vicinity!" shot back this Aniqdux̂six̂, my fanged captor.

The bewhiskered elder, an arbiter of sorts, gazed up at the lantern light in a moment of reflection. His face appeared leathery and weathered beneath his bentwood hat, and he, too, had fangs. "Is this true, Tayaĝukichax̂?" he inquired of the person who'd just crushed my legs.

Tayaĝukichax̂, a man whose visage was riddled with tattoos and piercings not unlike Aniqdux̂six̂'s, did not reply.

"Answer, Aĝnakax̂!" my colleen protector reproached him.

"The screw pickets were found in his pack," Tayaĝukichax̂ answered at last.

"Yes, brother," Aniqdux̂six̂ said, "and the stakes were all cut in half. He was removing them. This *igalix* has done us a favor."

"But he still must die!" the hotheaded Tayaĝukichax̂ repeated the dictate of Aĝnakax̂, the apparent chief among them.

"The *igalix* is faint from bloodletting," "chief" Aĝnakax̂ put in, "so can do little to appease your appetite. In fact, that would only make you thirst for more blood. You must stay away from the American camp. No stirring up trouble, remember?"

The elder then turned and addressed Aniqdux̂six̂ thus, "But you still haven't told me why you protect this *igalix*, and on what grounds we should grant his reprieve?"

"Give me time with this wight," said she, again using arcane terminology. "He will be my slave. If he tries to escape, I shall dispose of him quickly."

"You stupid *Americanchin!*" Tayaĝukichax̂ spat. "What will become of this!?"

"Get back!" the elder Aĝnakax̂ replied, and with one hand he pushed Tayaĝukichax̂'s chest, causing him to fly back into the shadows and hit an unseen something with a cacophonous report.

"This is a stupid idea!" Tayaĝukichax̂ called forth from the void.

"I'll deal with you later!" Aĝnakax̂ "the chief" shouted back, and then turned again to address my protector, "Aniqdux̂six̂, for now I shall grant your wish, only so that you might stay out of trouble. Remain at home and dote over your slave, if that's what pleases you. But I urge you to stay out of the others' way and keep him out of sight. I cannot provide any protection for

him. Once this *igalix* is healed, I shall poison his memory with
monkshood and deliver him back to the Americans. I only
hope this exercise makes you more respectful of my allowances
toward you. I know you didn't join us willingly, and so I shall
try to tolerate your childish desires until you know better. May
you learn the danger and futility of the game before you, and
remember, should this little plaything of yours try to escape, I
personally shall hasten his mortality."

Aniqduxsix glared back at him, answering naught.

Once Agnakax cleared Tayagukichax and the other men out of
Aniqduxsix's area, this last sequestered us from the rest of the
greater dwelling by means of movable, woven reed partitions,
and then she opened a portal in the ceiling, causing snowflakes
to come drifting freely in.

The peculiar young woman began warming a kettle over
an oil stove. At length, she asked me to hold still, and then she
carefully removed my splint. Grabbing the kettle, she poured
some of its contents over a sod sponge before applying it as
topical ointment on my leg. It felt warm and soft. "It's fox oil,"
she remarked. "It will help thee to heal."

"You must be hungry," she continued after some time. I
had slipped into a sort of delirium, a state of disbelief. She was
now bandaging my leg with a fresh dressing. I struggled to see
exactly what it was. "Wild geranium," she offered, reading my
curiosity. "Dost thou hunger?"

I barely understood her, but nodded nonetheless, at which
point she departed in a sprightly manner.

As snowflakes continued to drift down upon me through
the ceiling ingress, I struggled to comprehend the recent train
of events.

Cross section of an Aleut underground dwelling, or barabara, with notched log ladder extending through ceiling portal (Illustration by M. Muratov, Leningrad, 1937)

THE SOD HENHOUSE

IN ANIQDUX̂ SIX̂'s absence, another young woman who appeared to be of similar age—in her early twenties—came into the room and regarded me with a curious fascination. She looked similarly Aleut, her hair being sleek, black, and reflecting a dark bluish sheen not unlike that of the Aleutian crows; her eyes were wide but a little cross, and her lips were full and brown. She wore a long skirt made of dry, woven grasses, and a sleeveless vest that looked like it was fashioned from a potato sack. She was short and plump, and blended in with the earthen sod house better than did Aniqdux̂six̂, who I at first believed to be an enemy soldier. That is to say, while Aniqdux̂six̂ had something of the Japanese warrior about her, being svelte and slightly tall, this other young woman looked more like a squat, child-rearing homemaker. She touched my wounded leg and then slowly rubbed her fingers together, checking for blood.

Our eyes met and she smiled sinisterly, revealing a set of short but prominent fangs.

I gazed back aghast.

"I think you need acupuncture," she said.

Aniqdux̂six̂ came in holding a tray of food, and suddenly the two women were exchanging growls like alley cats staring one another down, displaying dripping, wet fangs in a threatening manner.

"Get out of here, Qihmux̂!" Aniqdux̂six̂ warned, throwing down her tray and chasing after her. "He's mine!"

"What are you going to do with him?" this other lass, "Qihmux̂" replied, dodging to my other side.

"Out!" Aniqdux̂six̂ hissed, and once again they rapidly switched sides around this wild rye bed of mine.

"Are you going to turn him?!" Qihmux̂ asked, sneering.

Aniqdux̂six̂ chased her around my bed station again, but to no avail. They were like twin sisters fighting in circles, not really getting anywhere. The scenario would have struck me as ridiculous had they not been bearing V-shaped fangs and speaking ungodly, incomprehensible things . . .

"You *are* going to turn him!" insisted Qihmux̂. "Otherwise you'd answer me!"

"Shut up!" Aniqdux̂six̂ spat. "Thou hasn't the slightest!"

"Thou, thee, this, and that!" Qihmux̂ mocked. "Stop acting like a fairy princess! You're no better or different than the rest of us, and you know it!"

At this, Aniqdux̂six̂ became visibly more vexed, tightening her shoulders while raising clenched fists.

"I can see it in your eyes and in the way that you protect him!" Qihmux̂ continued her attack. "But the next cycle is far off for you: seventy-four years to be exact! I'm going to tell Aĝnakax̂ what you're up to."

"Thou art wrong!" countered Aniqdux̂six̂, undismayed by her sister's quip regarding her unique vernacular. "And besides that, Aĝnakax̂ already knows: he's approved it. Now get out!"

"You know the rules!" Qihmux̂ wasn't backing down. "To turn a mortal before your gen-cycle warrants his swift execution and your exile! But you don't *want* to wait the required time, because by then, this *igalix* you've found will already be old and dead!"

"I told thee!" Aniqdux̂six̂ fired back. "I shan't turn him!"

"So you're going to drain him, is that it?"

"No, he's already bloodlet. You're the ones calling him *igalix*."

The sisters were at length calming down.

"'*Faint from bloodletting*,' okay, but then why are you keeping him?"

"Thou wouldn't understand." Aniqdux̂six̂'s countenance suddenly grew strained under a discomposing sadness.

"You can tell me Aniqdux̂six̂, I'm your sister."

"I'm tired of this life, Qihmux̂."

"What are you talking about?"

"See, I told you thou wouldn't understand. It'll probably take a million years before you get it."

"Get what? Don't tell me you've fallen for the slave."

Aniqdux̂six̂ rubbed her eyes and shook her head as if in uncertainty or disappointment.

"You have! I knew it! Well forget about it, Aniqdux̂six̂! Forget this *igalix*. You must wait seventy-four more years to find your forever-after. Then I'm sure you'll make a better choice, when you're more matured about the world."

"Go suck yourself, Qihmux̂!" Aniqdux̂six̂ spat. "You're not even a year older than me, neither in mortal years nor immortal centuries! So don't tell me about maturity. I'm the one who's matured beyond this endlessly boring existing just to exist. I miss the fruit of life, the ripening, the ageing, the true love that can only come with the reality of peoples' eventual dying. Why must my forever-after be chosen for me? It's my eternity to share with whom I choose, otherwise I'd rather die!"

"Don't go there, Aniqdux̂six̂," her sister urged with sobering earnestness, "just don't."

"Mortality is mine to choose, Qihmux̂. I was born under the sun of Agugux, and nobody can take that away from me."

"No, Aniqdux̂six̂, you cannot do this. You're of the cave clan now. What if Aĝnakax̂ finds out?"

"Don't tell the chief!"

"Oh, you've become so *Americanchin*, Aniqdux̂six̂!"

"If thou cared about me, Qihmux̂, if thou cared that I be happy, you'd help me instead of always getting in the way of what *I* want to do."

"Don't do this, sister," Qihmux̂ reproached. "Don't risk your life, everything we have over some stupid dream. You don't even know the way to proceed."

"But we can find the way!" Aniqdux̂six̂ pleaded, tears welling up in her golden-tinged irises. "I *know* it can be done. Maybe you call it a stupid dream because you have no more dreams."

"*Iidigidi* don't dream—"

"—because we don't sleep," Aniqdux̂six̂ finished her sister's sentence. "I know, girl, but I still have dreams, and if you can't see beyond this tiresome existence, if thou can't even imagine living out our natural lives again, then I feel very sorry for thee."

"No, Aniqdux̂six̂, it is I who feel sorry for you. Our natural lives died long ago, but you still can't accept that. We've been given eternity, and yet you still complain. Pathetic is what you are."

"Easy for you to say; thou hast a man."

"Keep Qagux̂ out of this!"

"But can he make thou warm, Qihmux̂?—didn't think so, slattern. You shall never feel warm like the mortals again, for thine heart is dead. But *I* will feel warmth again. I will gain the viviparous embrace of life once more, if it's the last thing I do!"

"It won't be the last thing you do," Qihmux̂ deemed, "because Aĝnakax̂ will never allow it."

"Just get out of my sucking room already!" Aniqdux̂six̂ scathed, bearing wet fangs and bony fists.

Qihmux̂ hissed in return, then fled as if on air.

FEEDING TIME

AS ANIQDUX̂SIX̂'s room glowed red from oil lanterns that she kept alight, she sat me up against a large wicker basket stuffed with dried muskeg and said, "You must eat. With all that's been going on in the barabara lately, I didn't have time to cook. But here, I brought some whale blubber and *pootchky*."

She lifted a slab of raw blubber before me. I was reluctant at first, but feeling almost starved, I bit off a small bite and began to chew. It tasted something like sushi.

"It's freshly cut this morning." she said, handing me a pannikin of water. "Sugangix̂ killed the whale."

After feeding me more whale fat, she presented an unwieldy bundle of meter-long celery stalks and said, "This is *pootchky* from my fumarole garden, but you can't eat it like this or thy mouth will burn for days. Thou first must peel it." She began removing the strands that comprised the outer layer of its skin. "I ought to shove a stalk of raw *pootchky* down Qihmux̂'s throat!" she griped as she peeled; "that might shut her up for a while. She could never understand why I brought thou hither. She's got Qagux̂, whose name means 'fierce' in our language." She laughed. "But he's just a commoner, cold like everyone else. But thou, thou art warm—and I'm going to make sure you stay that way."

She ran her forefinger into a stalk of freshly peeled *pootchky*, gathering a lump of delicate pitch within her long nail, not unlike a teaspoon. "Here, try some of this. It will help rebuild your blood."

I was hesitant.

Reading my reluctance, she pressed her finger against my lips, gently forcing my mouth open to deliver the spongy paste. But I wasn't resisting her like before. For whatever unfathomable reason, this woman had saved me from the cold, protected me from the others, and was trying to revive me further.

I chewed on the plant that tasted like dill, as I pondered my next move. Cooperation was prudent, at least until I could make a break for it. So long as Aniqdux̂six̂ protected me from her extended clan, she had my continued confidence. I was helpless without her, at least until I got better.

"When are you going to confer me thy name?" she asked.

"My name is Lieutenant Jake Harper, ASF."

"ASF?"

"Army Services Forces. When can I return to my base? There is a war going on and I am needed there."

"You're not well. You must stay here for now."

I could not deny either sentence. With a fresh williwaw roaring outside, travel would be hazardous by any means, especially for someone as infirm as me.

Aleutian Storm Blowing In—The apparent haze in the background is actually a storm cloud, called a williwaw, rushing toward the US Forces Seabee Camp on Adak. Within a minute of the taking of this picture, there was a howling gale of snow and sleet at this Aleutian base. (AP photo and caption, winter 1943)

Noticing my continued compliance with her administrations, my captor smiled. Her fangs protruded from her mouth, catching the reddish glow of burning embers. I shuddered at the sight.

She closed her mouth and turned away. "Be not afraid of me," she bade. "Once you understand me, thou shan't be afraid. Here, have some *alutiqqutigaq* pie. I made it myself, ere I found thee."

She turned around holding a flat stone, upon which sat a small pie resembling cobbler. Its dark blue stuffing overflowed with big berries, yet it smelled fishy, literally. She smiled, struggling to keep her mouth closed over her protrusive canines, but soon her lips trembled in the effort.

As terrified as I was, I responded, "You're all right by me, Aniqdux̂six̂—I'm not afraid of you."

She extruded her fangs in an unabashed smile. It was a sight I, for the life of me, could scarcely get used to, but I tried to play it cool and focus on her pie instead. I was establishing a bond of trust with my captor that I could later exploit to my advantage. Anyway, aside from her teeth she was not altogether unsightly. As for her pie, it turned out to be quite tasty, especially after the whale fat and *pootchky*.

"What's it made of?" I asked.

"Fish, whale fat, and dried berries, primarily."

MUMMY NEAREST

ANIQDUX̂SIX̂ HAD kept me cooped up in her room for several weeks—it was hard to know exactly how long because most of the time she kept me drugged up with various remedies. When she wasn't tending to me, giving me acupuncture, or going out for supplies, she was reading very old books (from where, I discovered, she gleaned her peculiar vernacular), or she was cooking, weaving baskets, or sewing parkas she called *sax*. For days I watched her weave the sinews of fish guts and seal intestines together with bird skins and sea otter furs to make the decorative robes. She would slice the skins using an *ulu*, or "Eskimo woman's knife"—an instrument with a broad stone blade and sturdy handle running across the top. The user needed only to apply a rocking movement of the hand backed by a downward pressure over the tool in order to achieve a clean cut through a variety of indigenous materials. For darning needles she used the sharp ends of bird wing bones, some of which were fashioned with animal head carvings at their blunt ends. These bodkins had a very fine tip, but didn't have an eyelet from which to thread the gut string. Instead, the stitching material was secured by means of a little notch at the blunt end of the bodkin. Aniqdux̂six̂ often had a friend over named Ayagaadax̂, and they would sew together, gossiping all the while in their native tongue.

Lord knows how many details of their work I observed to stave off boredom, right down to the twisted gut thread. For hours on end I watched them sew parkas and weave baskets, discerning the method by which they'd split apart whale sinews and grass fibers into ultrafine strips using only their long thumbnails.

"I need to leave this room," I told Aniqdux̂six̂ after weeks of mind-numbing observation began to drive me fairly batty—no pun intended; "I need to start moving again."

"Thou aren't yet ready to walk," said she, never looking up from her weaving.

"But I need to start exercising my leg muscles before they lose their strength completely."

"Oh, they won't," she replied cheerily, "so long as we continue acupuncture."

"But it will do no good without exercise, don't you see?"

She extruded her fangs over her lower lip, as she often did when contemplating things. As for the remainder of her visage, today she wore a nose pin made of walrus ivory, a blue lupine blossom in her hair, and her abundant ear piercings were woven through with little reed ringlets. "I don't know," she ruminated aloud, her almond-shaped eyes finding mine. Her irises cast off a warm reddish glow.

"Please," I begged, "I need to get up and move around. I know you've been helping me, but I really must walk before my muscles atrophy. You mustn't keep me down like this."

Another pensive moment transpired on her part. "Remain here," she said at length, and then she left.

I shook my head in frustration. *Remain here . . . Where the heck else could I possibly go?* I was so weak from drugs and inactivity that I couldn't even sit up without her assistance. The last time I tried to get to my feet, I wound up eating the reeds of her floor mat. Thus I lay, fixating on a daddy longlegs spider that was walking away from me, and soon I began to doze off . . .

"The men are out hunting," Aniqdux̂six̂ announced, rousing me from my stupor. "I shall take thee to the hot springs. Your physical therapy must start at the mineral baths."

She lifted me in her arms and carried me up the notched log ladder toward the ceiling portal, her superhuman strength a constant reminder that my eventual escape would not come easily.

She placed me on a sled outside and began pulling me across the ice, eventually turning toward an expansive valley, white with snow. My mind was sluggish and I thought I might be dreaming, but the familiar song of an Aleutian sparrow told me otherwise. We eventually came upon a hillside, whereupon she conveyed me into a rocky cave.

"Where are you taking me?"

"To the *umqan*, the resting place of my ancestors."

She carefully set me down against the cave wall, and when she stepped aside, I recoiled at the sight of several mummified bodies hanging from swings.

"Be not afraid," she entreated.

Easy for her to say. She reached over to the mummy nearest and touched its head. "But thou must never do as I am doing now. If you were ever to touch any one of them, their spears, bags, or any of their belongings, sores would open up in your skin and you'd perish erelong."

My eyes widened in terror. These were not the sort of mummies I'd seen at the movies, all swaddled up in white bandages and lain in gilded tombs. Rather, the corpses before me hung like giant spider victims wrapped in half-rotting cocoons, with some sort of dried gelatinous casing holding their shapes together. It was as if they'd been squeezed to death by the hand of Atlas, then their mutated bodies were stuffed with moss and tightly wrapped in saran wrap before literally being hung out to dry. On the floor beneath them sat their "mummy sacks"—woven baskets chock-full of their worldly belongings.

Aniqdux̂six̂ half spun the hanging corpse to show me its face. "This is mine father," she said.

The timeworn visage presented a most horrific display. The exposed skull and cheekbones had turned dark winter-green with arctic lichens and molds, while the mouth had been opened wide and stuffed with tufts of hay. The eyes were mere sockets, swallowing the light around them like black holes, while several ivory nose pins were crossed through the septum of the nose, not unlike Aniqdux̂six̂'s.

"My real father," she continued. "He died in seventeen forty-two."

"You mean to say," I corrected her, "your great-godfather, or great-grandfather."

"No, this is my biological father."

"But that's impossible! That would make you two hundred years old."

"We are Unangan," she replied cryptically, still touching the mummy's head, "the original people."

"Yes, I figured as much, Aniqduxsix̂, but that doesn't explain how he can possibly be your father."

"His name is Alix̂. He died when I was sixteen, four years ere the shipwreck." She looked upon the dangling body endearingly, then gently caressed the stringy hair of her so-called "father."

"Shipwreck?"

"The *Arkhangelsk*, a Russian seal-hunting vessel that had run aground near our complex."

The Arkhangelsk (*Exclusive art by Yury Zharov, USSR*)

"The seas were high and the fog was dense, but some men from the barabara organized a search-and-rescue party nevertheless. These were Chief Aĝnakax̂, his first son Tayaĝukichax̂, and Iĝanax̂, another sea hunter. The Russian vessel was fouled up badly on the rocks offshore, so the trio alighted in their separate *baidarkas* to encounter it."

"*Baidarkas?*"

"Like kayaks, made of seal gut. They can take a heavy sea. Remember we are Aleuts: we hunt sea lion, walrus, whales. My people know the currents; even in a blinding fog, they can find their way home. But this was different. It wasn't the sea that got them. It was something onboard the foundering ship."

"Something onboard? Like a disease?"

She did not summarily answer, nor would she make eye contact with me. Instead, she remained stooped over her departed relative, shaking her head in sorrow.

"You can tell me, Aniqdux̂six̂. I want to know what happened here. Maybe I can help."

With a peculiar reluctance, as if she were torn between remaining silent and revealing a deep personal secret, she looked at me contritely, her face flush with tears, at last answering, "It was more than a disease: it was something far worse."

"Some sort of plague?"

"It was something even more sinister than death itself. Before Chief Aĝnakax̂ had departed with the search party, he gave strict instructions to the men remaining in the barabara, telling them to guard the women from the *promuishlenniki* should they essay ashore with their guns and take over the domicile and its women."

"*Promuishlenniki?*"

"Russian sailors—fur hunters from the ship. The tribesmen who stayed behind to serve as sentries were loyal to the chief's wishes, even as time progressed and the likelihood increased that he and the reconnaissance party had fallen into a situation upon the stranded vessel. But then, just before dawn on the third day, Chief Aĝnakax̂ and his son Tayaĝukichax̂ returned from the ship appearing very pale and with small puncture marks on their necks. They took neither food nor water, saying they were exhausted and needed only to sleep in a dark recess of the barabara.

"That night, they awoke very thirsty, and that's when Chief Aĝnakax̂ revealed they'd encountered some sickly *promuishlenniki* onboard, and in doing so became exposed to a deadly virus themselves. The surviving Russians onboard, he explained, told them that only immediate bloodletting could cure them of the disease, thus the shipwrecked sailors drained them of their blood and sent them off in their *baidarkas*, saying that's all they could do for them and that only time would tell if they'd survive the virus. Iĝanax̂, the third tribesman in the search party, was lost in the fog on the return trip and never seen again.

"Chief Aĝnakax̂ told us that because he and Tayaĝukichax̂ were still sick, the disease had most likely already transmitted to the rest of us in the barabara. He thus ordered the immediate bloodletting of everybody, but claimed that the standard cut-and-drip approach wouldn't be quick enough to stave off the deadly contagion. Only by sucking the blood directly from the neck of the infected, he explained, did the inflicted have any chance of survival, while only those who'd already been bloodlet could do the bloodletting upon the newly exposed. His authority and urgency was such that his word was not questioned, and so he and his son proceeded to bite into our necks and suck out our blood."

"You talk as if you were there, Aniqdux̂six̂, but you don't look two hundred years old to me, so please, enough of the old folklore. This may be your father, but he cannot be deceased more than twenty years, which looks to be about your age. Obviously, he was preserved with some sort of wrapping."

"We use oiled sphagnum for preservation. But I am speaking to thee truthfully and your distrust in me hurts. I didn't have to convey you hither and expose myself like this. I didn't have to rescue thee from the survival barrel, or prevent my clan from harming you. But now when I open up to you, you still don't trust me."

"Trust that you're two hundred years old? Well, you're right, Aniqdux̂six̂, I can't believe that. How can I? Look, I appreciate all you've done for me. I owe you my life. But you've got to—"

"Be not afraid," she cut me off as bat-shaped, white feathered wings unfurled from beneath her parka.

I recoiled in terror.

She took wing, hovering several feet over the ground.

I looked again more closely. Her parka was flapping something like the wings of a hummingbird, but the clothing was merely a disguise, for her back had actually grown the pinions, and these seemed to attach into her parka from the inside.

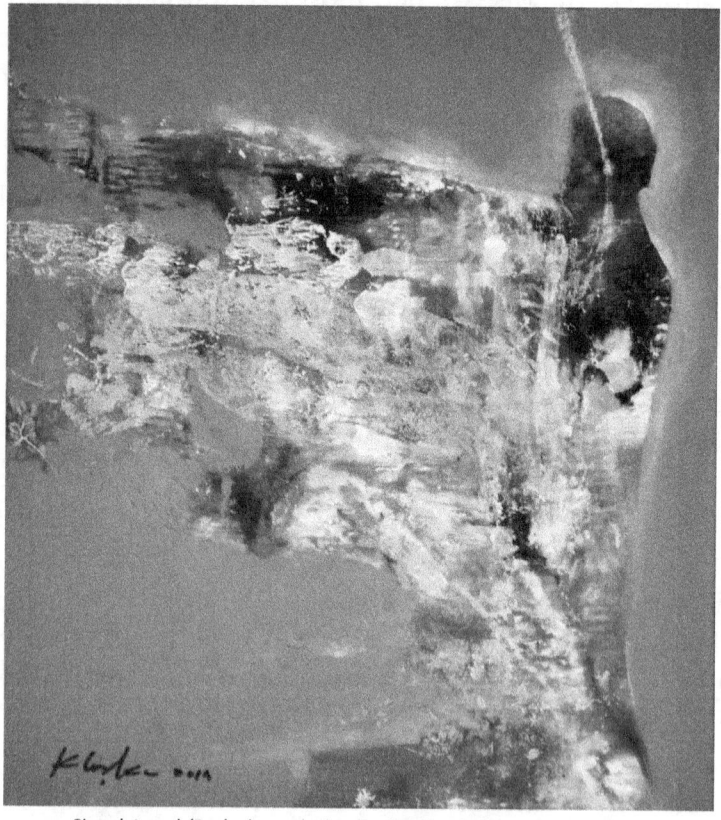

Signal Angel (*Exclusive painting by Ovidiu Kloska, ref#17.03.2014*)

"I'm sorry I must show you this," she said, "but it's the only way to convince you."

I shielded my eyes from the flying dust she was generating within the cave, and from the horror begot by her sudden transformation. Several beetles, metallic green in color, scurried across the floor to escape her blustery power.

"My human years are but twenty," she bellowed over the preternatural hum of her fluttering wings, "as thou have correctly surmised; and that they shall remain for all of eternity, for I am a vampire!"

Her eyes glowed red with rage as she bore her fangs. "Chief Aĝnakax̂ changed me one hundred and ninety-six years agone, and I shall *never* forgive him!"

Her shrill cry echoed seemingly without cease through the dark recesses of the *umqan*. I took to my heels and tried to flee her ancestral burial cave, movingly lamely over my sealskin-bandaged leg.

She landed in front of me, blocking my escape. "Be not afraid," she repeated, drawing in her wings. "I'm not going to hurt you. I just wanted you to see the truth."

"Please, send me back to my unit!" I pleaded, holding out a hand in defense while shielding her from my sight. "The ASF needs me! There's a war going on. Please just send me back!"

"I can't do that."

"Then . . . then what are you going to do with me?" I stuttered with dread.

"I'm healing you. Thou are still not well."

"Let the army doctors help me, then. Please, just take me back to Kuluk."

"I can heal thee faster."

She lifted me in her arms and took wing from the cave. We flew over miles of frozen tundra, and then high up beside a lofty volcano. I was helpless to resist her. To fall from those heights would've been my certain doom.

Once above the caldera summit, we dove into the simmering crater, and as we descended, the atmosphere grew significantly warmer; and then with a sudden flurry of her winged parka, she landed us gently upon the crater floor, where fresh green plants, lavender, fruit trees, and vegetable gardens spread abundantly in every direction over an alpine heath meadow. Smoky sulfur billows and swirling ash mists rose up willy-nilly about the hidden parterre, heating the air and enriching the soil with volcanic cinder deposits.

"Welcome to my fumarole garden," she said, unrolling a plaited reed mat over the verdant grass. "Most Aleuts take from the sea, but not me. I am of the earth, as thou shall see."

"This is incredible," I said, and meant it. "It's like a hidden oasis amid the fire and ice."

"It is forever unchanged," she replied, "even in the deepest of winter it is a sanctuary of warmth and life—a living example of all that I desire. I am not a monster of the caves, like those who came before. I am Unanga—I choose to live a fruitful life in the sun of my god, Agugux."

"I wish that you would speak plainly," I lamented as she lay me down upon the verdant glen. Aside from her archaic English tongue, she often peppered her prose with Aleut words that I strained to comprehend.

"Remain here but a moment," said she, taking to the skies, where, darting from treetop to treetop like a hummingbird, she gathered myriad fruits, which she returned to me in quick succession until I was surrounded with apples, peaches, and pears.

At length, she settled down beside me and offered me a peach, which I summarily devoured. It was the sweetest peach I'd ever tasted.

"I knew you'd be hungry," she surmised, procuring a dark red apple. "These are the best, but their skin is tough. Here, I'll get it started."

She sunk her fangs deep into the fruit. Sugary juices pooled up around her lips and dripped over her tattooed chin like crystalline strands of candle wax. "Take a bite," she offered, presenting the side of the apple opposite where she had bitten.

I was reluctant at first, but the temptation of the apple's juiciness still in evidence upon her lips proved too much to resist. I chomped a bite from the succulent fruit, chewed it quickly and then took another. Soon I had consumed all but the core, which I tossed over my head into a patch of lavender. "Thanks," I burped, wiping my lips. "You were right—that was excellent."

I reached for another apple that had fallen between us, but she held my hand and stopped me. "That will be enough," she deemed, and then she then rolled on top of me, straddling me like a horse.

I placed my hands on her thighs. She pulled off her bird-wing parka, tossing it aside, then ripped open her sealskin top, exposing her young, full breasts. The temptation was too much. I cupped my hands around her protruding womanhood and began squeezing fervently.

"*Oh Kayuu*," she moaned hotly, flinging back her hair. Her bare knees pressed hard into the wild rye mat on my either side, but her naked body felt cold to the touch, which put me at unease. I removed my hands.

"Please don't stop," she groaned, returning my hands to her breasts, and then she began slowly rocking her hips while unbuckling my pants. Soon the siren was riding me hard, once our real lovemaking began. She commanded me like a *baidarka* upon a stormy sea, each rise and fall of our bodies a tug-of-war of ecstasy, pushing, pulling, squeezing, and contracting at our groins as we interlocked together, tighter and tighter . . .

As she was bouncing her hips hard and fast against mine, I gripped the sides of her buttocks to maximize the banging effect, and while this was transpiring, we brought our chops together and kissed passionately in the French style, with open mouths, wet, red-apple lips, and rabid tongues.

We reached climax and I sat up quickly, causing her ivory nose pin to poke into my jowls, but the pain it inflicted only accentuated the explosive experience of our seeding together. Our collective scream of pleasure echoed deep into the fumarole garden's every recess and glen, until at last we fell side by side in the tall grass, totally spent.

"That was fantastic," she confessed.

"Unforgettable," I exhaled in a breath, succumbing to a long, restorative nap.

Aniqdux̂six̂ embraced me in her arms and took flight from her fumarole garden. Ascending over the crater rim once again, we dove sharply down along the outer side of the lofty cinder cone, coming to a breathless landing upon a rocky knoll overlooking the southern sea. Here and there about the craggy hillocks, sulfuric mists wafted up from bubbling springs. Steaming waterfalls and streams interlaced the mineral baths, while the shapes of the rocks provided natural stone seats.

"These are the hot springs," she revealed. "For many generations, my people have come here for their health-giving properties, bathing all the year round. We used to cook foods here, too. We'd put meats and roots in grass bags, then steep them in the cauldron zones. Boiled gorbusha with Eskimo potato was my favorite."

"I would like to go in," I chattered quite literally: the flight down the mountain had been frigid indeed.

She assisted me down to a water hole, then pulled off her parka before helping me remove my clothes. We slipped into the water together; it was immediately soothing.

"This pool is about the temperature of thine own body," she said. "I come often to remind myself of what a warm body should feel like."

I made my way over to her, asking gingerly, "Can I take a closer look at your wings?"

She turned around and then backed closer. Her wet, naked skin was well-toned and comely, even with a large, black-and-blue tattoo of a Harlequin duck stretching from shoulder to shoulder across her back, its wings in full display in a linear pattern. This bird, I knew from the many hours I'd spent along Adak's seashore while searching for screw pickets, seemed to prefer the ocean's more violent conditions.

Lieutenant Jake Harper, bottom right, and fellow soldiers stand before a shallow cave along the Adak shore. (Exclusive photo, 1942–1943)

Unlike other waterfowl, it didn't migrate south for the winter, but remained in the Aleutians no matter how bad the weather. Fortunately for the Harlequin duck, the Bering Sea ice floe never came this far south to infringe upon its habitat.

I glided my fingers along her shoulder blades and over the wingtips of the seabird, feeling the permanent pricks on her skin left from the bone needle used in the tattooing process.

"It watches over me and defends the spirit world," she explained.

I gently outlined the duck's body, then ran my right hand far down her spine to where the sliver between her buttocks began. "But where are *your* wings?" I inquired.

"It's part of necrogenesis."

"What's that?"

"The end result of the infection from the *promuishlenniki* ship. Those who are bitten undergo biological death, then full regeneration into a different kind of body—a process we don't really comprehend. I can grow wings at will and fly with the slightest effort; I never force myself. But I bemoan the day I ever became this hideous thing. My heart beats, but I do not breathe. My blood flows, but it is cold and black. Centuries pass, but I do not age. I can eat, but have nought hunger, while I thirst, but only for one thing."

"Blood?"

She turned and took my chin in her hand, looking deep into my eyes. "I thirst only for the love of a mortal." Our lips drew close and she added with a whisper, "Thy love." Our mouths interlocked widely, our tongues entwining together like mating snakes. "Be my slave," she breathed hotly into my ear, her wet tongue soon following.

I wrested her to the edge of the hot spring, tilted her back upon the steaming rim and slid on top of her. The black locks of her hair stuck chunky and wet over her face, collarbone, and jejune breasts. I grabbed the back of her head and peered unflinchingly into her eyes, and then I entered her, thrusting deeply into her pelvis.

We clutched our hands together over her head, her seal-skin bracelets sliding up and down roughly over her forearms as we slammed into one another's groins. Her irises flashed molten red; she screamed in immortal pleasure. Our climax was shared, unleashing pent-up longings, her centuries of pressure.

But still her skin was cold to the touch. The sudden thought that I'd just made love to someone dead in the flesh caused me to recoil involuntarily.

She spun away and buried her face into her bony hands, her body shuddering in a paroxysm of minute spasms, and then I heard her crying softy.

TO NAME THE OCEANS

"I'M HERE, Aniqdux̂six̂." I gently touched her shoulder.

"Get—get away." She shuddered. "I'm a monster."

"Hardly," I supplicated. "You saved my life."

"Thou knowest not the half of me."

"I think I do, I think I see you clearly now. It's not your fault what happened to you, and it hasn't changed who you really are."

"I am hideous."

"Quite the opposite. You've shown me how beautiful you are, inside and out."

"Why dost thou sayest these things? I am become a vampire. I drink the blood of men. It's no wonder you recoil from me in terror."

"I am not afraid of you, Aniqdux̂six̂. You have given me strength."

"Dost not thou think I'm childish?"

"Childish?"

"That's what 'Aniqdux̂six̂' means in Unangam Tunuu, my native language."

"You may be acting a little childish right now; Aniqduxsix̂, please just look at me." I grabbed her shoulder. She partially turned around to face me, not making eye contact. "Aniqduxsix̂, I think I love you."

Our eyes met again, but only for a moment before she slid off to the other side of the hot spring.

"Dost thou knowest what they call thee, Mister Jake Harper?" she asked, managing a little giggle through her sobs.

"Igalix. Why? What does it mean?"

"When I found thee"—regaining her composure—"you were so weak from blood loss, they named you 'Igalix.'"

I raised my brows.

"Faint from bloodletting, remember?"

I shook my head and shrugged my shoulders. I wasn't sure what she was getting at.

"But I always l knew you'd be strong, Jake. Unlike us, thou art a mortal survivor. That is why I'm renaming thee Kayuu, which is Unangam Tunuu for 'His Strength.'"

"Kayuu," I chuckled. "Not bad, but I've got a way to go yet."

"Not only outwardly, but you are strong on the inside, Kayuu. I've always sensed it."

"What's the gen-cycle, Aniqduxsix̂? I've heard you talking about it with your people. Does it have anything to do with your condition?"

"It has more to do with thine, I'm afraid."

She came and sat beside me again. She'd rubbed the last of her tears across her steam-moistened cheeks, and now appeared concerned and serious. She took my hands in hers, and continued face-to-face, "I can explain. In seventy-four years, my turn will finally come to choose an eternal mate. But this is not what

I want, nor can I wait another day. To me this life is eternal damnation. How could I ever visit such a fate upon someone I truly love? And if it isn't true love, it's pure blackmail. When I turn a human into a vampire, they must stay by my side forever—that is the one law of necrogenesis. I would rather die to know true love again, Kayuu. I wish to become human again, to bear children, to grow old with the one I love, and then to die a natural death."

I broke eye contact with her. I stared into the water in deep contemplation. "It's no small thing to abandon eternal youth, eternal life," I said.

"If only this *were* eternal life," she replied, squeezing my hand to garner my full attention, "but that's an oxymoron. Life cannot be eternal. Only death is eternal. My existence is thus an eternal living death."

"But maybe if you found the right person—a willing partner—immortality would be worthwhile. Nobody wants to die. Everybody wants what you already have."

"Until they have it, but as the centuries wear thin, priorities shift."

"Priorities?"

"Realities of existence. Dignity, how best to live. Vampires are not gods; we are not creators, yet we are pained to struggle eternally with such notions. Agugux is our creator, bringing light from the east, while we are barren. Life cannot come from us, yet we never die. The cave clan tribe is not of nature—we reek of abomination and evil."

"Only if you act as such, Aniqdux̂six̂. Whatever disease has befallen you, it cannot control your actions."

"This is where thou art mistaken, Mister Harper. We thirst for the blood of men."

"But you don't always act upon this urge, do you? You can control it. You have proven as much to me."

"The blood of sea mammals has been our substitute, but now that wights have arrived back on Adak, I can't be certain if we can control our most primal urge to feed on them."

"You've done a pretty good job with me."

"I am different, but I cannot speak for the others. Protecting you from them has not been easy."

"I know you're different." I drew her close. "I hear the way you speak—you are respectful to me, and sensitive. And through you, I know the others can show the same strength of character. They can help us—help the United States fight against the Japanese contention. The powers you possess would be a major asset."

"I would not ascribe the same desires of my tribe, as mine own. Qihmux̂, my sister, has her immortal mate, Qagux̂, the commoner, just as all the others have already created their gen-cycle partners. To them, humanity is long over; a non sequitur. The others are set in their ways: their permanent partners have been chosen for them; they've lost the sense of urgency in love that only comes with the reality of mortality. 'Until death do us part' hath no meaning to them. But to thou I hast already told: for I, true love, consensual marriage—a marriage cere-mony!—and having my own children, there's no substitute for that. Immortality is my biggest curse, and that's why I seek to become human again—I wish to once more become a wight. Kayuu, I *need* you to help me. You're all I've got, my only chance. Thou art my everything, and I know I can be the same for you, if only thou afford me the chance to prove it in your lifetime, not mine."

"But is it possible to reverse the virus?"

"There is a way."

Suddenly, two Japanese Zeroes came roaring around the volcano, bearing west.

"Japs!" I cried. I sprung up from the hot spring and tried to pull on my pants. But my leg was still subpar, and with the additional relaxant incurred from the mineral bath, I quickly fell back on my ass.

"The Aleutian Zero," or "Koga's Zero," as recovered from Akutan Island by U.S. forces in July of 1942, is pictured here at Ballyhoo Dock, Unalaska, awaiting transfer to San Diego, California for further study. The Zero was the most feared and awe-inspiring fighter plane of the World War II Pacific theater. (Photo by U.S. National Archives, 1942)

THE FALLIBILITY OF THE UNDEAD

PROCEEDING ON foot was futile: in my haste to fight the Japanese presence, I limped lamely away from the hot springs, not even knowing where I was going. All I knew was that the Japs were back, and I had to warn my fellow countrymen.

Aniqdux̂six̂ swooped me up in her arms and took to the skies, freeing me from the tor.

"Take me to Kuluk at once!" I demanded. "It's of vital interest to the war effort!"

"The planes were heading in the opposite direction from Kuluk."

"My base might be under attack! Please, Aniqdux̂six̂! I must get back to the ASF!"

She wrapped her limbs more firmly around my body to yoke me into safer submission, drawing me close beneath her beating wings. "We shall go and investigate," she said, cutting sharply toward the north. "But I won't let you go yet. I can't." She fluttered her wings more feverishly and we picked up speed over the frozen demesne.

"I won't abandon you," I said. "When the war is over, I'll come back."

"I beseech if thou art being earnest, Sir Harper," she formally replied, searching my eyes for any hint of truth or lies.

I kept a grim poker face, lips drawn tight, eyes steely narrowed against the cold Aleutian skies.

"Besides that, Kayuu," she switched back to the Aleut name she'd given me, "it's not that simple. If Chief Aĝnakax̂ finds out I've delivered you to Kuluk, he'll have my head."

I had no response.

"He'll literally have me killed," she added. "It amounts to treason of the vampire order to expose ourselves to the world at large."

"I promise not to tell anybody."

"I regret to inform that the promises of a wight mean nothing to my kind. Both our lives will be imperiled."

"But I thought you said you couldn't die."

"There are ways," she said cryptically.

Still flying fast, she dropped altitude and glided through a series of canyons and ravines. "We're about five minutes out," she said. "We mustn't be seen."

The skies over the Aleutians during wartime were a busy place indeed . . . (War Gum #82 insert, Gum, Inc., 1942)

We came upon a narrow valley, and as we glided along its foothills to evade detection, a man-made structure with a blue roof came into view. "No," Aniqdux̂six̂ uttered with dread and, as we drew closer, "*no*," again.

The sight beneath us was uncanny to behold. A double-domed, blue roofed church of the Russian Orthodox type sat decaying amid the muskeg, while in a small lake adjacent, a boy appeared to be drowning. A second child stood at the edge of the lake, waving his arms and screaming up at us in hysterics, but I couldn't make out what he was saying.

Aniqdux̂six̂ deposited me at the side of the lake next to the hysterical child. He appeared to be an Aleut not more than five years of age. He kept crying "Maguun!" as he pointed to the boy in distress.

I removed my bomber jacket, preparing to jump in to save the drowning one. Meanwhile, Aniqdux̂six̂ was trying to grab onto him from above, but amid his wild splashing, she kept backing off, and I soon realized why . . . the postage-stamp lake by the church wasn't a lake at all, but was a cauldron of piping hot volcanic water, and the boy caught at its center wasn't only drowning—he was being burned alive. Every time he splashed Aniqdux̂six̂, she lost her grip and recoiled in pain as scalding water visibly smoked off her flesh.

The sight of the scorching tarn alerted me to the harsh reality of trying to save the child. I got down on my good knee and carefully touched the water's edge, then quickly withdrew my finger, startled by the temperature. I reached for it again, now immersing my finger, then my hand. The lake wasn't scalding at all—it was freezing cold! Why, then, was it blistering the flesh of the boy and Aniqdux̂six̂? Perhaps he'd swum over a boiling vent? But then the whole lake would be lukewarm at minimum because it wasn't that big—it was more like a pond, really. It just didn't make sense. Whatever the case, there wasn't a second more to waste, so I dove in after him.

Upon reaching the distressed child, the water was still frigid. Aniqdux̂six̂ hovered a safe distance above me as I clutched the boy beneath my arm and began backstroking toward shore. The kid was in terrible pain and difficult for me to contain, for the water caused his skin to blister and sizzle. I kept glancing at my arms to check my own condition, fearing perhaps the lake was a dumpsite for chemical weapons materiél, or otherwise purposefully poisoned by the Japs during their retreat. But aside from the numbing cold that turned my skin bone-white, the water wasn't afflicting me as it was the child.

I finally reached the shallows, where I struggled to carry the boy up the muskeg. I kept falling over my weak leg and dropping him back into the water.

Aniqdux̂six̂ had landed beside the younger child onshore, but neither of them would come to my assistance—even as I was visibly succumbing to the effects of hypothermia.

Slowed by numbness and shaking uncontrollably, I gave a final, excruciating effort, at last hoisting the sizzling kid onto the icy reeds at Aniqdux̂six̂'s feet. She began rubbing snow over him and scolding him—apparently—in her Aleut language. She had sharp words for the other boy, as well, who assumed her strange duty of frosting the afflicted one with snow. Only then did Aniqdux̂six̂ tend to her own wounds, rubbing rough-hewn snowballs over an abundance of fresh blisters running down her arms and hands.

I reached a trembling finger up to them, trying to speak, but Aniqdux̂six̂ paid no attention to me. Apparently, she didn't realize I was freezing to death. My face hit the frozen sod, and just before I blacked out, I felt her claw around my shoulders, lifting me up.

TRUTH OR DARE?

"IT WAS a dare," I overheard as I regained consciousness. "Maguun bet Kitax he could fly over Ephraim's Lake! Don't you teach your kids any better!?" Aniqdux̂six̂ scathed.

I opened my eyes to find myself once again on Aniqdux̂six̂'s recovery table. My hands and feet were frostbitten and felt like blocks of frozen steel. The pain was relentless. Meanwhile, Aniqdux̂six̂ and Qihmux̂, her ever-cross and cross-eyed sister, were once again arguing back and forth over me.

"Is this true, Kitax?" Qihmux̂ addressed the younger of the two children, who was standing not far behind her. "Did Maguun say he would fly over the lake?" The little boy looked ashamedly up at his mother.

"I told you never to go there!" Qihmux̂ waved a finger in his face, and then she flew in a leap over to another reed table where a boy lay upon a bedding of dried reeds and mosses. His entire body was wrapped in waxy sealskins not unlike the mummification I'd witnessed in the cave. "Maguun, how are you feeling?" she asked.

"It burns all over," he quavered as he cried.

The partition separating Aniqdux̂six̂'s room and that of Qihmux̂'s family had been moved aside, temporarily connecting the two sectors. Beyond Qihmux̂'s area, toward the center of the barabara, I could see a fire pit filled with the embers of *pootchky* stalks. This, along with numerous stone lanterns and Aniqdux̂six̂'s oil stove, is what had been keeping me warm inside the barabara, a dwelling composed of sod [like peat moss], reeds, driftwood, and whalebones, primarily.

The Inside of a House in Oonalashka, *as drawn by HMS* Resolution's *artist John Webber (1751–1793) on James Cook's final voyage. The sketch shows the interior of an Aleut home as seen by Webber during Captain Cook's stop in Unalaska from June 28 to July 2, 1778. The ship's surgeon, David Samwell, later wrote that he and Webber observed several families living in the common area, but separated into individual "apartments" by mats, "which they let down occasionally like curtains to skreen them from the View of the Common Passage." Webber's notes remark at the early barabara's sturdy construction, its crossed ceiling struts, straw "insulation," and entry and exit ladders at front and in the center. (From* New, Authentic, Entertaining, Instructive, Full and Complete Historical Account of Captain Cook's First, Second, Third and Last Voyages, *by Alexander Hogg, published in serial format from 1784–1786)*

Qihmux̂ placed a hand on the forehead of her burned son, consoling him tenderly, "You must lie still. In time, you will get better. But may this be a lesson for the both of you. I told you to stay away from that place. If Aniqdux̂six̂ hadn't shown up when she did, the Holy Water would've fully consumed you, and Kitax would've been lost there on his own."

"It was Kayuu who saved Maguun," Aniqdux̂six̂ put in, "not me. And remember, sister, some secrets the wights must never know."

"Kayuu?" Qihmux̂ was perplexed.

"He's not Igalix anymore," Aniqdux̂six̂ explained. "His new name is Kayuu, Kayuu the Strong: he dove in and retrieved Maguun."

"Is this true?" Qihmux̂ canvassed her sons. "Did the mortal save Maguun from Ephraim's Lake?"

They nodded, uttering, "Yes," and, "He did."

"Will someone please explain what this is all about?" I asked with irritation, trying to sit up.

Aniqdux̂six̂ urged me back down, but I rejected her advance, at which point Qihmux̂ came to my other side and guided my legs over her side of the table, helping me to sit up. My skin all over was moderately frostbitten and stung to the touch, while the bulk of my muscles felt bruised and raw. My vision was blurred on the peripheries, and in sitting up I quickly became nauseous. I expectorated a driblet on the floor and girded my teeth, fighting through the many discomforts in order to get to the bottom of things. "Please?" I asked anew.

"Ephraim's Lake is toxic to vampires," Qihmux̂ began. "It's tainted with—"

"Stop, Qihmux̂!" Aniqdux̂six̂ snapped. "Wights are not to know such things! Chief Aĝnakax̂ will punish you for this!"

"Aniqdux̂six̂!" I reproached. "After all we've been through! Please, let your sister speak."

Ephraim's Lake (*Art by Edmund Dulac, 1907*)

"He saved my son!"—Qihmux̂ glowered at Aniqdux̂six̂—
"He deserves to know."

"Thank you, Qihmux̂," I concurred, at which point she gently squeezed my shoulder.

"*Hmmph!*" huffed Aniqdux̂six̂, shaking her head in disappointment.

I regarded her critically.

She folded her arms and turned her back to us in rage.

Ignoring her, Qihmux̂ took my hand and sat down beside me askew, so that we were more or less facing one another.

"Ephraim's Lake," she began, "is adjacent to Saint Ephraim of the Caves Church. The church was established in eighteen forty-four by a Russian priest who named it after an eleventh-century Russian bishop named Saint Ephraim of Pereslav. The onetime pilgrims in attendance were intermixed Russian and Aleut toions imported from Unalaska Island. Chief Aĝnakax̂ let them go about their business so as to not attract attention to our, well, our condition. But when the priest started coming to our barabara, seeking to convert us with his book, *The Way to the Kingdom of Heaven*, we were forced to dispatch the lot of them. We did it during a williwaw, and then we took their bodies to the top of Great Sitkin and tossed them into the volcano. Their *baidaras* we took for our own, stashing them away in our hidden boathouse, making it appear as if they got lost at sea in the williwaw, as sometimes happens in these parts. Only the priest, Innokenty Veniaminov, got away. Regrettably, transforming his flock had not been an option, because Chief Aĝnakax̂ wanted to keep our tribe small so that we are less visible to the outside and, frankly, easier for him to control. Besides, Aleuts aren't interested in growing their clans with the blood of rivals—we only want them as slaves. Because our numbers are permanent, membership into our barabara is especially guarded and controlled."

"Thus the gen-cycle," I surmised.

"That's part of it," she replied, then glanced back at her sister.

Aniqdux̂six̂ was leaning coolly against the reed-stitched wall, her arms crossed, shaking her head and biting her lower lip in a show of frustration and disapproval.

"Polygamy," Qihmux̂ continued, "as well as multiple husbands, were once common in our tribe, but are now outlawed. We simply must restrict our numbers. But back to the chapel: we went over to kill the priest and tear down his sanctum, but he was nowhere to be found. What we did find, however, was Holy Water, which you may have heard is lethal to vampires. A system of pipes ran into the sanctum to provide it with fresh drinking water and water for the sacramental—a receptacle for Holy Water. Furthermore, there were crosses, iconostases and Holy Icons all over, some forged in silver. The church was thus a major hazard for us: we could scarcely enter it, nor would it burn when we tried to set it on fire."

"What about the priest?" I asked. "He must have reported you to the authorities on Unalaska."

Qihmux̂ laughed. "Veniaminov did keep good records, but some things he kept secret from the Unalaska parish, and one of these secrets we knew about, so we threatened to blackmail him if he spoke or wrote a word about us: we knew he had a secret affair going with a young Unanga on Nikolski—the only woman he absolved from giving confession. He'd go there in the spring and summer to see her. He called the village his 'beloved Recheshnoe.' Outwardly, the Russian priest said he loved the township's sweeping plains and lakes, which contrasted sharply with the icy rock mountains of his winter polity in Iliuliuk. But we knew the real reason he loved Nikolski. We knew everything about his secret affair, and we had love letters they'd exchanged in Aleut prove it, thanks to Iganakuchax̂, his mistress's onetime confidante by way of old maternal bloodlines. We intercepted their letters, as well as sealed missives he'd send to Sitka and Irkutsk. Innokenty Veniaminov had no idea who we really were or the extent of our relations. He thought we were a band of notorious nomadic Aleut raiders who'd finally decided to settle on Adak in secret. He probably believed that because, unlike the other tribes he encountered—and there were many—we did not receive him and his religion gladly. His finding us was undoubtedly the worst thing that ever happened to his mis-sionary activities because, for obvious reasons, we couldn't accept his baptisms, his Sacraments of Confession, his Water Blessings, Catechisms, Divine Liturgies, and Communions. Beyond that fact that his presence here was a direct threat to our clan, the elders among us did not forget what the Russians had brought to us before—the plague, the decimation of sea life that is crucial to our culture, and the slavery of our people as we were shipped off en masse to work the fur seal trade of the Pribilofs. While Veniaminov was credited by other Aleuts as bringing them protections against such colonial exploitations, our elders remained suspect of anyone answerable to the Imperial Crown of St. Petersburg, and especially their merchant mariners, such as was Veniaminov via the diocesan office in Irkutsk—the Irkutsk Consistory, and the chief manager of the colonies. We had not forgotten the transgressions of the Shelikhov-Golikov Company, an imperial-merchant enterprise not long preceding him."

Kitax began pulling at his mother's reed grass skirt.

"Go keep an eye on your brother," she admonished him, and he went away meekly.

"The real shocker," Qihmux̂ continued, "was when we found the pond adjacent to the church, now dubbed Ephraim's Lake, also contaminated with Holy Water. After Veniaminov had consecrated the water within the sanctum, he went to the pond outside and blessed that as well. The potential danger this posed to us quickly became apparent. Adak Island, like all the Aleutians Islands, is extremely wet. Snow, waterfalls, waterways, and rain are common. Beneath the muskeg are entire lakes and rivers. Veniaminov's power was so great that there was a real possibility the contaminated water could spread to our barabara and perhaps over the entire island, forcing us to relocate. Then there was an even bigger question: Could Holy Water spread into the ocean, in turn contaminating the rainclouds and precipitation as well?

"Fortunately, fears of an extinction-level event for *iidigidi* were soon put to rest by further research into the polluted water's characteristics: Holy Water concentrated within a sacramental or other immediate source such as a lake acts like radiation, in that the further it is from its point of original distribution, the more rapidly it dilutes and dissipates. A priest, no matter how powerful, cannot consecrate an ocean, mainly because of its size and the fact that it is saline and not pure, just as many of the bodies of fresh water so abundant in the Aleutians are impure, containing varying amounts of minerals and volcanic sulfides. However, the sacramental water within Saint Ephraim of the Caves Church and its adjoining lake is very pure—the tarn's rain catchment geography keeps the priest's consecration perennially active and powerful."

"The Holy Water—the water in the lake—was frigid to me," I replied. "But to you it has the opposite effect. It burns. Can it actually kill you?"

Aniqdux̂six̂ huffed loudly and stomped a foot in a show of disapproval.

"What's your problem?" Qihmux̂ quipped back at her.

"This is my room!" Aniqdux̂six̂ returned fire. "Why don't you just take your kids and get the hell out?"

"We're all under the same roof here," Qihmux̂ answered calmly, then looked to me: "Can I finish our conversation?"

I looked back at Aniqdux̂six̂, the younger sister both in years and fragility, and said, "Please, Aniqdux̂six̂, she means us no harm."

"Whatever," she said, and then took wing out of the barabara.

"Aniqdux̂six̂!" I called, but she had disappeared into a fresh snowfall.

"Don't worry about her," Qihmux̂ bade. "She'll get over it."

"Over what?"

"Over you and I becoming friends."

Russian Orthodox Church, Aleutian Islands (Photo by News Press Wire Service, 1942)

I studied the features of Qihmux̂'s face. Previously, her cross-eyes made her look somehow feral and wild, but after getting to know her better, they now made her appear interesting and exotic. Her black hair was cut in a pronounced bang over her forehead that stepped down just over her ears, the remainder bunched up in a bun atop her head. Her nose was small and pudgy, with round nostrils that flared cutely back, and her lips were wide but thin, causing her fangs to show more often than not. Short, feather earrings hung from her narrow earlobes, while a sort of spirit-catcher necklace or amulet hung over her wide but relatively flat breasts. This observation of her features, however, should not by necessity signal an attraction to her on my part. Her younger sister was more readily becoming to me, or perhaps I'd just become more intimate with Aniqdux̂six̂'s personality and features.

"Holy Water can kill us." Qihmux̂ snapped me out of my reverie.

"Go on," I said as I lay back down. Truth be told, my body hurt like hell and I was becoming increasingly dizzy from sitting up.

She adjusted her position beside me. "Holy Water," she explained, "is incredibly painful. It burns our skin like scalding water. The scars it inflicts go away, though, usually in about ten days. But sustained exposure can be very dangerous, for when our blisters become open wounds our blood is exposed. Once Holy Water enters our bloodstream it can be lethal. You saved my boy just in time, Kayuu."

I looked up at her plainly. She'd called me the name that Aniqdux̂six̂ had given me. She smiled, and then continued, "Maguun dared he could fly over Ephraim's Lake. He was trying to show off to Kitax. He's always trying to impress his little brother, but he's not always smart about it."

"But if you're around the same age as Aniqdux̂six̂," I inquired, "that means your kids must also be nearly two hundred years old. Wouldn't all those years make them wiser than children?"

"Maguun is six and Kitax is almost five," she said. "They say the brain of a child is an open book, but in *iidigidi* years, nothing could be further from the truth. When a mortal is transformed into one of us, the developmental capacity of their brain is essentially locked in. *Ad infinitum* more years of experience on earth cannot bypass the mind's physical limita-tions—the brain's size, for one—especially for young children. We don't exactly have baby Einsteins flying around. Even for Aniqdux̂six̂ and me, we will forever be twenty and twenty-one, respectively, and while our brains are more expandable intel-lectually, our emotions, as you can witness with her especially, aren't fully matured, and never will be."

"So that's how Maguun could get into such a childish pre-dicament," I mused, "and why Kitax could just let it happen."

"Well, even the elders among us do stupid things from time to time. Just like old mortals, we're still limited by the biological deficiencies of the mind, and sometimes by plain dumb deci-sions. But experience does count for something. We've grown smarter over the centuries simply by trial and error. Kitax knew he couldn't save his brother without becoming imperiled himself. This is because the wings of vampire children aren't fully developed. They can fly only in short spurts, like lice or pigeons. Maguun may have been able to clear the chapel tarn, or maybe not. It was a dare of epic proportions. Had you not intervened, he'd be gone." Tears welled up in Qihmux̂'s eyes; she wiped them quickly. "Thank you, Kayuu,"—gently squeez-ing my arm—"that is all."

With that, she got up, gathered her children, and left, closing the partition behind her. The square portal above Aniqdux̂six̂'s room soon grew dark, even as white snowfall con-tinued to parry in through the dusk.

BACK FROM PATROL

"WHERE'S THE slave?" huffed an Aleut man, rumbling down the barabara's main ladder with heavy footsteps. It sounded like Qatxamax, a robust clan member in his late twenties with a bowl cut hairdo and a bone pierced through his forehead.

"Over here, you idiot!" Chief Aĝnakax̂ replied as he flew in through the portal above me. His son Tayaĝukichax̂ descended behind him, followed by Aniqdux̂six̂, who was Tayaĝukichax̂'s half-sister. "This is *my* room!" she protested.

The partition opened and Qihmux̂ entered, preceding Qagux̂ and Qatxamax, then shortly a whole host of other men from the barabara spilled in and surrounded me. Most wore bird-skin parkas that extended below their knees, but some donned a sealskin variety with breeches fashioned from seal esophageal skin.

"Make way!" the chief said, pushing his way through them. "Mortal! Tell me about your Allied base!"

"Why?"

"Because the Japanese are reconnoitering the west side of the island to set up defenses. Does not your military have radar or more scouts like you? It seems the Americans are not even aware of what is transpiring here."

A US patrol boat is shown on duty in the Aleutian Islands area, where Japanese warships are now reported to be operating in the vicinity of our naval base. (AP photo, December 31, 1942)

"My base is composed of Americans, Canadians, and other Allies," I clarified. "You must send me back to Kuluk to warn them."

"Just tell me the Allies' capabilities, and I will decide if we are to intercede. Does your base have radar? Do your planes? Are more planes scheduled to arrive, or other reinforcements?"

"If you want more information, permit me to return to Kuluk, not later, but now."

"How dare you seek to blackmail us!" Tayaĝukichax̂ raged, lunging at me with a javelin, its chiseled bone tip stopping just short of my eye. I glanced desperately between the projectile and the chief, who was just holding his son back.

"Stop, Tayaĝukichax̂!" Aniqdux̂six̂ came to my defense, pushing the tip away. "He saved Maguun's life!"

"Out of my way, *Americanchin*!" Tayaĝukichax̂ fought to push her aside.

"Go and see the child!" she cried. "And you, Qagux̂! Behold your son now!"

"What's this all about?" the chief inquired. "What happened to Maguun?"

"He's there!" Aniqdux̂six̂ fumed, thrusting a finger toward Qihmux̂'s quarters. "See his burns from falling into Ephraim's Lake! Kayuu saved him just in time!"

"Who's Kayuu?" asked Qagux̂, who was Qihmux̂'s boyfriend.

"The American! Now go! All of you!" She drove Qagux̂ clear out of her chambers, and then came back and laid a hand on Tayaĝukichax̂, attempting to do the same with him, but he pushed her to the ground.

"Hey!" I warned, trying to sit up, but Chief Aĝnakax̂ held me down with his staff.

Tayaĝukichax̂ lunged at my neck with his free hand, but the chief—his father—gave the young fighter a quick rap to his knuckles with his javelin stick.

"Aw!" Tayaĝukichax̂ groaned, shaking out his hand.

"Leave him be, you coward!" Aniqdux̂six̂ scolded the chief's bullheaded son. "Kayuu's frostbitten all over."

"His name is Igalix," Tayaĝukichax̂ grumbled back. "Igalix the weak, you dumb wight witch."

Aniqdux̂six̂ started after him again, but the chief, old but strong, blocked her with his staff.

"Don't you understand?" Tayaĝukichax̂ reproached both of them. "His people have already written him off as dead. They won't come looking for him, not out here. If we aren't going to make a slave of him, let's dispatch him now and enjoy the feast!"

I glanced around at the other Aleut vampires. Their faces were grim, many showing lips swollen by fresh piercings and the bite irritation caused by their protruding fangs. I couldn't ascertain their opinion of Tayaĝukichax̂'s dare, as they grumbled back in Aleut.

"No!" Aĝnakax̂ settled the matter, partially. "Not now."

"Maguun!" Qagux̂ shouted from the room adjacent, calling out his eldest son's name in shock and dread.

Several vampires went to see the burned child.

"I told you!" Aniqdux̂six̂ scolded the chief and a few others who had remained. "Maguun and Kitax were playing around Ephraim's Lake when Maguun fell in. I couldn't get a grip on him in the Holy Water. It was Kayuu who pulled him from certain doom."

I looked wide-eyed at Aniqdux̂six̂, taken aback by her admission. She had previously feared the chief knowing, but now, for my sake, was standing up to him.

Qihmux̂, standing with her mouth agape as she gazed at Aniqdux̂six̂, appeared completely nonplussed by her younger sister's about-face. Aniqdux̂six̂ had verily stolen her fire.

"This is blasphemy!" Chief Aĝnakax̂ declared, driving his staff hard against the ground. "The mortal is not to know such things, and the tarn is off-limits!"

"Kayuu did good by us," Qihmux̂ countered, placing a hand on my shoulder.

"I was there," Aniqdux̂six̂ added, maneuvering in front of Qihmux̂ to face the chief and in doing so, breaking her older sister's reach on me. It appeared they were vying to defend me. Aniqdux̂six̂ went on: "The mortal did not hesitate for a second to save Maguun, whom neither Kitax nor I could rescue. Kayuu risked his life in the freezing water and nearly succumbed to hypothermic shock because of it."

"They are lying," Tayaĝukichax̂ interjected, "lying to protect themselves and Igalix."

"That is no longer his name," Qihmux̂ countered, stepping beside her sister. "His name is now Kayuu."

"Kayuu the Strong," added Aniqdux̂six̂. "This wight I've brought in from the cold is no longer faint from bloodletting, for I have given him strength, and he has just returned the favor to us all."

Chief Aĝnakax̂ listened intently, weighing our arguments, while Tayaĝukichax̂ looked upon the old thinker with an air of disgust.

"*Hmpf*!" puffed Tayaĝukichax̂, flaring out his feathered bat wings with such force that a teenager beside him fell over. He ignored the youngster and stormed out of Aniqdux̂six̂'s sector.

"Tayaĝukichax̂!" the chief called out, but his firebrand son did not return.

"I'm going to see Maguun," the chief declared. "Everyone else, out of Aniqdux̂six̂'s room!—and that includes you, Qihmux̂! Aniqdux̂six̂, you stay here and watch over the wight. He looks blue in the face. He's still suffering from the effects of hypothermia, this much is certain. I'll deal with you and your sister later. And you, slave, there's no deal. You must stay with Aniqdux̂six̂ until I decide otherwise."

SHE-DEVILS, DOMESTICATED (SLIGHTLY)

THE LITTLE square portal above Aniqdux̂six̂'s room had become black with night, while several stone lanterns imbued her quarters with a soft golden light. She sat me up against a basket full of reeds, then began to hand-feed me sweet duck and stone-boiled mussels with chickweed, ending the meal with fried *alaadik* bread spread over with mossberry jam. My own hands were uselessly numb with frostbite, but the food was a welcome change from the staple of fatty whale blubber and yellow sea urchin eggs she usually prepared at that hour.

I again found myself studying the details of her features. She had become even more alluring to me, both physically and as a trusted friend. "Thank you for the food," I said.

"Do you like it?"

"I do. It's warm—just what I need."

She placed a palm over my forehead as if to check my temperature. I flinched on contact because her touch was so cold, and also I was taken aback by the many blisters on her hand.

She quickly removed her hand and went over to her stove, which she kept continuously burning. "I'll make you some *pootchky* tea," she offered. "That should do the trick. But I'm glad you liked the mussels and duck. They're not easy to come by this time of year."

Her kitchenware of choice consisted of an assortment of teakettles, heavy steel pots, cups, plates, and skillets, which, she revealed, had come into the clan's possession via a military supply vessel that had sunk in the Kagalaska Strait—a narrow pass that ran from Boot Bay up to Sitkin Sound and Kuluk Bay.

Japanese ship aground at Kiska Harbor (Dept. of US Navy photo)

Aside from cooking, Aniqdux̂six̂ used her stove to boil mysterious concoctions of flowers, fox and fish products, roots, and weeds, creating medicines, dyes, ointments, and adhesives for making things. Some of the plants and herbs she kept in dry storage, using wooden containers that were artistically carved over with rolling images of volcanoes, waves, spouting whales, and other local imagery. Fresh plants, such as white orchid, blue lupine, *pootchky*, monkshood, and chickweed, she culled from her fumarole garden, along with fruits like apples, blueberries, mossberries, and salmonberries. The berries she sometimes dried and stored in her ornamental containers.

Aniqdux̂six̂ never ate any solid food, at least not in my presence, but she, like all her ungodly cave clan tribe, frequently drank the blood of ocean mammals stored in seal-gut gourds, which hung ubiquitously about the barabara. The "hunting" expeditions the men went on were major fishing ventures, the choice bounty being larger mammals such as sea lions, seals, and whales due to their abundance of fresh blood (highest in the seal) and oil (highest in the whale).

She was relaying to me the manner in which whale oil is harvested, when suddenly Qihmux̂ burst in and slammed her against the barabara wall. "You despicable witch!" Qihmux̂ raged.

A large piece of peat moss came loose and curled down over Aniqdux̂six̂'s shoulder. She tore it from the wall and threw it at Qihmux̂, who easily dodged it.

Aniqdux̂six̂'s parka flared and she took wing over Qihmux̂, whose own wings began to unfurl, but not in time, for before she could take flight, Aniqdux̂six̂ drove her headlong into the partition on the opposite side; the woven wild rye structure gave way, the sisters crash-landing together into the adjacent sector.

I scarcely had time to register what was happening, when all at once the two women came cavorting back over each other in a bouncing ball of bat wings, rabid fangs, and flying fists, hissing and screeching like vixens in heat. It was frightening to witness, even more terrifying to hear. I no longer recognized their humanity. I froze with dread, while more of their extended family looked on from a distance.

"Get off of me!" Aniqdux̂six̂ spat at her sister, who had pinned her against the ground.

"Kitax has spoken!" Qihmux̂ shouted in Aniqdux̂six̂'s face. "I should've expected as much from you, you pompous tongue-twister! You made little effort to save Maguun!"

"I said, get off me!" Aniqdux̂six̂ struggled to break free, but Qihmux̂ had pinned her on her back and was holding her wrists.

"I should've known it was all for show!" Qihmux̂ declared. "You could've pulled him from the Holy Water, but you acted like the burns to your hands prevented such an action. *Bah!*"

"Acted?" Aniqdux̂six̂ shot back. "Look at my hands! And let go of my goddamned wrists!"

Qihmux̂ growled low into her sister's ear so that other clan members now gathered at the broken partition might not hear: "You've always been jealous of my family because you're unable to have kids yourself. And you're jealous that I have my mate, Qagux̂. That's why you've taken in Jake Harper, because you can't wait seventy-four more years to turn a mortal the proper way. And so how did you attempt your revenge on me?—you made a half-assed effort to save my son while hoping he would drown!"

"How stupid can you be, sister?" Aniqdux̂six̂ shot back. "You take the words of five-year-old Kitax as proof? Why didn't I stop Kayuu from saving Maguun, then?"

"You forgot all about your little Kayuu once he jumped in. You thought he'd drown as well."

"Rat shit!"

Qihmux̂ glanced back at me and said, "It's true: my sister left you for dead."

"No, Jake!" Aniqdux̂six̂ addressed me directly, as she struggled beneath her assailant's restraints, "—you know I love you and would never do that to you! She's only saying that because she's jealous of us, that we are going slowly and doing things the right way. She got pregnant with her boyfriend—"

Qihmux̂ fought to cover Aniqdux̂six̂'s mouth with her hand, but couldn't do so while pinning her down. Thus Aniqdux̂six̂ was able to continue her vindication: "—with her boyfriend when she was just sixteen, but he only stays with her because of their kids. The rules of the gen-cycle are strict about originally begotten children. Qagux̂ and Qihmux̂ are unmarried and always will be, because he refuses to propose—he only stays with her because of their children and our rules. It's a shotgun marriage without the marriage—only the shotgun, but Qagux̂ doesn't really love her."

At this, Qihmux̂ went ballistic, pushing Aniqdux̂six̂'s chin so far back that I thought she might break her neck.

I struggled to get up and intervene, when all at once Aniqdux̂six̂ emitted a terrible screech and arched forward so radically that she was able to flap her wings clear from the ground and take flight out from under Qihmux̂, whom she conveyed up with her through the ceiling portal, their bodies bouncing rudely off the doorframe as they passed.

"Stop them!" Chief Aĝnakax̂ ordered.

Numerous vampires took wing through ceiling egresses.

INAUSPICIOUS POLITICS

THE SMASHED partition was quickly rebuilt, effectively cordoning off Aniqdux̂six̂'s room from the rest of the barabara once again and, more significantly, from Qihmux̂'s sector. The two sisters now existed under an uneasy truce, or more like a forced separation, care of the chief. I was to remain with Aniqdux̂six̂.

But even amid my sequestration, many of the barabara members were gradually warming to me, not as food to eat, but more like a new member of the family. As the weeks passed, women would come in, bringing me strange dishes and sometimes flirting with me a little, all under the ever-watchful eyes of Aniqdux̂six̂. The men of the tribe also dropped by from time to time, sharing some words with me—but rarely did I see the chief.

Then one day in January or February of 1943 (in the barabara I'd been struggling to keep track of time), Chief Aĝnakax̂ came in to speak to me directly. "They now call you Kayuu," said he. "If you're named 'strong,' then you must work."

"What's happening outside?" I inquired. "Have the Allies found the Japs on Adak? Have the Japs hit Longview?'"

"Get up, Kayuu. Now you must work."

"What kind of work?" Aniqdux̂six̂ interposed. "He's already helping me here. See the walls and ceiling? Loose whalebones have been replaced, dirty reeds washed, and sod lining pressed. And look at the mats and baskets. I've taught him how to cure and sort the dune wild rye, and now we weave together. Regard the dyed elymus mullis fibers interlaced into the wicker. This is no easy task, Chief Aĝnakax̂. Next I will teach him how to make a *sax* jacket. Kayuu is becoming a skilled craftsman under my command."

"That is women's work. The mortal must do hunters' work."

"I know your men go out on hunting missions," I interjected, "and I know you have reconnaissance scouts. I would like to join them. I have skills outside that I can teach them for defense against the Japs."

The chief's brows curled in skepticism beneath his bentwood hat, his *chagudax̂*.

"It troubles me greatly," I added, "to be your prisoner while my enemies are making bold inroads here. You call me 'strong' while I sit here and grow fat from boiled whale blubber and *alaadik*."

"Thou dislikes my fried bread?" Aniqdux̂six̂ asked.

"It is not your turn to speak," the chief admonished, then signaled for me to continue.

"I didn't mean it like that, Aniqdux̂six̂," I responded to the other. "But Chief Aĝnakax̂, in all due respect, you seem content to let the war run its course so long as it doesn't affect you directly. Perhaps you believe that your location here in the south, with the Japs further west and the Allies up north, enables you to continue your existence out of harm's way. But I warn you, if the Japs are still amassing on Adak and the Allies at Longview don't know about it, the war on this island will significantly escalate and no place will be safe, not even this barabara in Boot Bay. The Japs' tactic is to dig in underground, to fight from foxholes and caves, while the Allies search for these very areas to burn them out. Your shelter here will inevitably be discovered and destroyed in the collateral damage of war."

The inroads of war expand throughout the Aleutians. Here US troop transport crafts are seen hauling men and howitzers up to newly created defensive positions. (Dept. of US Navy photo, 1943)

"We Aleuts have been living here continuously for nine thousand years," the chief remarked, none too pleased. "We don't like the Japs, and we don't trust you Americans, either. Your war means only trouble for us. I know that your navy burned down the village of Atka to prevent the Japanese from occupying it. This is how you treat us Aleuts."

"Yes, for their own protection against the Japs," I divulged. "The villagers of Atka were first evacuated to camps in southeast Alaska. We never harmed them."

"Evacuated?" huffed the chief. "You mean to say forcefully relocated, which is synonymous with death for Aleuts. We may be island peoples, but we're not ignorant about the world around us. Nine Aleut villages your government has uprooted. You forced every Aleut west of Unimak Island from their home, loaded them onto ships and then dumped them off at five mining camps surrounded by tall, soggy trees. Most Aleuts had never even seen a tree and were not prepared for the oppressive environment. We were once a proud and self-sufficient people until you forced us into your camps, where sicknesses, disease, and heartbreak daily do my brethren in, and you say we're not harmed? I know of your measles, mumps, pneumonia, of your whooping cough and tuberculosis. We will never allow ourselves such a fate."

I shook my head in doubt. How could he have known such things that I, coming from "the outside," didn't? I knew how many Aleuts had been relocated via information gleaned from an Army sitreps booklet, but it made no mention of the southeast camp conditions, or that the natives had to do any actual mining.

"I fear you may be misinformed, Chief Aĝnakax̂," I said, "but whatever the case, what if your barabara is discovered? You can't singlehandedly wage an all-out war against the Allies or the Japs, while retreat could only get you so far. Perhaps you could move further down the chain, but like the villagers of Atka, the tribes on every island have already been rounded up and sent to the southeast internment camps. Do you really want to go the way of the Atkans, the Nikolskis, the Akutans, the Makusins, and Biorkas? A vampire could not in any case live long in their camps without being discovered. Your only real option is to send me back to my base and allow my men to clear the Japs from Adak. You have my word that I will not disclose your whereabouts, and your existence will be made known to none. The Allies have no interest in long-term occupation of the Aleutians, and have only come in force because of the war. Once this madness is over, the troops will go home and the Aleuts will be repatriated to their homeland."

"The few that survive your concentration camps, that is," the chief growled in return.

"Hogwash!" I threw my hands up in frustration. "Now you're just being unreasonable. I'm trying to protect you."

"You are trying to protect us?" he laughed.

"You seem to know nothing about the seriousness of the Japanese contention," I warned. "They are currently acting out Phase Four of their blueprint for world conquest, The Tanaka Memorial, formulated in nineteen twenty-seven by the Japanese foreign minister, Baron Tanaka. Phase One was the Conquest of Manchuria, which they've already attained. Phase Two, the Conquest of China, has been bogged down, so they're hastening on with Phase Three, the Establishment of Bases in the South Pacific, and Phase Four, the Conquest of the United States, which is already well underway here in the Aleutians. Your ignorance of their plan is plain to see, otherwise you'd be doing more to join the war effort. You rail against America for evacuating the Aleuts, but pay no mind to places like Nanking, where hundreds of thousands of Chinese civilians were tortured and murdered by the Imperial Japanese Army in Phase Two of their twisted plan. Do you have any idea of what the Japs will do to you if they succeed with Phase Four? Yes, I stopped to save the boy Maguun, but had I only made it back to Longview, I could've resumed the duty I was sent out here to do—which is to stop the Japs dead in their tracks."

"You were stealing him back to Kuluk?!" Aĝnakax̂ glowered at Aniqdux̂six̂.

"I was on a recon," she said. "I wasn't going to free him."

"You!" the chief railed at her. "I should've known your underhanded and disingenuous ways! *Americanchin!* It wasn't enough to bring the mortal here, breaking our time-honored rules. You took him in, brought him back to health, and then sought to release him! Qihmux̂ was right! You're weak, and your transgressions have put our entire clan at risk. You couldn't wait for your gen-cycle, so acting like the child of your childish namesake, you kidnapped this wight, believing that would somehow make a difference. But seventy-four more years you shall wait, and this slave of yours can *never* be your chosen mate, for that timeline is an impossibility for him!"

Aniqdux̂six̂ began to cry. The chief's words hurt her but, ironically, both she and I privately knew that turning me into a vampire had never been her goal in the first place. She wanted to become human again, although she never told me exactly how she planned on achieving this. *It's possible,* and, *not yet,* was all she'd say regarding the mysterious process.

"You must be punished!" the chief lambasted her as she wept. "I'm taking the mortal away from you!" He grabbed me brusquely by the shoulder.

"*No!*" Aniqdux̂six̂ cried, coming forth for me.

Aĝnakax̂ beat her down with his staff, then jostled me out with the strength of five men. "The mortal works for me now!" he trumpeted back.

DARK SECRETS

CHIEF AĜNAKAX̂ conveyed me through the extent of the barabara. We passed about a dozen semi-partitioned areas that appeared to be family unit habitats a little larger than Aniqdux̂six̂'s room. Each had sitting and bedding areas, stone lanterns, woven wild rye floor matting, and abundant seal bladder gourds hanging conspicuously about. These last were filled with blood, I knew, from the purplish color of their bags and the crimson stains around their ivory spigots. I spotted two other stoves like Aniqdux̂six̂'s, but the majority of the families seemed to use the barabara's central fire if they needed something roasted, boiled, galvanized, or vulcanized for whatever reason. Even though the vampires had no need for warmth, I often saw them squatting over their stone lanterns while holding the bottoms of their parkas out like a funnel—so perhaps they did draw some pleasure from the sensation of heat, even though it served no practical purpose to their "undead" bodies. But I myself had come to adopt this technique, using my military jacket to capture the heat of the stone lanterns when the central fire and Aniqdux̂six̂'s stove just weren't cutting it.

Numerous stalls, I observed, were actively occupied by women and children, with some also containing elders. Several of the older women I saw weaving baskets, while one young lady seemed to be stitching an otter fur and bird feather parka that Aniqdux̂six̂ called a *sax*.

Close-up of The Inside of a House in Oonalashka, *showing natives weaving within a partitioned area of their barabara, as drawn by HMS* Resolution's *artist John Webber.*

It occurred to me that a tribe of Unangax̂ vampires, whose flesh was cold to the touch, would have no need for warm clothing, but then I thought of Aniqdux̂six̂, who showed little interest in being habitually naked before the inclement Aleutian elements.

Perhaps the *sax* and *kamleika* parkas, in being attached to a vampire's outer wingspread, served to camouflage the vampires' condition from the discovery of "wights" (mortals), should civilized men be happened upon. Or maybe they served as a protective shield from the sun, as sunlight—if traditional tales of vampires had any merit—had a profoundly hazardous effect upon the creatures. Alas, their reticence, indeed their very law preventing them from revealing their weaknesses to "wights" such as I relegated my theories to just that: postulated but untested assumptions. Even Aniqdux̂six̂, due to stern warning from Chief Aĝnakax̂, had learned to hold her tongue against me—although she often failed in this regard, engendering his recurring punishments.

My ruminations on such things were put on hold as the chief stopped before a darkened tunnel or cave. He grabbed an oil lantern hanging at the ingress and waved it before the blackness.

Fear struck my bosom as we entered the caliginous conduit. Death could come suddenly for me here, far from the watchful eyes of Aniqduxsix̂. The chief could end the major problem she had created for herself by keeping me alive.

I could not ascertain the length of the conduit, which increasingly appeared like a vast lava tube. There was no light at the end of the passage, and I spotted numerous secondary and tertiary cavities leading only to more darkness. It resembled the lava tube cave networks that the Japs were using to dig themselves in at places like Kiska and Iwo Jima, modifying readymade foxhole and trench configurations with several layers of habitable, defensive positions. Only it wasn't the Japs whom I feared in this frigid underworld, but the batmen creatures that I knew inhabited it. Should the chief turn on me now, or lead me into an ambush, I'd be all but defenseless against them; I was weak, wounded, and easy prey.

Suddenly, two Unangax̂ batmen darted past us from behind, startling me out of my wits as they raced forth into the black.

"I usually fly this stretch," Aĝnakax̂ said, breaking a long silence. "But this is just the sort of exercise you need, because you sure as hell aren't getting enough from Aniqdux̂six̂." He laughed.

His crass humor only underlined the fact that he wasn't her true father. A real father would never say such things, not unless he hated his daughter. I didn't care to reveal to him how much she actually took me out and all that we did together, both on the mat and off. Frankly, it was none of his business. "Where are you taking me?" I rejoined.

"To work, like I said," he quipped, "and not just with your legs. Hopefully your arms still work, too, and maybe even your brain. Or did that get frostbitten too?"

I'd actually felt a heightened sense of clarity since leaving Aniqdux̂six̂'s room. I suspected the things she incessantly brewed over her kettle served to keep me drugged to some extent, while the chill of the real world beyond the barabara helped to snap me back to alertness. The chief was nonetheless pushing my body hard. I was cold and needed rest. "How much further?"

"You will know when we get there." He was relentless. "Now pick up your feet, mortal, or true darkness shall be yours!"

He hastened his pace over the dried lava floor. I drew my ASF parka closer around my shoulders and tried my darnedest to follow in step.

TOOLS OF THE TRADE

THE LAVA tube cave terminated at a boathouse and workshop area as large as the barabara itself, but with no subdivisions whatsoever. There were dry-docked boats, primitive nautical gear, and workbenches around which dozens of Unangax̂ vampires slaved. Tayaĝukichax̂ was there working, too, and he became visibly angry when he saw me.

My hands were still numb from frostbite, but the chief put me into service anyway, right across the table from his implacable son. I was tasked to make whale hunting equipment. "Harpoons and throwing-lances," the chief said, "and if you graduate from that, you can repair *baidarkas*."

Tayaĝukichax̂ stood and reproached his father, "Why do you seat Igalix before me and entrust him with our trade? You know my blood boils at the sight of his face!"

The workshop went silent as the other Aleuts listened to the exchange.

Tactfully, the chief replied, "You'll be pleased to know that I've separated the American from Aniqdux̂six̂, and that he'll no longer be doing the work of women. You, Tayaĝukichax̂, can best keep him in line. But your insubordination to me ends here; this is a test of your restraint. Unless the mortal tries to escape or fails in his assigned task, you are not to harm him. Do I make myself perfectly clear?"

Tayaĝukichax̂'s brows sharpened and his face grew red with frustration and perhaps a twinge of embarrassment. "But chief," he addressed his father formally, "you can't expect me to show him how to make our weapons." His eyes darted furtively about his cohorts, and then he continued so softly that none but the chief and I might hear, "Not in front of my team."

"I don't expect you to," Aĝnakax̂ replied privately before continuing loudly enough for everyone to apprehend, "Sugangix̂ will put the mortal to work mending spears. Let this Jake Harper do a man's work for a change, if he can hack it. But if he fails, Sugangix̂ will let you know, son, and then you can put him back in line."

The young sea hunter Sugangix̂, who was sitting beside us, tipped his chin up to the chief and said, "No problem."

And this, too, I knew was an exchange of tact, working both in my favor and in that of the firebrand Tayaĝukichax̂, for the chief had publicly affirmed his son's might while secretly giving me a reprieve, as Sugangix̂, whom I summarily took a seat beside, had privately befriended me prior, as an associate of Aniqdux̂six̂. The chief knew as much, while the others may not have been privy to that.

*Sugangix̂, or likeness thereof (Drawing from the collection of
M. Muratov, Leningrad, 1937; no illustrator listed)*

"We're recycling harpoons," Sugangix̂ began, sliding various pieces before me. "You'll be refitting the four shafts of a compound harpoon back together. It's tedious work, requiring a lot of sanding of wood and retooling of bone ring joints that've broken apart. Nobody likes doing this job."

With a chorus of knowing sniggers from around the worksite, Tayaĝukichax̂ took his seat and the men resumed their work. Further down from my table I recognized Qihmux̂'s boyfriend, Qagux̂, a teen named Tix̂lax̂, and Qatxamax, a robust twenty-something warrior with a short-cropped bowl hairdo. How could I ever forget this last, whose name means "big penis" according to Aniqdux̂six̂, and who, in addition to his perfect bowl cut, now had a sea lion whisker running horizontally through his pierced forehead? Most of the other men in the room I'd seen before but had never actually met. As for Chief Aĝnakax̂, he'd already left.

"Pay attention!" Sugangix̂ sternly warned, probably for effect. "The thickest shaft terminates at the razor stone tip, tapering down from there to the lower sub shafts. You must re-sand the ends so they fit snugly into the sockets. Where the ends are split, you must saw them short, just below the crack, then retool them. Once you've finished that, I'll show you how to refit the bone rings. You will do this over and over until you've attained a tight fit, and only then will I show you how to fit the toggle-head spear tip, then braid the twine loop and connect it."

"I didn't know harpoons were so complicated," I said, eliciting chuckles from some of the others, but not from Tayaĝukichax̂, who sat opposite me, glowering as he broke seal vertebrae apart over the table.

"Very well, let's get started," I announced, grabbing two wooden shafts and testing their fit. My hands still hurt like hell from being frostbit, but I could just make a grip and figured the work might help the blood circulation in my fingers. "Was this harpoon damaged in a whale hunt?" I inquired of Sugangix̂.

"Probably," he said, "but it's not really damaged. The compound harpoon is supposed to come apart on impact. The four sections, once separated, cause the braided twine attached to rotate the spearhead into the prey like a corkscrew."

He gave me a handsaw made from sharks' teeth and driftwood, much like the Hawaiian *Lei-o-Manu*, explaining, "In case a shaft end is cracked and you need to sever it."

The sound of two stones knocking together further down the table garnered my attention. Tix̂lax̂, the teen, appeared to be shaping a pair of large arrowheads.

Sugangix̂ noticed my interest and said, "He's making toggle head spear tips from andesite."

Tix̂lax̂ regarded me with a sinister grin.

"And what are those guys doing?" I pointed over Sugangix̂'s shoulder to where a group of men were lifting rubbery mats out from soaking vats and stretching them taut with the strength of their hands.

"They're preparing the mammal skins to build and mend the *baidarkas*. The skins must first be soaked in urine and stretched."

"What kind of urine?"

Tayaĝukichax̂ slammed his jumble of vertebrae down on the table, one bouncing into my lap. "Are you here to work or to jabber like a woman?!" he raged.

"I'm just trying to learn the tricks of the trade," I replied nonchalantly, handing him back his vertebrae.

He snatched it and waved it brusquely before my face, saying, "Sugangix̂ told you what to do! You must cut and sand! Now do it before I make you!"

Several Aleuts rumbled in agreement, further bloating his overstuffed ego.

"Yes, sir!" I replied, reverting to my military training. I put my nose down and began sanding a wooden shaft end.

"Tayaĝukichax̂!" someone called over. "Give us a hand with this *baidara*!"

The ruffian prince dropped what he was doing and went over to help a crew of hunters move a large skin boat.

"Nice boat," I told Sugangix̂, trying to keep up the small talk in hopes of gleaning some new information. "Looks like it could hold a lot of people."

"Yes, the *baidara* can take us over the water to other islands. We trust it with our families. It's a very sturdy vessel, being made of walrus skin, and it has a large storage capacity. In Chief Aĝnakax̂'s mortal years, he led scores of warriors in *baidaras*, taking them as far as the Kodiak Islands to battle the Alutiiq. Our raids were legendary; they supplied us with many slaves."

"Do you hunt from a *baidara*, as well?"

"No, not usually. The *baidarka* is much faster and can keep up with a speared whale."

"What happens if the whale dives?"

Sugangix̂ regarded me with a raised brow. "You ask a lot of questions, *Americanchin*."

"People call Aniqdux̂six̂ that, too. What does it mean?"

"Too many questions, *Americanchin*. They call her that because she tries to act like you, a white American."

"Oh really? And how do white Americans act?"

"Nosy, like you're acting right now, and big-headed—you know how she can be. You should get back to work before Tayaĝukichax̂ gets on our case again."

Sugangix̂ did have a point—several, actually. I redoubled my efforts to hone and reconnect the various spear shafts.

⚬⚬

At length, Chief Aĝnakax̂ returned to check up on me. I'd made good progress with the compound harpoon, having reconnected the shafts into a solid-looking spear. He took it from me and closely looked over the bone rings covering the joints. "Did you retool these?" he asked.

"Yes, under Sugangix̂'s instruction."

"Not bad," said he, handing it back to me. "To further your training, you must now turn it into a throwing-lance."

"What's the difference?"

"The throwing-lance does not break apart except for the ring at the bonehead, so we can reuse the shaft. It is reserved for the largest of sea beasts, and to kill men. Sugangix̂ will show you how to make it."

"I want to join the hunt," I said outright. "The whale hunt."

The room, previously filled with low chatter, suddenly went silent.

"You want to hunt big fish?" the chief rejoined.

I held the spear in one hand to test its weight and balance. "I want to take down a whale with this."

"You want to see big fish up close, then?"

"Yes, sir."

"Sugangix̂, bring Kayuu the Strong some fish eyes!"

The Aleuts broke into laugher. I smiled with them.

Sugangix̂ shook his head as if to say *don't smile, you've been had.* He got up from his chair and went in one direction, the chief proceeded in the opposite direction, while I hung my head over my spear entirely deflated, but still wondering about its power.

BLOOD TIES

"MASH THEM together," Sugangix̂ instructed, handing me a human femur bone, while before me sat a stone bowl filled with freshly boiled fish eyes. "You must hurry before it cools."

I began crushing the eyes with the bone, but every time I hit them, the eyeballs just moved apart.

"Faster, like this!" he said, taking the bone and whip-mashing the eyes like eggs yolks. In no time at all he'd formed a bowlful of goo.

"Okay, got it." I seized the bone back. Hundreds of fisheyes glistened back at me. *I'll show them!* I thought as I smashed them hard and quick. *They haven't seen the start of me!* I imagined I was grinding the chief's quip into a gooey fisheye whip.

"That's enough," Sugangix̂ said, stopping my hands over the top of the femur bone. I'd been smashing like a madman. "Let it cool, then you shall glue the lance together.

As Lieutenant Jake Harper was smashing fish eyes together on the south shore of Adak, the Allied forces continued to amass innumerable warships at Kuluk Bay. Something big was going down in the Aleutians—something that would soon put the cave clan vampires squarely in its sight. (11th U.S. Army Air Force photo, 1943)

Another opportunity for "small talk," I thought, eyeing the men around us, who were preoccupied with their projects. I began rolling my spear back and forth over the table, creating an obtrusive sound with which I masked my next words: "Is it not dangerous for you to use these things?"

Sugangix̂ regarded me critically. "What do you mean?"

"You know, wooden stakes?"

He glanced around furtively. The other Unangax̂ vampires didn't appear to have overheard me. I kept the spear rolling at the same tempo.

"These cannot harm us," he replied inconspicuously.

"So the legend is false?" I quietly importuned. "Wooden stakes, silver bullets, and such?"

"You are not to know such things," he scolded without breath. But still our secrecy held.

"Try me. I'm a smart man. Why don't wooden stakes work?"

"Only the wood from a holy site can harm us," he replied, then covered his mouth in a display of self-reproof.

"A holy site? Like a church?"

"The adhesive is ready now." He changed the subject. "You must gather some to mend the lance together, like this."

He dipped his hand into the fish-eye muck and then gingerly rolled some into a ball with his fingertips. "You go." He motioned toward the bowl.

I tried to mimic him, but the goo was too tacky and soon formed an elastic web between my fingertips.

"Like this!" he repeated, rolling his fingers faster, but when I did the same, it only made my predicament worse, and soon my whole hand was webbed together.

"I saw how Holy Water could hurt you," I diplomatically revisited the subject, "when I saved Maguun. Just tell me what else endangers you, and I can be a real asset. If you refuse to fight the Japs, at least you can tell me this!"

I'd raised my voice. Alas, Tayaĝukichax̂ had been standing directly behind us for most of the conversation anyway. He spun me around and my gooey hand landed on the chest of his seal-gut parka, sticking there like flypaper. When I tried to remove it, I pulled the burly indigene even closer to me.

He pushed me back to arm's reach then proceeded to pound me in the face. He hit me so hard that my nose began to stream with blood and my adhesive hand separated from his body. A final, big blow sent me flying across the table and over his pile of seal vertebrae.

Landing on the other side of the bench, I saw him jump onto the table with unfurled wings and fangs in full display.

Struggling to get up, I reached beside me and my sticky hand inadvertently latched onto my lance, which had fallen off the table with me. I stumbled back against the wall, using it and the lance to get back onto my feet.

"A fine adhesive your blood will make for our weapons!" Tayaĝukichax̂ chided, rolling his head to stretch out the muscles of his burly neck. Tattoos of sea life in distress ran from his chin to his chest, while a mighty bird bone labret was skewered horizontally through his lower lip.

The other vampires laughed gurgling, salivating laughs.

My shirt, jacket, and army fatigues were splattered with blood. I pointed my lance at Tayaĝukichax̂, and then everywhere before me as a whole host of vampires closed in, their fangs drooling in hungry anticipation.

It seemed that Tayaĝukichax̂ himself would claim the mortal blow, so I trained my javelin back on him. Physically he was my superior, weighing probably two hundred and eighty pounds, while I was a relatively lean one-fifty. Sugangix̂ and Tix̂lax̂, meanwhile, had slowly backed away from the throng, not wanting to eat me, but unwilling—or unable—to intervene.

Tayaĝukichax̂, or likeness thereof (Illustration by M. Muratov, Leningrad, 1937)

Suddenly, Tayaĝukichax̂ jumped.

I broke my lance in two and made an X-shape with the pieces, just catching his neck in the wedge as he came down upon me. I threw him aside with his crazy momentum and his head careened into the reed wall behind, penetrating through the sod insulation up to his chin. As he struggled to free his noggin from a whalebone support worked into the wall, I whipped my two staffs around toward the others. They slowly backed off.

Tayaĝukichax̂ stood and removed a piece of peat that had gotten stuck to his cheek, throwing it aside with disgust. "Now you die," he sentenced tersely, his eyes glowing lava red. He raised his fists high over his head, his wings spanning out horrifically, then emitted a terrible roar.

I inched back onto the table, holding my staffs at him and all around me.

He grabbed my feet and threw me against the wall like I were a ragdoll. I bounced off the peat and rolled under the table. He tried to grab me, so I scrambled to the other side, and kept scrambling between a throng of vampires' legs. The hands of the undead clawed down by the dozens, attempting to snag me up. But I made it through the last pair of legs, or so I thought until one more appeared before me and spread out, blocking my way with an expanse of walrus gut skin stretched low in between. I looked up and beheld the chief, looking down at me while shaking his head disappointedly, *tsk-tsk-tsk*.

"Get up and fight," he said, grabbing my shoulders and lifting me to my feet as if I weighed nothing. But then he looked me squarely in the eyes with a glare of determination, encouraging so that only I could hear, "And show me what you're made of." He spun me around to face my nemesis, then gave me a little nudge.

I slightly stumbled over my onetime injured leg, then stood firm and shook out my shoulders, doubling down on my courage. The chief was right: this was my ultimate test with his hard-boiled tribe, and as a military man, retreat was tantamount to cowardliness, not to mention it was futile. I resolved to die like the Japs, running forward with lance in hand.

Having seen the chief's actions, the vampires before me cleared an aisle, where on the other side stood Tayaĝukichax̂, glaring back at me like some sort of demonic ox.

The hunters began chanting his name, and then like a prison gang spurring on their underground hero they began calling out his name in chorus, faster and faster, while clapping at each syllable: "*Ta-Ya-Gu-Ki-Chax! Ta-Ya-Gu-Ki-Chax!*"

As I marched toward the thick-headed prince that would likely be my "maker," Tix̂lax̂ and Sugangix̂ came forward in the phalanx. They were neither clapping nor calling out my executioner's name; rather, Sugangix̂ made a fist and surreptitiously pounded it against his chest in a show of strength and solidarity on my behalf. I nodded almost imperceptibly in recognition, then continued on my fated warpath.

Seeing Tayaĝukichax̂ before me, showing off his muscles as he stretched out his wings, I seized the initiative to throw him off guard, running at him at full speed.

He noticed my frontal assault all too late, enabling me to lunge my lance ends into his stomach before he could take flight. One bounced off his sweaty belly, but the other shaft— the one glued to my hand—penetrated into his gut. The force of the double-blow caused him to tumble back. As I flung forward over him, my spear extracted from his belly. He clutched his wound with a groan, then sat up and studied his hands, which were bloodstained black.

A collective gasp emanated from the spectating vamps. The meanest among them had been wounded. But as Tayaĝukichax̂ stood up again, my hopes of striking the mortal blow were dashed. Sugangix̂ had spoken plainly: the wooden stakes I held were not the kind that killed vampires.

The bastard son flew at me once again. I batted down one of his arms as he attacked, but he seized my neck with his other hand and began to squeeze the life out of me.

I jammed a lance end into his ear and began to twist it like a screw picket into the ground. He attempted to deflect the afflicting staff with his free hand, so I knocked him in the back of the head with my other staff.

He released his grip on my neck and slinked back from my counterattack, but before I could catch my breath, he wrapped an arm around me in a full headlock, the face pounding summarily resuming with his other hand.

I was seeing red as my blood splattered into my eyes, then strobes of unconsciousness flashed blackly before me. In a final, desperate attempt to stave off death, I jammed one of my staffs blindly into my nemesis.

He released me in an instant and we both fell to the ground in a bloodied, battered heap. He doubled over his chest and moaned, for my desperate, blind jab had landed directly into his old wound, and this time it hurt him bad.

I rolled this way and that over myself, short-winded, punch-drunk and unable to get up.

"It's a draw!" the chief called, answered by sporadic claps, first by Tix̂lax̂ and Sugangix̂, but soon the others joined in, and ere long the applause was accompanied by a chorus of whistling Unangax̂ vampires relishing in the blood sport's conclusion.

Shortly the undead fraternity came over and helped us both up, and soon had a hand, each from Tayaĝukichax̂ and me, raised high in celebration of the tie outcome. This exacerbated his puncture wound even more, however, so they helped him over to the skin boats instead, where he sat woozily upon the railing of a *baidara*, trying to regain his composure.

I was winded, too, so took an unsteady seat on the bench.

"Chief Aĝnakax̂!" Tayaĝukichax̂ called out, coughing and spitting black blood. "Everybody! The slave was asking Sugangix̂ how to kill us!"

A hubbub ensued throughout the workshop.

"Dare not test our powers, *Americanchin*," the chief warned, grabbing the lance end still glued to my hand, "for we are immortal."

He tried to remove my staff, creating an unforeseen tug-of-war. To counter the pain that his attempts had caused to my shoulder and arm, I kept pulling the pole back toward me. This back-and-forth dragged on to the point of ridiculousness, at which point Sugangix̂ splashed my adhesive hand with whale oil, dissolving the fish-eye bond and releasing my grip.

I looked at the chief sourly as I shook out my arm and hand. "It's not true," I countered Tayaĝukichax̂'s assertion.

"The mortal lies," said Qatxamax, aka "big penis."

"Speak," Aĝnakax̂ ordered him.

"I heard him, too," Qatxamax said, "asking Sugangix̂ about our weaknesses."

"Is this true, Sugangix̂?" the chief demanded, placing my ally on the spot, which potentially could be a very dangerous position for him, depending upon his response. To be ostracized in these parts was no small matter, as tribes were known to do to treasonous members—if the death penalty didn't come instead.

I quickly intervened: "I was trying to find out from Sugangix̂, yes! Because if your tribe isn't going to fight the Japs, then I need to know how to protect you from them! You don't know the enemy like I do. They show no mercy, not even to native noncombatants."

A mocking laugh ensued from Tayaĝukichax̂, a laugh cut short by his gurgling on black blood. He spat it out and said, "The mortal protecting us? Now that's the joke of the century, and a flat-out lie. Remember that it was his race that burned our villages and sent us to the death camps of the southeast. Now he comes into our barabara, spies on us and lies in the face of our chief, a proud Unanga. And you still believe this *Americanchin*, this imposter?"

The Aleuts grumbled in distaste.

Chief Aĝnakax̂ shot me an angry glance. "You say you want to protect us," he said, "but my son is right, you have no real reason to. You have a war to fight and we're in your way."

"I'm trying to find out how to protect you from the Japs," I finally admitted, "because I love Aniqdux̂six̂ and don't want to see her harmed by them."

The war the Japanese brought Fort Mears, Unalaska, under attack. Two barracks are ablaze on the right side of the photo, while three warehouses are burning to the left after the first Japanese bombing run on Dutch Harbor, June 3, 1942. (Photo by U.S. National Archives, 1942)

This elicited laughter from many, but not from the chief, who was Aniqdux̂six̂'s stepfather. He held a poker face. But as the mocking mounted, he silenced the crowd with a sharp wave of his hand.

"You have become a big problem for me, Mister Harper. In our tradition, men must prove themselves with deeds, not words. A chief's daughter is not to be trifled with, no matter how capricious she may be, while you bring me nothing but trouble and no dowry. There is only one way to resolve this matter, because I know she likes you, even though you will die anyway before her, as your mortal years are swift. You can in no way be her eternal mate, but you do calm her rockiness, I shall concede, and most here have got to appreciate that, including me.

"An Unangax̂ chief can only be lied to once," warned he, "because there's no second time for a dead man. You must thus prove these serious utterances you speak. You shall be on the next *qaqmiiĝux̂*."

Subdued chatter rose from the crowd. The chief silenced them with another wave of his hand.

"The hunt of giants is a life-or-death undertaking for an untrained wight like you," he continued. "Yes you, Mister Harper, have forced your hand to the ultimate test. You have unwittingly entered the world of the Niiĝuĝis islanders, which may have been your greatest mistake."

He gave the spear end back to Sugangix̂ and ordered: "You shall fix the throwing-lance for the mortal. Remember that his life depends on it."

I looked past Sugangix̂, to Tayaĝukichax̂. He was smiling at me sinisterly and licking the black blood off his fangs.

"Excitement's over," announced the chief. "Everybody back to work!"

I squeezed the blood from my shirttail before raising it back up to my nose to soak in more.

"You're coming with me," Aĝnakax̂ said, touching my shoulder. He proceeded toward the lava tube from whence we had initially arrived.

I was a bloody, shambling train wreck. He waited for me at the tunnel opening before we entered together.

"Who started the fight, anyway?" he inquired once we were in the dark recess of the conduit. "Let me guess, it was Tayaĝukichax̂. It seems he failed my test."

"Why'd you seat us together? You know he hates my guts."

"My son doesn't hate you. He's just looking out for the clan, and distrusts strangers—for good reason. But I thought you two bonded pretty well back there."

"I hope you're kidding." I spat out another wad of blood.

"Me, kidding? Never. That's why I sat you two together, so you could get to know each other better."

"I'll say."

He glanced behind us, toward the boathouse where all the drama had gone down. We were now completely out of sight of it. "This is far enough," he deemed, then grabbed my shoulders and took wing.

My legs were freed from the strain of gravity and the onrush of air enlivened my senses. All was dark, for he'd left his lantern behind. He darted this way and that through the black and bending lava tube, but I was not afraid. In that fleeting moment I truly and utterly felt free: free from time, from space, free even from my own mortality, nailed to the earth as I was as a "wight"—a sentient being.

"Thank you!" I called up to the vampire chief who conveyed me. I'm not sure if he heard me in the whooshing headwind, as he flew forth more expeditiously.

THE LIGHT OF EMBERS

AFTER DEPOSITING me by the central fire, Chief Aĝnakax̂ spoke with a woman who, like him, was excelling in years, but who held an air of power and grace. Her hair was long and white, and she was resplendent in traditional Aleut garb. As they conversed in Unangam Tunuu, they gravitated toward another area.

Aniydux̂six̂'s room. . . was all I could think. I shuffled through the barabara toward her quarters, but no sooner than I saw her partition did the chief land in front of me, waving a finger before my face.

"Like I said, I cannot permit you to see her," was his blunt reminder.

"Please?"

"Your mortal condition is showing pitifully, Mister Harper. Come, I'll help you get patched up, but you shall be spending the night elsewhere."

I hung my head in defeat.

He turned me about-face then marched me into another quadrant of the sod house, stopping before a partition. The plaited wild rye door slid open and the white-haired woman he'd been conversing with received me into her lair.

"My name is Iganakuchax̂," she said, taking my hand and guiding me to a soft peat moss chair. "The chief has instructed me to your care."

Tall, embroidered baskets were set here and there about her quarters. A little Aleut girl suddenly appeared behind one, gazing at me with big brown eyes.

"And what is your name?" I inquired.

She covered her face and giggled.

"She doesn't speak English?" I put to Iganakuchax̂, who proceeded to scold her in Aleut.

The child came out from her hiding place and replied shyly, "Datuu."

"And how old are you, Datuu?"

She looked from me to Iganakuchax̂, then back to me with her big almond eyes and replied, "Nine-and-a-half."

"Go get the poultice," the elder told her, pointing toward three pots simmering over a pit of red-hot rocks.

Datuu did as she was told, and soon Iganakuchax̂ was wiping the blood and dirt from my face with homemade sod sponges dipped in a strange-smelling brew. The bloodied sponges she passed down to Datuu to clean in hot water, from where the child transferred them back into the medicine kettle for Iganakuchax̂ to reapply to my head wounds.

It wasn't long before the two were helping me pull off my hopelessly bloodstained bomber jacket and shirt, which they tossed into a tall basket, hopefully to launder. Iganakuchax̂ proceeded to wipe my arms and chest while Datuu went to work on the fish-eye glue still stuck to my hand.

"I'm very thirsty," I told Datuu.

She got up, wrapped a cloth around her hand, took another pot from atop the coal pit and emptied its contents before climbing a ladder into the night.

"She's collecting snow?" I was a survivalist of sorts, and was keen to the trick.

Iganakuchax̂ cracked a smile, answering naught.

Close-up of The Inside of a House in Oonalashka, *showing Aleut descending down notched log ladder, as drawn by HMS* Resolution's *artist John Webber.*

Datuu soon came scrambling back down the ladder, a pot full of powdery ice melting all the while. She stirred the slush with a bone, then emptied it into a wooden bowl and offered it up to me.

"*Taanga*, Datuu." I thanked her in Unangam Tunuu—a language I was becoming slightly more familiar with.

She giggled self-consciously, covering her mouth and causing some of the water to spill onto my chest.

Iganakuchax̂ scolded her, sponging the water off my front.

Datuu stopped smiling and began administering to me in earnest, holding the bowl to my lips with both hands, being very careful to neither underfeed nor drown me. I held the bowl with her and drank all the melted snow, save a few chunks of leftover ice.

Iganakuchax̂ grabbed the remaining cubes and told her, "Bring more like this, but bigger."

As Datuu scurried back up the ladder, the elder placed a chunk of ice against my bruised face. "Tayaĝukichax̂," she sighed, handing me a piece of ice and guiding my hand over another bruise, "that boy."

No sooner had Datuu returned with a bowlful of ice did Iganakuchax̂ send her to fetch some new clothes for me.

"That won't be necessary," I remarked. "I'll clean my fatigues."

Iganakuchax̂ looked at the tall basket, shaking her head all the while. The rim and bottom were visibly bloodstained by my soiled clothes.

"Well," I reconsidered, "can they be repaired? The jacket at least?"

"Perhaps later we shall try," Iganakuchax̂ deemed, and then she unrolled a fiber satchel that concealed a steel knife. The blade gleamed lengthwise as she studied it in the light of embers.

Sitting half-naked and beaten before the crafty old woman as she held her prepossessing knife, I felt more vulnerable than I did standing before Tayaĝukichax̂. This woman had just studied my every weakness. I mentally readied my hands, watching her every move. "Where'd you get that?" I inquired, trying to ascertain her motive.

"By trade," she said, and then she pointed the knife at me, but only briefly before placing it beside the soiled basket. She procured from her fiber satchel another knife that partook of ivory.

"That's quite a little collection," I remarked. "What are they for?"

"This one's bone, nothing fancy, but it works good in slicing the fat and muscle from rubbery intestine walls."

I eyed her suspiciously in the waning glow of simmering coals.

"Seals and sea otters," she explained, pointing her white knife toward the shadows, whereupon Datuu returned with a stack of folded textiles weighing upon her arms.

"Now light some lanterns for the mortal," Iganakuchax̂ ordered, taking the clothes from the girl. "I'll teach you good hospitality yet, child."

"I knowest thee can see not well in the dark, Sir Jake," offered Datuu. "I may be but a bairn, but I still remember the ways of a wight. Dost thou wish for me to shew you how to effect a fire with quartz rocks and sulfur?"

"Kayuu!" Iganakuchax̂ rebuffed. "His name is Kayuu! Now go and do as your grandmother asked."

As Datuu slid away, I looked at Iganakuchax̂ with an air of surprise. "She talks like Aniqdux̂six̂," I remarked.

"Please be patient with us," entreated the elder. "We don't get many visitors, and have become all too accustomed to our own behaviors, I'm afraid. Datuu has taken up Aniqdux̂six̂'s hobbying with old English books and poetry. On one of the wrecks we salvaged long ago, we found a captain's library filled with classical playwrights and poetry, including a complete volume by William Shakespeare. Aniqdux̂six̂ has convinced Datuu that his is the best and most proper mode of English, and that by speaking it, we are made less defiled by our affliction—or that's how Aniqdux̂six̂ regards our condition, anyway." <Rolling her eyes> "Most of us tend to differ. But come, let me help you up. Datuu has brought you a competent *kamleika* to wear."

As Datuu illuminated the room by lighting more stone lanterns, Iganakuchax̂ helped me get dressed. "You must lose those." The elder was pointing at my soiled pants still hanging around my waist beneath the waterproof parka that she'd given me.

"I'll be fine."

"No." She held up a pair of sea mammal gut breeches. "You must wear these for the hunt or you'll freeze."

"When is the hunt?"

"Anytime; the men are now preparing. But don't worry—it won't be tonight. Now come, try on your new pants. I made them myself from seal esophageal skin, which Datuu helped me cure."

"Okay, if you insist." I didn't want to deny their hospitality. I was still in the business of making allies in this vampire den, because one thing I knew for sure—they made terrible enemies. I dropped my pants and pulled on the gut skins. They fit snug at the heels, but were a little loose at the waist, which a convenient drawstring fixed.

Iganakuchax̂ tossed my old pants in with my soiled garb, then reached behind her and grabbed a *chagudax̂* bentwood hat, placing it on my head. "There, now you look like a genuine hunter," she deemed with a twinkle. "Maybe Tayaĝukichax̂ will show you more respect."

I rolled my eyes. "Maybe not."

"You must earn it, Kayuu. Chief Aĝnakax̂ didn't become a chief by cowering down. He, too, was once a commoner, until he proved himself in battle and excelled in many a *qaqmiiĝux̂*— legendary whale hunts that left many dead."

"Kayuu!" Datuu pulled excitedly at my rubbery parka. "Come see my stitching floor!"

"Not now, Datuu!" scolded her grandmother. "The mortal is tired."

But with amazing strength for a nine-year-old, she was already pulling me away.

"Datuu!" Iganakuchax̂ warned.

"It's okay," I called back. "I don't mind."

The room Datuu took me through—the room I'd been hunkered down to one side of—was long, rectangular, and much larger than most of the other quarters I'd observed within the barabara. While the usual nuclear family habitat had just one overhead egress accessible by a notched log ladder (or simply by a mature vampire's flying ability), the dwelling of Iganakuchax̂ and Datuu contained at least three. Each opening overhead was met with an angular snowfall, indicating a williwaw had suddenly appeared, as was their fashion. The Aleut vampires, I knew, would soon close all but the main egress located above the central fire—a pyre always kept burning with crowberry, driftwood, dried *pootchky* stems, and the roots of the ground willow.

Datuu whisked me along, past macabre sights of sea mammal skins stretched taut to dry between driftwood and whalebones, past fetching visions of plaited grass baskets overflowing with walrus ivories, and past several semi-partitioned areas, a dearth of lantern light enshrouding their contents.

We stopped before an assortment of prepared skins, feathers, bundles of gut and reed twines, and several Aleut vestments laid out in various stages of completion. "This is my sewing ground!" Datuu announced with a leap in her step; and then she yanked me further, taking me before a small *sax* jacket made from white, blue, and black feathers draped in a decorative pattern.

"That must be for you," I said, taking stock of its size.

"Yes, Kayuu, I made it for myself."

"*You* made that?"

"She's been making her own parkas for practice," Iganakuchax̂ interpolated, having followed in our shadow.

"Once she perfects those, I'll teach her how to make *kamlei-kas*, such as the one you're wearing. Outfitting the tribe for the mercurial Aleutian environment is both a fine art and practice of consequence."

"Mercurial? How?"

"Listen," she replied, then went silent. The storm outside was whistling with increasing violence.

"Datuu, close the hatches. If Kayuu is to see our workshop, he must be comfortable and we must start correctly, according to the sequence of manufacture. Allow me, Mister Harper."

The sagacious olden one signaled for me to follow, and so we proceeded to backtrack a score of yards while Datuu scrambled dutifully up and down the various ladders, closing the hatches.

"The men bring us the intestines of walruses and other sea mammals to prepare," Iganakuchax̂ said. "We cut the tubes of gut into swathes, then clean them before stretching the membranes between stakes to dry."

Before us sat a small graveyard of skins stretched taut between pickets. Upon closer inspection, I noticed that some of the stakes were Rommel spikes. Bluebottle flies were also in evidence, scurrying about the outstretched swathes.

I followed Iganakuchax̂ around a partition to her sewing area, where several seal- and walrus-gut parkas were laid out, still in construction, across a reed mat, and where two were fully completed, dressed upon a rudimentary driftwood and mammal skin manikin. "Datuu," she called back, "bring me a completed *sax*."

While Datuu was off fetching the garment, Iganakuchax̂ expounded upon the parkas before me, "These are *kamleikas*: men's hunting suits. They're sometimes fitted for women, who frequently venture out to sea with the men to catch birds. It's highly durable raingear, replete with hood and drawstring; even the sleeves have cinches, closing the garment tight at the wrists. You can see where the patches of skin are stitched together with intestinal twine wrought from seals and other sea mammals, making the entire vestment completely waterproof against the ocean, and very resilient. Customarily, fox hair and sea otter fur is sewn into the seams for warmth. Neither storm wave nor williwaw can penetrate a finely stitched *kamleika*. We make our boots and breeches in the same fashion, using the esophageal skin of seals for the leggings and sea lion flippers for the soles. But most of us go barefoot year-round."

"Because of your condition?" I inquired, believing vampires had no need of warmth.

"Not just that," she revealed. "The Andreanof Aleuts and those of the islands further west have always gone barefoot all the year round. Some think footwear looks stylish, though, so we sometimes make it for fun. Aniqdux̂six̂ is a sucker for good boots. Sea skins are also used for our waterproof bags, for mummification, and for gourds in which we store whale oil, water, and other liquids. In times past, we've also used these items for trade."

She gestured to one of the ubiquitous purple-mouthed gourds hanging along the barabara walls. I knew it was full of blood. My eyes settled uneasily back upon hers.

"Trade with whom?" I sought to change the subject.

"With the Dena'ina and Ahtna Athabascans, the Yup'ik, Tlingit, and the Eyak, and we've had a few white visitors over the centuries as well. Some of the implements you see in this workshop came from Grigorii-Shelikhov's company, and from Captain Aleksie Chirikov's ship, which set anchor in Boot Bay on September 9, 1741. Unfortunately, these were two among a long line of Russian vessels that came, first with their explorers, then with their well-armed *promuishlenniki*, their merchants, diseases, religion, and subjugation, the end result being the near extinction of the Aleut people."

"No different than on the mainland," I added, well aware of the reputation of my European ancestors. "They called it Manifest Destiny."

"Aleuts lived good lives before we were invaded," she lamented. "We melded our lives so closely with these islands and adapted to the harsh environment so well that for us it was a paradise. As proud *Niiĝuĝis* people of Adak, we wouldn't sacrifice our lifestyle here for the world, and especially not for your death camps. Our existence here must remain a secret from your government at all costs, but if we *are* discovered, we shall repair to the Islands of Four Mountains, the birthplace of the Unangans, and there live out our lives in peace."

The Islands of Four Mountains, *birthplace of the Unangans (Exclusive art by Ovidiu Kloska)*

"You talk much of peace and paradise," I remarked. "But how could it have been a paradise with intertribal raids and such?"

"Few people are without a history of war."

She exhibited an uncanny knowledge of the world, given how isolated her people appeared to be. Then again, she was over two hundred years old and, furthermore, she could fly.

"Even as we speak, the opposing armies of your nation and Japan grope through the storm clouds above, frightening the ravens of our far-flung islands in the ebb and flow of world combat. But the battles Aleuts fought over our hunting grounds were of an entirely different nature. Hard and cruel, yes—intertribal battles were common, but remember, we're a highly localized people. Fighting was done via *baidara* boats and spears. It enhanced our lore and traditions, but was never by nature like your sweeping international conflicts that crush entire peoples beneath the gears of world conquest."

Datuu ran into the sewing area holding a homemade *sax* parka, which Iganakuchax̂ instructed her to display beside a *kamleika.*

"Notice the difference," Iganakuchax̂ offered, "between the *kamleika* and *sax* jacket. The *kamleika* generally contains no bird skin, nor decorative accents such as colorful treading and embroidered patterns. But sometimes we paint them with symbols of the hunt using vermillion paint. We make our boats with the same material, as well. The *qaqmiiĝux̂* is a perfectly closed system."

"The what?"

"The *qaqmiiĝux̂*—the hunt for food. The byproducts we gather enable us to embark upon further hunts and prolonged salvaging raids, which in turn bring back the core materials of our lifestyle, enabling us to effectively hunt again."

"The qaqmiiĝux̂ is a perfectly closed system." (Exclusive art, Aleut Whaler, by Ovidiu Kloska)

"The design and construction of a new *kamleika,* or a new *baidarka* or *baidara* boat is a laborious task, but fortunately it is highly recyclable."

"What do you mean?"

"Most of the materials employed are interchangeable. We can patch a *baidarka* with a *kamleika* parka, and vice versa, which goes a long way if trouble develops out at sea. Sea skins are built to last in this environment—the wetter they get, the better.

"*Sax* jackets, on the other hand, are not designed for rough ocean ventures, but are an everyday costume for men and women. This is Unangax̂ finery."

Datuu shoved her example in my face, proudly displaying her creation.

A Man of the Island of Unalaschka, wearing a *sax* frock, as drawn by William Wade Ellis (1756–1785), surgeon's mate during Captain Cook's third voyage (first on the HMS Discovery and later on the HMS Resolution). Cook recorded his own description of the Aleuts, writing, "These people are rather low of Stature, but plump and well shaped, with rather short necks, swarthy chubby faces, black eyes, small beards, and straight long black hair. Their dresses, both Men's and Women's, are made alike, the only difference is in the Materials, the Women's frock is made of Seal skin and the Men's of birds skin and both reach below the knee." (*From* An authentic narrative of a voyage performed by Captain Cook and Captain Clerke, in His Majesty's ships *Resolution* and *Discovery* during the years 1776, 1777, 1778, 1779, and 1780: in search of a North-West passage between the continents of Asia and America, by G. Robinson, published December 14, 1781)

W. Ellis del.   J. Caldwell sculp.

A Man of the Island of Unalaschka.

Publiſhed Dec:14:1781.by G. Robinſon.

"Notice the uniform lines of puffin and guillemot feathers," Iganakuchax̂ continued, "the decorative flair of the threads. Most *sax* parkas take up to a year for one woman to make, each jacket requiring the choicest feathers from hundreds of select seabirds. Unlike the seal, sea lion, and whale skins used in the *kamleikas*, the *sax* has a hidden layer of sea otter fur and bird skins to provide basic waterproofing, with reindeer hair sewn into the seams for additional warmth; we keep this tradition alive to give the parka its eminently wearable softness and puff, ideal for barabara wear and tooling around outside.

"Observe the colorful threads, inked from octopus bag, root and grass dyes, and the paint of vermillion. Notice the sea lion beard bristle accents, the feathered epaulettes and bird claws worked into the neckline. Datuu is off to a great start with this one, but will need to make a few more before she has a true command of the details. Aniqdux̂six̂ is the master seamstress of the *sax* jacket; she ventures far and wide to gather the precise materials she needs."

I ran my fingers down the feathers of the parka before me. "Nice work, Datuu," I said, and meant it.

She smiled coyly and effected a curtsy of sorts.

"What is the parka you're wearing made of?" I asked Datuu, because the one she had on seemed to be sewn from an entirely different material.

Her grandmother answered for her, "We use downy young eagle skins for the children's clothes."

"Me and grandma also make *qiigamisx̂atii*," Datuu put in, tugging my hand. "Come and see the baskets!"

I'd been feeling increasingly dizzy, so I released her hand and took a seat upon a bench a few paces away, which had been tempting me for quite some time. I rubbed my hand over its plush fur cushion, yawning all the while.

"That's fox fur," Datuu said. "We caught them outside."

"You must sleep," Iganakuchax̂ stated the obvious.

"I'm sorry." I rubbed my deadlights. "But I've had one hell of a night."

"Where do you wish to bed down?"

"With Aniqdux̂six̂," I said outright.

Datuu's eyes widened, seemingly bewildered by this romance I had with her kind.

I clarified: "She's set up nice sleeping quarters for me already."

"Go make a spindle of intestinal thread," Iganakuchax̂ ordered her granddaughter, "then color it red."

The little Aleut tromped off in a temper, apparently having been assigned no small task.

I got up to leave. "Thank you for your hospitality," I told Iganakuchax̂. "I'll see you on the morrow, perhaps."

"You know I can't let you see her, Kayuu." She was onto me fast.

"But why not? Don't you realize Aniqdux̂six̂ needs me?"

"Do you need her?"

My heart weighed heavily. We'd been separated so suddenly, and since then, I'd been thoroughly battered. I needed her now more than ever. I slumped back down onto the bench and rubbed my temples while covering my eyes with my palm.

"The mysteries of youthful romance," the matron offered, reading my longings, "are never easily fathomed, not even by immortals. Be more patient with the process. I know that's hard for you to do, but time is all she has."

"What process?" I suspected she was referring to the mysterious transformation process whereby Aniqdux̂six̂ could become mortal again.

"The love process; it's the same for us as it is for you: the magical and mysterious beginning; the spells of fear, fear that it may all just be some wishful dream, that it will not sustain; the belief that you've found your one and only, a belief soon plagued by doubt, doubting such joy can happen to you, that you are worthy of being loved forever. Fulfillment of one's gen-cycle is the highest calling for an *iidigidi*, and all the emotions a mortal feels when faced with the prospect of a love that never dies, are amplified to the extreme for us. Selecting a mate is the single most important thing we can do for all of eternity, and that's why the gen-cycle has been set for two hundred and seventy years, to teach the eligible *iidigidi* patience and wisdom in choosing."

"Set by whom, and who is deemed an eligible member?"

"The clan chief has determined the gen-cycle."

"Chief Aĝnakax̂? Aniqdux̂six̂'s stepfather?"

Iganakuchax̂ regarded me critically. "I advise you to not feign to know about our relations or to speak of them publicly. You are new to this barabara, and thus incapable of wisdom regarding our internal affairs."

I wasn't exactly in the mood to get into a row with my endearing old hostess, so replied disarmingly, "Very well, then, but perhaps you can at least tell me the definition of an 'eligible member'? It is my understanding that Aniqdux̂six̂ is one such person, waiting for her opportunity."

"By 'eligible' we mean an *iidigidi* that, when turned, was turned alone and not in conjunction with a significant other such as a spouse or lover. Aniqdux̂six̂ was turned before she'd ever fallen in love, so yes, she would qualify as an eligible. She has seventy-four more years to wait, and praise the law of Chief Aĝnakax̂ for that, because Aniqdux̂six̂ is still maturing emotionally and is clearly not yet ready."

My expression grew cross at her suggestion. She was basically insinuating that Aniqdux̂six̂'s love for me, and mine for her, was mere child's play and not the genuine article.

"That's a pretty harsh assessment," I replied, "especially after we were just discussing the strong emotions that come with a fledgling romance, and moreover among your kind, as you have said."

She slowly shook her head. "You are missing the point entirely. I was telling you how the gen-cycle requires two hundred and seventy of our years to teach the eligible the necessary patience and perspective an eternal relationship commands. The most significant shifts in our psyches typically come after the two century mark. That's something of a magic number for an *iidigidi*. Our worldview tends to stabilize then, especially for elders who have the retrospect of additional mortal years. Until then, an *iidigidi* has a tendency to hold onto its old recognizance of time, whereby there may be a rush to gain certain life events such as marriage or attainment of worldly knowledge. At the two century mark, however, one's acceptance of eternity becomes better understood, and then one is able to make the right decisions based upon our timeframe, not the timeframe of mortals."

"That is clear to me," I replied. "Your kind need more time to better appreciate the gravity of eternity. But I don't see how another lifetime for Aniqdux̂six̂, in human years, will make her any less lonely or desperate. I'm not saying that I want to be like you. What I really want is to return to my people and fight the Japanese contention. But you just can't marginalize Aniqdux̂six̂'s feelings as some sort of earth echo that needs to die out before she can understand her emotions. I find that to be cruel and misguided. Frankly, in many ways Aniqdux̂six̂ seems more mature and capable of a serious relationship than many of your timeworn cohorts who are already hitched. You assume that age inevitably leads to wisdom, and in most things, I would agree; but I would not hold this as law in matters of the heart, where age can just as easily stifle genuine insight and intuition."

"Insight and intuition, you say? Finding you, Jake, has created for Aniqdux̂six̂ the most painful confusion and longing imaginable. If only she would have abided by our sound dictates instead of setting out on her own to prematurely seek a mate. You, I hate to say, just happened to be the first commoner she should find."

"*Bah!*" I rejected that notion.

A Young Aleut Woman, *and likeness of Aniqduẍsiẍ (Steel engraving from* The Natural History of Man, *by James C. Prichard, first published by Hippolyte Balliere, London, 1845)*

"Might I remind you, Mister Harper," she sharpened her tone, "that we have strict guidelines about transforming mortals, and not just to ensure the successful union of forever-after mates. We used to number eight males to every female, and it's taken a long time to correct that imbalance. We no longer permit polygamy or vice versa. An eligible can only have one forever-after partner, so the choosing process is no trifling matter. We must consider very seriously who will be a good fit for the clan as a whole. Successful hunters from within our tribe are given preference, and especially cross-cousins. To change the wrong person such as a slave—someone who might turn against the tribe—could prove disastrous for both parties. It's happened before."

"So basically what you're telling me is that marriages here are prearranged."

"You could say that."

"Do you think perhaps Aniqdux̂six̂ and I could be exempted from the chief's law if I further prove myself to him, such as on the whale hunt?"

Iganakuchax̂ went silent for a moment, her eyes squinting in deep thought, and then she answered, "The question has been floated—if you were dispatched now, might that amount to a wasted opportunity for Aniqdux̂six̂ and the cave clan? What sort of mate will she find once her gen-cycle is up, and how might he compare to you?

"The love Aniqdux̂six̂ displays for you no longer appears as juvenile as many here once believed. The sacrifices she makes for you, even at risk of her own exile; and the trust you show in her, your willingness to protect her and our kind, even at your own mortal risk—these things are not so easily overlooked. The problem with you is that her gen-cycle is not yet fulfilled, while your very being here creates an acute risk to us. But be under no false illusion: the chief's dictates are final; they can neither be questioned, nor changed."

"Respectfully, Iganakuchax̂, I don't believe he's so draconian, no pun intended. I've seen Aniqdux̂six̂ reproach him on more than one occasion, while I myself have questioned him without undue persecution—unless his current separation of Aniqdux̂six̂ and me becomes lasting."

One of the larger stone lanterns had been burning low, and finally its moss wick puffed out a final smidgen of smoke.

Iganakuchax̂ went to refill it, going first to a wooden receptacle to obtain more oil, replying all the while, "There's no question that your rescue of Maguun, and in-house diplomacy overall, has gone a long way to earn the tolerance of the tribe, while your taking on Tayaĝukichax̂ has undoubtedly gained the respect of the warriors and hopefully even Tayaĝukichax̂ himself. If you ask about Chief Aĝnakax̂, I will say that, unlike me, he is strict and taciturn—as is becoming of men in his high station. But I must concede, inwardly he's not made of stone. You should know that he is a chief and I am an elder, and in our world, elders hold more power. While you must never publicly oppose him, he can be swayed privately. If anybody knows this, it is I."

"Why?"

"He's my husband."

Datuu ran in carrying a spindle half-wound with intestinal thread, the other half trailing off behind her.

"You can't be serious?" Iganakuchax̂ said. "You're finished already?"

"Here it is." The little *iidigidi* held up the spindle.

"I told you to dye it red!" Iganakuchax̂ was strict. "And look, that's no way to a wind it!"

Datuu was crestfallen.

"Here, I'll take that!" the matron wrenched the spindle from the little one's hand. "Fix Kayuu's boots while I fetch more oil. Excuse me, Mister Harper."

With that, the elder hastened out holding an empty wooden bowl under her arm, respooling the spindle all the while.

"I'm sorry, Mister Kayuu," Datuu said, looking up at me with sad, puppy dog eyes.

"Sorry about what?"

"About grandma."

I laughed.

She giggled, then sat on the reed mat before me and began adjusting the cinches of my sea lion boots.

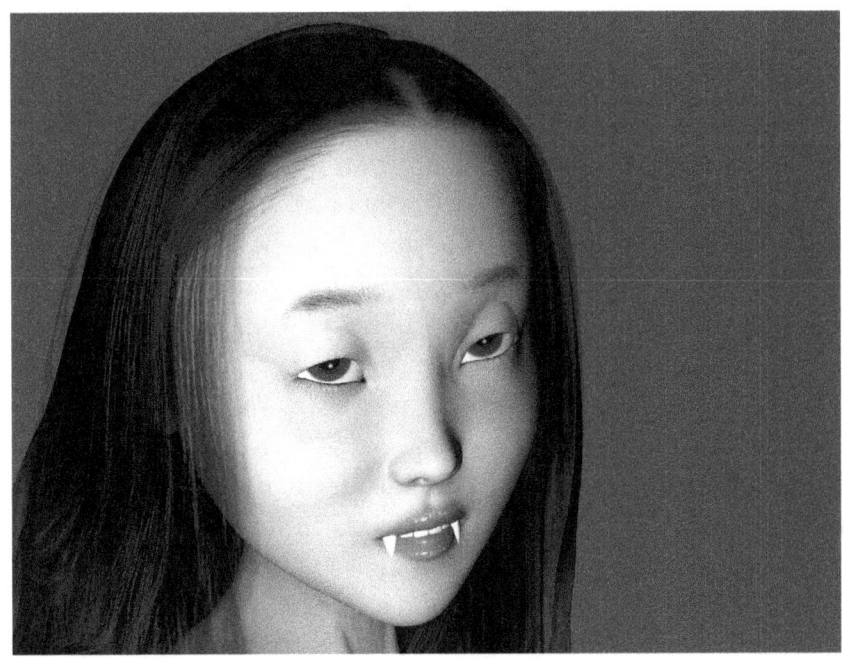

Datuu *(Illustration by Gerrit Hein)*

I felt my swollen face and sighed. "Tayaĝukichax̂ smashed me up pretty good, didn't he?"

"Thou got him good, too, my lord," Datuu said in a tongue that humored me.

"How do you know that?"

"I just do."

"Is he going to be okay?"

"He'll get over it."

I had to smile. This little one had a way with words.

"All right, Datuu, if you're so smart, then tell me how else I can fight him off if he comes at me again."

She yanked a cinch tightly over my foot and shot me a narrow glance. "Grandpa says I'm not supposed to tell you those things."

"Wooden stakes?"

"No." She cinched again.

"Silver bullets?"

"No!" She cinched even tighter.

"Sunlight?"

"Thou knowest the answer to that, Sir Jake!" she tempestuously surmised, yanking at my boots like she were stitching a corset up the back of a bulging queen bitch.

"I do?"

"You didn't notice her skin when you went outside?"

"Aniqdux̂six̂'s skin?"

"When you two were naked at the hot springs?" She tightened my boots more violently.

"*Ouch, ouch*, okay, okay!" I held out my hands, pleading for mercy, at which point she stopped assaulting my feet.

"And so?" She was glaring up at me with a black look.

How did she know about Aniqdux̂six̂ and me at the hot springs?

"*And so?*" she said more forcefully, her hands pulling at my boot strings once again.

"And so,"—pausing to clear my throat—"well, as far as sunlight, when it does break through the endless train of cyclones here, the only effect I notice is that it makes her skin appear lighter. But the sun makes everything look lighter anyway, so maybe I'm just being falsely impressed."

"What kind of answer is that, Sir Jake?"

Iganakuchax̂ returned with the bowl, now filled with whale oil, and handed it to my little inquisitor, telling her to top off all the lanterns.

"We'll finish this conversation later," warned the little one, her big deadlights honing in on mine.

"Conversation about what?" asked her grandmother.

"Lord Jake's feet are smelly," Datuu said.

Iganakuchax̂ laughed. "Don't forget this one," she instructed, holding up a lantern.

"I know that a mortal can become an *iidigidi*," I told the matron of the house, essentially changing the subject. "But can an *iidigidi* really be changed back into a mortal?"

Iganakuchax̂ dropped her stone lantern, almost on my feet.

Datuu picked it up and went about her business, but Iganakuchax̂ remained motionless and silent as the grave.

"Madam?" I inquired.

"Why do you wish to know?"

I thought about Aniqdux̂six̂ in her plight, the plight of a vampire, or *iidigidi* as they called themselves, and now it was I who fell silent. Perhaps her kind wouldn't understand her desire to change back, and might even persecute her for disparaging their condition. It pained me to think of her internal struggle and the constraints she was under to keep her true feelings secret. I looked bleakly up at Iganakuchax̂ and replied at last, "Nothing."

"No, Kayuu, your eyes tell me differently. This is about Aniqdux̂six̂, isn't it?"

I looked down again, my despondency over my lover impossible to mask.

Iganakuchax̂ then called over to the little rascal, who was refilling the stone lanterns with whale oil, "That's enough, Datuu. Go back to your room and remain there until I get back."

"Where art thou going, grandma?"

"Just do as you're told!"

"But grandma . . ."

"Now go!"

Datuu shuffled out, totally nonplussed.

Iganakuchax̂ watched her closely as she left, and only when she was long gone did she address me again: "I'm no stranger to Aniqdux̂six̂. I've only wanted what's best for her."

"I know," I replied, unimpressed, "the gen-cycle. We've been through that."

"No, even before then, I've only wanted her to be happy."

"Before she was changed, you mean?"

"Even before she was born a wight. You see, Kayuu, Aniqdux̂six̂ is my daughter."

"Your natural daughter?"

"Yes." She paused to glance around her extended dwelling. All was quiet, too quiet, perhaps, so she drew close beside me and spoke into my ear, lowering her voice so that only I could hear. "I know that her love for you is real, Kayuu, and I trust her in your charge, if you truly love her, too. I know she wants to turn back the clock and live out her natural life with you. As her mother, I cannot deny her the opportunity to start a family of her own, which is her deepest desire. You know that Aĝnakax̂ is not her natural father. After her real father, Alix̂, my first husband, died in seventeen forty-two, Aĝnakax̂ took me for his own, and while he's been good to me, I don't feel beholden to his dictates on matters of my child. Do you truly love my daughter, Mister Jake Harper?"

I nodded sullenly.

"Do you truly want to spend your life with her? Please consider the reality of what I am asking. Do you wish to spend the rest of your mortal days with Aniqdux̂six̂, even it amounts to one hundred years?"

It took me but a few seconds to respond, "I do."

She took my hands in hers, saying, "Then there is a way. Our rules regarding the gen-cycle leave but one choice, a forbidden choice, because she cannot change you prematurely or you'll be executed on the spot, while she'll face banishment or worse. But if you truly love each other, I will help you live together as mortals. But you must promise, at the pact of death, never to tell, because if anyone finds out what I'm about to show you— and I mean *anyone*—both our lives will be summarily ended. Can I really trust you, Jake?"

*Editor's Note: By duty of impartiality, it is worth noting that several photos unearthed
from Lieutenant Harper's private collection are of this unnamed woman, in whom he
apparently sailed with to Dutch Harbor on the SS Cordova in 1942 via Seattle and Kodiak
before he transferred to Adak. Was it a romantic interest? A relative? Or simply a friend?
This he never made known. However, there is abundant evidence that places him at Dutch
Harbor prior to and during the June 3-4 bombings. (Exclusive photos by Lt. Harper, 1942)*

"If you're saying that you'll help Aniqdux̂six̂ become mortal again so that she and I can stay together, then yes, you can trust me absolutely. I know she wants this more than anything, and once she's changed back into a human, I shall request her hand in marriage without delay."

Iganakuchax̂'s eyes welled up with tears and she firmly squeezed my hands. "Good, good!" she whispered loudly. "Then we have a deal! But you are to tell no one, not even Aniqdux̂six̂, or we'll both be killed. Do you completely understand that, and promise to remain silent?"

"I shall never forget the gravity of this," said I. "You have my sovereign promise and full confidence. Now, please tell me how to proceed. The sooner we get this done, the better. She's your daughter, I now know, but trust me when I say that she and I will both be better off the moment we leave here to start a normal life together. Time is of the essence, *madame*."

She wiped the tears that periodically streamed from her eyes, replying, "You speak the truth, a truth that has not come easily for me. But come, I agree, it is time: follow me."

She got up to lead me away, but my boots were tied together and I fell flat on my face.

"Datuu!" Iganakuchax̂ held up a fist, but the little fiend was long gone.

Swiftly, furtively, Iganakuchax̂ took me through the dark recesses of the barabara, other vampires lurking always on our periphery. Unbeknown to them—otherwise we chanced the penalty of death—their most sacrosanct secret would soon be revealed to me. This was risky business indeed, but a necessary blitz on my part to increase my chances of escape. I hadn't forgotten my mission with the ASF. Being kidnapped had made me soft, but now I was seeing clearly. I did have strong feelings for Aniqdux̂six̂, but stuck here in a barabara was not how I intended to spend my future, especially while there was a war to be won for the free world, Aleuts included. To wed my captor was a shameful arrangement for the both of us. I would marry on my own terms and not according to the predicament we found ourselves presently in. A man must do all he can to take charge of his future, even if that means eloping, or so I had presented the argument to the mother of my lover.

BLOOD OF THE INNOCENT

AT A dark, distant corner of the barabara, Iganakuchax̂ reached her hands into the peat covered walls and gave a mighty push. With the sound of massive, sliding stones, a passageway opened behind the curtain of overhanging muskeg. She pulled apart the vines and told me to stay close as we stepped through the hole.

Once inside, she removed a stone lantern hanging from the corridor wall, ignited the moss wick and gave the beacon to me to hold, after which she readjusted the curtain of sod behind us and closed the weighty stone doors.

"Watch your head," she warned, guiding me through the secret corridor. The walls were roughhewn and narrow, as if chiseled by escaping prisoners. Suffice it to say, the going was slow.

Some fifty yards on, there was an abrupt turn to the left, terminating in a chamber whose surroundings were completely transformed. The room was roughly ten feet square on all sides and composed of pure red adakite, a rock formed from young ocean crust, or so my guide explained. The "slab melt rock," as she called it, had been cut and polished to an immaculate sheen, casting off a shimmering red gleam. An object at the center of the room, however, commanded the greatest attention.

Glinting in every direction like a massive jewel stood a silver suit of armor. "Yes, silver," Iganakuchaî countered my remonstrations, my disbelief, "not iron."

I stood, gawking at the costume before me; a work of art, the work of gods. As if smelted from the Excalibur itself, King Arthur's legendary sword, the armor appeared symmetrically perfect. Each line, from the crucifix of the breastplate to the cornices of the eye slits gleamed in the reflecting lantern light, harnessing the sparse brightness around it and magnifying it to an extreme. The silver suit stood as if readying to march, gripping in its right hand a sort of javelin or jousting pole that stretched from the floor almost to the ceiling.

"This was made, or so we believe," remarked the brave matron who'd taken me before it, "by Innokenty Veniaminov."

"The priest of Saint Ephraim of the Caves church," I recalled.

"He may have been more than a Russian Orthodox priest," she replied. "He may have been a bishop."

"Remarkable."

"And here . . ." She showed me a weathered book at the base of the armor, "these are the instructions."

"Instructions?"

She carefully picked up the timeworn text and read its cover, "The Way to the Kingdom of Heaven."

She opened to a page individuated by a thin red string. "This is chapter five, which he redacted before formally publishing the book. Besides his original manuscript, this handwritten copy is the only other one in existence that contains the fifth chapter, which he entitled *Exorcizing the Undead by Means of Fire Witching.*"

Arms and Armour *(Illustration by F. Grose, London, 1785)*

My lantern's wick almost blew out, although there was no draft about.

"The Undead?" I inquired uneasily.

"For lack of a better translation," she said. "The word he uses is *iidigidi*, but he means to refer to my kind."

"Vampires."

She nodded.

"What is fire witching?"

"Listen as I translate for you. He wrote the book in Unalaskan Aleut, which you're not yet versed in."

I shook my head.

"By the power of our Lord and Savior," she began, reading from the text, "and His Majesty the Emperor, has the Shield of Repentance armor been forged to drive Satan from one so possessed, for a man in such a dire predicament has only one need: that of salvation. Salvation is Divine Providence in action, testifying to God's insuperable power to save a mortal soul.

"By urgent order to the Crown of Saint Petersburg has the armor been shipped to the Unalaska parish via our most trusted company mariner, and assigned to my care directly by the chief manager of the colonies. The process by which fire witching is accomplished holds all manner of dangers that can prove fatal for all involved; however, no risk is too great in endeavoring to extricate the Prince of Darkness from a soul who is anyway given over to eternal damnation, while those who risk their earthly lives to assist in the exorcism shall summarily gain the Kingdom of Heaven."

"The exorcism must be performed in sovereign secrecy on the thirteenth Sunday after Pentecost. It requires a clergyman, such as a priest or bishop, and two assistants, the first of whom must be very strong physically and both of whom must unquestionably be of Christ's flock, and all of whom must be donning the cross. Finally, the *iidigidi* must be present and stripped bare, not wearing a cross.

Choir of Angels Presenting the Holy Lance, ". . . And there they saw angels . . . and a spear which bled marvellously." (Painting and quote by Helen Urquhart, London, 1920)

"In order to drive the devil away from the *iidigidi*, the possessed soul must first be yoked into submission using Holy

Water, and kept in control by the clergyman's reciting, in verbatim, any of the spiritual instructions of the previous four chapters herein.

"Once subdued by the clergyman, assistant number one, henceforth 'the porter,' must lock the *iidigidi* into the Shield of Repentance and transport it together with the *caelum divinatorius* rod to within forty-two sazhens [300 feet] of the windward rim of a resolutely erupting volcano, the clergyman at point and assistant number two, henceforth 'the operative,' following behind in a single-file queue. There the *iidigidi* and the operative must be laid squarely on their backs beside each other with the operative at a slightly higher elevation.

"The clergyman must then connect the operative to the *iidigidi* via a blood transfusion reed, attaching the transfusion tube to the conical siphon tip located on the Shield of Repentance's neck on the heart side, or left side of the armor facing forward, which feeds directly into the bloodstream of the possessed. A cinch must be kept on the reed until the precise moment the transfusion is to commence, as shall be indicated below.

"The porter must then make haste to retract the telescoping *caelum divinatorius* to its full extent of five sazhens [about 35 feet], then attach its base end—shaped like a plus (+)—into the crucifix latch located front and center of the shield's breastplate. This is accomplished by lining up the crosses, then pivoting the *caelum divinatorius* rod until it locks into place, being careful to keep the full extent of the lightning shaft balanced straightly over the *iidigidi*. Large adakite stones should be employed to better secure the possessed subject, and to protect the exorcists from the effect of lightning as it strikes the rod and enters down into the Shield of Repentance."

"In order to drive the devil away from the iidigidi, the possessed soul must be transported to the windward rim of a resolutely erupting volcano . . ." (11th US Army Air Force photo, 1942)

"If the clergyman has chosen the appropriate volcano and correctly followed these steps on the thirteenth Sunday after Pentecost, then the fire witching shall shortly commence. The electromagnetic force begot within the volcano's bowels will strike up through the smoke and cinders as blue lightning. The exorcist and the porter must lie low until a rabid bolt finds its target, which tends to happen quickly. The 'dirty lightning,'"— Iganakuchax̂ looked up at me—"for lack of a closer translation, will strike the *caelum divinatorius* rod and enter down into the breastplate of the *iidigidi*. The electromagnetic force, when drawn into the Shield of Repentance's holy crucible, will cause the heart of the *iidigidi* to stop while simultaneously killing the virus within its bloodstream.

"The clergyman must then immediately remove the cinch from the transfusion tube so that the blood of the operative can flow freely down into the blood system of the *iidigidi*, henceforth called 'the patient.' This stage must be undertaken with all due haste, because lightning will soon again strike the *caelum divinatorius*, funneling through the rod and restarting the patient's heart. Once this happens, the healthy blood of the operative will immediately start pumping into the patient's body, circulating throughout his heart, brain, and bloodstream. After this occurs, the porter must remove the *caelum divinatorius*, throwing it clear of the area as the clergyman keeps the two subjects connected long enough for sufficient blood to be transfused. The risk at this point is greater for the operative than it is for the patient, for many an operative has perished by overmuch bloodlet in saving the soul of the damned.

"As soon as the transfusion is sufficient, which you shall know by the coherence of the patient, the clergyman must disconnect the tube and unlock the Shield of Repentance, removing the patient from it and dressing him immediately with a cross. The porter must then gather the abandoned armor and rod, weighing a total of three poods (about 110 lbs), then the entire party must depart from the volcano at once, the clergyman helping to assist any infirm souls back down the mountain.

"The patient and operative should recover in a warm house or heated dwelling under the administration of the porter, who must have ready access to good food and water. Much time should be spent in prayer, in pondering the eleventh and twelfth statements of the Nicene Creed concerning the reckoning of the righteous versus the unholy and, weather permitting, in exposing the infirm subjects to daily sunlight. Full recovery for both can be anticipated after approximately seven moons.

"The clergyman, meanwhile, must privately reconsecrate the Shield of Repentance and *caelum divinatorius* with an admixture of warm Holy Water, tin, sea salt, and baking powder, using an antimins to buff any discoloration from the rod and armor, then the suit must be returned, together with the rod in its right hand, to the red adakite chamber within the inner confines of the Adak Island sanctum, hidden from the eyes of men and from the *iidigidi* especially."

"What is an antimins?"

"A cloth upon which are set the silver chalice and bread for Holy Communion," Iganakuchax̂ explained. "The antimins is extremely powerful, having been brushed over the relics of saints. You'll know it by abundant icons of Christ embroidered throughout."

She continued with the scripture: "The process of fire witching is not a failsafe proposition for the Lord's contractors. Several attempts on Amchitka Island were met with total disaster, where the entire exorcism party was lost. However in all cases the *iidigidi* have been either healed or destroyed, thus the Shield of Repentance's power to conquer over Satan has been proven with certainty—Glory be to God!"

Saint Innocent of Alaska (*Exclusive painting on wood by Miko Petrov Stoyanov of Sofia, Bulgaria, undated*)

"The way to the Kingdom of Heaven is narrow, and even more so for the undead, but the Word of God maketh all things possible for people of His faith, not exempting those individuals since commandeered by Satan, whose souls by the aforementioned method can be seized back from the brink of eternal darkness and resurrected into the light. Although driven out of paradise, these damned souls are still not without hope, for the Kingdom of God is present for all ages, and the Second Coming of Christ is always nigh. Remember that it is through suffering that we are purified, and a wight thus pained by Satan's possession, once impaled by the light of heaven through the *caelum divinatorius*, is given back to God and shall thenceforth bear the holy cross with exemplary power, even if he does not survive the process."

"'Many years' for His Majesty the Emperor for vouchsafing these divine tools, entrusted to the Imperial Crown by the Lord's mysteries, to my acute battle against evil shamans still haunting the Unalaska parish.

"Signed, Priest Ivan Veniaminov of the Ascension Church of Unalaska. July twenty-one, eighteen thirty-four."

Iganakuchax̂ closed the book.

I gazed upon the silver suit of armor, speechless at its professed power.

"Now I know why Aniqdux̂six̂ has been flying the chain," Iganakuchax̂ said, her eyes wet with tears. "Of our forty-three active volcanoes, she's been seeking the most promising one."

CRADLE OF STORMS

LAUNCHING INTO the wild Pacific, I experienced a sudden surge of adrenaline. The whale hunt was on, even amid the stormy seas. But the real cause of my excitement was a secret known only to me.

I was seated in my own *baidarka*, and as the Unangax̂ tribesmen preceded me out of Boot Bay, I hurried my pace, but only to test my speed. Once the kayak before me rounded the southern tip of Elf Island, I broke swiftly to the east.

Boot Point was my first objective. I paddled with all my strength, giving focus to my forward speed. The skies were cloudy and the seas were grey, but it wasn't until I neared the promontory that the open ocean bared its roughshod face. Sideways and contrariwise currents ripped at the hull of my sealskin craft like slithering snakes trying to squeeze a slippery fish into their hold; and then came the waves, which increased in size and frequency as I rounded the eastern promontory. Great combers, one after the next, rolled mightily beneath my kayak before lunging shoreward, morphing into giant walls that came smashing down against the rocky cape with a thunderous *boom!* and horrendous splash. But even amid this protean calamity, the shouts of angry men could be heard behind me—angry vampire men with harpoons and fangs and wings and who knew these craggy convoluted fjords like the back of their black webbed hands.

I didn't bother to look over my shoulder. This was my final chance at escape, and they were already onto my spurious advance. I redoubled my efforts over my double-bladed paddle.

Providence was with me, for as soon as I rounded the cape leading unto the Kagalaska Strait, a great williwaw blew in from the south, reducing visibility to fifty feet while driving me rapidly up into the narrow pass. This was a blessing because it meant the vampires in pursuit would have difficulty flying, not to mention sailing or seeing, and may even find themselves smashed up on the reefs I'd recently passed. Meanwhile, the waterway I'd gained was smooth and swift, like a river made for inner-tubing, so much so that paddling itself became a hindrance. I lifted my oars and lay back against my seatback, riding the current toward freedom: the garrison at Kuluk Bay.

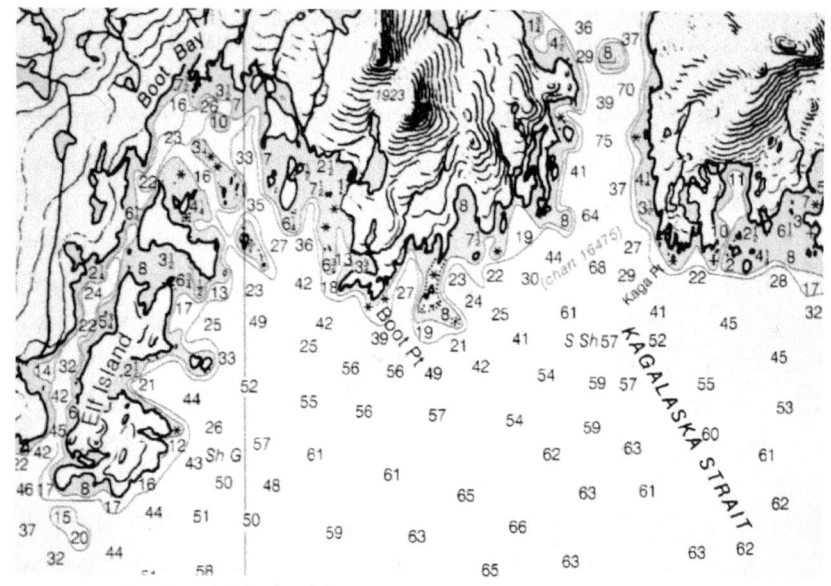

Boot Bay, Adak Island (NOAA map segment; soundings in fathoms)

"Marauding vampires be damned!" I howled with the wind at my back, but no sooner had I sounded victory did vampires appear to port, casting off from Adak Bight in a large *baidara*. I knew they were *iidigidi* because Aniqdux̂six̂ was among them, along with Iganakuchax̂, Datuu, and four-year-old Kitax. They appeared to be embarking upon an interisland journey at an ill-timed moment, for the williwaw was strengthening by the second.

I dipped my paddle into the water, turning my craft toward theirs as I scudded by. Alas, Adak Bight, in its stormy temperament, had already drawn their *baidara* into its grasp, sucking them into a large whirlpool that'd formed at its center.

I paddled hard against the raging torrent, but headway proved futile.

"Kayuu!" Aniqdux̂six̂ cried as her *baidara* was flung rapidly around the bottomless maelstrom.

"Mister Harper!" screamed Datuu, while little Kitax stood beside her in the boat, holding the rails for dear life.

I stroked hard, groaning, growling, at times shutting my eyes and frothing at the lip as I sought to gain an edge against the river driving me away from my loved ones. The veins of my forearms bulged blue and stretched clear up to the dual red pillars of my extruding jugulars as I clenched my teeth in a terrible grin of agony, giving my all to save my newfound family, of whom I knew some couldn't swim.

"Jake!" Aniqdux̂six̂ shouted, trying to take wing, but she was beaten back down by the williwaw, smashing her head against the *baidara*'s driftwood rim.

"Aniqdux̂six̂!" I hollered, raising high my paddle in defiance of the heavens as her *baidara* got taken, all hands, down into whirlpool.

"Nooo!" I cried, the whisk of the williwaw erasing the bight in a blinding mist as I ghosted around Blind Point, the end of the pass. Northwestwardly to bow lay Kuluk Bay, Sweeper Cove, and Longview Station. Freedom was mine, but inside I felt dead.

"Mister Harper! Mister Harper!" I heard, waking in a pool of sweat. "Mister Harper!" implored Datuu, who was pulling at my arm. "I think you were dreaming a bad dream."

I reached out and touched her face with tenderness. "Yes, Datuu, it was just a bad dream. Thank you for waking me."

The storm outside had become a full-blown williwaw, blasting away undiminished for five days and five nights. This type of wind was technically a powerful downdraft emanating from the snowy mountains, whose thick, cold air descended toward the coast, gaining on itself exponentially as the force of gravity pushed it down. Typically a williwaw appeared suddenly and blew itself out after a few hours, but in those early spring days of 1943, it blew without cease.

Emerging from the barabara during this event was an experience I'll never forget. I'd been outdoors in serious Aleutian weather before, so I knew well why the Aleutians were often dubbed the "Cradle of the Storms" and "Birthplace of the Winds." This particular tempest, however, was the most ferocious I'd witnessed.

I sat up in my reed mat bed, pulled on my ASF goggles, and then lumbered toward a notched log ladder in Iganakuchax̂'s sector, where'd I'd remained more or less sequestered. While climbing the near-vertical ladder, my sundry injuries continued to plague me, until at last I attained the ceiling portal, braced my knees upon the ladder's high rungs, and then pushed open the sod and whalebone door above.

The hardly flap instantly whipped back, the incoming wind and sleet being so severe that, had my knees not been secured beneath me, it would've blown me down. Twenty feet was no small distance to tumble back from roof to floor. I grasped the doorsill and forced my head out further from the barabara, my attempt to gauge the weather now passing into the masochistic.

The view through my goggles was all but scuttled by precipitation and pellets of ice blasting sideways into my face. The wind appeared to be surpassing one hundred miles per hour: I'd spent enough time in Longview and environs to have a good sense of what breaks an anemometer. My bentwood cap, recently sent to me by Aniqdux̂six̂ while I was in sequestration, and which I stupidly thought would buffer me against the ridiculous onslaught, immediately whipped back off my head, its walrus gut string lanyard wrapping around my neck and chocking me half to death, but at least sparing the supposed "fortune-bearing hat" a one-way flight to Midway.

"Holy Christ," I thought as I steeled my lips against the Aleutian cyclone, for to open my mouth even a centimeter would invite the wind to pry it open further—much further, like a torturous doctor instructing "say aah" before cramming a dozen-and-one snow cones down my throat. This was nasty business outside, and even if I spoke or yelled or screamed, the roar of the williwaw would've gobbled up my words the instant they parted my lips. One thing I knew for certain: there'd be no whale hunt today, not even for the living dead. They never got cold, true, because they were already cold in the flesh, but fortunately they had enough wings to beat some sense into them regarding the local environment and when it was truly too perilous to navigate—even for an immortal, whose forever-after days were preferably not spent bobbing about the brooding north Pacific with broken pinions.

I grabbed the hatch behind me and went to close it, but with one hundred miles per hour winds, the pressure per square inch on a door thirty inches square equated to a ninety thousand pound lid, or so it seemed as I yanked, in vain, at its pull cord. The bloody thing would've snapped in half—and I mean the door, my arm, and the cord, each to its own accord—had the lid's plaited reed screen not allowed for some diffusion of air.

When the wind let up from one hundred and eight miles per hour to ninety-two (or so I calculated by my beard's sudden but fleeting popping back into shape), I groaned and curled my arm like an arm-wrestling marine, at last succeeding in slamming the door over and into the top of my head.

In my fall down the ladder, I bounced all the way down the rungs like a plastic army man caught inside a pachinko machine, at last eating the reed mat below the bottom notch. This hardy green flooring I came to fully appreciate as woven dune wild rye, a mildly peppery mélange of dried summer grasses. As far as I was concerned, the Japanese had already infiltrated this sad, sod house, because they had invented the pachinko contraption to begin with; and it was a sad house because, well, I was a real fine mess.

"Your *chagudax̂*!" noted Iganakuchax̂, who came to my hat's assistance. "It's completely smashed!"

Oh, never mind about me! I thought, none too pleased. I would thenceforth remember the supreme importance Unangans bestowed upon their bentwood caps.

"I'll help you fix it before the hunt," she winked, "so you can tell the men you worked on it." What she was referring to was that a sea hunter should personally make his *chagudax̂*. A necessary accoutrement to guard the eyes from the sun's glare and falling rain, the bentwood hat was also supposed to bring good luck on the hunt. But a woman having had constructed mine could amount to a great deal of embarrassment for me, for men took great pride in making their own hunting hats—and the tribesmen very well might ask, because the design and decoration of the *chagudax̂* was a popular topic among them. "Besides that," Iganakuchax̂ explained as she looked over the smashed headwear, "you'll need something more suitable for winter."

I looked up at her sheepishly.

"Oh, I'll help you up," she offered at last.

Oh! The mortal just fell about three sazhens [20 feet] *down the ladder. No matter!*

She led me through her sealskin drying area and then past Datuu's stitching quarters to a partitioned workshop of an entirely different nature. Here upon extensive shelving were kept choice pieces of driftwood in various stages of bentwood hat production, the lower shelves containing raw woods and the top shelves displaying completed hats. A row of nearby baskets stored walrus ivories in similar fashion, starting with raw tusks and ending with baskets overflowing with decoratively carved volutes. Further along was situated a table made of driftwood and lined with plaited reed mats, with three chairs composed of like materials set before it. The table itself carried several wooden bowls (whose rims were stained with dried paints), a collection of bone tools and brushes, assortments of sea lion whiskers and other things that Iganakuchax̂ identified as materials for making *chagudax̂*.

Datuu came in and smiled coyly. He mouth was stained red from the contents of a seal-gut gourd she was carrying, engendering a sickly feeling in my stomach. As cute as she may have been otherwise, it was a stark reminder of the kind of people— or creatures—I was dealing with. Back home, a smile like hers would be lined with milk, but here in the land of Aleutian vampires, little girls drank blood for sustenance. I counted my lucky stars they'd been able to subdue their preternatural inclination for human blood by settling instead upon the sustenance that ocean mammals provided. How long that would last, however, was anyone's guess. My bout with Tayaĝukichax̂, Datuu's bloodthirsty father, had been evidence enough never to turn my neck on them.

"Ah, there you are, Datuu," Iganakuchax̂ noticed. "Please boil me some water. We're going to make Kayuu a *qayaatx̂ux̂*."

"Just call me Jake," I offered, subtly seeking to differentiate myself in namesake from these heretical scrub bunnies.

"Kayuu!" replied Datuu with a leap in her step, skipping off with her blood-filled gut sack. "Kayuu! Kayuu! Kayuu!"

"Kayuu it is then," Iganakuchax̂ laughed.

"What's a *qayaatx̂ux̂*?" I asked, seeking to change the subject.

"A full-crowned hat. Unfortunately, the *chagudax̂* that Aniqdux̂six̂ gave you, which was really just a visor, is damaged beyond repair. We'll have to start from scratch."

She grabbed a large piece of relatively flat driftwood from the bottom shelf, placed it on the table, and then with her bonzer knife proceeded to carve a pyramid-shaped outline into it.

"This will suit you better anyway," she said, "because it's still wintertime. You know my husband always wears his *chagudax̂* visor around the house, but on a winter hunt, he'll don his *qayaatx̂ux̂*."

"The chief takes part in the *qaqmiigux̂*?"

"The hunt is for more than just sustenance," she revealed, "it brings men power and they enjoy the competition. Now pay attention if you want to learn the skills of a bentwood hatter. Once the outline is drawn, you must carve the wood thin enough for bending, like so."

With shocking rapidity that came with her supernatural condition, she shaved the wood down with a steel file to a thickness of between one and two centimeters.

"Only one piece of wood is used in the construction," she said, "so we leave some areas thicker than others in order to achieve the proper bend. Datuu?!"

"Coming, grandma!" The little vampire shortly arrived with a wooden barrel steaming over with boiling water, which she set on the floor beside the table.

"Once you've prepped your outline," said the elder as she dipped her piece of carved wood into the water, "you must soak it until it's eminently bendable. If you've shed it to the proper thinness, this stage shouldn't take long."

As the wood soaked, the matron explained, "The bentwood hat—the *chagudax̂* and the *qayaatx̂ux̂*—will give you vision on the *qaqmiigux̂* and make you a better hunter. But to wear it you must be strong and brave. You must not be afraid to kill even the greatest beasts, including men. Are you up to the task?"

"This *qaqmiigux̂* is a whale hunt, is it not?" I anxiously inquired.

"That's the primary goal, yes, but you could happen upon anything, including raiding warriors, whom you must be ready to kill without so much as flinching."

"Yes, madam." I chuckled with relief, knowing fully well that all the Aleuts, save for her clan, had already been relocated.

Bentwood hats weren't the only things bendable when soaked, in the Aleutians. This Catalina (PBY) long-range flying boat came skidding hull-first into the muskeg after sliding off the Marsden matting during an intermittent rainsquall at Longview AFB, Adak. (Dept. of US Navy photo, 1943)

She read my flippancy and added, "Including the Japs."

I went silent. I had not considered that. If we were to happen upon them in our little kayaks, what good would harpoons and bentwood hats do against a submarine or warship?

"And so I shall ask again," she said, "are you up to the task?"

"If joining your men will help my case, then yes."

"And what case is that?"

"Aniqdux̂six̂!" piped Datuu, turning toward us with several used paintbrushes in hand. Iganakuchax̂ hushed her quickly, telling her to clean the brushes.

"Well?" inquired Iganakuchax̂ after a stretch of silence. "Is Datuu correct? Are you doing this to win the hand of my daughter, or do you have an ulterior motive?"

"I do love Aniqdux̂six̂," I said unconvincingly.

Datuu giggled.

"*Sshh!*" Iganakuchax̂ admonished her.

I glanced back at the little vampire with an unsympathetic grimace, then continued to Iganakuchax̂: "But for my love to have any real merit, there's a bigger picture here. If I'm to marry Aniqdux̂six̂, of course I must first earn the respect of Chief Aĝnakax̂ and the tribe, and that's why I'm going through with the hunt. But what good is marriage if the fascists win the greater battle? If only your clan could see it: the fascists are taking over the world, and if we don't try to stop them here in the Aleutians, we're doomed to a future so grim as to render even the noblest of vows as futile. If I can't convince your people of this, at least I can show them my commitment to the world I love, to a free world that your daughter inhabits.

"Once I win her favor, Iganakuchax̂, we must get on with the plan as soon as possible so that I can take her back to base with me, for only there can I help to win the real war—the war that must be won if any of this is to have any lasting meaning."

Iganakuchax̂ was fervently gesticulating for me to keep it down. I glanced back at Datuu, who was staring at me wide-eyed. Had I said too much or spoken too loudly? I never mentioned a thing about fire witching—not even close. Verily, the old matron would sooner draw attention to our hidden agenda with her jittery paranoia than I would with my rather nonexistent comments about it.

"We're well aware of the danger your war poses to our people," Iganakuchax̂ replied to the bigger issue. "Look at what it's done to us so far on the outer islands. The American era here has been very difficult for my people. When your government purchased Alaska in eighteen sixty-seven, it threw out the measures the Russians had finally put in place to protect the fur seals. The hunting of pelagic seals as they migrated to their

Bering Sea rookeries almost wiped the species out completely, while the sea otters, already greatly depleted by the Russians, were also driven to the brink, until finally in nineteen eleven, your government got wise and drafted an international treaty banning pelagic sealing, which also included measures to save the sea otters. Since then, the Pribilof seal herds have returned and the sea otters have come back from the edge of extinction. But just as things were becoming more tolerable under your government, war came to us in the Aleutians and my people were forced out completely by the warring adversaries.

"But we are not ignorant to the fact the Japanese started the war here, not the United States. We have heard that the entire village of Attu has been raided by the Japs, its inhabitants relocated to prison camps in Japan. [*Editor's note: This is correct. When Major Matsutoshi Hosumi led his infantry of 1,140 soldiers in a takeover of the island on June 6, 1942, three Aleuts and one American civilian (a schoolteacher) were killed in the invasion, and the remaining forty-two Aleuts were sent to a prison camp near Otaru, Hokkaidō, where sixteen soon died from the harsh conditions. A second civilian, a nurse named Etta Jones, who had been married to the murdered schoolteacher, was taken to the Bund Hotel in Yokohama, Japan, and held prisoner there.]

"And so believe me when I say that many an Unanga is eager to join the Allies in their fight against the Japanese, and many are enlisting, even as own your government treats us poorly.

"But if it is not your wars that are wiping out our culture here," she continued her expostulation, "it is your religions. Long before Alaska ever belonged to the United States, the strain of humility imparted to Aleuts by the likes of Innokenty Veniaminov and the Russian Orthodox Church supplanted any remaining inclination the natives might've had to resist their occupiers, teaching them instead a philosophy of patient forbearance toward those committing crimes against them; and so it begs the question: was the religion of Christ a blessing or a curse to Unangans, whose indigenous practices included appropriate self-defense mechanisms in the face of recurrent genocide?"

It seemed like she was rambling, so I offered a general but genial reply: "You cannot blame the Aleuts for that."

The Church of the Holy Ascension in Unalaska. Built in 1894 (upon the remnants an 1826 chapel), this Russian Orthodox church is one of the oldest existing churches in Alaska, and played a major role in the formal evangelization of the Aleut people. (Exclusive photo by Lt. Harper, 1942)

Iganakuchax̂ paused, and in a pensive measure she gazed into a stone lantern, its subtle glimmer casting a rufescent glow upon her orbs. She drew a hand over her countenance, stretching her face long in thought, at length replying, "Perhaps you're right. The Aleuts did fight back on occasion, but they were vastly outnumbered and outgunned by the colonialist's modern weaponry, and in these instances they were massacred."

"If such is the case," I offered, "then it's terrible to insinuate the Aleuts didn't do more to resist their occupiers when every occasion to do so invited their own pogrom. But what I was referring to is Russian Orthodoxy. You cannot blame the Aleuts, or anyone else, for finding the glory of Christ."

150

She quickly reproached, "This is an impossibility for *iidigidi* and you should know that by now. But your question is one the Aleuts of today may anyways be afraid to ask, because they were ultimately co-opted into their occupier's religion—a religion that told them their sufferings purified them if endured humbly. Perhaps the natives had little choice but to accept the teachings of Christ in order to help them cope with the sundry injuries the colonialists were causing them. That being said, the Christian missionaries fought to protect the Aleuts from the exploits of other foreigners. Many of the proselytizers were Aleuts themselves who'd either ventured overseas and returned with Christianity, or were born with mixed ancestry—Aleut and Russian. Which brings us to the question of whether the Aleuts were falsely impressed by the arrival of the white man and his religion, perhaps not realizing that their traditional ways and beliefs, while seemingly primitive in comparison to those of the colonialists, were legitimate enough practices in their own right to continue to live by. Living in harmony with this terrific natural environment is no small accomplishment and, in my opinion, our shamanism was not worth sacrificing for the white man's religion, which anyway was borne from some far-away desert. But I'm an *iidigidi* and I digress."

"I beg your pardon?"

"I'm a vampire, for lack of a better translation. I shall never see eye to eye with Christianity, not while it continues to see my kind as evil shamans with a devil inside that needs to be cast out; as appalling primitives that must be exorcized of their 'hideous' customs. What an indignity! Indeed! For lack of a confession to their colonial toions! For a shaman's refusal to abandon his profound knowledge of nature!

"As you wish, but until this war—"

Suddenly, the barabara shook violently, causing driftwood and other construction materials to fall from the ceiling and walls. I surmised we were being bombed by the Japs. A hefty whalebone nearly fell on my head, and so I ran for cover.

Iganakuchax̂ grabbed my arm with the strength of a two ton anchor, stopping me dead in my tracks. "An earthquake," she said. "Stay here, it will pass."

Indeed, the initial *Boom!* that had dislodged parts of the underground shelter soon reverberated away, leaving us in a modest cloud of dust. I kept staring wide-eyed at the ceiling, expecting more calamities.

"Don't tell me this is your first earthquake in the Aleutians?" the matron asked almost mockingly.

I nodded in the affirmative.

"Then get used to it," she laughed, "otherwise you'll be scurrying off at every little tremor."

"That felt pretty big to me." I grabbed the end of the whalebone still resting upright on the ground like a giant anchor.

"I think you may have been mistaking some of our usual tremors for our common thunder," she chuckled. "Now Datuu, would you please clean up this mess?"

The little vampire jumped into action, grabbing the other end of the whalebone and pulling the entire fossil away from my grasp like it were light as a feather (it probably weighed fifty pounds), from where she jumped clear up to the ceiling and wedged it back into place. This process she repeated with other large detritus that had fallen. I could only watch in amazement.

"Now where was I," her grandmother said, snapping me out of my gawking stupor. "Oh yes, until this war brought outsiders back to our shores, your government was beginning to permit us measures of freedoms and independence that we quickly realized the Japanese were not planning to duplicate—and I can see by your bunker-hunker reaction to that earthquake that you'd probably agree. So, while the Aleuts of today have mixed feelings about being citizens of the United States, we know that a Japanese takeover spells the total destruction of our race; thus, as I've said, most Aleuts are eager to join with the Allies, if only to push the Japanese out."

Up close and personal at Dutch Harbor. This quaint and remote U.S. fishing village/ naval garrison was the surprise far north target of the Japanese on their early morning (04:07) bombing raid of June 3, 1942. (Exclusive photo by Lt. Harper, 1942)

"Then why don't you join me? Have your men come back to Longview with me and enlist! The women can serve as nurses and seamstresses. To protect operational secrecy, our soldiers are being conveyed here after having been trained in deserts— not the Arctic. They aren't prepared for this environment and are often poorly equipped with insufficient clothing. We could use your skills as textile manufacturers, as hunters, as healers, using local materials to help gain an edge against our common enemy."

"Do not forget," she rebuked sternly, "that our tribe is hiding for a reason, and you know what those reasons are. First, all patriotism aside, we are realists. We shall not become victims of your mining camps, and neither shall we become victims of the Japanese. Second, if our true nature were discovered, there'd be no end to our suffering at the hands of your scientists and to secret military experiments. We'd forever be on the run, forever in hiding, because the alternative, even if the wights deem us a work of evil, is unthinkable to us."

"And what alternative is that?"

She winced and looked away, finally beholding me again to say: "We could infect the entire human race with our disease."

"A world of vampires," I gasped.

"That is correct, and so for the protection of your kind, we choose to remain here in hiding. Come now, we digress. We're constructing a proud *qayaatx̂ux̂*, and the wood is ready to bend."

She lifted the soaked driftwood fascia from the barrel and held it before a stone lamp. "You can see the light through the areas we've prefabricated for bending. That's how thin you need to shed the wood in order to attain the requisite pliancy."

She placed the soaked panel of prepared wood on the table, then used a sharp bone awl to bore small holes along one edge of the template she'd cut into it. "Now," she said, taking the sheet between her arms, "we bend it into shape."

She drew her arms together and the semblance of an elongated cap took form, looking something like a duck's bill with a conical top. After strong-arming the angles to perfection, she drew the rear ends of the hat together so that the holes she'd bored were more or less aligned, and then while sitting down with the hat between her knees to hold it into shape, she sewed the seams together with a sturdy twine.

After looking over her work thoroughly, she set the hat on the shelf, satisfied with its progress. "Next it must be painted, but it needs to dry first. Datuu, aren't you about to paint yours?"

The little vampire was half-lying over the table, organizing her brushes and bowls. "This one," she said, lifting a small *chagudax̂* before us.

Aleut in gut-skin parka and bentwood hat fitting a toggle-head lance (Photo card from Peter the Great Museum of Anthropology and Ethnography [The Kunstkamera] in Leningrad)

"Excellent," noted Iganakuchax̂. "She can show you how to paint and decorate a bentwood hat, but we're running short of sea lion whiskers. I know there's a bunch at the boathouse. Datuu, please go and fetch fifty more."

"All the way to the boathouse?" She wasn't thrilled about the directive.

"How else will you decorate your *chagudax̂*?"

"*Oh, all right!*" Datuu grumbled, and then left in a temper, at which point I discovered the hidden motive in her grandmother's order. After snooping around to make sure we were truly alone, Iganakuchax̂ drew close beside me over the painting table and said furtively, "The fire witching will require some trustworthy assistants, which may take a while for me to gather. But even should I find them, the task before us will remain extremely difficult. The environment we must work in is eminently perilous, especially for a mortal, while the Shield of Repentance is pure silver and quite heavy in conjunction with the *caelum divinatorius.*"

"Why not let me recruit some of the guys from Longview—strong military men from the eight-o-seventh? By now the engineering battalion is probably running out of things to do anyway. And there are pastors at A-2. I could get all this arranged from Kuluk, I guarantee you. I could do it in such a way as to mask the true situation." My case was passionate, but perhaps a little farfetched.

"That's a tall order," she laughed, "recruiting some of your military men along with the pastor-in-residence without raising any red flags—not unless you intend to kidnap them, which would entail dispatching them afterward." She searched my eyes for an answer. For her this was a serious consideration—or was she just fucking with me?

"Out of question."

"Then forget it. I can't risk the exposure of my clan. It will be better for me to assemble my own exorcism party, but need I remind you, you must be patient and keep this in utter secrecy. It may take some time."

I slunk my head in regret. Time was the one thing I didn't have, not with a war at hand on the shores of my homeland, and more so in the birthplace of my budding lover. But Iganakuchax̂ had told me the reasons her clan was staying out of the fray, so it was useless to try to convince her further. "But where will you find a priest?"

*Lieutenant Jake Harper, far left, with some of the guys of the 807th out of Longview,
proudly displaying some whalebones they'd found near Kuluk Bay on Adak, with
muskeg-laden hillock in background. Absolutely not available for cave clan "dispatch."
(Exclusive photo from Lt. Harper's collection, 1942–1943; photographer not listed)*

"I have my connections," she said cryptically.

A distant rumble of planes sounded faintly though the earthen walls and williwaw beyond like a drum roll of cotton balls upon a sodden tom-tom. I wondered if they were Allies, lost in the blinding blow of snow and fog, searching for the apron girder I helped to build in order to welcome them safely home after endless Kiska bombing runs. Or perhaps they were Japs who'd just bombed Longview or Dutch Harbor, only to get caught in the williwaw on their homeward run. In either case, the dying sound of departing planes made me feel lonely and depressed.

"Here are your whiskers!" Datuu suddenly arrived, both hands full of the long black spines. "Where dost thou wish for me to put them?"

"Give me half," Iganakuchax̂ said, "and keep half for your hat. Now you can show Kayuu how to decorate a *chagudax̂*."

B-52s return through fog to field on Adak after raiding Kiska, while
B-24s wait in revetment (Painting by Ogden Pleissner, 1944)

After surrendering half of her stash, Datuu scurried over and took a seat beside me at the painting table. "Ready?" she asked excitedly.

"I—I . . ." I stuttered, then looked over to Iganakuchax̂.

"Pay attention to her," the elder advised. "The kid is good. I'll bring some lunch by afterward." With that, the matron of the house walked out, leaving me alone with the little rascal vampire.

Datuu pointed out variously hued paints in wooden bowls, explaining, "We get the colors from flowers, berries, octopus ink, and even from blood—but don't worry," she giggled, "we rarely use human blood. Now pay attention, Kayuu! First thou must sketch where you want thy colors to go. Most hats have a horizontal rainbow pattern stretching down from the crown."

With impressive speed, the centuries old nine-year-old sketched out a pattern, carefully painted along the edges of her lines, then handed me a brush to help fill in the wider swathes at center.

"Why does my brother despise you so?" she asked as we painted.

"Tayaĝukichax̂? You tell me. He's never liked me, although I never did him any wrong."

We soon were adding fancy blue-black swirls to the hat's brow, using squid ink for the unique pigment.

"Why dost thou like my auntie so much?"

"You sure ask a lot of questions, Datuu."

"No I don't. Why dost thou like her?"

"What can I say, I just do."

"You can't just like someone without a reason, Mister Harper. Is it her hair? Or dost thou like her tattoos? Maybe it's her eyes. Dost thou like mine eyes?"

"I'm trying to paint, Datuu."

She shoved her head before my line of sight. "Dost thou know that Datuu means big, beautiful eyes?"

I had the mind to paint her ear. "Are you sure about that?"

"Big eyes." She blinked a few times for emphasis. "So dost thou like mine eyes, Mister Harper? Dost thou think they are pretty?"

"Yes, Datuu, you have very pretty eyes. Now please, I don't want to mess up your hat."

She removed her head and apologized, "Sorry, Kayuu. But thanks for saying I'm pretty. You still haven't told me why you like my auntie so much."

I resumed painting, giving her question some thought, to which I finally replied, "There's no one thing that explains why I like her, but more like a million little things. Like this hat, I like the way she's molded, molded by the creator; I like her array of colors, the moods and emotions that make up her character; the wide swathes of simplicity embellished by complex details, the darker and more defining colors that tell a deeper story. I love the warmth she shows me, sheltering me from the williwaws. She is tolerant, pliable, and not easily broken by my pitfalls. She stays by my side and over me, protecting me from my own shortsightedness; that is to say, she is loving and wise.

"I love her decorative flair, her hair, and yes, her tattoos, too." I chuckled. "The pretty stuff about a woman is like the pretty stuff in this hat: its shape, the lines, the unique outward embellishments that display its inner personality. But what I love most about Aniqdux̂six̂ is the strap she keeps beneath my chin. It used to feel like an uncomfortable restraint, before I knew any better. But in the stormy seas of life, she has reached around me to keep me safe, to hold me tight. She wants us to stay together through the ups and downs because that is what it means for two people to be made for each other. And even though it took a while for me to accept that, I realize now that we belong together, that our lives fulfill a greater purpose together, and that I love her very much. She is willing to die for me, as I am for her. That's why I need to leave here as soon as I am permitted. There's a war I must fight that, if lost, will turn hats like this into scrapwood and destroy my chance at returning your auntie's love. Hats as special as this must be protected at all costs."

"I understand, Kayuu," Datuu replied as she embellished the *chagudax̂* with the semblance of a seal's nose, mouth, and eyes. "Aniqdux̂six̂ is like the chief's crown to thee."

"What do you mean?"

"She's the most prominent thing you have, and makes thee very proud."

"Yes, Datuu," I laughed, "you could say that. But like this *chagudax̂*, you can only possess love if you take care of it, or give love back."

"Dost thou love me, Mister Harper?"

"The pretty stuff about a woman is like the pretty stuff in this hat: its shape, the lines, the unique outward embellishments that display its inner personality."
(Exclusive pencil art "Angel" by Ron Russell II, Utopia Productions, 2001)

I chuckled. "Love's not that simple, Datuu. Sometimes, it takes time. But one day when you find someone closer to your own age, you will know. I was going to say I'm too old for you, but the truth is, you're too old for me!"

"What sayest thou?"

"It's complicated. We're a little different, that is all. But how about this, Datuu: I will love you as a friend."

"It's a deal, Mr. Harper!" She held out her hand and we shook on it in the western fashion. "I love thou, too, as a friend."

I smiled. She was too much.

"Now that that's settled," she deemed, "let's finish the hat. This is my favorite part. We get to add ivory flanges, glass beads, feathers, and sea lion whiskers. Open those baskets thither—they're full of my decorations."

She showed me the best size and placement for the final embellishments, explaining how a real hunting hat should only have whiskers protruding from one side so as not to interfere with the spear throwing.

"Sugangix̂ is finished fixing thy harpoon," she said.

"Is that so?"

"Yes, but you still must poison the tip. You are very brave to do that."

"Why, is it dangerous?"

"The poison is boiled from the bodies of mummies, the really powerful mummies who were once great hunters and chiefs. I'd never be a whaler, because you know what happens when you mess with a mummy?"

"Aniqdux̂six̂ did mention something about that."

"You said she is willing to die for thee." Datuu caught me off guard. "What did you mean by that? Thou knowest we do not die, right?"

"Oh, it's been a long day, Datuu. What I meant was that Aniqdux̂six̂ considers my welfare before her own. She has made me a priority in her life, even above herself. She may have her own reasons for doing so, but the fact is she has proven that her commitment to my well-being is worth the ultimate risk, and it's a commitment that she knows never ends. She has no need to tell me any vows, for her actions speak for themselves. As for me, I intend to finish the war I was sent here to fight, and only then I will be able to honor my own commitment to spend my life with her."

"But she's not ready yet: her gen-cycle—"

"Look at these lovely ivories," I cut her off. "Please, show me how to apply them to your wonderful hat."

We continued to work, speaking thenceforth only of the finer points of bentwood hat construction.

EMBEDDED

"IT IS time to prepare for *qaqmiiĝux̂*," the chief said, referring to the hunt.

I took this as good news. I missed Aniqdux̂six̂ dearly and had been cooped up in Iganakuchax̂'s quarters for days, seeing only the chief on the rare occasion, his wife, and Datuu. Now I could finally move forward with the challenge that'd been set before me, to earn the chief's stepdaughter in holy matrimony. But there was one thing I found curious about the chief's announcement.

"I checked the weather not too long ago," I told him, "and it was still as stormy as can be. Do you usually go out in these conditions?"

"We do not discuss the weather," he said. "It does not bode well for us to do so. Follow me, Kayuu, the men are waiting."

We walked to the entrance of the lava tube leading to the subterranean boathouse, at which point he stopped to say he'd carry me the rest of the way to make things quicker. I agreed, and appreciated his warning me first instead of just picking me up and flying, as the Aleut vampires had a habit of doing. We rocketed through the black portal at great velocity, as could be ascertained by an incredible onrush of air, arriving at the boathouse moments later. From there, he led me through some overhanging reeds and into an adjoining chamber that I hadn't yet seen.

Perhaps two dozen hunters were seated in a semicircle around a large clump of volcanic stone that partook of black adakite or obsidian. Steaming water bubbled from the monolith's rocky crown and streamed down its craggy sides, terminating at a porous base of shale, from where it disappeared into the ground. Each hunter was seated upon a great whale vertebrae, one of which had been reserved for me. At the chief's instruction, I took a seat.

The room was roughly circular in shape, with numerous stone lanterns set into shallow crevices along the wall. The light was sufficient to see the faces of the men around me and, as I looked at them, each in turn regarded me. I recognized some, such as Sugangix̂, who gave me a little nod, and Tayagukichax̂, who actually was smiling at me. How he was recovering from his wound I could not say, but his very presence at the meeting indicated he was hale enough to join the whaling expedition.

Others in attendance were Qagux̂, who, again, was Qihmux̂'s supposedly unloving boyfriend, the youngster Tix̂lax̂, and Qatxamax, aka "big penis." There was but one woman present, whom I'd initially mistaken for a man. Her hair was styled in the same manner as many of the warriors, with a straight, black bang cut just over the brows; and like the men, she was dressed in a *kamleika* hunting parka and wore bird beak labrets through her lower lip. She'd been sitting next to me, and only when she surprised me with a formal introduction—"My name is Igasix̂, Unangam Tunuu for *wing*"—did I realize her gender. I returned the greeting, introducing myself as Lieutenant Jake Harper.

"You are Kayuu now," she said, eliciting grunts of agreement from the others.

Someone wearing a frightening mask appeared before the great monolith and spoke, "Rainbows are appearing, while

Qagux̂ has seen sea beasts on the move. The time has come to prepare for *qaqmiiĝux̂*."

The speaker's face was completely masked by a painted wood vizard, while a *sax* parka composed of red feathers covered the greater part of his body. By his stature and the sound of his voice, however, I believed it to be the chief.

"Let us begin by remembering the ones who lived before," he continued, "the beings of the caves that were here even before our ancestors."

"Then came Agugux, rising in the east to create light for the Aleuts to live. Even though the *promuishlenniki* from Siberia have made us more like the cave dwellers who came before, Agugux has not turned against us, but allows us to continue to live like Aleuts in his world of light, the only side effect being a slight whitening of our skin."

A collective murmur of agreement rumbled around the chamber.

"The *promuishlenniki* from the *Arkhangelsk*," Igasix̂ whispered to me so that I might better understand, "the ones who infected us, could not go into the light. The sun would cause them to catch fire."

I nodded in solemn recognition.

"The ritual before us," the disguised chief continued, "is to honor the giant we are about to kill, for it is only in the beast's sacrifice that we are able to live so abundantly. This ceremony is reserved for you, the select group of sea hunters gathered here, who by blood and experience are entitled to practice the ritual and throw the first spear, if you be so fortunate. But I offer a stern reminder for the benefit of our veterans and initiates alike, that the ceremony before us and the actions we take in preparation for the hunt are exclusive only to us and must never be shared with the uninvited."

The Aleuts place their origin at the Islands of Four Mountains, where dwelled their primordial generation, the "beings of the caves," whose bodies were said to be formed of wood. (Exclusive wood art, Memory Mark, by Ovidiu Kloska)

He glanced back at the corrugated rock bubbler and continued, "Just as the monolith before you fountains in perpetuity, so, too, do the creatures we shall take enable us to continue steadfast in our ways. We, the Niiĝuĝis, are the last holdout of the Unangax̂ people. Our Andreanof Islands brothers on Atka have been relocated to the Killisnoo evacuation camp, their village burned down by the Americans—wiped clean off the face of the earth. The Qax̂us, those seafarers of the Rat Islands, have disappeared before the secret atomic bomb tests conducted by that same rapacious superpower.

Atomic Energy Commission James R. Schlesinger and his nine-year-old daughter, Emily, stand at ground zero on Alaska's Amchitka Island a mile above where the AEC will detonate a five-megaton nuclear bomb the next day. The AEC official said he brought his wife and two daughters to the island to demonstrate his faith in AEC safety precautions. (AP Wirephoto and caption, date classified)

"The Qawalangin, who had lived on Umnak uninterrupted for nine thousand years, have been rudely uprooted from their lake and prairie homeland of Nikolski and shipped away in barges to the tree-lined death camps. The Qagaan Tayaĝungin of the east, who once lived harmoniously among the world's most formidable bears, now die by the claws of an unpredictable beast that swallows villages whole: the US government. The Sasignas of the Near Islands, who, in waking one morning to find they were too near the rising sun of the East, have been taken prisoner to Imperial Japan. The Naahmiĝus of Tanaga and the Delarof Islands, who have been completely displaced by fox trappers from both hemispheres. The Qigiiĝun of Unalaska, the Fox, and Krenitzin Islands, whose precious whaling depot of Akutan is but a memory, as they mine the concentration camps of Ward Lake instead, digging their own graves. And finally the Akuuĝun, our brothers of the Islands of the Four Mountains, whose disappearance from that place of power remains a mystery even to us Unangans. The Aleut people once numbered twenty-five thousand, but now only our small cave clan, hidden beneath a fingernail on the greater hand of Adak, remains as the final hope of all Unanga.

"In the sunset of our peoples, the ceremony before us has more significance with each passing day, and as an exclusive minority entitled to participate, you have a solemn responsibility to forward these duties with bravery and honor. The fountain that symbolizes the renewal of our world through *qaqmiiĝux* is now endangered, and will dry up completely unless we maintain the traditions that we have gathered here, once again, to perpetuate.

"It is my sincere belief that Agugux shall smile over Beringia again, retuning to our emerald chain those who by no fault of their own have lost their way."

En route to Adak is the rarely seen, emerald green, south shore of Amlia Island, east of Atka. (11th Army Air Force photo, 1942)

"But until that day comes," the old impresario explained, "it is up to us, the Niiĝuĝis of Adak Island, to keep the necklace strong and gleaming, so that when our brethren return over the gemstone bridge with the sunbeams of Agugux hearkening their advance, their hearthstone shall still be here, whispering with the tender voice of a mother, 'welcome home, Unanga, to your beloved cradle of storms.'

"And so we begin with the poisoning of the spearheads. As is customary in our barabara, I shall personally initiate the novices. Once this is completed, I will pair initiates with experienced paddlers, then each man shall inspect his watercraft. The initiates will get their piercings, at which point the others can test their buoys, or trade and polish their bird beak labrets. Then you can return to whatever you were doing, remembering to frequently clean yourself, for the hunt may be announced at any moment, but never during the evening when you should rest and conserve your energy. Take a moment to reflect on these things, to make your silent vows to Agugux, and we'll reconvene in the boathouse shortly."

With that, the chief turned toward the monolith and offered a reverential bow, and then left the chamber in silence, while those seated around me had closed their eyes and many were moving their lips, partaking in some manner of prayer.

I closed my eyes and wished for a successful hunt, that I might see Aniqdux̂six̂ again and take her hand in holy matrimony. My ultimate goal was to return with her to Kuluk as man and wife so that she could be provided the protection of our Allied base without being deemed a refugee and shipped off to the abandoned mining camps of the southeast. I could devise a scenario to my high command, saying I had found her alone, thereby sparing her clan from discovery. I surmised that if she were truly immortal, the fire witching could wait. Once the war blew over, we could covertly repair back to Boot Bay, and by then I could recruit the requisite officiates, such as a priest and retinue of strong men—personal friends of mine—to perform the requisite action. As things stood, I knew that Chief Aĝnakax̂ would not go along with the latter half of this plan, for the Shield of Repentance and fire witching were forbidden secrets. That being said, he'd already conceded it was possible for me to win the hand of Aniqduх̂six̂, showing that perhaps he could be flexible about other taboos as well. If he could break his sacrosanct rule about the gencycle, he may be cajoled into abandoning his other dictates such as the classified moratorium on fire witching. Perhaps his wife, Iganakuchax̂, could help convince him. Alas, to even broach the subject to him at this point could backfire severely, so I resolved to tell him naught for the time being.

To prevail in the whale hunt was paramount, then, for once I won over Aniqdux̂six̂ we could steal away to Longview. Presently I considered the barabara a lost cause, for if the Japanese were to take Adak, the island wouldn't be a place worth living. Even now, the cave clan's existing clandestinely under the American military occupation seemed tantamount to imprisonment, but if the Japs prevailed in their horrific agenda, the Unangans would assuredly be murdered or otherwise shanghaied back to Hokkaidō as slave laborers, just as the chief and Iganakuchax̂ had reported of the Sasignas of Attu, likely never to return. If the Allies won, however, I was convinced the Aleuts would be repatriated, their present displacement being a temporary necessity and not the underlying agenda of the US government, contrary to what many of my hosts were inclined to insinuate.

I wanted more than ever to help the barabara clan, and all Aleuts, regain the measure of self-determination they'd enjoyed before the Japanese contention. But it was clear that I could be of little help to them here, buried beneath the sod, far from my unit. I'd come to Adak to remove muskeg and Rommel stakes—impediments in the fight for freedom, but a screw picket had snagged me bad and now the peat had become a permanent fixture over my head. All these calamities I was intent on changing.

My vow, then, which rolled off my lips as a silent mumble beside the rest, was probably no different from a pledge: I swore to kill the biggest whale I could find, for only this would keep the world I loved in motion. If I could attain this one victory at sea, I could return to the ASF to fight the bigger battle. I reminded myself of the words of George C. Marshall, US Army chief of staff: "Victory of the democracies can only be complete with the utter defeat of the war machines of Germany and Japan."

The whalers got up from their vertebrae stumps with the last of my thoughts and, conversing in low tones, they shuffled out of the chamber. I followed in their footsteps.

Back in the boathouse, the chief invited me to sit at a table as he introduced me to two other initiates: Igasix̂, whom I'd already met, and Algax̂ Malihnax̂—a smooth-complexioned boy of perhaps sixteen years of age. This latter looked green like me, with no visible tattoos or piercings, yet unlike me—I am somewhat tall and lanky; Algax̂ was bullish in stature, being short, squat, and muscular. Igasix̂, on the other hand, looked like she'd already spent a great deal of time upon the water for, in addition to sporting the tattoos and bird beak labrets so common to Aleut mariners, she had the leathery face of a weathered sailor. Her hunting *kamleika* was of the make more commonly worn by seamen, while her formidable harpoon propped up against the table evinced she was serious about becoming a whaler—a predominantly male-oriented activity. As she peered at me coolly past her slate point spearhead, a chill rolled down my spine. This girl could swallow my liver whole, and undoubtedly would put me to shame in any ocean contest. But when her stern gaze suddenly cracked into a smile, she radiated the unfettered beauty of her youth, notwithstanding her fangs. She must've been in her late teens, but perhaps centuries old. With these people you never really knew.

Another Aleut bedecked in hunting garb came by with a large woven basket and distributed from it monkshood roots, placing one before each participant; and then were issued finely twined mats, stone and bentwood bowls for holding boiling water, and finally various pestles, mortars, and other tools from which to make the poison.

A Woman of Unalaschka, *as drawn by William Wade Ellis (1756–1785), surgeon's mate during Cook's third voyage, first on the HMS Discovery and later on the HMS Resolution, providing a fair likeness of Igasix̂. (From* An authentic narrative of a voyage performed by Captain Cook and Captain Clerke, in His Majesty's ships Resolution and Discovery during the years 1776, 1777, 1778, 1779 and 1780: in search of a North-West passage between the continents of Asia and America, *by G. Robinson, published December 14, 1781)*

Chief Aĝnakax̂ instructed us on how to extract deadly aconite resin from the monkshood roots and meld it with water; however, I was already familiar with the process from watching Aniqdux̂six̂ do it. Still, something that Datuu had said confused me, so I asked the chief: "Excuse me for asking, for I don't intend to be disrespectful, but Datuu mentioned the use of mummy fat in making the poison. Is that true?"

While the others regarded me with wide-eyed terror, the chief emitted a knowing chuckle and then answered: "That is what you must tell the uninitiated. We tell them that our dead ancestors provide the lethal power as a way of keeping the greenhorns a good sea mile away [6000 feet], but it's just a ruse."

My cohorts were visibly relieved, with more than a few chortles to go around. As for me, I remained a little confused.

"Dead bodies," Igasix̂ relayed surreptitiously. "Bad news."

"*Ah . . .*" I remembered. "Not to be touched."

Then the chief, using Igasix̂'s harpoon as an example of how to lace a spearhead, smeared a thick coating of aconite resin over it. Afterward, he fitted the poisoned tip with a pre-fabricated reed sheath to keep the resin moist, warm, and contained until it was time to throw the lance.

As Algax̂ Malihnax̂ smeared his spearhead, the chief asked me where my harpoon was.

"I don't know," I replied. "I think Sugangix̂ still has it."

"Sugangix̂?"

"I have it!" announced Tayaĝukichax̂, who'd overheard us.

"*You* have it?" Chief Aĝnakax̂ inquired with surprise.

"Yes, I shall retrieve it," Tayaĝukichax̂ said.

And then to the amazement of all of us, my onetime greatest enemy left the room, only to return to personally hand me my lance, blunt end first. Its ground slate point had been sharpened to a formidable degree of accuracy; Sugangix̂ It had refurbished it finely.

I thanked Tayaĝukichax̂, who replied something akin to, "Don't mention it," but when I scanned the room for Sugangix̂ to thank in kind, he was nowhere to be found.

After lacing my spearhead with poison, I joined the others to the *baidarkas*, where Chief Aĝnakax̂ was partnering initiates up with seasoned veterans. He placed Algax̂ Malihnax̂ with Qagux̂, and Igasix̂ with an older, graying, but robustly built seaman named Altixum. He then invited me before the largest two-person *baidarka* in the boathouse and said, "You shall be piloting this one with Tayaĝukichax̂."

"Tayaĝukichaх̂?" I was completely nonplussed. "Are you serious?"

"Tayaĝukichaх̂!" he called out, his burly vampire son lumbering into my midst once again.

"Yes, chief?"

"On this *qaqmiiĝuх̂*, Kayuu shall be your partner, and he'll be riding point in this *baidarka*."

I was certain the cocksure Aleut would react the same as I had at the preposterous idea, but he seemed to be perfectly fine with it, or the first half of it, anyway. "Sure, I'll show him the ropes," he replied nonchalantly, "but chief, there's got to be a better *baidarka* available. This one's ancient."

"That's exactly so," countered his father. "They don't make *iqyах̂* like they used to. Enjoy the ride!"

"*Iqyах̂*?" I inquired.

"That's what the old-timers used to call their *qayaqs*," answered Tayaĝukichaх̂, "but they're total *baidaras*! Just look at it—it could hold ten people. This should be used to transport fat women to Blind Cove, not for men to hunt whales. Look how wide it is: we'll never be able to keep up with a pluming beast."

"No *iqyах̂* is wide enough to hold your head," Chief Aĝnakaх̂ quipped, "so deal with it. I personally had this boat refurbished. It will do just fine."

"It will wind up on the rocks," countered his recalcitrant son.

"That would be your fault then," replied the chief. "After all, had you not wrecked your own *baidarka* in precisely that fashion, I wouldn't have had to dig this *iqyах̂* out of the woodwork to refurbish for you."

Tayaĝukichaх̂ huffed loudly, rolling his eyes in frustration.

"Enough pouting! Inspect your new *baidarka*—I bet this is the one that lands the greatest beast."

"If you say so, chief," Tayaĝukichax̂ replied unconvincingly, and then he went about inspecting the craft, which was erected upon a short driftwood gantry.

"Well, show the new initiate what to look for," prodded the chief.

"Oh yeah, sorry," remarked Tayaĝukichax̂, sounding like he meant it, and then, "Come here, Kayuu. Let's see what's under the hood."

"Under the hood? Really?" I was intrigued by his parlance.

"I wasn't born yesterday," grumbled he.

"That's right," laughed the chief. "You were born the century before last! So show this Aleut wannabe what a real *qayaq* is made of, son!"

"Whatever, pops," Tayaĝukichax̂ said without breath, motioning for me to come closer for the inspection, which I did. "Just ignore him," he remarked of his father.

"Is that possible?" I replied furtively, and we both had a laugh.

"What are you two talking about?" Aĝnakax̂ asked. "I hope it's about the *iqyax̂*."

"Relax, dad," replied Tayaĝukichax̂. "I got this."

"It's Chief Aĝnakax̂, boy, and don't you forget that!"

Tayaĝukichax̂ rolled his eyes, then continued with me: "Okay, so we start with the hull and work our way in from there. This particular dinosaur is about a foot wider than it should be—but no matter, it was built for fat, lazy chiefs."

"What?!" railed Aĝnakax̂.

"Not you, dad," Tayaĝukichax̂ said with a wink that only I could see. I was happily relieved to be getting along better with the beast of a batman that'd previously tried to kill me. "This *baidarka*," he continued, "if you could call it that, is a double-seater, the average length of which should be about thirteen cubits [about 20 feet], but this one appears more like fifteen cubits [about 23 feet]. Its width is a little wide: only about one cubit [2 feet] should be the average for a two-man *qayaq*.

"The frame is built like that of a sea mammal, like the skeleton of a walrus—just replace driftwood for the bones and you get a general idea of how it's constructed. Heavy thongs are used to tie the driftwood together. This particular dinosaur, I can tell you right off, has plenty of internal structure. The woods of the hull are not supposed to bulge out like the bony knees of a lanky *Americanchin*—the frame should have a smoother appearance; but in all likelihood this *iqyax̂* is of sound constitution; a little extra weight never hurts, if only it were more supple—a *baidarka* should bend with the waves. At any rate, the important thing is for the sides to be nearly vertical, the bottom to be rounded, and the skins to be taut. Come, we must inspect beneath the hull to make sure it's sound."

As we bent to look down, he gripped his chest and groaned.

"Are you okay, Tayaĝukichax̂?" I knew he was suffering from my harpoon jab, but what else could I say?

He ignored me and resumed the business at hand, gliding his fingers over the hull and saying, "The frame itself is covered with seal or sea lion skins, and then we apply boiled seal oil to make it watertight. Whoever refurbished this *qayaq* did a good job with that. See the translucency? The hunter should be visible within the craft like a heart within a ribcage. For Aleuts the *baidarka* is a living being—an extension of one's own body, if you will."

"Aniqdux̂six̂ skinned it," added the chief. He was milling about with his arms crossed, inspecting us performing the inspection.

"As wives do?" Tayaĝukichax̂ laughed.

"What are you talking about?" I was flabbergasted.

Tayaĝukichax̂ remained silent, while the chief just shook his head.

Igasix̂, who'd been inspecting the *baidarka* adjacent, gravitated over and remarked, "I saw her down here earlier as she was finishing up. Her hair was combed real pretty-like and she kept washing her hands with urine, Kayuu. A good Aleut woman does that before making things for her man's hunt."

The chief signaled for her to get back to inspecting her own boat with Altixum, the wise old seaman.

"In my time," the chief addressed Tayaĝukichax̂ and me again, "women weren't even allowed to step over the hunting boats, let alone pilot one. It's their body. A female's sexual energy was too powerful and could easily contaminate a craft. Even one strand of her hair left on the vessel could make a sea lion jealous and vengeful, which spelled bad news for the hunter stuck in his floating *baidarka*. Those were the days of our ancestors, before the *promuishlenniki* fundamentally changed us, and so now it doesn't matter that Igasix̂ is a woman."

I pondered his words in silence.

"At any rate, Kayuu," continued his son, "for comparison, one-person *baidarkas*, like that one over there, are about ten cubits [16 feet] long and—"

"How about your wife?" I interjected.

Tayaĝukichax̂ drew in his shoulders as if reacting to a sudden chill, then dropped them resignedly and said: "Long gone, Kayuu, long gone. I take care of Datuu now, with the help of Iganakuchax̂."

"He'll get a new wife on his next gen-cycle," the chief interposed, rubbing his scant white beard while focusing on his son.

"We need to finish inspecting this *baidarka*," Tayaĝukichax̂ grumbled, clearly irritated about the direction the conversation had taken. "After going over the exterior," he said, "we must look at the inside. The first thing to inspect is the gut skin circling the rims of each hatch. This must be checked for cracks and tears, because, like the boat itself, the gutskin hatch extensions form a waterproof cocoon that is pulled up beneath the paddler's armpits and tied off there, preventing water from getting through. In this way, the hunter forms a seamless bond with his *baidarka* via his *kamleika*, made of the same or similar waterproofing materials. But it must have enough excess guts-kin to allow the hunter to stand fully on deck, from where he will cast his spear with the aid of a throwing board."

Seated within his baidarka, an Aleut prepares to cast his spear with the aid of a throwing board, which he is gripping beneath the shaft (Library of Congress Prints and Photographs Division, 1929)

"Next are the seats themselves," Tayaĝukichax̂ explained. "Made of woven mats, they should not have too many holes or frayed edges, which could lead to failure under duress."

I felt the seats. "They look brand new," I remarked.

"Blame Aniqdux̂six̂ for that," the chief answered, still lingering about. "She wanted to make sure you two were comfortable. You might go fifty leagues [150 miles] out to catch your monster, and hunt for twenty hours without rest."

Tayaĝukichax̂ shot him a wry glance, but in rubbing the seats, he came to the same conclusion as me, saying: "She *is* good at weaving—probably the best here, actually. Anyway, once you have looked over the seats, check within the hull to make sure that none of the driftwood poses a puncture risk. If the craft was constructed well from the start, this should not be an issue, but heavy seas have compromised frames in the past. You also should check to make sure you'll have enough leg room. Look for loose stones on the floor, which we sometimes use for ballast when going out alone. Any stones should be removed and, if need be, replaced at the beach just prior to launch. The ballast can stabilize an underweighted craft and helps in attaining the maximum flanking speed of nine knots (10 mph)."

"In a kayak, really?"

"Going downwind, yes, even in a *qayaq*. Also regarding stabilization, some of the newer boats have bladder bags on deck that serve as buoys to prevent them from capsizing, but none of this need concern us, because this old *Hydrodamalis gigas* isn't going anywhere but slow."

The chief uncrossed his arms, and gawked at his wayward son.

"The what?" I had no idea what Tayaĝukichax̂ had meant.

"We're finished." He dodged the question. "The chief's *iqyax̂* has miraculously passed."

"Enjoy the ride," his father put in again, unfazed by Tayaĝukichax̂'s quip. "I hope you catch a sperm."

"Any questions?" Tayaĝukichax̂ inquired of me.

I was still digesting their peculiar vernacular and family feuding, so drew a blank.

"Good. We'll go over the rest when we launch. For now, we get to drill some holes through your lip, right dad?"

"That's *chief*," replied an unimpressed Aĝnakax̂, "and yes, you are correct—the initiate can now get fitted with labrets."

I shat my sealskin breeches, figuratively speaking. By the looks of Tayaĝukichax̂'s lower lip, abundant with ivory, bone, and shell bead adornments—all requiring piercings—I was in for a seriously painful makeover. But I was already committed past the Rubicon, because I was committed to Aniqdux̂six̂ and my ultimate escape back to Longview.

I'd been through a lot since getting lost in the tundra, so the piercings, while painful, were nothing to carry on about. The Aleuts gave me three. Qihmux̂ began by explaining that Aleuts enjoy the pain of receiving piercings and tattoos because it prepares them for the far more painful rigors of childbirth, and for the men, a hard life at sea. Thus without any anesthetic, she pulled my lower lip far back and shoved a seagull bone pin up through its underside in three places. I was sweating profusely and drooling red until she plugged the holes with a walrus ivory and two bird beak labrets, these latter supposedly having the power to bring me luck on the *qaqmiiĝux̂*. The lip piercings were traditionally performed by a close relative—thus the employment of Qihmux̂, who, again, was Aniqdux̂six̂'s older sister. She held her seagull bone before my face and asked if I wanted a nose piercing. I politely declined.

Most of the Aleuts had all sorts of piercings and associated jewelries in their lips, noses, ears, and forehead, the most common adornments being either a lion whisker, bone, or eagle's feather shaft worn horizontally through the nose; amber, shell beads, and/or sea lion whiskers worn as earrings; and for decorations in the lower lip and cheeks they wore walrus ivory studs, beads, bones, and/or garnets. The forehead was occasionally crossed with a white bird bone or black walrus whisker extending horizontally through the flesh not unlike their nose pins.

Woman of Oonalashka, *donned in traditional sax parka and adorned with facial piercings, jewelries, and tattoos (First printed in London circa 1770–1780s)*

Some of the Unanga I'd met wore six separate labrets, for the more piercings a clan member had, the higher the respect s/he was said to command. But beyond social and decorative functions, Chief Aĝnakax̂ explained that for a sea hunter, piercings and tattoos served to meld or camouflage the wearer in with his or her surroundings, thereby warding off the evil spirits that inhabited the coastal region—pernicious *khoughkh* that were constantly trying to enter through one's facial orifices.

Whatever the natives' fancy, I'd survived my first round of initiation, and with a bloodied chin that served little to ward off the "evil spirits" in my midst, Chief Aĝnakax̂ passed around a seal bladder gourd filled with mammal blood for the *iidigidi* to drink, christening the "hazing" of the initiates while underhandedly keeping the Aleut vampires from feasting upon my own bloodily swollen lips. But the chief had the courtesy to requisition for me a gourd of salmonberry wine and a bentwood bowl full of pure Aleutian ice. The former burned my lips going in, so I just sucked on the irregularly shaped ice chunks instead, which helped bring the swelling down significantly. In fact, the hospitality I was receiving was unprecedented, at least from those present, who were mostly adult male hunters and a few young acolytes.

Tayaĝukichax̂ called me over, conspicuously before all present, to his table, where he sat with a bunch of squat and burly whalers trading swigs of blood while swapping labrets. He picked out a shiny white stud from his pile and tossed it up to me, saying, "No hard feelings, Kayuu. I know we had a rocky start, but let's let bygones be bygones. We're going to make a strong and fearless team!"

I thanked him, receiving a great *ballyhoo!* from the other whalers.

At long last, I returned with Chief Aĝnakax̂ to his and Iganakuchax̂'s quarters, bloodstained and sweaty from the rigors of the initiation, which had also included "feats of bravery" with our weapons, but that's another story that I'd already forgotten about after drinking the entire gourd of salmonberry wine by day's end. Nevertheless, I was able to stand up straight enough to thank Aĝnakax̂ for his boat, stating that it looked "good enough for me."

He responded with a shit-eating grin, telling me to go clean myself up. The *qaqmiiĝux̂* could start at any moment, and a hunter must always cleanse himself before he goes. He handed me off to Iganakuchax̂, who directed me to a big water gourd hanging near a smaller gutskin filled with urine, which she reminded me was to be used as soap. I began removing my *kamleika* to take a piss shower, but she said my face and hands would be sufficient enough to wash for now because a *qaqmiiĝuŝ* is never launched at night. I've anyway had too much to drink, she chided like a doting mother, and needed rest. As she saw me to my sleeping quarters, I asked a quiet, "Can I see Aniqduŝsiŝ real quick?"

"*Nangaa, hlas qingunaaŝs aguu, asxinus anaan ngaan hixtada,*" she said. I knew only the first word, which meant "no." But then she clarified: "The young women are dancing together naked beneath the moonlight in order to bring good fortune to the *qaqmiiĝuŝ*. The penalty for a man to interfere with the ceremony is death."

"Naked, outside, in this weather? That's okay, I think I'll stay in tonight."

As she helped me onto my plaited reed bed, she warned, "You should pray the dance will help you. Mortals always die on *qaqmiiĝuŝ*." She procured a necklace from her *sax* pocket and placed it over my head. It was attached with feathers, beaks, and carved bone trinkets.

"What's this?"

"An amulet that will help you avoid certain doom. It contains ravens' beaks and the feathers of the rosy finch, which are indispensable to your protection. But no one must look at it." She tucked it beneath my *kamleika*. "I must be the last woman you have contact with before the *qaqmiiĝuŝ*. You must stay away from young women especially."

Smiling tenderly while bearing her fangs, she tucked me beneath my muskeg blanket, and then left.

I lay staring at a stone lantern that seemed to flicker with the rumble of distant storms. But as I listened more carefully, I couldn't ascertain what I was really hearing. It could've been a storm, a battle raging from afar, flying fortresses reconnoitering, or mysteries yet unknown . . .

When I awoke, the distant rumble was still recurring, so I scaled the notched log ladder to survey the out-of-doors, expecting to see a thunderstorm approaching; but just as I opened the reed and whalebone door, Chief Aĝnakax̂ appeared there with several other men.

"Look out below!" he warned as they pushed a huge pile of seaweed over the rooftop portal.

I did a half pachinko (I was getting better at it) back down the ladder as the mass of kelp loomed overhead, and then like a spider in full retreat, I scurried away backward on all fours as the first ropes of seaweed came bouncing weightily over the floor, lashing at my feet.

After the totality of incoming algae came to a standstill upon the reed mat floor before me in giant, ropey bundles, Aĝnakax̂ poked his head though the portal above and warned, "Look out!—there's more!"

"Look out!" "Stay there!" "Get back!" and "Bomb's away!" the chief repeated as the dumping continued unabated, until at last I stood back-against-the-wall with a massive mound of kelp piled in front of me, where'd I'd only minutes before been sleeping. My hands were gooey and gummy from haphazardly helping to consolidate the mass as it was poured in, while my bed was completely buried.

Aĝnakax̂ carefully climbed down the ladder, followed by two vampires who jumped through the portal one after the other, bouncing and rolling off the rubbery mound like overgrown children, laughing all the while. They were wearing *kamleika* hunting suits, as was I, which provided effective enough armor against the stinking blob of maritime flora.

"This is Olean," the chief said, pointing at the first Unanga who'd jumped in, a short, squat man in his thirties with a tattooed nose, somewhat fair complexion, and a belt ringed with large, hanging bone hooks. "And Tix̂lax̂, who I believe you've already met."

I nodded in recognition of the teenage hunter, and then said hello to Olean, who glared back at me with coal-black eyes that were slightly crossed. He looked as if he may've been mad (like literally insane), and I thought he'd shortly charge me, tackling me like an Unangax̂ halfback, but he just smiled and laughed: "Kayuu, *qahngus.*"

"Pardon?"

"He's talking about the seaweed," offered Aĝnakax̂. "You three are going to turn it into a fishing line."

I was a little perplexed at how this could be achieved.

"How'd it go?" inquired Tayaĝukichax̂, suddenly appearing from behind a partition.

"*Sakang akus igax̂tax̂ waaĝanax̂*," the chief replied.

I had no idea what he'd said.

Aĝnakax̂ walked out with his son—my shipmate, as it were—but not before Tayaĝukichax̂ turned around to say, "Enjoy the job, Kayuu—it's all part of being an Aleut."

"What were they talking about?" I asked Tix̂lax̂, who'd been amicable to me once before.

"Airplanes," was his curt and mysterious reply, then, "We must get started making fishing rope. The *qaqmiiĝux̂* could start at any time." He leapt up through the portal and disappeared.

"So we're going to catch a whale with seaweed?" I quipped. "You can't be serious?"

Olean eyed me with displeasure. "You're right, *Americanchin*, we can't catch a whale with this, it's much too strong—the seaweed, that is, so the chief has drafted you to help us soften it up. Are you ready to do some gardening?" He laughed.

"Incoming!" cried Tix̂lax̂, and no sooner than he sent the warning did gallons of brown liquid come pouring in through the portal, soaking the kelp mound beneath it.

"Fish oil," Olean revealed with a grin, but my nostrils could've surmised as much by the offensive, briny smell. He handed me a knife and showed me how to prune the seaweed so that only the central rope remained, with Tix̂lax̂ jumping in to join the "gardening" phase.

The prodigious ropes of kelp were remarkably long, the strand I was working on taking about forty minutes to prune before I met Tix̂lax̂'s knife trimming up from the other end. We now had two coiled piles connected at the center, the total length of line amounting to approximately one hundred meters.

Olean, for his part, was an experienced pro, singlehandedly finishing his coil only minutes after us, his total length of cable equaling Tix̂lax̂'s and mine. Then came the hard part: we had to make the cord pliant by smashing it inch by inch between two stones. This stage explained the fish oil offense, which was merely an additive to soften up the kelp. Thankfully, I was working with vampires who went into high gear when pounding, and with blurring speed we completed both lengths of line in about thirty minutes.

Afterward, Olean detached a curved bone hook from his belt and made a motion of throwing it at me. I jumped back, holding my hands up in defense. He and Tix̂lax̂ had a laugh, and then he gently tossed the hook to me and handed one to Tix̂lax̂ as well. It had a green barb like an oxidized nail attached to it, and I became angry at the pudgy Aleut for not having warned me about it before throwing the hook up for me to catch. The jocular Olean couldn't care less about my huffiness, but immediately launched into an instruction on how to attach the hook to the rope end.

Once we'd fitted our lines with the formidable barbed bones, Olean dragged in a basket full of pre-notched stones that served as sinkers, which he showed me how to attach to the ropes before placing them back into the basket.

"I'll admit, Olean," I remarked as I looked over the burly coils of prepared sea cable, each with a pernicious-looking hook emerging from its center like a cobra's head, "I'm impressed with these cords. But can they really pull in a whale?"

"Who said anything about a whale?" he laughed. "I'm going after halibut!"

THE GREAT WHALE HUNT

EARLY THE next morning, a large whale was sighted off Elf Island and the signal was given to go. The *qayaq* teams met in the boathouse, from where we gathered the equipage and began heading out from the cave.

I wished Tayaĝukichax̂, "Good morning."

He laughed at my bentwood hat, telling me it was the wrong kind. He wore a *chagudax̂*—the visor type, open-crown variety, claiming it was better for paddling because it helped to keep one cool.

I asked him if he got hot while paddling, knowing fully well he didn't, due to his condition.

"Your *qayaatx̂ux̂* looks ridiculous out here," was his evasive response.

"Well, your mother helped me make it."

"Iganakuchax̂?" he laughed. "Eh! You can make your own next time. Just forget it. Let's go hunting."

Exiting from the lava tube, we trudged out over an alpine heath meadow abundantly patched with fresh spring snow. While Aleutian sparrows sang all around us, a strange fallout greatly reduced our visibility. I assumed it was snowfall, but soon noticed the flakes were neither cold, nor did they evaporate when rubbed.

"Is that—?" I began, then stopped to listen to a distant rumble—the same reverberation I'd heard all night, only now, outside, it was much louder and didn't sound so distant.

Man of Oonalashka, *a likeness of Tayaĝukichax̂, in chagudax̂ hat and kamleika parka (First printed in London circa 1770–1780s)*

"Volcanic ash," replied Tayaĝukichax̂, marching past me with a weighty coil of kelp slung over one shoulder and carrying two large baskets in his hands. "Watch those spear tips," he cautioned. "Keep an eye on the scabbards."

"We're going to hunt in this weather?" I asked disbelievingly as I tried to keep apace.

"It is a gift from Great Sitkin," he replied, and left it at that.

I was perplexed, but kept focused on my steps through the water's edge tundra, fearing for Rommel spikes. The last picket that'd snagged my leg could not be easily forgotten.

"We only hunt under heavy fog or ash," he explained in his own time, "to avoid detection by aircraft."

Allied bombing runs to Kiska were sometimes delayed for days due to a thick cover of fog. Air support for ground troops in the Aleutian theater was likewise often hampered by uncompromising weather and difficult flying terrain. (Panel from World War II comic strip, Kiska Surprise, *1946; no illustrator listed)*

"Before the war," Tayaĝukichax̂ continued after a pause, "we encountered a lot of Japanese trawlers who were probably spies surveying our islands in preparation for using them as military bases. The Aleutians, we knew, could serve as their ultimate land bridge from which to conquer America. But they wouldn't bother us, and we sometimes traded with them. But now that the war has actually arrived, things are much different: there are planes all over the place, none of which can be trusted or ignored— only in a heavy fog is there a reduction of aircraft. And forget about the Japs! With the completion of Longview came great squadrons of Allied bombers and reconnaissance aircraft, and you *know* what your military will do to us if we're discovered."

I knew all too well what would happen. They'd be evacuated to places like Ward Lake. My having helped build Longview suddenly put me at odds with the burly Aleut and what he was presently trying to accomplish—to simply go fishing in a traditional manner without being deported. But I felt no shame. This was wartime, and so what would you expect? The islands had to be cleared of natives for their own safety. Until the Japs were defeated, we'd need every runway and aircraft we could get—and this in itself had proved an incredibly difficult task: forging airfields in muskeg and requisitioning enough planes from the greater Pacific battle to protect this forlorn northern flank.

US Army Air Forces aircraft (Lockheed P-38 Lightning & Curtiss P-40 Warhawks) undergoing maintenance in a revetment somewhere in the Andreanof group of islands in the Aleutian Islands in southwest Alaska. (USAAF photo and caption, 1943)

I sought to change the subject before it got heated: "I'm surprised so much smoke and ash can fall from a distant volcano."

"It's normal. If it's not Great Sitkin, then it's Kanaga, Tanaga, or Gareloi. Even ash from Chuginadak and Okmok reaches here on occasion. The shoreline of Boot Bay would presently be useless to us without our great smoky sentinels, our blinding fogs and whiteout snowstorms."

"But how can you navigate in these conditions?"

"Centuries of practice. We read the winds, tides, and currents like the white man reads his Bible. We put the phrases to heart, memorize them, and can act on them in all situations. Only standing waves truly scare me—the Devil in disguise, they break all the patterns."

"Standing waves?"

"Have you ever seen a wave crest up and curl without dissipating? The funnel just stays there, slithering back and forth atop the wave like a serpent. To get a *baidarka* through that is a deathly proposition. Many a paddler has lost his life to the chilling whip of the standing wave."

"Can they be avoided?"

"Usually you can see them forming or already formed. They tend to occur between islands due to the opposing tug of currents. You just have to wait until the tide changes and they dissipate, but sometimes they appear without warning, rising out of the sea like a rippling serpent's back, creating a wall of water a mile long with a ferociously roiling tube at its crest."

"How big can a standing wave get?"

"I've seen them at ten to twelve cubits [14—17 feet]."

"Jesus, where?"

He stopped and stared me down. "Don't use that word!"

I froze in place. He resumed walking in giant steps.

"Easy, big guy," I uttered under my breath, struggling to keep apace. He slightly turned his head. Those vampires could hear a pin fall in China.

"Between the Islands of Four Mountains," he replied to my initial inquiry. "The rips can be bad there, real bad."

We at last arrived at a small stretch of beach—a spread of brown sand deposited by a stream meandering down through the muskeg to the ocean. Cawing ravens, the source of many an Aleut myth and legend, traipsed and hopped about the moist sand. We set our equipage down on the beach beside that of other teams' deposits, and then turned back to the boathouse to retrieve the *baidarkas*.

Tayaĝukichax̂ and I mostly kept silent on our return trip to the boathouse and then back to the beach, which was probably a good thing. The boats, although fairly lengthy, were not too heavy to carry, especially with the help of the super-strength *iidigidi*.

On the shoreline, other vampires were already outfitting their kayaks, and to a certain degree the *qaqmiiĝux̂* had the aura of a race. I for one was eager to spear a whale, for only then could I prove my worth to the cave clan and thereby win over the hand of their most cherished rebel, Aniqdux̂six̂.

Most of the equipage was secured to the *baidarka*'s deck. There was plenty of room between the front seat and the bow to lay our harpoons, throwing boards, floats, and darts. My initial assumption was that Tayaĝukichax̂ was going to place his seaweed cable over the aft deck, because directly to our west was the *qayaq* commanded by Olean and Tix̂lax̂, whose kelp line was already coiled up neatly astern their craft. But then, to my surprise, Tayaĝukichax̂ took our coil of seaweed over to the kayak to our east and handed it to the "big penis" Qatxamax and his deckhand Sugangix̂, who were partners on the *qaqmiiĝux̂*. I didn't care much for Qatxamax, but I liked the young Sugangix̂, so didn't wage a protest about the apparent donation.

Natives of Oonalashka, and their Habitations, *as drawn by HMS* Resolution's *artist John Webber (1751–1793) on Captain James Cook's final voyage. Sketch shows the homes of Aleut people as seen by Webber during Cook's stop in Unalaska from June 28 to July 2, 1778. The ship's surgeon, David Samwell, later wrote that he and Webber were invited to "an Indian Town in a low valley close to the water" where they saw houses built in earthen mounds with entrances via notched log ladders from the top. Traditional kayaks and a fish drying rack can be observed near the shoreline. (From New, Authentic, Entertaining, Instructive, Full and Complete Historical Account of Captain Cook's First, Second, Third and Last Voyages, by Alexander Hogg, published in serial format from 1784 to 1786)*

All told, nine *baidarkas* lined the shore, six of which were two-seaters and three of which were singles. We were rather uniformly lined up along the fifty meter stretch of beach, with the furthermost crafts on our either side barely visible in the falling ash and misty morning chill wafting in from the ocean.

In observing my fellow hunters preparing, I noticed that one of the tall baskets Olean and Tix̂lax̂ had placed beside their *qayaq* was wobbling. I rubbed my eyes and looked again, and sure enough, unbeknown to them it was becoming increasingly ungainly, while the wind was too light to explain it. Suddenly, the basket fell over and a large octopus crawled out on all eights, making haste directly toward me!

"Hey! Hey!" I exclaimed, backing up and almost falling over my *baidarka* as the purple cephalopod closed in, wild as can be.

"Grab it!" Tix̂lax̂ shouted, but no sooner than he gave this unenviable command did the octopus take a sharp turn toward the sea.

"Don't let it escape!" Tayaĝukichax̂ upped the ante, undoubtedly humoring himself at my expense.

Not wishing to appear the coward, I scrambled after the cephalopod and tackled in a few inches of water, mere seconds from its emancipation. But in those following seconds, several mighty arms squeezed around my head and arms with the horrible sensation of innumerous suckers cupping into my skin. I rolled about the shallows in a wrestling match with the eight-armed demon, finally succeeding in stretching its head to arm's length from mine, but aside from that, it wouldn't let me go and I wouldn't let go of my quarry, so we were both sort of stuck in limbo about what to do with each other. But then when I saw its beaked mouth and grinding teeth, I began pushing its head away with increased vigor that was in reality terrific panic.

"Don't grab the back of the head!" Olean warned, coming to my defense with a bone knife. "Or you'll kill it!"

"I can't exactly mollycoddle the damned thing!" I countered in exasperation, using a word I'd garnered from Sabine Baring-Gould's, *The White Fang*—a book I'd borrowed from Aniqdux̂six̂'s collection.

The other hunters gathered around to watch the drama, and they were all laughing.

Thankfully, Olean and then Tayaĝukichax̂ wasted no time in using the blunt sides of their knives to free the suckers from my *kamleika* and wrest the bait off of me—"bait" I discovered when they handed the sprawling thing to Tix̂lax̂ to return to the "bait basket" from whence it had escaped. I could only wonder about the type and size of fish they were hoping to land with such a sprawling enticement. Images of killer whales and sharks soon came to mind—large toothy monsters attacking us in our vulnerable skin boats, which anyway resembled the big game seals that the apex predators probably sought as lunchtime morsels.

Like the jocular asshole he was, Tayaĝukichax̂ adjusted my hat—the one he liked to laugh at—and said, "Looks like you're just warming up. Okay, you take point. I paddle, you spear."

We slid the fully loaded *baidarka* into the gently lapping waves, and partially floating in the sandy shallows just off the beach, we took our seats. As I stretched my legs deep into the hull, Tayaĝukichax̂ handed me a double-bladed wood paddle and offered to tighten the cinch around my seat's gutskin waist extension. I felt the sack pulling snugly around my trunk.

I dipped my paddle into the water and experienced a peculiar mix of queasiness and excitement. This was it—we were entering the realm of sea beasts, engaging in an activity that had reputedly killed even the best of Aleut hunters.

Tayaĝukichax̂ pushed his oar into the sand until the hull was free enough to advance, and soon we were paddling out into the cold, grey waters off Boot Bay, an onshore breeze ever so subtly filling in as we progressed.

A cold, grey brume blows over a typical Aleutian main (Exclusive photo by the author, looking south from Adak shoreline)

As we moved further offshore, the onshore wind increased and sharpened the updraft against the cliffs that fringed the bay, where all sorts of birds were at play. Geese soared in circles with motionless, outstretched wings, ravens engaged in wild acrobatics over the tundra-clad steppes, while gulls, puffins, and other sea birds darted back and forth, nesting, feeding, and singing in myriad ways.

While the rest of the fleet gravitated toward the center of the bay, we cut crossways toward Elf Island. Tayaĝukichax̂ was steering from the stern and I didn't question his piloting, although it did concern me a little as to why the rest of the pack was consolidating in one area while we were breaking away. The answer to this riddle came shortly . . .

"*Tweee!*" sounded a whistle from Altixum, who sat behind Igasix̂ in a double-seater as she held up her oar, which was barely visible to me through the ash. All the other *qayaqs* closed in and formed a circle approximately thirty meters wide around their location.

I stopped paddling and asked Tayaĝukichax̂ what was going on.

"They've spotted something, maybe an otter," he replied as he kept pulling at his paddle.

"So we're going to continue out?"

He sank his oar to one side and turned us about; we began ghosting laterally with the wind, but nevertheless he said we could stay and watch for a minute.

Olean baited the end of his kelp cable with octopus before tossing it overboard. As the line ran out, he periodically clipped stone sinkers to it. It took several minutes for the rope to fully uncoil, at which point a fisherman in a single-seater paddled over and secured his *baidarka* with that of Olean and Tix̂lax̂. They crossed their paddles over one another's decks, stabilizing their *qayaqs* together like a double-hulled catamaran.

"Halibut, most likely," remarked Tayaĝukichax̂.

"How can you tell?"

"Because that's what Olean told you, didn't he? Besides that, their lines have been run out deep, probably to the bottom. The halibut come into the passage this time of year to feed on mackerel."

Suddenly, the cable drew taut and began dragging their formation this way and that, but by shrewd paddling and careful control of the rope, Olean and Tix̂lax̂ succeeded in pulling the line in, hand over hand, until at last a giant fish broke the surface with an incredible splash.

"Christ!" I exclaimed. "That's a halibut?!"

"Don't use that word!" Tayaĝukichax̂ shot back. "Yes, they've landed a halibut of average size, by the looks of it."

"And how big is that?"

"About three hundred and fifty pounds, from what I can tell through the ash."

The other paddler who'd joined their hunt procured a mighty club and held it over the water, readying to strike the mighty fish as Olean struggled with the line and Tix̂lax̂ endeavored to keep their two crafts stabilized.

Aleuts Catching Halibut at the Mouth of Island Passage (1887; artist unknown)

The *baidarkas* encircling the action drew in closer, tightening the noose, their paddlers procuring all manner of spears, clubs, and throwing boards—spear extensions about two feet long. The throwing board resembled a dugout two-by-four upon which the javelin rests. A notch at the butt end of the javelin firmly secured it to the top of the throwing board. When ready, the hunter simply had to sling his spear with the action of his arm, the additional catapult effect provided by the throwing board resulting in a stronger, faster, longer, and more direct flight pattern.

Several compound harpoons were launched by the surrounding fleet, some successfully finding their target. These harpoons had barbed dart tips made of bone that detached from their shafts upon impact into the fish. The hunter who'd made the hit would then pull on the other end of the line to draw in the quarry.

Excited by the action, I reached for my toggle-head spear attached to our *baidarka*'s foredeck, but Tayaĝukichax̂ scoffed, claiming it was a waste of our time. He told me to keep paddling instead.

Abandoning the fleet, Tayaĝukichax̂ turned us south-by-southwest toward the southern tip of Elf Island and the open ocean beyond. Not long after setting course, he groaned.

I kept silent, knowing by now that the subject of his chest wound was about as palatable to him as the mention of Jesus Christ. I glanced back at the hunters we'd left behind, and could faintly see through the volcanic brume their bladder floats now attached to the fish, undoubtedly to keep it on the surface and to further tire it out as they clubbed it to death.

"Why'd they go after halibut?" I asked, but my bullheaded partner didn't bother to reply.

"I mean, how much blood can you really extract from a fish like that?" I qualified my inquiry.

"It's the meat they're after, Kayuu. Halibut are abundant in meat that's good for trade. It's a failsafe proposition. Catching a whale, on the other hand, is not an everyday occurrence, and is an endeavor fraught with great peril."

I stopped to glance back at him, and he was grinning from ear to ear. I suddenly grew very concerned, thinking this man in whose craft I was literally stuck was completely mad. But when I looked at him anew, his face was once again stern, as anybody whaling the Aleutian main from a *baidarka* should be.

Continuing further out, the chief's son was now paddling in lockstep with me, and when I regarded him once more, his eyes were steeled to our surroundings, apparently paying close attention to the minute details of wind, swell, and current, and he even appeared to be observing the flights of birds. In seeing that he was keeping the navigation of our vulnerable craft under careful command, I breathed more easily as I turned back around to face the bow. A volcano rumbled in the distance, and we soon lost sight of the other *qayaqs* in the fall of ever-swirling ash.

Not far offshore of Elf Island, we spotted a Steller's sea lion, but decided not to go after it. A whale was our due. Tayaĝukichax̂ said that he'd been noticing fewer and fewer Steller's sea lions—as much as 80 percent fewer, while the sea otter had also been in significant decline for no apparent reason, all within the past few decades. But he had his own theory for this depletion, explaining it as a "top-down depredation" being caused by a significant rise in the resident great white shark population—an apex predator not as conspicuous as orcas, per se, but as just as prevalent throughout the Aleutian archipelago, according to him.

Dipping my paddle into the cold, grey deep, I laughed nervously, "You're just trying to spook me."

"They rarely surface," chuckled he, "unlike the *Hydrodamalis gigas*, which used to come up all the time. But it would be a grave mistake to think there are no white pointer sharks out here."

"What are *Hydrodamalis gigas*? Whales?"

"It was the Steller's sea cow. Too bad you can't see one of those anymore."

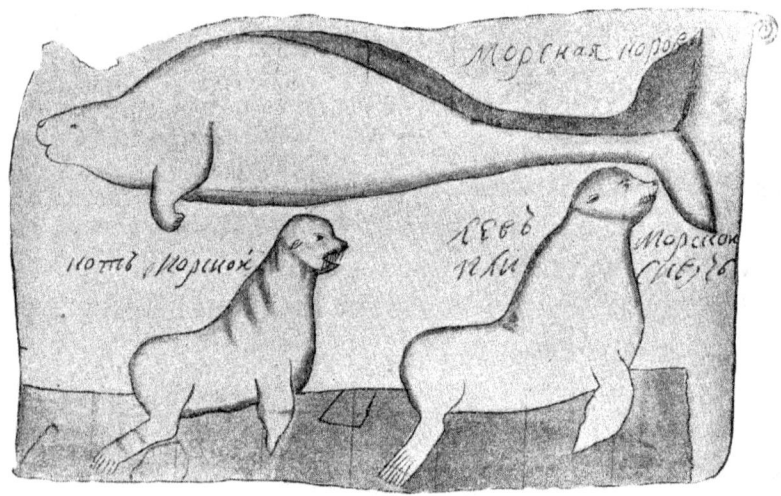

A Steller's sea cow rendered above a Steller's sea lion (lower right) and northern fur seal (lower left) for size comparison. (Illustration by Wilhelm Steller, 1740s)

"Steller's sea cows were seventeen cubits long [25 feet] and weighed three tons. They liked to come in with the tide, right up to the shore to graze on seaweed, just like cows. They were harmless creatures, just too easy to hunt, so were totally killed off by the *promuishlenniki* in seventeen sixty-eight. The *promuishlenniki* liked the taste of dugong meat—the Steller's sea cow didn't stand a chance."

"The *promuishlenniki*. I've heard of them before. Can you tell me more?"

"They were heavily armed Siberian fur hunters who came like a flood in the wake of Bering's second voyage. The sea otter pelts Bering's crew brought back from their epic adventure sold for forty rubles apiece, fetching a grand total of three hundred thousand dollars. It was a goldmine for the white man, a disaster for the Aleut. The fur seals were almost completely wiped out in Bering's wake, as were the sea otters, while *Hydrodamalis gigas* became extinct."

"How tragic," I lamented.

"Indeed, Kayuu, but what I meant about Bering's final exploratory voyage being epic was its unprecedented ambition and scope. The expedition has rightly been deemed 'the most gigantic geographic enterprise undertaken by any government at any time.' It took eight years of preparations before Bering's two vessels could finally launch from Kamchatka in seventeen forty-one."

"Eight years to prepare? Why so long?"

"Because at the time," explained my guide, "the Kamchatka peninsula was an isolated no-man's land: there was absolutely nothing out there. Bering had to organize a team of hundreds of people, blaze a trail out from Russia proper and construct everything from scratch: the two vessels—the *Saint Peter* and *Saint Paul*—the shipyards, lighthouses, mines, an entire town was forged from the seafront forest in order to outfit the expedition and its vast population of builders."

As we conversed, we kept paddling further out to sea, the tip of Elf Island—our last view of land—now barely discernible through the ash. "Where are we going?" I asked.

"Further out," replied the stubborn prince, "to where the big whale was spotted earlier, before the fallout thickened. The biggies like the deeper water. Here, let's take a break from paddling for a moment while I adjust your seat cinch. You've been turning around too much and so it has become loose around your waist and water will get in, especially if things get rough."

Navigator Vitus Bering (AP, 1964)

I felt the mammal sinew cord tighten around my upper waist, providing a seamless waterproof seal between the gut skin of the *baidarka* and the skin of my *kamleika* parka. I resolved to keep facing afore, as much as I could help it.

"Vitus Bering," he continued, "was the first white man to see most of our islands, but scurvy, heavy seas, and perhaps even hostile natives did his expedition in. Bering wrecked the *Saint Peter* in a williwaw five months into his voyage, running aground on an uninhabited island. Castaway with the remainder of his crew, he died of scurvy a month later. Today that island is called Bering Island, located in the Commander group of islands."

A Hadean vision, "Behring Wrecked on the Aleutian Islands," *but one that is probably not an exaggeration of the horrors Bering and his crew experienced in shipwrecking on such inhospitable shores (Steel engraving, 1882; artist unknown)*

Tayaĝukichax̂ continued to tighten the cinch around my waist, so much so that I wondered how I was supposed to stand and throw my lance. But I didn't want to interrupt him, as he spoke with great interest about Vitus Bering . . .

"The following spring, the remaining survivors built a smaller vessel from the wreck of the *Saint Peter*, and that August they set sail again, making it safely back to Kamchatka to tell their incredible tale. Wilhelm Steller, a famed naturalist, botanist, and physician, was among the surviving crew, but while he brought back some stunning information about the Aleutian region, such as its flora, fauna, and inhabitants, his crewmates returned to Petropavlovsk with nine hundred sea otter pelts, which at forty rubles apiece hauled in a grand total of over three hundred thousand dollars. The flood of Siberian fur hunters—the *promuishlenniki*—came shortly thereafter. That was the beginning of the end of the Aleutians as we knew it."

"What happened to the other ship?" I inquired. "The *Saint Paul?*"

"The *Saint Paul* had set sail from Kamchatka at the same time as the *Saint Peter*, on June four, seventeen forty-one, under the command of Captain Alexei Chirikof, but on June twenty, the two ships became separated in a heavy fog, never to see each other again."

"Then on July fifteen," Tayaĝukichax̂ continued, "while exploring near Chichagof Island in the far northwest Gulf of Alaska, Captain Chirikof dispatched from the *Saint Paul* an investigative party of ten sailors to go ashore at Lisianski Strait, just south of Cross Sound. When the cockboat didn't return, he launched a second party of five men to search for them. This second tender likewise never came back. Bereft of further landing crafts and unable to wait any longer than was prudent in this Cradle of Storms, he reluctantly made the choice to weigh anchor, writing the fifteen men off for dead at the hands of Tlingit Indians who occupied the region."

"That's rather presumptuous of him," I countered. "Maybe the search parties got lost in the forests or fog, or were otherwise somehow delayed."

Captain-Commander Vitus Bering had always been extremely reluctant to sail too close to the Aleutian shoreline, and always to the great disappointment of his conscripted botanist, Wilhelm Steller. However, a number of glaring factors lent credence to the captain's prudence, such as the dangerously unpredictable Aleutian weather and hidden reefs (the two of which ultimately wrecked his ship and killed him), the relatively unknown nature of the Tlingit Indians on shore (who may have been responsible for the disappearance of fifteen of Captain Chirikof's sailors from the other ship), and finally, the Aleutian Islands themselves were so precipitous and colossal in appearance as to present a pressingly alarming obstacle for any captain at the mercy of the elements alone. The above photo of an Adak Island escarpment typifies the Aleutian typography, and to get a true scale of the bluff, you can make a pen dot at the base of the mountain, and even this dot would be about five to ten times larger than a normal human. (Exclusive photo by the author)

"Perhaps," replied Tayaĝukichax̂, whose true intelligence, wrought by two centuries of existence, was at last making an appearance, "but unlikely. Tlingits had been seen tooling around the shoreline in canoes, but when the Russians drew near, they quickly disappeared—not exactly indicative of welcoming behavior. Remember, Chirikof's men were the first Europeans to enter Alaska. It's not like their coming ashore followed a precedent of white men who'd already been exploiting people and resources there, which would perhaps have caused the Indians to paddle away in retreat. No, these Tlingits were up to something, and Chirikof, devoid of lighter crafts, could do naught more to investigate. Thus, fifteen of his crew were abandoned—dead or alive."

"Jesus." I was chilled by the account.

"Hey!" Tayaĝukichax̂ exclaimed, poking his paddle into my back.

"Oops, sorry—got it! You don't like that word."

"Anyway," he continued as we plowed slowly forth over an increasingly choppy sea, "the real problem Chirikof faced was that he now had no landing craft from which to replenish his water supply, for a ship his size could not so easily maneuver close to shore, especially with the coming of autumn's tumultuous storms, while the water in these parts, as you know, hovers around forty degrees Fahrenheit—even colder in the winter. So swimming to the shore to fetch fresh water was simply not an option, even where streams were readily in view. Thus he returned to Kamchatka on the tenth of October, four months after first setting sail."

"Casting anchor in the cold, grey depths of Avacha Bay once more, the *Saint Paul* had returned less twenty-two hands: the fifteen lost in Alaska, plus seven who'd succumbed to scurvy. As a matter of fact, every soul onboard the *Saint Paul* had contracted scurvy. The seven who'd perished before making it back to Kamchatka were consigned to the deep before the noxious spores wrought from their decaying bodies [anthrax?] could be transmitted to the other sailors."

A plane could be heard overhead, overcoming my guide's discourse and distinguishing itself from the intermittent rumble of the distant volcano by its incessant drone. Alas, nothing could be seen through the ceiling of soupy brume.

Avacha Bay, Kamchatka Peninsula, Russian Far East.
(Illustration by M. Muratov, Leningrad, 1937)

"The *Saint Peter* got hit even worse with scurvy," continued Tayaĝukichax̂, ignoring the unseen aircraft, "which ultimately killed its Captain-Commander Vitus Bering. Had he only listened to the naturalist onboard, Wilhelm Steller, he and many more of his crew likely would've survived. Steller warned him against replenishing his stores' barrels with brackish water, but was ignored, and was ignored again when he suggested to the captain that he and his crew eat green weeds found in the

Aleutians, which would've supplied them with the necessary nutrients, such as vitamin C, to ward off the ravenous high-seas disease. Steller, for his part, avoided the brackish water and ate the flora that he had recommended, surviving the year-long ordeal scurvy-free and with relative ease.

"Ultimately, though, the Aleutian seas were what really drove the *Saint Peter* and its resilient captain to their untimely fate, because all the while he was trying to return to Avacha Bay from his easternmost discovery—Mount Saint Elias on the Alaska mainland—he'd been beset by the cruelest of storms, storms so terrible that his ship was left tattered and ruined long before he drove it aground on the island that now carries his namesake and grave."

"Holy—" I began, then remembered Tayaĝukichax̂'s warning about uttering the Lord's name, so ended it, "sea cow."

We laughed. The chill between us, which ebbed and flowed like Bering Sea ice, at that moment receded.

"I was wondering," I posed, believing it was a suitable time, "if your kind can fly, why even bother paddling *baidarkas*? Why not just do your hunting from the skies?"

"We maintain our traditional ways as much as possible because it builds character and integrity, and besides, the way of the Aleut is extremely effective, being borne of this technically challenging environment. For example, how could we fly with all our ropes and baits, our floats, spears, and clubs for catching fish? And as for whaling, the old ways still dominate. Centuries of hunting at sea level has worked well, while whaling from above, with fogs and the towing of massive sea beasts through unpredictable winds is not as advantageous as one might believe."

"I think I see what you're saying, but—"

"Look there!" He was pointing dead-ahead over my shoulder. "*Alax̂.*"

"*Alax̂*?"

"Whale," said he, and then I saw it—a wide grey hump barely appearing over the waves, followed by a misty blast of water, almost invisible in the ash, which quickly disappeared in the wind.

"What kind of whale?"

"A sperm whale. We've been tracking it for quite some time."

"We have?"

"I've been talking and watching, but you've been only listening, not observing. The *alax̂* in these parts are sly. They like the fog and rough seas, like I was explaining. You seldom see more than a portion above the water, and they usually appear unexpectedly."

I squinted over the bow and saw another blast of mist some eighty meters distant. "How big do you think it is?"

"We'll find out ere long."

As Tayaĝukichax̂ gave firm leverage to his oar, I became nervous. I didn't expect things to happen so nonchalantly. What we were doing had something thieving about it, and the whale would undoubtedly become alarmed once we were discovered. "How can you tell it's a sperm whale?"

"Its head is long; observe the way it cuts through the water. And the spouts occur diagonally from the snout, angled between about ten o'clock and eleven o'clock, as opposed to straight up from the top of the head like with other *alax̂*. The beast is traveling west, as I had suspected: it's their usual spring-time pattern."

We came to within forty meters, a distance at which the brume lightened between us, and then I saw it: the large grey head plowing up from the surface like the bow of a submarine. This creature was massive. Then came the shot of moistened air, blowing out from its forward-facing snout with such volume that the trailing mist kissed my face moments later.

"It's a male," Tayaĝukichax̂ remarked. "This is auspicious."

"How do you know it's a male?"

"By its larger size. This *alax̂* looks to be about thirty-five cubits [52 feet] in length. Prepare your throwing-lance."

A knot welted up in my stomach. This seemed totally crazy. Even if we could get away with a spear shot, what then? Would not the creature thrash about wildly, smashing our little skin boat? I reached forward and began to slowly unfasten the armaments from the foredeck, barely overcoming my hesitance. "Should I use the throwing board?"

"No, you won't be needing the *haasxuĝ*," the prince commanded, "not for the harpoon. I shall steer the craft to a close striking distance, and then when I give the signal, you will throw from your seated position. You must throw hard and aim for the eye. This will increase your chances of hitting the head."

I put the arm-length throwing board back, then freed my throwing-lance. "Shall I remove this yet?" I asked of its reed scabbard.

"Yes, but take care not to dip the spearhead into the water."

I pulled the sheath off, exposing a warm and wet, razor-sharp tip, dripping with aconite poison. We were now within thirty meters of the monster, and every time it surfaced, its back appeared larger and slicker.

Tayaĝukichax̂ began chanting something in Aleut, a chant that soon morphed into a plaintive moan that bordered on the histrionic. I could only wonder if, in his often crass and untimely sense of humor, he was humoring me once again, even on the threshold of our harrowing task. I meant no disrespect, but had the nerve to ask, "What are you saying?"

"I'm calling upon the spirits of deceased whalers," (—interjecting another Unangam Tunuu moan—) "asking for their assistance. We are but one *baidarka* weighing perhaps five hundred pounds in all, while a *spermaceti* of this size is close to forty tons (80,000 lbs)."

Maybe we ought to rethink this, I thought as the behemoth plowed steadily through the sea preceding us, causing our *baidarka* to list to and fro in the slipstream of whirlpools left by its heavy undertow.

Tayaĝukichax̂ ceased summoning dead hunters and resumed paddling with great vigor. It gave me renewed respect for the traditional Aleut hunters, who, like my superhuman boatswain, could single-handedly propel a *baidarka* forward with the necessary celerity to catch a whale. "Look behind us," he said, "others are coming."

The thought of being trapped between of pod of massive whales was a terrifying realization, but then I turned around to see the faint silhouette of other Aleut kayakers through the ashy brume.

"Prepare your harpoon," he warned. "You must throw a good first shot or our mission is doomed."

I held my throwing-lance over my shoulder, testing its weight and bearing. All I had to do was heave one strong shot at the monster's head. The poison tip would lodge and we could peel off, return to shore and wait for the beast to wash up dead. An engraving worked into the spearhead designating it as mine would prove me the victor, winning me more respect, power, and leverage within the clan. Such was the whaling strategy outlined to me during my extensive training in the boathouse.

Tayaĝukichax̂ had maneuvered us out of the whale's roiling wake and forward abreast its body. The beast outsized our *qayaq* by three boat lengths, its head alone some twenty feet long and shaped like a giant, elongated torpedo.

We'd made such a furtive advance that the whale did not appear to be aware of our presence, even as I found its eye groping between the grey heavens and frigid Aleutian main.

During one forward lunge it made over the sluggish ocean, I beheld a formidable row of teeth lining its lower jaw, the water spilling through each fang as it surfaced, creating a nightmarish impression that would forever haunt my memory. Each spout from the beast's forward-angled blowhole blasted us with mist, and each time I wiped my eyes with my free hand, the black eye of the titan became more equidistant to our craft.

"It will see us," I noted furtively back to Tayaĝukichax̂.

"It already has. They're usually the ones that sneak up on us, coming alongside our *qayaqs* when we're loaded down with sablefish, trying to steal from our lines."

This did little to placate my terror. I was sure that at any moment the beast would discover us, and in its surprise, turn *us* into the quarry. I heaved my lance back over my shoulder, preparing to launch on command.

Tayaĝukichax̂ stopped paddling for a moment and grabbed my harpoon's butt end, better adjusting my aim. "Do you really love my stepsister?"

The timing of his inquiry threw me off guard. I didn't know what to think, or say. A surreal moment transpired, where all the world and time seemed to move in slow motion. I watched the behemoth's glossy black orb lazily scanning its surroundings and suddenly felt a strange affinity to the giant, as if it were my eye innocently surveying the world, my life inextricably woven into a vulnerable web of existence. The eye settled upon us and our *baidarka*.

The monster flinched, a slight spasm of its head that continued down its body, soon to terminate in an explosive splash of its tail that would toss us from the water like we were a pesky fly. But before this could transpire, my boatswain sounded the command, whereupon I released my weighty lance.

Two Men Hunting: Aleuts Planting Darts in a School of Whales (1887; *artist unknown*)

The titan was already beginning to roll when the spear-head connected, just catching its narrow underjaw. But to my shock and horror, a line had run out from the back of the harpoon, connecting somewhere to our *baidarka*. This wasn't supposed to happen with a throwing-lance. Only the simple harpoon and compound harpoon were meant to be fitted with braided twine, enabling the hunter to pull in an otter or seal close enough to his *qayaq* for him to club it to death, or otherwise to help him track and tire the wounded mammal by means of bladder buoy attachments. Throwing-lances, on the other hand, were designed specifically to hunt whales. Once the poison projectile penetrated, the whale would sound and the lance shaft would break away from the spearhead and float to the surface. The whale would then die in its own time, drifting to shore a few days later. Each hunter's spearhead was marked with engravings, making it possible to know who made the kill.

All these teachings flashed before my mind in a few short instances as the mammoth continued to roll, running out the twine as it unknowingly or otherwise spooled it around its snout. Tayaĝukichax̂, for his part, was ferociously back-paddling, causing the line to discharge even faster. But we had little other option, given the magnitude of danger wrought by the rolling titan.

"We need to cut the line!" I cried back.

"I already did," he said, loosening the gut sack that sealed me within the *baidarka*.

He had cut the cinch. I thought perhaps he meant to free me from the craft should it be pulled down with the whale, but then to my horror, I discovered, as the twine snapped taut, that the line wasn't connected to the *qayaq*: *the line was tied around my waist!*

The giant jerked its head, flinging me headlong out of my seat toward its mouth, and the last thing I heard from Tayaĝukichax̂ was a booming laugh.

I landed in the frigid water next to fifty grinding teeth as big and sharp as axe blades. The monster glanced at me with a black look as it continued its roll, my spear end jutting skyward when the beast went upside down, chomping madly in an attempt to extricate the projectile from its jaw. I was pulled up alongside the monster's flank via the twine still attached to my waist, the cinch yanking tighter and tighter, squeezing the air out of me as I got dragged up out of the water. I struggled to free myself amid the maelstrom, but the line was sturdily inter-woven through my *kamleika* like a belt.

Sperm Whale Versus Whalers with Harpoons (*Painting by Louis Sargent, 1912*)

I was nearly out of breath and about to black out when the cinch momentarily released, leaving me splayed out on the whale's belly, lying on my back and beholding an ashen sun. Then with a terrible moan the monster sounded, diving back-ward into the depths, pulling me down with the weight of a forty ton anchor. My predicament was now obvious: Tayag̃ukichax̂ had secretly equipped my throwing-lance with a twine at its center like a compound harpoon before furtively tying the other end of the line to my parka. His intention could only have been to kill me, as was presently transpiring.

The bubbles escaped from my mouth as the Gargantua continued its spiraling dive into the black. I closed my eyes and tried to suspend all thought, not wishing to struggle in my death. The image of Aniqdux̂six̂ appeared in my mind, reaching down to pick me up as she'd done so many times before. Her wings outstretched over us and we flew up toward the light, the drag of temporal existence pulling strongly at our extremities, but ultimately failing to halt our heavenward thrust. The gravity of the world suddenly snapped free, the existential weight of my mortality at once ceasing to be. I opened my eyes to find myself staring through the sky at the black orb of the beast.

All at once I filled my lungs with oxygen and twisted my fist into the monster's eye. I was overwhelmed at having to perform such savagery upon the terrific creature, but now that we'd resurfaced, "survival of the fittest" was at play, and so I took my only chance, knowing fully well that "the fittest" wasn't me.

The whale splashed its tail wildly about, spraying me as I climbed the line entwined around its head. *But behold!* by the time I mounted the giant's snout, it was near death, the monkshood poison, eye gouge, and chance strangulation having gotten the better of it. The cinch now slack at my back, I tore off the shirt portion of my *kamleika* and tossed it "overboard" from where I stood upon the beast's head, unquestionably in full command.

In the final throes of life, misty, bloodstained geysers shot from the beast's blowhole, pluming back in the wind to pepper the arriving kayakers red, while beside them sat Tayaĝukichax̂, grumbling in his failed attempt to mortally trick me.

I was now the clear victor of the *spermaceti* monster, for in its dive it had barreled around and hogtied itself by accident, then resurfaced—probably for air, only to quickly die after I devastated its eye, presenting me in the light of sovereign command as I climbed upon its back, still holding the appendage of its sight.

Tribe Hunting *(1887; artist unknown)*

There was a great ballyhoo of whistling and cheers as the Aleuts approached through the mist to collectively behold my conquest. Their chase after halibut having ended, they'd followed Tayaĝukichâ and me into the ash, and now in classic *qaqmiiĝux̂* fashion, they were forming a circle around the giant from which to throw spears and club it to death. Everyone wanted a piece of its head, for the spear closest the eye determined the winner. But it was a done deal—the whale had already stopped spouting and moved not a mite more and, besides that, I'd long since extracted the very bulls-eye in question. The cave clan, in taking account of this, ceased their rabid swarming upon my quarry, replacing their war cry with excitable chatter and praise—all save for my boatswain, who slowly back-paddled to the outskirts of the circle, seeking to remain anonymous in the mist.

At that moment I realized how careful I'd have to remain of this trickster prince, who now would certainly make my offing his quick priority, lest I expose his foul play while upon *qaqmiiĝux̂*. If his gaming me to such an extent would be deemed acceptable among his tribe I could not readily ascertain, but by his current behavior—silently slipping off into the fog—that he had something to hide could not have been better dramatized.

Suddenly, a second, smaller sperm whale surfaced between the cave clan and my escaping boatswain.

"A female!" shouted a whaler.

"Thirty tons!" cried another as the beast rammed the *qayaq* of Igasix̂ and Altixum, taking the frame of the elder seaman up into its maw.

His spear-thrower at point, Igasix̂, utilizing her freak-ish *iidigidi* abilities, vaulted from her seat and landed on the lady-whale's oblong head. She raised her spear high, and then drove it down into the creature's skull cavity with the force of lightning.

This sudden counterattack caught the whale off guard, and with a poisoned lance twisting into its brain, it increased its chewing action upon Altixum with intense vigor.

The wise old mariner, for his part, could do little but lie there as mincemeat, struggling in vain to get a good grip on the monster's maw, from where he might perhaps force the jaws open. But its snout and chin were slippery as sea moss and allowed him no such opportunity.

Igasix̂ then procured a club from a sheath at her back and proceeded to pound the whale's head, and soon other Aleuts encircled the creature and joined in the attack, assaulting it with all manner of weapons.

Clubs, axes, darts, and spears struck at the mammal, these last armaments showing the occasional line with bladder float attached, helping to buoy the creature, preventing it from summarily diving as mine had.

Aleuts Planting Glass, Obsidian, and Jade Darts in a School of Whales (*1887; artist unknown*)

Altixum grimaced in heroic pain as the little giant continued to chomp at his midsection, releasing black blood from
his body until at last the lady-beast was too afflicted to keep
snacking on the old vampire, and so slackened her jaws and let
him slip away.

As Altixum made his way over to his *baidarka* and pulled
himself over the rails, large chunks of flesh hung from the
back of his *kamleika* where it'd been rent open by the sea beast's
lower flanking teeth. *How little mind did the other vampires pay to
his plight, swept up as they were in the high seas blood sport!* Perhaps it
was a given that Altixum would be alright (I was still uncertain
how a vampire could die). At any rate, Igasix̂'s and my whales
were dead or dying, the hunting party in attendance relishing
in the dramatic open sea climax of the *qaqmiiĝux̂*.

The next step was to haul in the quarry. Seven *qayaqs* were
employed: four for my catch, three for Igasix̂'s. Thank goodness

most of them were doubles, otherwise it would've been a strain, not so much on the Aleuts, whose vampire strength seemed to know no bounds, but on the *baidarkas* themselves, whose hulls audibly creaked with each pull at the oars.

As Tayaĝukichax̂ had long since disappeared from the field of combat, it was decided that I would return in the craft of Altixum and Igasix̂, with her sitting on my lap because she was the sparest set of the party. My lips were turning blue with hypothermia, so Qagux̂ offered me his *kamleika*, buffering me against the chilly spring air.

On the return trip, I had no oar, so could not paddle and thus had no place to put my hands, so Igasix̂ suggested we'd both be more comfortable if I simply held her around the waist, which I did. Her paddling further warmed me up, because while her flesh was cold, the repetitive movement of her posterior upon my midsection created heat by friction. It was a long journey back—two hours in all, and she was stroking hard because Altixum, sitting in front, was in pain from the whale attack and mostly resting. This gave me time, too much time, to study the back of the girl sitting on my lap. I could not help but sense her bubbly buttocks gyrating over my groin. Beads of cold sweat soon appeared on her neck and steamed up inside her gut-skin parka, making the garment practically see-through. Her posterior was wet and bare through the folds of her *kamleika*, and as she continued to circulate over my crotch, I couldn't help but to become aroused. Petrified she'd notice, I fought hard to bring things under control, but she was young and attractive, which only added to my quandary.

Just as I was trying to keep my sensations in check, she glanced back with a smile and asked, "I can paddle harder if you want. Do you want me to stroke harder? You must be in a hurry to get back to Aniqdux̂six̂."

As her words, "harder, harder," echoed through my mind, I couldn't help but to steal another glimpse *lower.*

"No hurry," I practically gasped, releasing my bear hug from around her. She may've been a coldblooded hatchling, but she was too hot to handle.

DANCE OF VAMPIRES

THE RIGORS of *qaqmiiĝux̂*, two hours of Igasix̂ on my lap notwithstanding, had all but exhausted me. I arrived back at the barabara feeling seasick and tired. By direction of Chief Aĝnakax̂, I was handed over to the care of Iganakuchax̂ once more, taking lodging in their extended chambers. As the old confidante lay me down upon a reed mat bed, her grand-daughter, the wily Datuu, appeared with a cooked root vegetable resembling a yam, along with a gourd of water, which she placed beside me.

"Thou hast done it," she said, rubbing the tuber in my hands to help warm me up. "Thou hast killed thy giant."

"His first whale," added Iganakuchax̂ as she circulated about, lighting stone lanterns. The day was growing late, the temperature dropping fast.

"Where's your son?" I inquired. "He was my *baidarka* partner. Did he make it back?"

"Tayaĝukichax̂?" Iganakuchax̂ posed. "He's the son of Chief Aĝnakax̂ and his first wife, who passed away a long time ago, but he's not my boy—and I emphasize boy."

"Dad got back a few hours ago," remarked Datuu.

"He did?" I asked. "Did he tell you what happened?"

Iganakuchax̂ took the helm at answering: "He said that while you two were battling the *spermaceti*, the *baidarka* was punctured and taking on water, so he left you to finish the kill so that he could return the *qayaq* before it sank. Chief Aĝnakax̂ has seen the vessel and said he was amazed that Tayaĝukichax̂ got it back in one piece. Had you remained onboard, the chief said, the additional weight would've caused it to founder. By the way, Tayaĝukichax̂ mentioned you rode back with Igasix̂ on your lap. How did you two victors get along?"

"Tayaĝukichax̂ and I?"

"You and Igasix̂."

"Good, I guess. Why? What does that have to do with anything?"

"Just asking," the matron replied with a curious lilt. "Are you still looking forward to seeing Aniqdux̂six̂?"

"Of course. When will I be permitted to?"

"Tonight when we celebrate the success of the *qaqmiiĝux̂*. Do you feel up to it?"

"Absolutely."

"Good. Remember what we talked about. We take our commitments very seriously."

"Are you talking about Kayuu and Aniqdux̂six̂, grandma?" Datuu probed.

"Ask Kayuu."

"Do you still love her?" the nine-year-old going on two centuries put to me directly.

"Of course!" I snapped back. "Now give me that!" I wrenched the tuber from her hands and tore my teeth into it. After chewing on it a few times, I chugged down some water, then kept on chomping, absolving myself of further small talk.

"It's good to see you regaining your appetite," Iganakuchax̂ offered somewhat wickedly, and left it at that.

While Lt. Harper remains relatively close to the naval garrison at Kuluk Bay,
his continued activities with the Aleutian vampires keep him worlds away
from the war effort there (Exclusive photo by Lt. Harper, 1942-1943)

The celebration for the first whales caught in the spring *qaqmiiĝux̂* took place at the seamen's ceremonial chamber adjacent the boathouse. Everyone from the barabara was invited—men, women, and children. The festivities started off informally. People milled about, conversing and swapping hunting stories. I happened upon Tayaĝukichax̂ doing just that, bandying a group of Aleuts with his version of events.

"Kayuu had grabbed the wrong spear," he said, shooting me a wry glance, "but that wasn't the worst of it. He had mistakenly tied the other end of the toggle-head twine around his waist, believing it was his seat-bag cinch."

The Aleuts laughed, Qatxamax the dickhead going so far as to pat me brusquely on the shoulder like I was a real buffoon.

"And so out of the *iqyax̂* flew my spearman," (—Tayaĝukichax̂, sharing in their humor at my expense—) "but not before ripping up the hull with his throwing board, which he'd improperly placed astern."

"Are you really such a mooncalf?" sniggered Qagux̂. "How'd you ever kill the beast?"

He had put the question to me directly. Tayaĝukichax̂ looked on with a shit-eating grin, awaiting my response alongside the rest.

I replied analogous to a wide-eyed psychopath, "After I jumped from my seat to lash its jaws shut with twine, I tore its fucking eye out with my bare hands. But then when I looked back, my boatswain was back-paddling away into the mist, scared shitless, so I had to ride back with Igasix̂ on my lap. But I didn't mind; I prefer her kind anyway."

"Women?" bandied Olean, who was standing beside Tayaĝukichax̂.

"I prefer to ride with victors," I said.

The crew burst into guffaws once again.

"Funny version of events," Tayaĝukichax̂ put in; "too bad my boat was sinking, thanks to you, so I had to split. But glad you and Igasix̂ had such a cozy time together. She's all ass, ain't she? And Aniqdux̂six̂'s all ears. To the victors!" he cried, holding his blood gourd high.

"To the victors!" the vampires responded in kind, quaffing at their purple gut sacks.

"Asshole," I quipped under my breath, continuing with a soliloquy of muted imprecations. I was pondering how to cajole these louts to my way of thinking, when suddenly Chief Aĝnakax̂ appeared, telling us to be seated because the ceremony would shortly commence.

As wild rye mats were brought out to where we were standing, I shuffled off to the side, where I'd seen Sugangix̂ conversing with Tix̂lax̂. The mats were placed facing the adakite fountain in the center of the chamber. A group of elders shortly entered and sat down on them. Iganakuchax̂ was among their retinue, as was Altixum Taĝaacha, his torso wound concealed beneath a *kamleika* robe. There was also an elder I was familiar with, named Kuuyux, who was said to be a powerful shaman. Apparently, he was a driving force in keeping the cave clan vampires steeped in Aleut traditions. He and the other male elders were wearing handsome, full-crowned *qayaatx̂ux̂* hats, while the women of all ages generally wore soft *sax* jackets and ravens' feathers in their hair.

"Have you seen Aniqdux̂six̂?" I asked Tix̂lax̂.

"No, not yet—but Igasix̂ is just over there."

He pointed across the room to the nineteen-year-old whaler, the only female of the hunting party, who at a distance looked very much the warrior of her temperament, apparently still wearing the same gut skin parka she'd worn while on *qaqmiiĝux̂*, and she was still walking around with a spear in her hand. She happened to glance over at me. I could make out the outline of her weathered but cute face beneath her straight cut bangs.

"And so?" I at length answered Tix̂lax̂. "I was asking about Aniqdux̂six̂. Hey Sugangix̂," I addressed the other young man, "what happened to my harpoon, anyway? I thought we were making a throwing-lance, but it was fitted with an internal twine."

"I didn't do that," he said, then told me more privately, "but maybe it was Tayaĝukichax̂. He insisted on personally giving you the spear. He said he wanted to make amends. When I handed him the lance, I swear to you it was unthreaded. But possibly, because your throwing-lance was modified from a toggle-head spear, maybe he thought he was doing you a favor by fixing it back. I really don't know—but you should check with him, and tell me what he says."

I glared around the chamber, searching for the rough-neck prince, when suddenly the chief announced the start of festivities.

"*Qaĝaasakung huzuu haqakux̂*," he began, meaning something akin to, "Thank you all for coming." He continued entirely in Unangam Tunuu, of which I could decipher a few words only, such as *qaqmiiĝux̂* (the hunt), *alax̂* (the whale), and *chagix̂* (halibut). But the elders sitting before him were pleased by his delivery, frequently making "*Hmm!*" sounds and nodding in agreement. At one point when the chief mentioned my Aleut name, Kayuu, all eyes settled upon me; he continued in English, "You have surprised us all and earned your due. We hope you enjoy receiving your first tattoo."

Was he trying to be humorous? Alas, nobody laughed. When he mentioned Igasix̂, all eyes settled on her standing at the opposite side of the room; and then he mentioned my name again.

"She's good for you," Tix̂lax̂ informed me surreptitiously. "You should go for her."

I ignored him, asking instead, "What's the chief saying?"

Sugangix̂ frowned upon our speaking, indicating with a downward motion of his hand that we must remain quiet for the time being.

Chief Aĝnakax̂ concluded his oration with something about Agugux and the beings of the caves, at which point he stepped aside and a low, measured drumming began. As the music increased in tempo, all eyes settled upon the adakite monolith; and soon the sound of rattles could be heard accompanied by a peculiar, animistic call of Aleut vampires, cawing out like crows from unseen positions.

"What's going on?" I inquired of Sugangix̂.

"Our music begins. Do you like our instruments? The drums have bone handles. And listen to the rattles—they're made from bird beaks that are filled with pebbles."

"That's all very interesting, Sugangix̂, but what shall happen next? Where is Aniqdux̂six̂?"

He motioned for me to watch, and shortly, a troupe of women entered adorned in beautiful *sax* costumes, colorful bentwood masks and feathered tiaras. "This is *unangam taliĝx̂*, our native Unangax̂ dance," Sugangix̂ said. "Aniqdux̂six̂ is one of the performers. See if you can spot her."

The women danced around the central monolith in the manner of certain birds during courtship rituals, performing half twirls, flaring out their *sax* wings, and doing little curtseys before the spectators. Some of the actresses were more flirtatious than others, but for the life of me, I couldn't make out Aniqdux̂six̂ behind their half-face masks and headdresses overflowing with feathers.

Suddenly, one of the temptresses handed me a mask and said, "*Txin iĝamaĝal taliĝing ii?*"

I stood mute with raised brows, having had no idea what she'd meant. She then mimed a bird by tilting her head from side to side while dipping her chin, effecting a sweet-and-sour look of disappointment, and then she went prancing affectedly on her way to the guffaws of the crowd.

"What did she say?" I asked Sugangix̂ in a sideways manner, trying to be inconspicuous.

"She asked if you wanted to dance."

"Was that Aniqdux̂six̂?"

He shrugged his shoulders, and then advised, "Just put on the false face."

I pulled the bentwood vizard down over my front, securing its band of twine to the back of my head.

Sugangix̂'s eyes widened in jovial terror. "A horrible hunter god you are!" he remarked with a smile.

"Oh, thanks," I sniggered from behind the musky-smelling mask.

Meanwhile, back at Longview, Curtiss P40-D Warhawks were donning their own fearsome "Aleutian Tiger" masks. This single-seat, all-metal fighter could reach speeds of 360 mph and had a pair of 12.7 mm guns concealed within each wing. (USAAF 11th Fighter Squadron photo, 1943)

As the flirtatious dancers continued to circle about, one stopped before Igasix̂ and gave her a bentwood mask not unlike mine. The way this deliverer of costumes moved caught my eye. She was all at once tall and graceful, comely in gait yet masterfully in command of her pantomime. I scanned her face below the mask, detecting prominent, upturned lips and a tattooed chin. I surveyed her stately body, distinguishing a pair of long, sylphlike legs bedecked in white sealskin boots.

"Aniqduxsix̂!" I said with a start, knowing she fancied stylish thigh boots beyond all else.

She glanced my way, but only briefly, perhaps not having entirely heard me amid the rabid drumming, rattling, and general ribaldry of the revelers, who numbered near sixty. As she proceeded around the central monolith, I was struck by the sight of a glistening, red liquid bubbling from atop the fountain. As the viscous *taille* flowed sappily down over the adakite's many little escarpments and crags, the crowd's excitable din grew to a feverish pitch, until at last the mucilaginous fluid covered the entire stanchion, all the way to its base, to where it slowly sank into a bed of shale.

The dancers procured bentwood bowls and gut skin sacks from somewhere in the back, and these they filled with the red substance in a libidinous, swooning, if not altogether erotic manner.

I began to feel queasy. "Is that what I think it is?" I put to Tix̂lax̂.

"The fruit of your quarry," replied he, bearing his fangs in sublime anticipation: and then, to my unabating horror, the blood was drunk freely by the vamps.

Now the dancers' chins ran red with blood!—as did the upper flanks of each and every Aleut in attendance, as they quaffed upon their liquid trophy. Thus what had started out as an exotic tribal dance had quickly descended into an ungodly ceremony of horrors, the strange shriek of ravenous vampires echoing without cease through the tenebrous underground chamber.

Lieutenant Harper's false face mask, or semblance thereof, front and left profile views (Shumagin Islanders death mask example, found in rock shelter near Delaroff Harbor, Unga Island by Dr. T. T. Minor, U.S.R.M., from The Third Annual Report of the Bureau of Ethnology to the Secretary of the Smithsonian Institution 1881–1882, *by J. W. Powell; Washington Government Printing Office, 1884)*

As I beheld this unholy procession wide-eyed through my mask, Chief Aĝnakax̂ suddenly approached through the blood-ied, reveling mass with Igasix̂ at his hand. "You two must partake of blood from the same bowl," he officiated. "This is how we honor multiple winners of the *qaqmiiĝux̂*. When more than one *alax̂* is killed, the victors become fraternity and consum-mate their pact with this sacrament—an offering to Sugangix̂."

I lifted my vizard to better meet the eyes of Igasix̂, who had also slid her mask up over her head. Her straight black bangs just grazed the top of her eyelids, beneath which I found a sheepish stare gazing back at me. But her chin evinced her true nature, as did her bloodstained lips. This was not some shy teenager, new to the ways of the world. Beneath that coun-tenance of coy innocence I knew existed a fierce whaler, and a vampire who drank the blood of her quarry.

"Okay then," I said, surrendering to their tradition, as resis-tance was impolitic, if not downright futile, "let's get on with it."

As Igasix̂ and I partook of the same blood bowl, I was drawn in by the dark allure of her coal black eyes, her wet, red lips, and on occasion, her tender upper chest, which was likewise becom-ing saturated red. And her eyes suffered no hesitance in find-ing mine. She frequently glided her glistening red tongue over her crimson fangs, which were just dripping with blood as she impulsively quaffed. *What did she want of me, really?* I pondered. She could rip my heart out, or my throat—for her it would be child's play, for me, the forever-after.

Now it was my chin and upper flank that were becoming bloodstained, and any happenstance visitor—a mortal in cer-tain terror—would not have been able to tell me apart from the others, so much had I become steeped in the ways of a vampire.

At last, my long-lost love and age-appropriate mate came between us, half pushing Igasix̂ away. They exchanged some sharp words in Aleut, then the chief, still standing behind the bloodthirsty little popsy, chaperoned her away to some other activity.

I reached up and touched Aniqdux̂six̂'s shoulder, saying her name aloud: I wanted to be sure, because she was now ornamented with an ivory nose pin, from whence colorful pieces of coral hung on strings before her chin, further disguising the woman I once knew so closely.

She took my hands in hers and said with a childish skip, "Congratulations, Kayuu, thou hast prevailed!"

In spite of her coral adornments, she'd taken more care than the others with her feasting, for while her lips were red with whale blood, naught had spilled over her tattooed chin, her small bead labret, or her stunning *sax* parka. She removed her bird-eyelet mask, resting it atop her feathered tiara headdress.

"I did it for you, Aniqdux̂six̂," I declared, my heart suddenly quickening now that she was standing before me in all her ravishing exoticness. Igasix̂ had been a huge diversion, a silly little non-event cooked up by others. Yes, she was young and pretty, and yes, we'd prevailed together on *qaqmiiĝux̂*. But ultimately, Aniqduх̂six̂ was for me. This woman who had saved me from an icy grave many moons agone was also my equal in maturity and temperament, not some childish crush invented by impulsive longings. Aniqduх̂six̂ had that special quality of intuition, while the faith she had in me—that I was worthy of her complete dedication—I'd also shown to her, even if sometimes inadvertently.

"Come," she said, all gladsome grins, "I have prepared some delicacies for thee."

She took me aside to a group of driftwood tables, where we seated ourselves on whale vertebrae chairs, and then she proudly pointed out various dishes set upon the plaited reed tabletop. There was *kuliich* Easter bread, white orchid bulbs boiled in seal fat, grilled halibut, and a bowlful of *pootchky* pith not unlike Hawaiian poi, all skillfully prepared from her own kitchen. She suggested I help myself, and so I thanked her and without further ado tore off a copious piece of Easter bread to use as a utensil from which to scoop up some of the other victuals.

Datuu came by and asked her if it was time to bring out the whale blubber.

I nearly choked on my bread and *pootchky*. "No need for that," I begged, "really, there's more than enough here for me to eat, thank you very much."

"Oh, but you must!" Aniqdux̂six̂ insisted, squeezing my shoulder. "It's part of the hunt. I've prepared it differently for thee; you shall see. Yes, Datuu, please fetch the blubber for Kayuu."

"Yes ma'am!" Datuu replied with a histrionic curtsy before turning to leave.

"And fetch the salmonberry wine!" Aniqdux̂six̂ added.

The vampire babe stopped to hear the appended order before skipping off on her way.

"So what's so particular about your whale blubber?" I inquired as I dipped my *kuliich* bread into the *pootchky*.

"It's *thy* whale blubber," she emphasized. "I know you don't particularly care for it raw, so I've roasted a prime cut between hollow stones."

"*A prime cut of blubber!*" I parodied under my breath.

"I beg your pardon?"

I had forgotten how well my gracious hostess (and her kind) could hear, and so I replied simply, "Oh, I was saying thanks for all this."

She pecked my cheek and blushed.

Before Datuu could even return with the fat, a slab of raw whale liver was brought before me on a stone plate by Qihmux̂. "I prepared this from thy quarry," she said, affecting her sister's poetic vernacular. "There's whale blood and product enow for everybody, thanks to thy kill and that of your partner Igasix̂. We are all very appreciative."

She glanced over at Aniqdux̂six̂, but her younger sister held her best poker face, not giving Qihmux̂ any reaction she may've been trying to elicit.

"Igasix̂ wasn't my partner;" I put the matter to rest. "Tayaĝukichax̂ was, or was supposed to be until he rigged my arrowhead with a line and tied the other end around my waist, basically trying to kill me."

"Is that what happened?" Like everyone else, Qihmux̂ appeared totally surprised by my account. "Well, at least you hitched a ride with Igasix̂—I heard she sat on your lap the whole way back."

With Easter bread in hand, I banged the table roughly and shot her a stony stare. "Hitched a ride?! Who's telling you people these things?"

"Your trusty *baidarka* partner, of course," Qihmux̂ replied flippantly, sliding the slab of liver before me.

"Tayaĝukichax̂, or Igasix̂?" I probed.

She turned and left, evading my inquiry.

"Just ignore her," Aniqdux̂six̂ said. "Qihmux̂'s just jealous. Her boyfriend hasn't caught a whale in about a decade, and here come thee, landing a giant on your first time out. And to think that Qagux̂ means 'fierce' in Aleut," she laughed.

"Well, can I just ignore the raw liver, too? I usually don't eat these kinds of things, especially from the likes of her."

"Oh don't worry about her. And you should try the liver—it's the best part. Nobody will understand if you don't at least take a bite."

I reluctantly consented. She sliced off a piece of the liver and told me to open wide.

Surreptitiously glancing around, I discovered we were being watched by many a clan member, some of whom had been on *qaqmiiĝux̂* with me. Not wishing to stir the boat among the party of the undead, I did as asked and took a methodical bite out of the raw liver. I chewed on it orderly-like, pretending to like it, all the while uttering to Aniqdux̂six̂ under my breath, "Yeah, well, thanks, but can we save the rest for later?"

"I understand." She smiled candidly, and then, perhaps to satisfy the onlookers that I was one of the clan (at least as far as their Aleut customs went), she continued more loudly: "The liver is so good that you want to stash it away to eat all by yourself later." She cast me a stealthy, wry wink.

Datuu soon returned with the salmonberry wine and roasted whale blubber, at which point Aniqdux̂six̂ told her to fetch a seal-gut wrap and reed basket to pack my "leftovers." Datuu appeared more than a little frustrated at all the commands being levied upon her, so I gave her a firm squeeze of the shoulder and thanked her with a twinkle, telling her how much I appreciated it. Her unduly sour countenance waxed again into the carefree grin I'd come to know, even love.

"Please, drink," Aniqdux̂six̂ offered, pointing to the seal-gut gourd of berry wine. "Thou hast earned it—you truly have; I want thee to be happy."

"But I *am* happy, Aniqdux̂six̂. It's so good to see you again." And furthermore, I was most happy about imbibing copious amounts of the sweet salmonberry spirit, which went a long way to kill the aftertaste of the Aleut delicacies, which I demonstrably wasn't yet fully acclimated to.

While the main dance performance was over, the festivities continued with songs being sung and stories told about the Aleuts' ancestors. Then came feats of juggling and games involving rings and sticks, such as the ring-and-pin game, where a ring is tossed and others must try to catch it with a stick. There was also a blanket-throwing game enjoyed by the women, and then women and children challenged one another in balancing contests. The boys, for their part, liked wrestling and donning the more frightening ceremonial masks.

While eating with true relish (the emotive kind—*not* the raw seaweed variety) the fresh roasted halibut (*not* the whale blubber) that Aniqdux̂six̂ had prepared, I was occasionally cajoled into partaking of the aforementioned diversions. Regrettably for me, the tribe was well-practiced and I often found myself on the losing end, but nevertheless the amusements won me the smiles of the children and perhaps the acquaintance of some new friends.

One particular wrestling match with Maguun really did me in. This was the six-year-old boy I'd saved from Ephraim's Lake, and it appeared he was having his revenge. Even a child *iidigidi*, when not beset by Holy Water, possessed incredible strength. I laughed about this fact with Aniqdux̂six̂, as I swigged my salmonberry wine in the aftermath.

"Makes one appreciate a mortal child," she replied somewhat cryptically. "They're easier for the parents to pin down."

Her statement was funny, true, and perhaps not so flippant, for in it was an intimation of her greatest longing—to bear children, which from my understanding was presently impossible for a vampire, not unless it was by means of "adoption," i.e., by transforming them with the *promuishlenniki* plague.

Chief Aĝnakax̂ approached with an attractive bentwood bowl. Kuuyux, the shaman elder, was with him. "It is our custom," the chief said, "that he who delivers the fatal lance to the *alax̂* gets the first allotment of *spermaceti*."

I was unsure about what he was referring to, for as I knew it, *spermaceti* was the Latin name of the sperm whale itself. Perhaps he was talking about yet another precious organ for me to (un)happily consume? Kuuyux correctly read my vacant expression as a sign of ignorance, and so he added, "*spermaceti* is the greatest gift of the *qaqmiiĝux̂* and should be received with the highest reverence."

"Ah yes, well, thank you then," I replied straightaway, still not knowing what the heck it was they were giving.

"Reverence to *alax̂*," Kuuyux explained, looking entirely unimpressed by me.

"I understand;" I answered in an attempt to ease relations with the shaman, "*alax̂* is central to Unangax̂ culture. I appreciate having taken part in *qaqmiiĝux̂*, and have the deepest gratitude for the whale's sacrifice."

"*Hmpff!*" he huffed, snubbing my essay at diplomacy.

"*Cachalot*" Sperm Whale (*Original engraving for encyclopedia, 1882*)

"*Spermaceti* has many uses," continued the chief, placing the bowl before me. "Aniqdux̂six̂ can show you what to do with it. It is very valuable to us and has been for centuries, especially because it does not freeze."

"What are some of its uses?" I asked, still trying to break the ice the shaman had brought to the impromptu meeting.

The elders remained silent as the grave, so Aniqdux̂six̂ took the initiative: "We use it for making candles and ointments; as a lubricant and in fabrics; we employ it in our sealskin creations and leatherworks, and personally, I like to use it as a cosmetic."

She slid the bowl before her to behold the waxy substance, which resembled chilled honey or butter.

I turned and asked her, taking the opportunity to leave the circumspect men out of the conversation, "What part of the whale does it come from?"

She was more than happy to reply: "The waxy oil is extracted from the sperm whale's head."

"Does the poisoned lance tip taint the oil, or the whale blubber for that matter?"

"Not really. Over the centuries, Aleuts have become immune to any residual effect left by the monkshood poison."

The chief and shaman had grown visibly flustered. "You're not supposed to speak such things," the chief warned his step-daughter, the shaman offering his trademark "*Hmpff!*" for emphasis.

"Her speak, or me know?" I asked, none too pleased.

"You are not to reproach the chief," the shaman coolly replied.

"Publicly, or privately?" I inquired (I'd imbibed quite a bit of wine).

"Not at all!" trumpeted the shaman. "Know your place here, *Americanchin*, and take heed! You may have gone on *qaqmiiĝux̂*, you may have killed an *alax̂*, you may've played with our children and fallen in love with this child here, but you're still not one of us, and never will be."

Aniqdux̂six̂ went to get up and talk the shaman down, but I grabbed her hand, encouraging her to remain seated, then reproached Kuuyux and the chief thus: "Since we're on the subject of *qaqmiiĝux̂*, I was wondering if it was common-place for the kayaker seated abaft to affix the point man's throwing-lance with twine, then covertly tie the other end around the waist of this thrower seated afore? Is this customary while hunting for *alax̂*? Is it acceptable practice for the spear thrower in front to be forced overboard by the shenanigans of the paddler in back? Because that's exactly what Tayaĝukichax̂ did to me. The line went taut when my harpoon connected with the whale, and when the *alax̂* dived, I was dragged down with it."

"Is that what really happened?" Chief Aĝnakax̂ inquired, his eyes widened like a madman, either in anger, shock, or both. "And you survived?"

"More than survived," Aniqdux̂six̂ came to my defense. "He hast prevailed over the monster, and I'm not just referring to the whale."

"Why did you bring him here?" Kuuyux scolded her, thereby changing the subject. "You know he doesn't belong with our kind."

"I believe that's for mine to decide, right father?" she put to Aĝnakax̂, who was actually her stepfather.

"Who gave you that amulet?" the shaman continued his verbal attack, noticing my rosy finch necklace, which, now that *qaqmiiĝux̂* was over, I felt no need to conceal.

"None of your business," I said.

Now it was Aniqdux̂six̂ who grabbed my hand, encouraging me to scale things back, while the chief remained silent. *Perhaps he knew that his wife had given me the amulet?*

"Thank thee, Chief Aĝnakax̂ and Shaman Kuuyux," Aniqdux̂six̂ addressed them formally, "for bringing Kayuu his *spermaceti*. As thou, chief, have mentioned, I shall be pleased to shew him its many uses." And then she added without breath, so that I only I might hear, "beginning with its use as a lubricant."

We were unable to hold our lips, simultaneously erupting in hysterics.

"What did she say?!" steamed the shaman, but the chief encouraged him away, although not before privately warning his stepdaughter, "I'll have a word with you later," and offering me a sour grimace.

"Bye, chief!" I said, waving back.

Aniqdux̂six̂ and I bit our tongues until they were out of earshot, then erupted in guffaws again.

"Pay no mind to that stodgy old dinosaur," she trilled as we were calming down.

"Which one?" I asked, and we shared a chortle once more.

Olean came to our table and said, "It looks like you got your *spermaceti*. Good stuff! Come on, it's time to get your facial tattoo!"

"Oh, that . . ." I was not particularly enthused to remember this ritual, which was standard fare for all hunters after their first big kill. I looked from Olean to Aniqdux̂six̂ with some strange false hope that she might come to my rescue once again, but received only a nod of encouragement backed by a twinkling smile over her tattooed chin. To resist now would probably seem like a slight to her tribe, not to mention an overt rejection of her style as well. And so, once again, I feigned enthusiasm for undergoing another exotic Aleut tradition, following Olean to my hard-boiled fate.

The Aleutians theater proves a hard-boiled experience for most all enlisted servicemen, such as here, where, "Rough seas batter a small boat transferring a plane crew, illustrating the battering taken by US Navy officers and enlisted men in getting from ship to shore and ship to patrol plane as they scout and hammer Jap forces invading the Aleutians." (AP Wirephoto and caption from Dept. of U.S. Navy, August 17, 1942)

IGASIX̂'S TRAGEDY

AT THE tattooing table sat several seasoned hunter-warriors already decked out with abundant tattoos, and Igasix̂, who was presently receiving a permanent marking on the side of her face. We exchanged greetings, and shortly I was offered a whale vertebrae seat opposite her.

"Chin, cheek, or forehead?" inquired my tattoo artist, a short and pudgy guy brandishing a slightly curved bone needle with a fine, sharp tip. His own face was generously riddled with piercings and prick marks.

"How about my back?" I said, thinking of Aniqdux̂six̂ and also the smooth facial complexion I'd carefully managed to keep with a shaving kit she'd given me, salvaged from a wrecked Japanese trawler.

"How about along here," he countered, gliding the tip of his bodkin from the side of my mouth, up along my cheek to almost my ear. "This is the most traditional."

"Go for it, Kayuu!" squeaked Igasix̂ from across the table. "That's what I'm getting, both sides of course, like a big smile—*hee-hee-hee.*"

Her nineteen-year-old complexion was already weathered beyond repair, so what did she care? It occurred to me that I could always wear a beard along the prick line, if I ever made it back to civilization.

"Okay, how about a row here, just like you said," I conceded, retracing my jawline for the tattoo artist, "one on each side in perfect symmetry. Can you do that?"

The coal-black eyes of the tattooist smarted with pleasure. I'd cast a limelight upon his bailiwick. "Perfect symmetry," he affirmed with a wily grin, then took my face in one hand and carefully went to work with the other. The pricking sensation was a little unpleasant, and I only say a little because, fortunately, I'd downed most of the salmonberry wine from the seal-gut gourd and was feeling benumbed around the edges ('twas the fruity spirit I shall freely place blame on for many of my transgressions, including my capitulation to the facial tattoo, which was more akin to scarification).

"Is there any significance," I inquired, causing the artist to pause his steady hand, "of having the line along the cheek?" I genuinely wanted to know, since the said line would be mine forever, and perhaps forever-after if I didn't escape the bloody barabara alive.

"Try not to speak if you want your perfect symmetry," warned the chubby stylist of pricks before he went back to work on my face; "but yes, the tattoo will please the animal spirits and ward off the *khoughkh*."

"The what?"

He withdrew his needle again and waved it before my face. "No talking!"

"The *khoughkh*," offered Igasix̂, unconcerned if her lines became crooked. "They're evil entities—like truly evil, rotten to the core. They exist everywhere outside and will seek to harm you to increase their power."

I thought about Igasix̂'s description of these evil entities and dared not voice it publicly, but the tail end of it seemed to match the bloodsucking ways of her own kind, the *iidigidi*. But then I mulled it further and realized I was wrong in that assessment, for the cave clan made all effort to avoid contact with humans, choosing instead to feast on sea mammal blood rather than harming people. While there were truly wicked types like Tayaĝukichax̂, and people like Kuuyux who understandably were wary of outsiders, the example of Aniqdux̂six̂ and many others who'd taken me in and tried to help me showed that the *iidigidi* did have a heart, even if cold, black blood was what it pumped through them. Furthermore, the *promuishlenniki* plague was not their own making, but had been visited upon them by savage colonialist poachers.

"A fine pair you two make," commented Olean, no doubt taking account of Igasix̂'s and my freshly pockmarked cheeks and similar (by happenstance) labrets; and by now there was also no doubt that he and his *baidarka* partner Tix̂lax̂ had been trying to outdo one another in hooking me up with the young female whaler. I could not deny that she was attractive, and at nineteen she wasn't much younger than me. Also (if you might pardon my asseveration), I'd drunk my fair share of salmonberry wine, enhancing the sense of enchantment I now had for my opposite-sex initiate. When it came right down to it, I was attracted to her bravery, such as I'd witnessed firsthand on *qaqmiiĝux̂*. This was the sort of person who would insist on being on the frontlines in an assault against the Japs. And now that I was drunk, I could readily admit, if I'd been privately asked, that embracing her sweaty body through her wet skin suit as she sat on my lap and pulled hard at her oar, giving a little grunt with each stroke, had left a deep imprint on my animal core—if a man truly has such a thing.

At Olean's titular suggestion that she and I made a "fine pair," Igasix̂ beamed at me freely, and the lines of her freshly carved tattoo seemed to eerily extend her smile from ear to ear not unlike "The Joker" character from the Batman comic series.

"If we can please the animal spirits together," I replied to his suggestive quip, "then we're off to a pretty good start, I guess."

With that seemingly insignificant little ode to our undeniable compatibility as like-hearted warriors, the hunters around the table erupted in ribald cheer.

Igasix̂'s smile (her real smile) remained and her stare held firm, our steady eye contact throughout the suggestive exchange telling me one thing: she did not have a problem with the ideas being expressed. The insuppressible fact was that we were the primary victors of the day's sea action, which meant we'd won similar esteem together, even if the naysayers about me refused to concede it. As far as the greater tribe was concerned, our concurrent breaking through the rite of passage bonded us together on a very fundamental level. (Perhaps this is why it had been determined that we paddle home together?)

But I felt an underlying unease about these realizations, because Aniqdux̂six̂ was here, and in the end she was, in fact, probably better for me. I scanned the room and glimpsed her seated at a table not too far distant, conversing with other women, the entire group stealing glances back at me. I felt a little embarrassed. I guess I was too much of a flirt for my own good, and they probably noticed. Alas, at the end of the day, Aniqdux̂six̂ may've been *too good* for me.

"You look great!" Igasix̂ remarked from across the table.

"As do you," I replied out of politeness, having regained my composure.

"How about a sea lion whisker through your forehead?" the tattooist offered. I knew this was the pinnacle adornment of respect and honor for a hunter, so could not so easily refuse. Only I calibrated the offer, saying, "Okay, but give it to me as an earring instead."

The whalers around the table were pleased. A sea lion whisker worn through the ear was imminently wearable, as many of them proved with theirs.

"Let's us proceed!" replied the beautician of pain merrily, and then he pierced my ear through with his bloody bodkin.

Shortly after the whisker was inserted, Aniqdux̂six̂ came over with some of her friends and they all had a giggle in beholding my makeover.

"That bad, eh?"

"No, it looks good!" she entertained. "We're just not used to seeing a non-Aleut in our fashion, but really, thou art fetching!"

Her best friend Ayagaadax̂, whom she liked to sew parkas with, touched my shoulder and said, "It's perfect; just give it a few days to heal and you'll be amazed at your transformation."

I gingerly rubbed the side of my face and felt numerous little pockmark protuberances, and then I tapped the tip of the hard whisker now skewered through my right ear. In military terms, I'd been given a mortar makeover, but thanks to the wine (*a-hem!*), I was sufficiently wasted to take it all in stride. My relaxed attitude through these painful initiations seemed to please the men at the table as well. They no longer looked upon me as a curiosity, but had visibly eased in my presence. For all intents and purposes, I was now "one of the guys." Of course, the likes of Kuuyux and Tayaĝukichax̂ were not taking part in Igasix̂ and my facial shindig.

Aniqdux̂six̂ smarted her upper lip in a sexy sneer, revealing a fang at one side, which she slowly encircled with her tongue. She was watching my hand as I withdrew it from my face, for my fingers were wet with blood. I came to my senses and lowered my hand beneath the table, not wanting to tempt her in such a manner.

"Well," I offered nonchalantly, "thanks everyone, but I had better go get washed up."

"You look great!" Igasix̂ said again from across the table. The drummers, rattlers, and some masked dancers had gravitated toward our area, almost putting her out of earshot.

I smiled and gave her a mindless wave. Aniqdux̂six̂ was here now with her friends, so I wasn't too eager to shout out another compliment to the popsy young initiate.

"Enjoy the rest of thine evening," Aniqdux̂six̂ told her instead, loudly enough for all to hear, "as shall I." She rubbed the top of my head as if I were her little boy, and then she took my hand and conveyed me up from the table.

Igasix̂'s bandying expression became undone by Aniqdux̂six̂'s action. She was clearly put off, and clearly jealous, if I might say so.

"Bye," I said, giving her another rote wave. I had few other viable options, but didn't want her to feel bad. At the end of the night, I'd be shacking up with the twenty-something Aniqdux̂six̂—an inevitability now palpable to many, it seemed.

My mate-to-be guided me by the hand into the group of dancing revelers, then pulled her bird beak vizard back down over her face and unfurled the wings of her *sax* parka.

Sugangix̂ handed me my mask to wear, and as I was putting it on, Aniqdux̂six̂ circled around me enticingly, grazing my body with the tips of her feathers.

Once disguised by our false faces, Aniqdux̂six̂ wrapped her plumage around me and guided me in a slow dance, even as the drumming and festivities continued to blur around us in rapid tempo. I embraced her with like intimacy and, a few timeless moments later, she lifted her snow-white wings clear over our heads, sheltering us completely from the world around us. But a glimmer of stone light breached her feathered sanctuary, a single, slanting beam that fell upon her pearly fangs and luscious red lips, lips wet with the blood of my quarry, lips quavering, ever so subtly, while they caressed her ivory canines. She edged her mouth open further, and then she whispered through the muffled, distant drumming, "I love you, Jake Harper."

Aniqdux̂six̂ (Oil on canvas painting; the artist chooses to remain anonymous)

Mesmerized by her tender words and luscious mouth, I went to kiss her, when suddenly a cacophonous sound startled us both, causing her to drop our cover. The dancers and musicians were destroying their masks and instruments, smashing them against the central monolith.

"What's happening?" I asked anxiously, confused and concerned by the natives' behavior.

"Don't worry," she consoled, even as blood from the fountain splashed all around us in the violent onslaught. "It's our tradition."

I lifted my vizard from my face and asked her if I, too, should smash it upon the adakite stanchion, but she quickly took it from my clutches and stashed it beneath her *sax*, doing the same with her bird beak mask. "Let's go," she said. "Party's almost over."

She took my hand and led me swiftly though the throng toward the side egress. Chief Aĝnakax̂ was milling about the exit there and regarded us curiously as we fled, but made no effort to interfere with our leaving together.

Upon attaining to the boathouse adjacent, Aniqdux̂six̂ could hardly contain her excitement. We were finally free of her clan and the elders. She whisked me off my feet and darted into the adjoining lava tube, flying at a breathless pace all the way back to the barabara, where she delivered me unto her chamber, laid me down upon her wild rye bed and fucked me like an animal.

Aniqdux̂six̂ and I lay side by side, staring up through her ceiling portal. The winds had shifted, clearing away the volcanic haze, and now stars winked down through the cobalt heavens. I asked her what she'd been doing since we were separated by Chief Aĝnakax̂, and she explained that she'd been keeping busy with her usual activities, such as making parkas and weaving baskets with Ayagaadax̂, visiting her father's tomb (his *umqan*), tending to her fumarole garden, cooking, and reading. She said that Chief Aĝnakax̂ had notified her whenever I was sleeping, so that she could help re-skin his *iqyax̂* for Tayaĝukichax̂ and me to use. He'd determined early on that he wanted Tayaĝukichax̂ to take me on *qaqmiiĝux̂*, and it was customary for the hunter's wife to skin the boat, so long as she wasn't menstruating. As Tayaĝukichax̂'s wife was long deceased, Aĝnakax̂ called upon his stepdaughter—my "desideratum," as he called her—to help out; Aniqdux̂six̂ was obliging. "Anything to help ensure your safety," she told me, noting how perilous whale-hunting could be, "especially riding with Tayaĝukichax̂."

"You know your half-brother all too well," I replied with a shit-eating grin. "What I told Aĝnakax̂ is true: his son tried to kill me on the hunt in a very sly, underhanded, and cowardly way. Do you think your stepfather's going to do anything about it? Tayaĝukichax̂ should be publicly called out and chastised."

"Aĝnakax̂ would never do such a thing in public," she replied. "Tayaĝukichax̂ stands to succeed him, should he ever die."

"Tayaĝukichax̂ as clan chief?" I laughed, aghast. "Now that would be a disaster."

"Perhaps," she deemed, "or perhaps not. It's a brave new world out there, and Tayaĝukichax̂, while immature at times, has the sort of resolve and backbone we need. I think if it came right down to it, he would modify his behavior and start doing the right things."

"You can't be serious?"

"Tell me what happened on *qaqmiiĝux̂*. I know your version of events about killing the whale, but I want to hear what happened thenceforth. Tayaĝukichax̂ said that you and he had an argument over you puncturing the *iqyax̂*, and then thou refused to get back onboard his craft, insisting instead on repairing with Igasix̂."

"Puncturing the boat and insisting I return with Igasix̂? *Really*! Is that what he's been telling people? And you believe that crap!?"

"Look, Kayuu, I can understand you not wanting to get back into an unsound *baidarka*—believe me, I can; I'm very particular about skinning them. But did you decide to ride back with Igasix̂ because she was the victor over the other *alax̂*? I can only imagine your mutual excitement."

"Hey, Aniqdux̂six̂, what's this all about? Tayaĝukichax̂ wasn't even there at that point. He totally abandoned me, and then someone, I don't know who, decided I ride back with Igasix̂ because she was the smallest of the party, while her partner at point, Altixum, had been badly injured by their quarry."

"So let me get this straight," Aniqdux̂six̂ ruminated, "Altixum was presumably too injured to paddle, and so your joining their *baidarka* as a third occupant, without even being given an oar to help Igasix̂ paddle, was propitious? And some unknown, well-trained mariners are making these decisions?"

"You think I'm lying?"

"I just want to know what really transpired."

"I couldn't paddle because she was sitting on my lap! We would've crossed oars at every stroke!"

"Why was she sitting on thy lap to begin with? She could've just flown back."

"As it is my understanding," I replied, mottling every syllable, "the entire purpose of the hunt is to encourage your clan to remain true to the traditional *qaqmiiĝux̂*. Flying back on vampire wings is not exactly traditional!"

"The sole purpose of the hunt is whale blood, oil, and sustenance, just as it's always been," she replied in an even temper. "Everything else surrounding *qaqmiiĝux̂* is fluff and pretense."

"How can you say that?" I countered. "These are your time-honored traditions!"

"It was true ere, even as it is now: all culture is a by-product of survival, making a pageantry of the acquisition and use of necessities. We court each other at dance with silly bird masks, but in the end it's the fuck we really need."

"What are you saying, Aniqdux̂six̂? Culture is the spice of life, it's everything."

"Tell me that after you are many centuries old and tired of human posturing and affectation."

"It sounds to me like perhaps you're jealous of mortals," I paused to deliver the trump card I'd never wanted to play: "and Igasix̂."

"Did she give thee an erection, Jake?"

"It was nothing!"

"What was nothing?"

"Nothing was nothing!"

She rolled over, half on top of me with her naked body. She touched her forefinger to my nose and said, "Okay then, Lieutenant Harper, I believe you. It was nothing. Just take it easy."

"I am taking it easy!" I scoffed, still sufficiently peeved.

"You're right, Kayuu, right on both accounts: I am jealous of both mortals and that little hunter of yours." She wrapped her hand in mine, our fingers naturally interlocking. "I've lost my way and am losing all of humanity. I need you, Jake, need you more than thou may ever knowest; and you may not see it at present, but you need me just as badly, just as you did when I found you, lying in the snow."

I thought she was being a little unfair and was going to tell her so, but when my eyes settled upon hers and I saw her corneas glow, her ageless love enveloped me like a warm home. Our bond, while unexpected, was undeniable; our love was inescapable—eternal.

"Dost thou desire to play a little game?" she asked as she straddled me fully, the tips of her jet-black locks just gliding over my lips.

I held her by the waist, which was slowly beginning to rock. "What kind of game?"

"Blanket tossing while wearing false faces. I could never stand watching them destroy their masks, so I always sneak mine out. They're such precious works of art, don't you think?"

"Totally, along with the bentwood hats—they belong in a museum."

Chief Aǵnakax̂'s false face mask, or semblance thereof (Shumagin Islanders death mask example found in rock shelter near Delaroff Harbor, Unga Island, by Captain Charles Riedell, from The Third Annual Report of the Bureau of Ethnology to the Secretary of the Smithsonian Institution 1881–1882, *by J. W. Powell; Washington Government Printing Office, 1884)*

She laughed. "For now, the blankets and masks belong with us, in bed."

"Sounds kinky," I said, nibbling the ends of her hair. "What'd you have in mind, exactly?"

She pulled on her bird beak mask, and then handed me my hunter god vizard and one of the rye grass weaves that the Aleuts used as bed coverings. "You must catch me with this blanket."

"That will be easy, little birdie!" I huffed through my fearsome false face, emitting a boorish laugh.

"Dream on," she quipped, and then took wing to the ceiling.

We were both totally nude save for our false faces, which did naught to halt her vampire proclivities. I should've remembered she could sprout wings in an instant and wasn't dependent upon a *sax* jacket to fly.

"Hey, that's cheating!" I called up, all the while curling the edge of the grass blanket clandestinely into my fist.

"Come, great hunter god," she teased, "shew me what you've got!" She darted down and hovered just beside me.

I flung the blanket at her, but she was too quick, fluttering to my other side. "Missed me, missed me, now thee must kiss me!" taunted she.

"When I catch you, pretty little bird, the punishment shall be more than that!"

"Then I shall make it easy for you. Here, I'll close my eyes."

Indeed, behind the eye sockets of her bird mask her own eyelids lowered shut.

I got out of bed and grabbed the blanket from the floor, saying, "Okay, but let me—" and midsentence I threw the blanket up toward her head. My surprise attack caught her left wing, but wasn't enough to bring my quarry down.

She flittered about me in a counteroffensive, poking me here and there while teasing me with a nursery rhyme: "*A little cock-sparrow sat on a high tree, and she chirped, she chirped so merrily, for this little cock-sparrow would make a nice stew, and her giblets would make a nice pie, too. 'Oh, no,' says cock-sparrow,*

'*I shan't make a stew,' and she fluttered her wings, and away she flew . . .*"

"Bite me, little cock-sparrow!" I spewed, then lunged up from where I knelt, whipping my wild rye blanket clean around her. As she struggled to fly away, I seized her ankle and pulled her down onto the bed.

She continued to flap her wings, so I climbed up over her legs and onto her back, at last pinning her down against the stuffed grass mattress.

"It appears my little cock-sparrow's been had," she capitulated, and then she reached back between her wings and grabbed my hand, pulling me closer.

I slid up over her rump and she began stroking my penis. She tugged and tugged until my dong was as hard as adakite, so I took the invite and entered her from behind.

"Oh yes, Kayuu," she groaned, arching her back and flaying her wings by degrees as I pumped ever harder into her posterior. "*Oh yes hunter, take me!*" she moaned. "*Take me higher!*"

I clutched her shoulders, disencumbering her wings. "Fly me to the moon!" I bade of my poetic vampire lover.

Our bodies left the bed, lurching toward the stars. We stretched our heads through the ceiling portal, where at the pinnacle of ecstasy we unleashed a collective cry, her peaking scream a full octave above mine. The unabashed report of our intercourse echoed off the volcano summits and over the milky black shores.

Settling down again upon her bed, some of her white feathers that were liberated in our feverish lovemaking continued to drift in the air. We laid there watching them float before the midnight sea of stars. She took not a breath, for though I could feel her heart pumping strongly in her chest, necrogenesis had voided her need of life-giving oxygen.

"You're my whaler man," said she, cuddling up beside me, her vocal chords powered by an accordion-like action of her neck muscles.

"Does that mean I'm getting fat?" I joked.

"Aleuts aren't fat," she laughed. "We're just a little chubby."

"Chubby from all the whale fat," I teased with an air of persiflage.

"Chubby and cute," she bandied back.

"I'll give you that."

"Are you certain you can't bear children?" I asked.

"Not in my present condition," she lamented.

"You know that for a fact?"

"Yes," she said. "We reference the Wongs as a definitive case study. They are a couple from China who were the sole survivors of a shipwreck here in 1880. We summarily turned them into *iidigidi*, and Mis'ess Wong miscarried almost instantly. They've been trying to bear children ever since, but to no avail—as *iidigidi*, they simply are incapable of carrying natural offspring. They're our proof positive that two Wongs don't make a wight."

As Aniqdux̂six̂ smiled at me glibly, I was unsure of what to make of her anecdote. "Two Wongs don't make a wight?" I asked incredulously, at which point she burst into guffaws.

"Wait, listen," she said, gently touching my lips. "Dost thou hear it?"

"Hear what?"

"*Sshh . . .*"

Vampires had an acute sense of hearing, so I settled down and concentrated on the dead air . . .

Sure enough, I could just make out a strange, moaning howl in the distance, and in the moments that followed it became louder and more anguished. "What *is* that?"

"Igasix̂ in mourning," Aniqdux̂six̂ revealed. "Alone by the sea she will splash the water and make the dying calls of a whale. *Alax̂* gives us its sustenance freely, but to kill one for the first time is a profound thing for a young initiate, and can affect them deeply."

Listening further, I became enchanted, almost haunted by Igasix̂'s tragedy, and wondered why killing a whale didn't have the same effect upon me. But then I remembered how close my alax̂ had brought me to death, thanks in large part to Tayaĝukichax̂'s trickery, so realized that I perhaps felt less remorse or compassion or whatever it was Igasix̂ was experiencing over her quarry. While the two giants of the sea had already been partially cut open for their goodies, their carcasses remained hauled out on the beach, awaiting further processing. Igasix̂'s moaning was both deeply sensual and gut-wrenching.

"Perhaps she's just missing you," Aniqdux̂six̂ said in earnest.

I raised a brow, peering at her with glum skepticism. She held a poker face, at length breaking into guffaws and slapping me with a stuffed reed pillow.

The pillow fight continued, I donned my mask and launched into *Fee-fi-fo-fum*, changing the lyrics some:

> *"Fee-fi-fo-fum*
> *I smell üdigidi blood*
> *Be she alive or be she dead*
> *I'll grind her rump until we're wed!"*

She was none too pleased by my crass nursery rhyme, and in her shock I mounted her again, this time in the Russian missionary position, or so I joked.

To defend her virtue, she licked the blood from my pock-marked cheeks and delivered it back into my mouth. All was fair in love and war.

BLASPHEMOUS RUMORS

THE NEXT morning, Aniqdux̂six̂ mentioned something about visiting the quarry site with her friend Ayagaadax̂, leaving me in my peaceful slumbering. I lazed in bed for hours, listening to Aleutian sparrows singing outside. I was lucky I didn't have a hangover, which was a miracle considering how much wine I'd consumed. But I'd eaten a lot of food and made a lot of love, too, and so by balance of excesses I came out relatively sound. Alas, I could scarcely ignore the pain in my swollen face. I'd yet to see my "mortar makeover" in a mirror, but already knew I'd surely look as ruffian as my savage hosts—at least until I grew a beard.

I was just trying on a new *kamleika* parka that Aniqdux̂six̂ had made for me when Algax̂ Malihnax̂, one of the teenage whalers, appeared in the ceiling portal and said the chief wanted to meet me topside posthaste. I asked him what about. He said he didn't know. With genuine curiosity, I pulled on a new pair of sea lion boots—also courtesy of Aniqdux̂six̂—then climbed up the notched log ladder.

Chief Aĝnakax̂ was standing in a patch of snow not far from the barabara; he signaled me over when I saw him. The first thing I noticed when I approached was his bare feet. I still couldn't believe the cave clan went barefoot year-round, but such were the ways of the Adak Aleuts, and not just the *iidigidi* among them. This was reputed to be common practice among all Andreanof Islanders. "*Qilachxizax̂!*" I said with a spring in my step, wishing him *good morning*, practicing my Aleut. He was unsmiling, which was nothing new. "It is no longer morning," he said.

"How can you tell?" I never saw any of them with timekeeping devices.

He glanced up at the sun and said, "Don't be stupid, but come, let's take a walk. We must talk."

"Talk about what?" I queried as we began strolling over the subarctic tundra.

The subarctic tundra of Adak Island (Exclusive image and caption by Lt. Harper, dated 1943)

"I've spoken with Sugangix̂, Tayaĝukichax̂, Igasix̂, and others about the *qaqmiiĝux̂*." The chief paused, leaving only the sound of my boots scrunching over the snowpack.

"Yes?"

"I was growing suspicious about the conflicting rumors. The *qaqmiiĝux̂* is a serious matter. It completes our existence and determines ranks of honor. Then there was the subject of my *iqyax̂* and how it became damaged, and why you abandoned Tayaĝukichax̂ in favor of Igasix̂. She may seem like a nubile, ripe for the taking, but I warn you, her gen-cycle is further off even than that of Aniqdux̂six̂."

I shook my head. "You know chief, no disrespect, but I've had to listen to this garbage ever since I got back. It's all a bunch of BS fabricated by your son Tayaĝukichax̂. He's never liked me and has always had it out for me; I have no idea why. I've always been nice to him. I thought he was finally being cool, you know, on the level, but then he goes off and tries to kill me on *qaqmiiĝux̂*, so maybe you should talk to him about what really happened."

"I'm meeting with you privately because I knew you'd be angry," he said. "Publicly you must never raise your voice at me like that. You need to become a better listener. I told you that I have spoken with Tayaĝukichax̂ about what happened, and in light of the evidence I am permitting you to return to Kuluk."

"*You are?* So you finally believe me?"

"I am deeply frustrated by your continued presence. You really don't belong among us and are causing too much trouble. You are complicating matters with my son and heir-to-be. This last incident proves it beyond question."

"In light of your son's behavior," I reproached, "you might want to reconsider handing him the keys to the kingdom."

The chief gave me a long, cold stare, as we trudged over the snowpack and heath.

"I know he's your son and you're just trying to protect him," I added, "but by your own admission, a man must prove himself to gain respect, while he goes around lying to his tribe, cheating on *qaqmiiĝux̂*, and backstabbing me at every opportunity. You, Chief Aĝnakax̂, are made of different stuff, and it pains me that the love you have for your son should blind you to your significant differences of character. You are chiefly by nature, while he is very immature."

"Once you return to Longview," he continued, disregarding my opinion, "you must not disclose our existence or location, ever, because if you do, that will set in motion a scenario too terrible to fathom."

"I won't compromise your clan;" I vowed, "but out of curiosity, what scenario is that?"

"We are the last remaining Aleuts in our homeland, and if we are discovered by your government, you know fully well what they'll do to us; but we could never accept submission and relocation. We will fight to the death."

"You cannot go up against the US military. Your numbers are too few, your weapons too primitive—even with your special abilities. You'll be wiped out."

"I always said you were a poor listener," he countered. "Have you not been paying attention to the effects of the *promuishlenniki* plague? After having lived with us, do you still deny its power? We can infect your army, who in turn would infect the world. You allude to my wisdom, which is so: the sole reason I established the gen-cycle was to ward off such an event ever from occurring. Perhaps you can see now how egregious was Aniqdux̂six̂'s crime in keeping you here alive and risking any of this from happening. But I am a man of my word and promised you a measure of respect if you were willing to earn it, which I will concede you have. So call me the greater fool for allowing you safe passage back to A-2, but I give you my stern warning about what will happen if you expose us. If you can so easily perceive the folly in my son's ways, this master of all follies I know you're not going to make."

"As I said, I shall not expose you here, because I have come to like and respect many among you and don't wish to see you suffer the same fate as your Aleut brethren on the other islands. But the promise you made before *qaqmiiĝux̂* was that, if I prevailed in the great and perilous task, I'd be permitted the hand of your stepdaughter, Aniqdux̂six̂. So if this is a manner of the mutual honor we speak, you must allow me to take her back with me. At Longview, I can get approval for her to be transferred to the lower forty-eight, where we shall marry without further ado once my tour of duty is completed. They will not deny a man his wife-to-be, I can assure you."

"You can assure me? I think you overestimate the allowances of your commanders. A GI can't just pick up a native girl and ship her home. We're not some war prize, some artifact that you can stuff in your rations bag. I am angered by your demand, but don't wish to pontificate whether it's blackmail or not, because I know how much you love each other; we've all had enough of hearing your nighttime trysts. But the fact is, it's too dangerous a time for her to elope with you now. When the war is over and you're ready to settle down, return to Boot Bay and you can marry her here, then you can do as you please. That is my promise."

I pondered the seriousness of his intention, but was unconvinced in light of his recent remarks that I didn't belong among his people. "Do as you please, as in, take her back down south with me?" I probed further.

"That is my promise," he repeated.

I stopped walking, and so did he. I really wanted to get back into the war effort. My country needed me and I knew Aniqduх̂siх̂ could wait. She wouldn't want to, of course, but all she had was time, while the free world didn't. The Tanaka Memorial was in full swing, along with the Third Reich. These were greater battles that couldn't wait, for to lose either meant the loss of all free peoples' dreams. The chief may not have been able to see this, hiding away in his house of muskeg, but it was eminently clear to me.

"Agreed," I said, offering my hand in the American fashion. "You take me back to Kuluk without delay, I never reveal a thing about you to anyone, and once the war is over, I return here secretly to marry Aniqduх̂siх̂, at which point she and I are free to leave."

Aĝnakaх̂ looked at my hand curiously. "I am familiar with this gesture," he said, then grabbed my hand and shook it histrionically. "We have decided this together, and shall honor it to the end."

"You've got a deal, buster!" I replied eagerly, then looked back toward the barabara, which by now was indiscernible among the rolling snow and heath.

TXIN YAKTAKUG

"SO IS that all I mean to thee?!" Aniqdux̂six̂ scathed, bearing her fangs while jabbing a finger into my chest; "a mere heath-stone—leverage to buy your ticket out of here?" Obviously, she'd found out about my deal with her stepfather, even before I could tell her.

"No, Aniqdux̂six̂," I replied calmly, trying to be the level head in the room, "I must complete my tour of duty with the ASF, and then I'll return for you and we can marry."

"Well isn't that a convenient excuse to leave me? Anything can happen between now and then. I thought we were in this together?"

"It's not an excuse, Aniqdux̂six̂. I've always wanted to return to base and fight the war, and you know that. I've made an agreement with the chief and received his formal approval for us to be wed once the war is over. This is cause for rejoicing, my dear, not worry."

"Oh please, once the war is over!" she shot back. "Don't 'my dear' me! Have you ever heard of the Hundred Years' War? You may *never* come back. It seems you never really loved me, but were only using me to get your way."

She was right: for a long time I'd been using her as a means to my own ends. But over time, I'd come to love her deeply, and it pained me she didn't realize how much I'd changed.

"Don't say that, Aniqdux̂six̂," I pleaded. "I do love you, and I trust you completely. It was you who saved my life and brought me back to health on numerous occasions. You taught me about selflessness, compassion, and sacrifice, and I'm not willing to throw all that away to be the person I was before I met you. You complete me, Aniqdux̂six̂, but I've made a prior sworn duty to serve my country, and just as you wouldn't want me to break my solemn vow with you, you mustn't allow me to break my solemn vow to fight the scourge of fascism.

Seabees Fight a "Winter War"—For two years, the Navy's Seabees—Construction Battalions—have built and rebuilt along the road to Tokyo. For many of them, the war has been a long struggle with stubborn tundra, an Herculean day-by-day routine of doing skilled work with cold hands, as they construct the springboard for ousting the Japs from the Aleutians. Seabees have "commandos," too. Here, Rear Admiral J. W. Reeves, USN, reviews a graduating class of the advanced combat school at Dutch Harbor, Alaska. (Department of U.S. Navy photo and caption, 1943)

"And so I promise you, when the war is over, I will return and we shall be espoused. From there, the world will be ours. If we choose to leave Adak, I've already received approval from the chief to take you back to the lower forty-eight. But not now—it's too soon. There are greater workings afoot. How can you people not see that? Soon the Japs will come knocking at your door in the form of a bomb, and I must, at all costs, do all I can to prevent that. I meant what I said when I told your elders that I was only trying to protect you. I think Chief Aĝnakax̂ sees that now, so why can't you?"

"I appreciate that you want to protect me, Lieutenant Harper, I really do. But do you truly want to spend the rest of your life with me, is the painful riddle I daily contemplate."

I didn't answer, thinking about how the gen-cycle and Shield of Repentance complicated the matter. I'd promised Iganakuchax̂ not to tell a soul about this latter subject, not even Aniqdux̂six̂. How could I craft a response to my distraught lover and not allude to it? In my silence, she turned and covered her face, breaking down in tears.

I couldn't bear to see her cry, to hear the continual suffering of her eternal soul. While I hadn't come to the realization in a straight line, I had discovered that she was the most cherished thing in my life. I had no choice but to break a lesser vow: "The Shield of Repentance," I began.

She spun around with an air of shock, her octopus ink eyeliner dripping down her face like immortal black tears.

"And fire witching," I continued boldly, knowing the rest of the barabara had gone down to the beach to continue harvesting the whale (Aniqdux̂six̂ had told me as much, when she had returned from the festivity early, only to find me in her room arranging my belongings to leave). "You must tell no one," I grimly warned; "but Iganakuchax̂ has revealed to me—and me alone—how to make you mortal again, and I promised to assist with the operation as soon as I return from the battlefront."

Aniqdux̂six̂ lunged at me, slightly spreading her wings to move faster, and took me in her downy embrace. "Thou shalt do this for me, Kayuu?" she cried softly, her body trembling with each word, "so that we can be together as mortals?"

Holding the back of her skull with one hand, I rubbed my fingers through her hair and drew her ear close to my parting lips, speaking the words she longed to hear: "I shall be the operative. With the beating of my heart, my blood shall flow through you, and when the galvanizing force of light strikes down anew, your heart shall beat in concert with mine until our dying days."

"Assistant number two," she affirmed knowingly, weeping over my shoulder while trying to wipe her face.

"Yes, the operative," I repeated. "I promise you, Aniqdux̂six̂, our time will come."

She backed away, and holding my hands while crying black tears, she disclosed, "I've found the volcano we seek: Mount Cleveland, in the Islands of Four Mountains."

Mount Cleveland on Chuginadak Island (11th US Army Air Force photo, 1942)

"With the help of Iganakuchax̂, we can fly all the supplies to the caldera rim; it reaches exceedingly high, reaching into the sunlit heavens beyond the clouds."

"Hidden from the eyes of men," I offered.

"Yes, Jake, oh yes! We shall be espoused as mortals! All I ever wanted was to grow old and die with the one I love, which is thee, my *ugi*."

I'd heard this word before. It meant *husband* in Unangam Tunuu. While growing old and dying was the furthest thing from my mind, I knew I didn't want to live forever, and that she was the one for me. "*Txin yaktakug*," I replied in Aleut for *I love you*—a phrase I'd learned from her.

BROKEN TREATISES

"WHEN SHALL you be leaving?" Aniqdux̂six̂ asked, after a long embrace.

"Soon," was all I really knew.

"Then I must give you this." She lifted a *sax* jacket out from a wide basket. It was an exceptional piece of finery, replete with white guillemot feathers, pleated red flouncing, and brown sea otter fur.

"It's very handsome." I glided my fingers over the handiwork and feathers, then thanked her in Aleut: "*Qaĝaasakung*."

"I took me a year to make."

"Wow," was all I could say.

A distant drumming became audible.

"It's the cave clan," she said. "They're returning from the beach. I guess this will be our last bit of privacy for a while."

I knew fully well what she meant. Our time together was counting down in unknown measure until my fated departure. I held out a hand and offered, "*Txin iĝamaĝal taliĝing ii?*"

She effected a little curtsy and replied with a coy twinkle, "Yes, I shall take this dance with thee, Lieutenant Harper." We embraced again in the center of her room, at the side of the barabara, at the edge of an island in a far-flung archipelago known as the Aleutians, on a planet that was at war; and there we began to shuffle our feet in concert, slowly moving as one, our hearts beating together to the song of approaching drums.

About thirty minutes later, I was summoned to meet with Chief Aĝnakax̂ in his chambers, situated adjacent to the quarters of his wife Iganakuchax̂ and granddaughter Datuu, who were nowhere to be seen. Only Kuuyux, the shaman elder, was there with him. I was invited before a circular fire occupying the center of the partitioned roundhouse, where we sat down on plaited reed mats more or less facing one another.

"Nice *sax*," the chief said to break the ice, which sometimes he did, sometimes he didn't. "It looks like the work of Aniqdux̂six̂."

"Yes. It took her a year to make."

"Impressive," put in Kuuyux.

I was wondering where all this was going, and assumed they were merely happy I'd soon be leaving.

"She's always been creative with things," remarked the chief.

The shaman nodded in agreement.

"Jake," continued Aĝnakax̂, reverting to my American name, "with your departure being imminent, I wanted to talk more with you about the Japanese contention."

To me, his was a significant admission. Finally he was willing to talk reality beyond his vulnerable Boot Bay settlement. "I fear for my clan," he admitted, leaning over to give me a gourd full of purple liquid.

"What is this?" I inquired.

"Spring berry juice, made just today by Iganakuchax̂. It's her specialty, and does well in trade. She wanted you to try some before you left; something to sweeten your memory of her, she said. But as I was saying," (—as I sipped the juice—) "I've come to consider more seriously what you say about the Japanese, and I can tell you, now that you will soon be departed, that they are currently on-island, amassing at Three Arm Bay."

I practically spat out my juice.

"On the North Arm, to be specific."

Imperial Japanese Forces on Aleutian Islands (Photo first issued by the Japanese Newspaper Publishing Company on December 8, 1942 in commemoration of the first anniversary of the DAITOUA war. DAITOUA is the name of the Pacific War of Japan)

Now I was spitting up for real, and not only because of what he was saying. My mouth was foaming and my vision was starting to swirl. I held out the gourd and demanded, "What the hell is this?! What have you given me?"

I called out for Iganakuchax̂ and then to Aniqdux̂six̂, but it was no use: I was gurgling on the poison mix and quickly losing consciousness. The last thing I remember was the chief and the shaman seated before me, patiently waiting for me to black out—or worse.

I awoke in a semiconscious state and, like in a bad dream, I was unable to move or speak. Kuuyux stood over me, chanting some diabolical-sounding incantation while Aĝnakax̂ proceeded to strip my boots from my feet. "Aniqdux̂six̂ was always a good cobbler," said he, throwing the boots into the fire, "but only we can fix the problem she's created in bringing you here."

I struggled to move, but could only twitch my eyes, for my body felt as if it were frozen stiff.

"You can hear me, Jake Harper," the chief continued over the shaman's chant, "but your body has been petrified by an age-old remedy, a variant of the monkshood root poison."

He removed my bentwood hat, made for me by Datuu, and tossed it into the pyre. "You may act the part and dress up in our style," he deemed as he extracted the sea lion whisker earring I'd won in battle, "but you'll never be one of us." He flung the whisker from his fingertips like a spear into the flames, and then he pulled out my three labrets and flicked them into the fire, as well. "We've known all along you've been testing our powers, searching for a weakness—an Achilles heel for you to strike at, but you've gravely underestimated our abilities."

He began removing my new *sax* jacket, which I'd been trying on for the first time when I was summoned to meet him. "The *promuishlenniki* plague did more than bestow us with wings and superhuman strength," he said, "it gave us centuries of time—time to test and retest our secret ways." He finagled Aniqdux̂six̂'s *sax* masterpiece from over my arms and head, holding it before the fire. "*Tsk-tsk-tsk*," he snickered cruelly, "what a shame to waste such finery. If only you hadn't worn it. But now it's tainted."

He cast it over the pyre. It momentarily floated upon the heat before settling back into the flames, its precious white feathers curling into black.

Tears spilled from the sides of my eyes; I could feel them trailing down my face.

"The monkshood root potion," he revealed, "in conjunction with the shaman's hex, shall erase your memory of Aniqdux̂six̂, because we don't want you returning for her. I believe your people call it hypnotism, but for you the spell is immutable."

"As for spells," put in Kuuyux, ceasing his chant, and then while crouching down over his timeworn reed sack, he lifted several volumes of Shakespeare into his bony hands, "there shall be no more wight magic from your insipid little wench." He tossed the books onto the fire.

Rage exploded from my core, breaking through my frosty stasis. I reached up for the shaman's neck, but he seized my arms and pinned me down. Kuuyux was unduly strong, belying his once-mortal age. His hoary face filled my sight, his coal-black eyes flaring red at their sides. "You don't belong here!" he scathed.

I curled my fingers and wriggled my arms but could not overcome his stone-heavy grip.

"You're a threat to our way of life!" he growled.

I spat in his face.

He wrapped his knotty fingers around my jaw and began squeezing it with a viselike grip. "I shall throw you into the fire!" He lifted me by his one hand attached to my face.

"*Nangaa!*" warned Aĝnakax̂, meaning *no!* in Unangam Tunuu. "We must stick to the plan!"

Kuuyux squeezed my jaw near the breaking point, glaring at me like a madman before throwing me back down against the reed mat. "Increase the aconite then!" he demanded. "This *Americanchin* won't know what hit him!"

"Enjoy this final word I speak to you, Jake," put in the chief, "because it's the last time you'll ever know it. Good-bye, Aniqdux̂six̂."

He struck me with a heavy blow and everything went black.

CHAPTER II
ADAK VAMP ATTACK!

DISTRESSED

I AWOKE in a snowy tundra bowl feeling numb all over. I was wearing my worn-out military fatigues, replete with weathered bomber jacket. My pistol was in its thigh holster, loaded and ready. My face and chin were pockmarked and sore, and I was beginning to shiver from the cold. I had no idea where I was, other than in some forlorn heathland depression.

I crawled up to the edge of the grassy knoll and looked down upon a large airfield situated beside a bay hemmed in by rocky, snowy mountains. Numerous warships lay at anchor, and several tenders were moving to and from the shore. A Flying Fortress lifted from the airstrip and buzzed by overhead, whereupon the gleam of sunrise illuminated a white star/blue circle insignia on its fuselage.

"Longview," I said groggily, settling my weary eyes back upon the expansive steel apron I'd helped to build by hand. With great effort, I forced myself to my feet and stumbled down the hill toward the Kuluk garrison.

This general view of the settlement at Adak with the barren Aleutian hills in the background suggests the bleakness of this American outpost. (AP photo and caption, Now It Can Be Told, Adak, Aleutian Islands, ref#A-55604, 1945)

"Jesus Christ," remarked a flight mechanic as I shambled onto his airplane revetment. "I don't believe my eyes."

"Is that Jake Harper?" said another, sliding off the wing of a Flying Fortress. "Holy mackerel! He's alive!"

They came to my either side and half-carried me through a maze of petrol drums, aircraft maintenance equipment, and debris. I was taken past the Canadian encampment to the Navy Seabees barracks—a small city of pyramidal tents pitched deep into the snowy tundra. The campsites themselves were further shored up by black oil barrels stacked into low, circular walls. The cantonment beyond housed the slightly better off tents and Quonset huts of the heavy-bombardment squadron, but I had no such luck in continuing down there: I was taken into one of the pitiable muskeg hovels occupied by the US Navy Construction Battalion (aka Seabees) and Army Corps of Engineers, the general sodden condition of which had hardly changed in my absence. And so too, were the rugged men who existed inside them fundamentally unchanged, or rather, the deprivations I'd left behind had only grown worse with them, in this far-off base where provisions were always in short supply.

Three servicemen, partially unshaven and wearied by the harsh Aleutian conditions, studied me over with great curiosity. "What happened?" one asked.

"Who is he?" inquired another, whose face was blotched with oil stains.

"Lieutenant Jake Harper," replied the carrier on my right, "from Rommel spike recon, remember? He went missing last fall."

"Jake, can you speak?" inquired an engineer named Steve Nelson who I recalled from the 807th.

"I, I—" I coughed.

*Tents and Quonset huts of heavy bombardment squadron
on Adak (Painting by Ogden Pleissner, 1944)*

"Just take it easy, Jake," he said, surrendering his cot to me, "we'll get you warmed up. Hey Charley! Bring us a cup of joe, will ya?"

Shortly a serviceman wearing a blanket as a scarf came over and introduced himself as: "Charley Hawkins, E-2 Seabee Constructionman. Pleased to meet you, Lieutenant Harper." He handed me a steaming tin cup of coffee, which I cradled in my hands to help warm me up. "Sorry about the low altitude chill," he said. "The hot air gets stuck at the top of the tent. Sitting down here, you're in Antarctica."

"Just as I remember it," I mumbled, barley able to move my lips. "You gotta defrost yer boots on the stovetop."

"Atta boy!" exclaimed Steve, pulling off his wool-knit cap and placing it on my head. "Your brain hasn't gone numb after all!"

"Where you from anyway, lieutenant?" Charley asked.

"Ohio," I said. "Yourself?"

"Brooklyn. I thought by now I'd be at some white sand beach in the South Pacific, partying it up with the Japs. Who woulda guessed I'd wind up in Snow White's crapper? This is worse than winters back home."

We all shared a knowing chuckle.

Alaska US Engineers Corps Member during World War II (News of the Day newsreel image by International Sound Photo, 1943)

One of the guys pulled on a pair of flight goggles and said he was going down to the command post to inform General Buckner that I was back. I wondered why he needed flight goggles for that. But then minutes later a williwaw blew in, stretching the tent like a lean-to.

Steve was rubbing his arms fast—even through his thick bomber jacket he was trying to stay warm as the tempest ripped at the tent flaps. I offered him his hat back, but he refused, explaining he'd warm up soon because the collapsing tent was starting to circulate the air more equitably, "like inside an accordion," he said. "I'd feel a heck of lot better if I was in a Quonset hut!" he remarked over the roaring blizzard. "A few weeks ago six tents just like ours were ripped clean from their foundations, leaving the guys inside wide open to the elements. It's a miracle they survived the whiteout with all their toes intact. Would you believe their tents were never found?"

"No kidding?" I tried to mutter over the storm.

"That was when the wind meter at the command post snapped off its pole," Charley added. "They found it in the snow eighty feet away with its pointer frozen solid at a hundred and thirty-four miles per hour."

"It's a good thing you're dug into revetments," I said. "I still can't believe the planes make it through this shit."

"Keeping them anchored down is tough enough," put in Steve. "I fear for the pilots who get stuck flying in a williwaw."

"Many never make it back," added a guy in a Seabee jacket, just awakened from his cot by the storm's commotion.

"Tom, this is Lieutenant Harper," Charley introduced us. "He's the guy who went missing last year while on Rommel spike recon. Jake, you made it back just in time, judging from this storm."

"Lieutenant Jake Harper?" Tom said. "Lord have mercy, you're still alive! What happened? How'd you pull through out there for so long?"

They were all watching intensely for my response. I sipped my coffee and said, "I got snagged by a screw picket, then became lost in a williwaw. I made fires, shot birds and seals for food; that's about all I can remember."

"Frozen water tanks at foot of Mt. Moffet" (So reads Lt. Harper's cursive on the back of this exclusive photo dated 1943. His survival alone, outside in such a mercurial climate for an extended period of time, would not go unquestioned even today)

"What the heck is a lieutenant like you doing on Rommel stake recon?" inquired Tom, whose jacket patch indicated his rank as Seaman, First Class.

"Or tinkering with Marsden matting, for that matter?" added Charley, the other enlisted constructionman.

"Go easy on him, boys," said Steve. "He's still a little adaky-wacky—even worse than us after what he's been through."

"Nah, I'm all right, Steve," I replied. "But to answer you guys' questions, I got my rank from West Point, but I got my jobs from volunteering. I was with one of the first units on Adak. I was keen to roll up my sleeves and help build the runway—there was only so much a lieutenant could do out here without an operational front. I took the screw picket gig to keep useful until some sort of land operation materialized. I can't fly airplanes and am not one to sit around pushing papers while the Japs are tromping around these islands of ours."

"You graduated from West Point?" asked Charley with a twinge of excitement.

"That's right, soldier. All grads exit as second lieutenant."

"Jake here's the humble type," remarked Steve, who knew me from my time with the 807th Aviation Engineering Battalion. "The way he gets his hands dirty, you'd never guess he's two hash marks [service stripes] above us."

"Thanks, Steve, but if I'm above you, it's only in rank. In this war, every man is of equal importance to the overall effort."

The guy who'd gone to the command post came in from the blizzard, a horrendous flurry of snow blowing open the tent flaps as he entered; it took all hands to wrest the whipping canvas doors back into submission. The messenger's goggles, meanwhile, were frozen so stiff with snow and ice that he was as good as blind and could barely remove them from his head. I helped him through his conundrum. He thanked me with chattering teeth, and then thanked the Lord for the guide ropes outside, saying that without them, he would've "wandered all the way to Jack Frost's funeral." As it turns out, Jack Frost was his name. He was a Private First Class (Pfc) in the army. After formally exchanging chatters, he relayed an order from General Buckner that I be brought forward for immediate processing.

"Buckner's gonna have to stew his ass for the moment," Steve growled.

"We can't send you back out in this crap," Charley explained, refilling my tin mug with steaming hot coffee. "Or you," he added, pouring Jack Frost a fresh cup, as well. Poor Jack was so rattled with cold that he could barely keep the coffee inside his mug.

Charley helped Private Frost over to the burning stove and said, "What do y'all say I whip up a few hotcakes?"

"You do that, Charley!" Tom replied eagerly, wrapping his woolen blanket more snugly around him.

The U.S. military establishes a cold foothold in the far western Aleutian Islands, where ice-box like conditions prevail. (AP photo and caption, 1942)

"Hey guys," I asked, "what day is it, anyway?"

"April twenty-six, nineteen forty-three," frosty Jack chattered between sips.

"When did I go missing, exactly?"

"Early last December," Steve recalled.

As Charley's watery batter sizzled over the griddle, the guys filled me in on the war's progress. Steve Nelson began with himself, stating he'd become a Tech/5, which was one of several new "Technician" ranks designated for army engineers. I then learned that Simon Buckner Jr. was still in command of the Alaska troops and was now overseeing Brigadier General William Butler's Eleventh Air Force. Adak had become a major airbase in the operations against Kiska and Attu, but the ever-changing and mostly terrible flying weather often thwarted daily objectives. Bombs would stick to the tarmac and planes would freeze over. Much of what these boys did, aside from defrosting frozen pancake batter, was to keep the planes warm and combat-ready—which was hard enough. Aircraft were impossible to defrost at 40 degrees below zero, oil froze solid, and rubber and metal parts cracked like fresh Christmas brittle. In Adak, it was said that only pilots ever saw the sun, when they flew above chilling fog.

Fighting the weather is part of Aleutian job. Gale rages about planes on Adak—Consolidated Catalinas (PBY) long-range flying boats weather a 60-knot wind and snow storm on Adak Island, American base in the Aleutians. Crouched low, a ground crewman makes his way against the wind. (US Navy photo and caption, 1943)

A major big ship duel had transpired in my absence: The Battle of the Komandorskis went down on March 26 near the Soviet Komandorski Islands, where our naval fleet went to break a Japanese resupply convoy heading to the Aleutians. What our navy didn't know at the time was that the Jap convoy was being escorted by numerous cruisers and destroyers, outgunning them by a long shot. Rear Admiral Charles McMorris and U.S. Fleet Commander Admiral Kinkaid, through sheer tactical ingenuity, managed to outmaneuver Admiral Hosogaya's convoy and break the supply line, sinking *forty* enemy ships in the process. "The Japs haven't tried to deliver by boat since," joked Tom, an enlisted navy man. "Sub-mail only."

We laughed over our steaming hotcakes and coffee, even as the williwaw continued to bend our tent like Gumby's head.

"How about Miles?" I inquired. "Corporal Miles Perkins with the eight-o-seventh?"

"He was sent to build a new airfield on Amchitka," Steve acknowledged. "It's just seventy miles from the Jap stronghold at Kiska."

"Marsden matting?" I asked, having become a believer in its versatility and strength.

"It appears so."

"By comparison," put in Pfc Frost, his clanking teeth now under control, "Adak is two hundred and fifty miles from Kiska, so the Amchitka apron will greatly reduce fly time."

"Yeah," Brooklyn Seabee Charley added, "and over two thousand guys were sent to build it, so it must be an A-level priority. Most of us fellers were needed to stay back here in Adak, though. This is still the big forward base on the chain; we're the only guys with any real harbor facilities west of Dutch Harbor. There's something hot brewing in these parts. We've been told to get ready for a big jump in activity soon, in ships, planes, and men, but haven't been told exactly what's afoot."

"Has there been much harassment here by Jap planes?" I inquired. "I saw some Zeroes buzzing around over no-man's land."

"Their bombing and strafing has dropped off a lot in recent months," Tom replied. "We're pretty well defended now, thanks in large part to the Two Hundred and Sixteenth Coast Artillery and the addition of Canadian flyboys. Meanwhile, the Japs' nearest fighter strip on Kiska has been bombed to shreds by our Flying Fortresses. But sometimes the Japs still make awkward attempts at recon here."

"Their Zeroes and Rufes have suffered strong attrition," added Pfc Frost.

Soldiers at a US Army observation post on Adak Island in the Aleutians chain watch an American plane winging over Kuluk Bay. Adak has been developed into a strong US base for air attacks on Japanese-held Kiska 244 miles away. Moments after this photo was taken, a williwaw blew in. (US Office of War Information photo and caption, August 29, 1943)

AFTER THE WILLIWAW

ONCE THE screaming downdraft of sleet had passed, I went to see Major General Simon Buckner Jr. in his central command post. I stood in salute. He ordered "at ease." I placed my feet about sixteen inches apart. His office was very busy, with people coming in from adjacent rooms to deliver reports and communiqués. As for the man himself, he appeared very much the general of renown I'd always heard about. He had an oval-shaped face and ruddy complexion, but with dark eyes and a stern gaze. His hair was short, white, and parted to one side, giving the fifty-four-year-old an almost boyish look. That he was fond of the great outdoors was evident in his broad shoulders, giving him the girth of a lumberjack, while his wind-burned cheeks evinced a man bred for action. "Do you know who I am?" he asked, never getting up from his desk.

"Of course, sir—you are the army commander of the Alaska Defense Command."

A GI of negro descent came in with an urgent dispatch. Buckner looked at him critically before snatching the communiqué from his hands, telling him to remain there for a moment while he read it.

While the general was scanning the document, the messenger began to shiver on account of an open window nearby, so he went over and closed it.

Buckner obstreperously pushed back his chair, vaulted up, and angrily marched over to the window, throwing it back open with a *slam*! "This window stays open!" he spat. "It always stays open, even in a williwaw! And if the Japs fly over, I'll sooner turn out the lights than deny myself fresh air! Go, make yourself useful, and fetch me some blackout paper, Buffalo Soldier!"

"Yes, sir," replied the colored GI. He turned to leave and I saw his expression go sour.

Lieutenant General Simon Bolivar Buckner, Jr. commanded our forces in Alaska since he arrived there in the summer of 1940 to fortify and garrison the vast area. Gen. Buckner is a former commandant of the Military Academy at West Point, honor graduate of the Command and General Staff School, and former Executive Officer of the Army War College. (AP Newsfeatures photo and Wide World caption dated March 4, 1943)

Buckner was an old Southerner, you see, and his father, Simon Bolivar Buckner Sr., had been a confederate general and onetime governor of Kentucky. That was no excuse for his prejudice, but still he made little attempt to hide it. I'd heard about this sentiment of his from some of the guys in the 383rd

Port Battalion, whose job was to unload ships coming into Adak, but this was the first—and not only—time I'd be privy to it. "What else do you know about me?" he asked.

If he only knew what I was really thinking! But I held to the formal response he was probably seeking: "You command the troops in Alaska, including Brigadier General William Butler's Eleventh Air Force."

"Very good, lieutenant," he acknowledged, looking very pleased. "Yes, General Butler is answerable to me, and I am answerable to Lieutenant General John L. DeWitt, the head of Western Defense Command, while we are answerable to Admiral Kinkaid, who is responsible for coordinating our collective forces to retake the Aleutian Islands from the Japanese."

Key Men in the Aleutian Campaign, *pose for a group photo on Adak Island's newly constructed Marsden matting airstrip, from left to right: Admiral Thomas C. Kinkaid, Lieutenant General John L. DeWitt, Rear Admiral Charles McMorris, Lieutenant General Simon Buckner, Brigadier General William Butler, and Colonel William O. Earkeckson. A significant missing person is General E. M. Landrum, Commander of the Aleutian Island Forces on Attu, whose role would take on greater prominence later in the engagement. (Official photograph of the U.S. Navy, 1942–1943)*

"As for you, Lieutenant Harper," Buckner continued, "I have reviewed your file and know you militarily, but what happened to you here on Adak? Where the hell did you go?"

"I was on Rommel stake recon. I'd been hiking for several days, working my way west, when I stepped on a screw picket hidden in the muskeg. I'd scarcely time to free my leg before a nasty williwaw blew in."

"They're all nasty, lieutenant, but go on."

"My tent got carried away in the storm as I was trying to set it up, so I cut a flap in the muskeg and peeled the sod back, then slipped beneath the muck like a knife in a scabbard, and there I slept. It kept the windchill out, probably saving my life in those first few days. I eventually raised the peat flap up on Rommel stakes, making a lean-to of sorts, then expanded the space beneath it into an underground den, building small fires to keep the tight quarters warm."

Buckner's brows curled inquisitively. I pressed my shirt pocket, and sure enough my Zippo was still there. It felt as if it'd been refueled. I showed the lighter to Buckner, who wrested it from my hands and flicked the flint. It still worked! The gas smelled strange to him, but I easily recognized it as whale oil.

"What'd you find to burn out there?" he probed.

"Wild rye and driftwood, mostly."

"Wild rye? In winter?"

"I'd gather the brown grass from beneath the snow and dry it out. It makes great kindling. Even muskeg will burn after a time."

"What'd you eat, Wheaties?" he pried. "Your fatigues look tired, but I see a hale stature beneath them."

"Fowl, fox, murre eggs—whatever I could get my hands on. I was able to shoot some birds and sea lions, supplying good protein."

He eyed my pistol in my thigh holster strap, his suspicious glare soon waxing into a look of utter fascination. "Remarkable," he conceded.

"When you have limited ammo," I qualified, "you learn to use it wisely."

Buckner drew closer, then grabbed my jaw and studied my face and ears. "You have fresh prick marks on your face and holes in your chin and ears. Explain yourself, lieutenant."

"I must've been cut up by the icy muskeg as I crawled back to base. Toward the end of my ordeal, I was half frostbitten and in a real bad state. This morning's williwaw would've done me in, had I not made it back when I did."

He studied my ragged clothes and they seemed to add credence to my story. He raised his shoulders and brows, then dropped them with a resigned exhale. "Remarkable;" he repeated, shaking his head in lingering disbelief, "truly a remarkable story, lieutenant."

He went over and closed the two doors connecting his office to the adjacent rooms, then said, "As second lieutenant, you should've been cleared on the classified objective regarding the Rommel stake assignment here on Adak."

"Yes, sir," I confirmed: "To terrestrially scout out possible enemy presence on-island."

"Well, did you find any?"

"Enemy? No sir, only Rommel spikes and screw pickets, but I did spot a Zero or two flying overhead on rare occasion, and I found test holes where the Japs had explored possible airfield sites."

"But you saw nobody out there?"

"Not a soul."

"No enemy ships, subs, landing craft, or tents, even abandoned?"

"No sir. Why, do you think the Japs are on-island?"

"That's classified."

"I take that as a yes, general."

He chuckled wryly.

A missive came floating in over the transom, landing on the wood beam floor. As Buckner went to pick it up, he asked if there was anything else I cared to report concerning my ordeal.

"No sir, nothing of military interest anyway, but I am concerned about the war effort. I've been gone far too long at this critical time."

As he scanned his latest communiqué, he replied concurrently, "What I have time to tell you, lieutenant, is that until recently our primary objective was to bomb the hell out of Boodle, weather permitting." He was referring to the island of Kiska. I hadn't been gone *that* long.

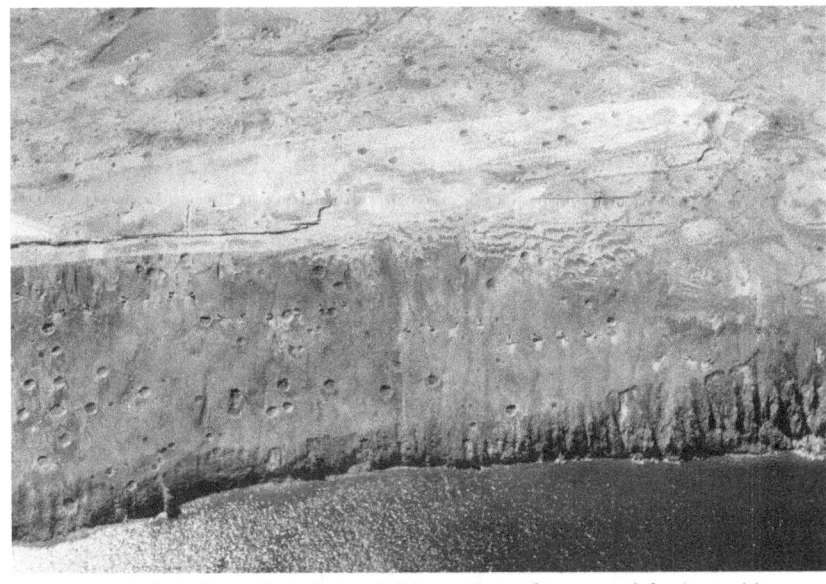

". . . Bomb the hell out of Boodle." Aerial recon photo of Japanese defensive positions on the US Island of Kiska, where a major Jap airstrip in construction is seen cratered by 11th US Army Air Force bomb blasts, along with the coastal bluff adjacent (Exclusive 1943 photo as part of the "magnetic album" [photo #26] attributed to Clyde Royden sample, Rank: PHOM c/3, Photographers Mate 3rd Class)

"You'll see Flying Fortresses around here these days," he added, "but the primary objective has recently changed with a major action already underway."

I pressed him for details.

"In due time," he said, setting his dispatch aside, "you'll learn the details concerning Operation Landcrab. For now, I'm ordering you to the infirmary for a full physical."

"I feel fine, general. I'm ready to return to service in Operation Landcrab or any other action against the Japs." The fact was, I still felt groggy as hell, but did my best to raise my chin and steady my line of sight.

"I appreciate your dedication to duty, lieutenant." He resumed his seat behind his desk. "We have much in common, it seems. Did you know that I graduated from West Point exactly thirty years before you?"

"Is that so?"

"Yes, in nineteen-o-nine. As a colleague of sorts, I know what you're made of and, like me, you seem to thrive in the great outdoors. But for now, I'm standing by my orders to send you to the Naval Hospital to get fully checked out. You've been through hell, soldier, and while you appear to have come out on top, we need to know for sure that you're not harboring some sort of illness and that your leg has properly healed. If and when you're confirmed healthy, I'll personally grant your request for redeployment."

"Yes, sir."

"It's been a real pain in the ass getting troops and materiel up here, lieutenant. Our northern front has been given a backseat to the South Pacific and European theaters, which is a tactical mistake in my book. The Japs may've taken Tarawa and Guadalcanal, but they're already here occupying American soil, for Christ's sake! Why have we been constantly on the defensive here when we should be on the offensive? With a little more backing from CINPAC, we could just as easily be driving the

Japs back to their naval base at Paramushiro, from where we could launch a direct invasion on Tokyo."

Heavy bombers take off from Adak to raid Japanese naval base of Paramushiro in the Kurile Islands (Painting by Ogden Pleissner, 1944)

"True, general. I am in full agreement."

"Thank you, lieutenant, but let's not get ahead of ourselves. To the medical station with you; they'll look you over and give you a warmer bed than what most troops have here at present." He got up from his chair. "For now I have an important lunch to attend with General Butler and Admiral Kinkaid."

PRIDE AND PREJUDICE

THE MEDICS at the field hospital were amazed that, aside from my grogginess and pockmarked face, I was in exceptional health and my leg had healed perfectly, with only a faint pink scar remaining. I attributed it to the cold, preventing infection, and a splint I said I'd made from whalebones, plus daily exercises I did to keep warm.

While I was lazing about my cot, reading a six-week old newspaper, the guys from the airfield tent came over with cigarettes and booze, which were real rarities out in Adak. Charlie even brought me cold pancakes with two sugar packets. While sugar was also very rare, cold pancakes were becoming all too common around here, as were cold green beans eaten straight from the can. The resupply ships often had to wait out stormy weather and seas before coming ashore, while ovens, even in the field hospital, frequently failed.

Jack Frost kept cajoling the navy nurses; the other fellers never ceased offering the white birds hearty smiles. You see, women were also a rarity in these parts, but we all respected their duties and didn't bandy them *too* much. The nurses often gossiped together, but it'd be disingenuous to say that we guys didn't frequently engage in the same wartime pastime as well.

All levity aside, my fellow soldiers were about to deliver a report of great consequence, for they'd just been filled in concerning the details of Operation Landcrab: "The Japs are deeply entrenched in Attu now," explained Private Frost. "Last month, CINCPAC and General DeWitt issued a joint directive to Admiral Rockwell to plan a large-scale operation against Attu, with Admiral Kinkaid to coordinate the whole thing."

"Kinkaid?"

"There's been a change in command since you've been gone. Rear Admiral Theobald had been muddying the army brass's blue suede shoes, so they got Admiral Kinkaid to replace him as commander of the North Pacific Force. Thomas Kinkaid was already serving as commander of Allied Naval Forces."

"I know who he is. I'm just surprised to hear Fuzzy got canned."

"So were we."

Hard-working navy nurses, assigned to the Naval Hospital at Adak, Alaska, spend their off hours hiking over tundra covered mountains and old volcano peaks. Overlooking one of the many bays on their Aleutian Island are (left to right) Ensigns Gertrude Merz, Eleanor Miller, Margaret Allen, Lt. (JG) Mildred Terrill, who is the Chief Nurse, and Ensigns Alberta Krape, Stephanie Kore, and Bettie Eberhardt. (New York Bureau Press photo, 1943)

"When is D-Day for Operation Landcrab?" I inquired.

"Nobody's been able to figure that out yet," answered Tech/5 Steve. "But we've been told to anticipate a sharp increase in our planes, boats, and men any day now, so I reckon it's imminent. The Fourth Infantry are already under sail, bound for Adak, and rumors are afoot of a much larger convoy of ten thousand infantrymen, maybe the Seventh, presently stopped over in Cold Harbor en route."

"So this is it—finally the big *putsch*."

"That's exactly what Buckner called it," replied Pfc Frost. "The big *putsch*."

"Well, the general and I went to the same military academy, so go figure," I explained. "That's how we sometimes describe a secretive attack."

Bizarre Battleground: Attu Island. This is an aerial view of Attu Island, with Cape Wrangel, the westernmost tip of the North American continent, in the foreground. The photograph reveals the mountainous terrain. Fogs that usually enshroud the island prevent all but the rarest opportunities for making a picture such as this. (AP photo and caption, 1943)

In Private Jack's estimation, the general and I had a way with words that none of them had. As he got to talking about Buckner, he said the general was always to the point with his subordinates, while the real point was always something different that only the general and his high brass knew. Regardless, Jack said he'd follow Simon Buckner to the gates of hell, because the general had a sharp gleam in his eyes "like a steel sword driving straight at the Japs."

"I guess it takes a stiff-ass to run the army," grumbled Steve.

I had to chuckle, but both these fellers had Buckner right: the general was sharp-witted and eloquent, but sometimes came off as uncompromising in a bad way.

Seabee Tom, for his part, reckoned Buckner was a fitting commander for the army forces in Alaska, noting that he'd been protecting Alaska since 1940, when he was made commander of the army's Alaska Defense Command. Tom was also a constructionman, which meant he spent a lot of time out in blizzards, digging through the snow and muck of Adak as he laid down runways and built revetments. He said he often saw the general milling about the garrison, the brutal climate never seeming to faze the ruddy-faced Kentuckian.

I relayed to them my story of Buckner's insistence on keeping a window open in his office, "even in a williwaw." The guys had a hoot. That should tell you how intense a williwaw was.

"Yeah, well no disrespect to the old man [i.e., the commanding officer: Buckner]," offered Charley, "but he's not out there shoveling the mud out of his tent or digging up screw pickets like the rest of us. I heard he got all his experience from West Point academics; it's not like he plucked his medals from frontline trenches."

"Give the general a chance, fellas," rejoined Private Frost. "Even with his high-heeled gummies, I still wouldn't take this post if you paid me."

We all had a yuk at that, too. The fact was, the guys were stuck out here in Adak purgatory, wearing wet leather boots and getting paid a hell of a lot less than the general. Our salary was doled out in script on a monthly basis, and the script was redeemable for cash at the military exchanges. Problem was, Adak was always so short on provisions that there was nothing to buy on base, and our base being an island meant that if the salmon weren't running, cold pancakes with sugar and rum syrup was the best a guy could ask for on Christmas Day.

"Buckner seems alright by me," I deemed, "but he's really got it out for the blacks." The US military barred African Americans from higher ranking positions such as commissioned officers, segregated their units from those of whites, and kept them mostly in secondary service and support roles. Even with over one million African Americans serving in the war, top brass establishment holdouts such as Buckner still clung to their age-old prejudices. Blacks were not permitted to join the marines or carry weapons, and very few were allowed into the army and navy air forces.

Private Bates, an African American serviceman stationed at Adak Island (Exclusive photo by Lt. Harper, 1942–1943)

The general's prejudice did not sit well with guys like me from the northern states, however, nor with the squids who brushed shoulders with the negroes of Company A down at the docks and found them to be just like everybody else at heart—or friendlier. But it was 1943, and such impartial sentiments about African Americans had a narrow audience among whites. The question that really haunted me about Buckner was, given his treatment of blacks, what would be his treatment of Aleuts? As army commander of the Alaska Defense Command, his power over their territory was disturbingly vast.

The very next day, on April 27, 1943, Adak Central Command declassified the news across the garrison that the Japs were here on-island, deeply entrenched in Three Arm Bay. An imminent joint Canadian/US offensive was set to jump off at first light tomorrow, April 28. This was startling news, even more nail-biting than Operation Landcrab's pending jump on Attu. As many as 10,000 Japs were confirmed on west Adak, merely a day's hike from Longview.

"... The Japs are confirmed deeply entrenched on-island." (Propaganda postcard issued by the Imperial Japanese Army, showing its soldiers well acclimated to the Aleutian environment, deeply entrenched, and eager to defend its new foothold on American soil)

I tried to get the nurses to organize my medical report to forward to General Buckner, but a flurry of recent trench foot cases made it difficult for me to pin any of them down. It was only when I demanded to speak with the head field nurse "on behalf of General Simon Buckner" did I get my case moving.

The chief nurse, Lt. (JG) Mildred Terrill, was quick to wrangle in some of her subordinates, who procured my abstract in no time. She was surprised to find nothing checked on my chart aside from "bed rest." She prodded one of her minions for an explanation, and the nurse in question confirmed that I had no medical indications aside from signs of scarring on my leg and face, and a general lethargy. I'd been submitted to the hospital by request of General Buckner, she noted. Given that, I knew I'd probably stay there until I rotted, lest he submit another directive ordering my discharge.

Lt. (JG) Mildred Terrill stuffed my chart into a manila envelope, along with a note I'd scribbled out to Buckner requesting my immediate release from the Naval Hospital in order to join in flushing out the Japs from west Adak.

Ten hours later, I'd yet to receive a reply. I'd attempted several times that night to leave the Quonset hut on my own accord, but wasn't allowed so much as my fatigues without an official discharge notice from Buckner—and I wasn't going to get very far without my boots and jacket on a wintry Adak night. I eventually learned that my fatigues had been discarded on account of their abhorrent condition, but that still didn't answer my question of how long I'd have to remain there dressed in woolen socks, long john pajamas, and a beanie hat. I'd kept wishing the fellers back at the 807th barracks would come back for me, but that never transpired. At least they'd left me a quarter pint of rum and a couple of cigarettes.

Finally on April 29, after I'd dozed off, Buckner returned a missive. His cursive was so perfect that I had no problem reading it with my bleary, bloodshot eyes. He wrote that he'd taken stock of the sanguine report from the chief nurse regarding my condition and was consenting to my discharge. Furthermore, I was to be embedded with combat team 12-2, a composite group set to deploy the following morning, April 30. He was ordering me to their command post at once, directing me to check in with them and get outfitted. He'd already notified the field sergeant about my inclusion and pending arrival to the unit.

A pretty ensign nurse named Eleanor measured my waist with tape and took a close look at my feet, her Army Nurse Corps cap riding atop her brunette curls like a destroyer through heavy seas. The hat rolled from beam to beam but never lost its head-on bearing, steady as she goes. She left my bedside all too soon, only to return with some fresh fatigues and gummies—the latter courtesy of Buckner's private provisions, she relayed.

Fortunately, I had more in common with the general than a BS from West Point, which, without rubber boots, amounted to useless BS on this godforsaken island. The gummies fit swimmingly—so much so that I could wear two pairs of woolen socks inside them, which I deemed a great benefit judging from the GIs checking in with trench foot. I thanked Ensign Eleanor and she smiled back, casting a rare, warm glow over that cold, sepia-toned spring of 1943.

At long last, I was discharged from Adak's fledgling 179th Station Naval Hospital. I kept my beanie for the memories, but also to keep my noggin from freezing.

COMBAT TEAM 12-2

THE ELITE nature of composite group 12-2 became readily apparent, as I entered one of the few Quonset huts on base. In addition to the dedicated staging area, the operatives themselves—a mixture of some three score Canadian and American infantrymen—showed every sign of specialty and discipline. There were sharpshooters priming their low-profile, high caliber rifles; flamethrower operators adjusting the weight of their fuel packs; field medics wearing camouflage berets embroidered with red cross patches; and soldiers like me of higher rank who'd volunteered for a frontline assignment for no other reason than to bring our experience and grit directly to the Japs. My rank of second lieutenant was never publicly broached, but did not need to be, for before my discharge from the field hospital, Ensign Eleanor had fitted my fatigues with the dual gold bars of a commissioned officer. But only in the Quonset hut was I fitted with the accoutrements that would evince my pending break from the windy camps of Seabees and runway engineers. I was issued a "steel pot" helmet, a repetitive rifle, a belt of grenades, and two 200-round bullet links, which, for the time being, I draped across my chest in an "X" formation.

In a final briefing, I learned the details of our mission. Our detachment was to hike west across the center of the island, reconnoitering for Jap foot soldiers in the Adak hinterlands before taking part in a pincer movement to purge the enemy from the Three Arm Bay area, where they were reportedly deeply entrenched with Coast Defense guns. Due to operational concerns in the greater Aleutian theater, Buckner would not personally be taking part in this action he had ordered, but would ostensibly remain back at his Adak command post, communicating sitreps from there.

We jumped off at 04:00 the next morning, boarding an attack transport craft at Sweeper Cove, which took us around Lucky Point to the south, then southwest into Finger Bay, where we disembarked and began hiking west.

Our pack train (Exclusive photo and caption by Lt. Harper, Adak Island, 1943)

Trucks and transport vehicles were out of question, for besides alerting possible enemy positions to our advance, heavy machinery didn't stand a chance over the terrain. Hiking west alongside Lake Constant, we sank almost to our thighs into volcanic ash muck that lingered just beneath the icy topsoil. Some medium artillery that we tried to drag along was quickly abandoned to the quagmire, scuttled barrel-first to prevent enemy commandeering.

Infantry co. en route to Expedition Harbor pulling toboggan. Soldier in foreground has a loaded packbrack. (Exclusive image and caption by Lt. Harper, Adak Island, 1943. His peculiar spelling of "backpack" has not been altered from his original handwritten cursive as penned on the back of the photo)

Our advance was thus forcibly slow-going, allowing us abundant opportunities to scan the surrounding ridges for enemy snipers. We stopped several times at the foothills of slopes abounding with hillock caves but, in reconnoitering them, found no evidence of human presence, save for a few Aleut mummy bones.

The lowland muck began taking its toll on some of the men, who fell back with complaints of trench foot, their gummies caked with frozen mud.

A member of our group carrying rations sinks to his ankles in muck
(Exclusive photo and caption by Lt. Harper, Adak Island, 1943)

As Expedition Harbor came into view over the heathland tundra, it was a scout out in front who suffered the worst foot affliction. With an agonizing cry from the frontlines that caused the entire line behind to hit the muskeg for cover, believing they'd fallen under surprise attack, I spied the injured one ahead, still standing over his foot nailed fast to the sod; it could only have been an antipersonnel spike.

I rushed lamely through the muck toward the front, and sure enough, a Canadian GI had stepped on a Rommel stake. The pernicious steel rod had driven clear through his foot, frozen gummies and all, with the top five inches glistening red over his icy boot. As several fellow soldiers helped him reduce his weight over the affliction, I scanned the immediate area and spotted another spike poking above the sod several feet preceding me. With a great cry back, I warned everyone about pickets in our midst, telling them to use their rifles to sweep the heathland before each step.

Two unit medics arrived at the front shortly thereafter. I instructed them on what to do, then led the remainder of the regiment carefully forward.

Moments later, the GI left behind emitted another terrible scream: the field medics had dislodged his foot from the anti-personnel device, which had probably already become frozen stuck to his flesh, making the extraction all the more grisly.

Arriving at the small beachhead of Beverly Cove, several US warships were silhouetted in Expedition Harbor amid a 22:00 sunset. It'd been an all-day hike with no enemy spotted and only minor casualties sustained.

Two landing craft shortly arrived and shuttled us west across the waterway, to where we disembarked on a black sand beach and made camp above the high tide line.

Making camp along Ex. Harbor in 2-man mtn. tent (Exclusive photo and caption by Lt. Harper, 1943)

We'd have but one night to rest in pyramidal mountain tents and thick wool sleeping bags tendered in by transport crafts. Canned food was also delivered to our beach party. We cooked chili and beans, corned beef mulligan, and made hot coffee and cocoa on propane stoves within our tents; no external fires were permitted on account of the nearby enemy forces. Cigarettes had been provisioned for our enjoyment, along with ever-disappearing match packets.

The day's weather had been clear but cold—in the low teens—but as night fell, the temperature dropped even further. While four soldiers circulated on watch, the rest of us bedded down in the tomblike peace of our shelters, knowing fully well that on the morrow we'd be marching headlong into battle.

THE THREE-ARMED MONSTER

MAY 2, 1943. We broke camp in the black and donned our equipage. At 06:45, as the cobalt twilight gave definition to the snowcapped eastern ridgeline, we began our fateful march across the mile-long land bridge connecting Expedition Harbor to Three Arm Bay.

The Aleutian sunrise emerged all at once, jettisoning its fiery rays between the icy mountaintops and a low ceiling of clouds, clarifying targets for our maritime contingent. The preinvasion naval bombardment shortly commenced.

We halted our advance at the first report of shelling, which came in conjunction with sitreps to our radioman. Just as the enemy was deeply entrenched along the three-pronged peninsula ahead, so too were our forces peppered everywhere around them, presently serving them a military breakfast of scrambled munitions. For Combat Team 12-2 it equated to a full hour's rest made all the sweeter by the report of the hellfire the enemy was under. We sat back against the volcanic rocks, pointing our weapons lazily toward North Arm, our specially issued long johns helping to keep our asses from freezing off.

Train of U.S. infantry near 3-Arm Bay (Exclusive photo by Lt. Harper, 1943. It is not clear by the photo or caption if this is his unit, or other Allied brigades')

A repetitive rainsquall with no certain end cut short the softening-up bombardment, at which point the green light was given from the warships, via Buckner back at Longview, for the foot soldiers to continue forward.

With sporadic gunfire sounding from distant, unclear directions, we continued warily into the North Arm area, following the waterway's south shore out toward Central Point. Our mission was to flush the Japs from the Middle Arm peninsula—a thousand yard wide promontory extending to our south, reportedly deeply entrenched with enemy forces. We were to march along the North Arm halfway to Central Point before pushing southward across the fortified cape.

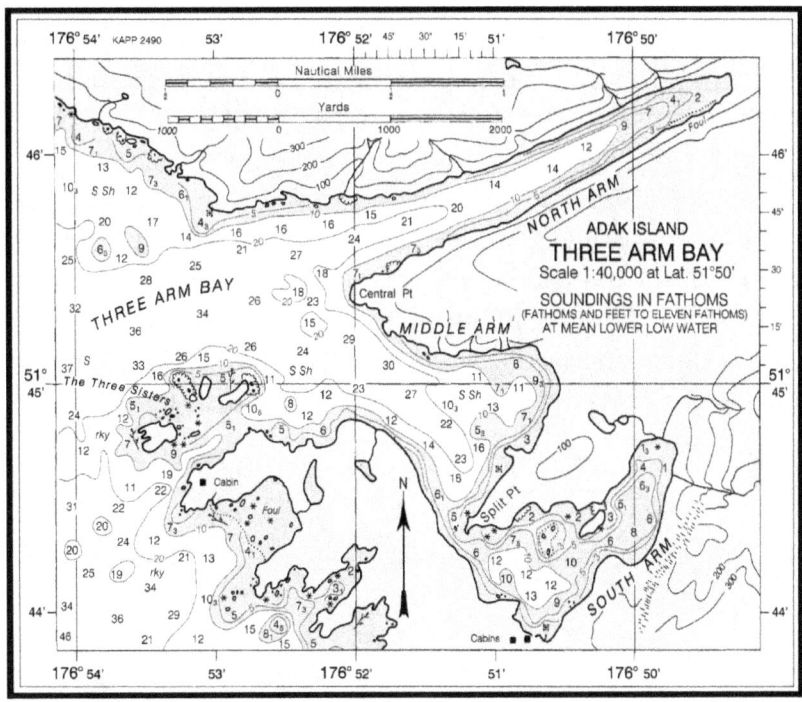

Three Arm Bay (Inset map courtesy of NOAA)

Other Allied brigades had already been deployed onto an opposing peninsula that stretched perpendicularly out into Three Arm Bay, culminating in series of islets called The Three Sisters Islands, and yet another detachment was to march on Split Point soon. But it'd been made clear to us that, notwithstanding the preinvasion softening up and possible air support, there'd be no other infantrymen but us to neutralize the Middle Arm entrenchments.

It wasn't far along North Arm beach that we came upon a series of smoldering craters marking the site of an enemy battery that'd been bombed to shreds. Bloody limbs and broken big guns littered the muskeg shore embankments, with one dying Jap still trying to pull himself out of a hole. Discovering that his legs had been blown off at the knees, one of our men quickly put him out of his misery with a bullet to the head.

In response to the merciful bullet crack came a barrage of enemy fire from Argonne Point, some 500 yards across the North Arm waterway. We dove for cover along the shoreline embankments, slowly slithering back into the Middle Arm heathland. It would've been a waste of ammo trying to combat the Argonne Point contention from our position due to the sheer distance and our lack of long-range munitions: our armaments were primarily M1 rifles, machine guns, flamethrowers, and grenades.

(This uncaptioned photo was part of Lt. Harper's Adak Island collection, but it does not appear to be the North Arm waterway, due to no visible beach. However, it does serve as a general likeness of the area in question. Lt. Harper exclusive, 1943)

Our weapons were suited primarily for the close-combat needs of our expeditionary assignment, which was precisely what occurred next, with a surprise attack from the rear.

Diving into smoldering craters and muskeg holes for cover, we trained our arms south in an effort to counter the sudden blitzkrieg. Enemy artillery and machine gun fire was heavy, resulting in several swift unit 12-2 fatalities. Meanwhile, increasingly accurate artillery fire from Argonne Point caught us in a north-south pincer. Taking heat from both sides, we were squeezed into a westward retreat along Central Point, leaving three of our dead behind.

We took position among the rocky reefs and boulders fronting the open ocean, regrouping for a tactical reassessment; a phalanx of machine gunners stayed back to protect our rear. We hadn't anticipated a double-flanking spanking, which was a no-win situation for us due to the long-range weaponry being employed from the northern flank, which we did not possess.

With a lucky break in the rainsquall appearing to the west, our field commander, Sergeant Terrence Malloy, radioed for air support. Even as he was requesting flyover assistance, our machine gunners began opening up on advancing Jap foot soldiers to our east. The battle for Central Point had reached a critical state: we'd soon be driven off the land.

In the eight nail-biting minutes we waited for our request to relay through high command and back, a third of our remaining unit fanned out along the reefs in a secondary phalanx, providing backup for the beleaguered machine gunners at the frontline.

At last the reply came, courtesy of Buckner, that the army air forces were not to be used at present due to deteriorating weather.

"Deteriorating weather!" Sergeant Malloy spat, thrusting a forefinger toward the crack of blue sky appearing on the eastern horizon. Indeed, the forces on the ground had a visual of the improving meteorological conditions that apparently Buckner didn't, for a windward breeze was already pushing the gale over.

Air support for ground troops in the Aleutian theater was often, if not always, hampered by difficult terrain and uncompromising weather. On Attu especially, air support would have been almost entirely lacking if it were not for the expert flying and squadron guidance of Colonel Eareckson. He was not adverse to flying into tightly hemmed, fog enshrouded mountain valleys to deliver provisions to stranded troops, or to flying low enough to intentionally draw enemy antiaircraft fire in order to give away their positions. (Panel art from World War II comic strip, Kiska Surprise, *1946; no illustrator listed)*

As Malloy went to mount his protest over radio, he was beaten to the receiver with better news at last: Buckner was ordering the resumption of naval bombardment of all three east-west promontories. The Allies had yet to send ground troops onto the adjacent Split and Argonne Points, while we were ordered to "stay put and take cover" at the tip of the center fork, for the shelling was imminent and would be delivered directly over our heads.

Field Commander Malloy embellished upon this directive some, because we were still under attack from the east. To take cover now was tantamount to an open-door policy regarding the enemy advance on our rear. So we held our position on Central Point, which was ostensibly to remain beneath the trajectory of the naval gunfire, but we tripled our line against the enemy approaching from the east over greater Middle Arm.

As a task group of four US destroyers began hammering the three-pronged coastline and well inland over our heads, our recalibrated ground offensive forced an east-west pincer movement back upon the Japs, reversing them into the Middle Arm shelling zone with a blazing eastbound counterattack.

The Japs returned heavy fire seaward with big 4.7" Coast Defense guns mounted on the surrounding shores, scoring a visible hit on a destroyer, rendering it *hors de combat.*

Our three remaining warships continued to deliver a ferocious barrage of neutralizing fire with 14 inch shells, and, as we forced the enemy back into the Middle Arm kill zone, we drew perilously close to the incoming munitions ourselves.

After having driven the enemy back some three hundred yards, Sergeant Malloy ordered us to fall back half that distance, where we remained safely beneath the umbrella of falling ordnance.

The Japs didn't advance on us again, but continued their retreat eastward past the curtain of bombs, toward the sunrise hinterland.

"The Japs didn't advance on us again, but continued their retreat toward the sunrise hinterland." (Exclusive photo from the collection of Lt. Harper, 1943)

Thirty minutes into the engagement, a swift-moving fog closed in again from the west, and the heavy guns went silent from land and sea. As the blinding mist crept over the heathland, the report of small arms fire likewise fell off. All grew silent on the western front as we listened to Jap casualties moaning in agony in the killing fields to our east.

After radioing central command, Sgt. Malloy consolidated our forces to resume clearing out the beleaguered enemy, relaying the navy would hold its fire as we conducted mopping-up activities. Target areas on Middle Arm were believed to have been thoroughly covered by the naval bombardment, but frequent fogs made it impossible to verify this without ground reconnaissance. Malloy warned us to be on the lookout for sniper holdouts and booby traps.

I wasn't sure how all this would be possible in the fogbank, but I knew that an Aleutian fog could last for days and so I couldn't be too critical of the directive to advance if we were to secure any headway against the enemy. We'd taken only a few casualties, while the bulk of the opposing forces on Middle Arm were either dead, dying, or on the run. The weather shall not dictate to us at this juncture, such was the conviction of high command.

Sergeant Malloy devised a sweep of the half-mile wide peninsula whereby our unit would proceed up from the south shore of Middle Arm in a parallel line dragnet, clearing out the remaining Japanese forces from the promontory. Once Middle Arm was confirmed as silenced, we'd be poised to track the enemy who'd retreated into the eastern hinterlands without risking a counterattack from our rear. Flushing the Middle Arm peninsula had always been group 12-2's primary objective in the Three Arm Bay theater of operations. A further push into the eastern hills would require a forward command tactical reevaluation and resulting change in orders, the latter of which had not yet been handed down.

The south shore of Middle Arm had an abundance of rocky cave formations, which took some time to clear. On three separate occasions, Jap sniper holdouts opened up on us from the convoluted cavities, killing another of our troops and badly injuring two more.

Employing hand grenades and flamethrowers, we eventually purged the enemy from the rocky strongholds. Captured Japanese documents in the vicinity suggested the enemy forces in the Three Arm Bay theater numbered 8,000, but did not offer clear size numbers for Middle Arm specifically.

Once safely emplaced along the south beach, our phalanx proceeded north over the Middle Arm cape, each soldier responsible for ten meters of ground on his either side—about the distance of visibility in the blinding fog—totaling twenty meters apiece. This advancing "line interval" technique generally worked well in mopping-up operations.

The lowland peninsula was mostly bereft of snow, with only an occasional crusting of ice wedged betwixt the rocks. To my east sounded sporadic gunfire and the shouts of soldiers cooperating in my unit, but my biggest quandary thus far had been in negotiating around the many muddy, smoldering craters left by the naval bombardment, some of which were ten meters across, their slippery rims camouflaged by smoke and mist. In addition to this, frequent pockets of mangled bodies appeared around enemy entrenchments that'd been upended by our navy's heavy artillery. Moving around the dead and dying Japs required utmost vigilance—indeed, well into my march I was targeted by one of them. The Imperial Japanese soldiers had a nasty penchant of fighting to death, and on this instance a mortally wounded enemy gunner lobbed a grenade at me, which fortunately bounced down into an adjacent crater before going off. A piece of shrapnel tore through the cheek of the ally on my left flank, however, destroying one of his molars, which fortunately may've prevented further serious injury to him.

Nevertheless, the pain inflicted from such a wound sounded horrendous as he did his best, in vain, to mask his moaning. I told him to fall back to the field medics and that I would cover his ground ahead. He slung his rifle back over his shoulder and proceeded awkwardly but swiftly to the rear, holding his bloodied jaw with both hands. As for the offending enemy, I'd unloaded an abundance of rounds into him in the immediate aftermath of his ambush. He rolled back, dead, into the crater from whence he'd crawled.

Such was the general tenor of the advance, with sporadic gunfire and the rare explosion sounding through the fog on my peripheries. But all the while, I also heard the hale commands of my team, indicating that our northward sweep was gradually succeeding. Alas, as we came to the hillocks separating us from the North Arm waterway, all hell broke loose once again.

During our last pincer movement, when we pushed eastward at the enemy from Central Point, driving them back into the curtain of incoming ordnance from our combined naval gunfire, the south shore of the North Arm waterway had been left open due to the enemy's early crippling of the warship that'd been targeting it. Our compromised destroyer had commanded a superior volume of fire, and thus its neutralization resulted in a large number of Japanese soldiers fleeing up into the now unprotected beach corridor. Now, as our advancing line mounted the hillocks separating the heathland from the North Arm beachhead, believing our sweep was a foregone conclusion, we were met with a sudden barrage of enemy fire backed by Japanese shore batteries still intact on the opposite side of the North Arm fjord.

In the blitzkrieg, casualties suffered by composite group 12-2 were many and severe; we lost perhaps twenty infantrymen in those first short minutes. The terrific irony of the enemy's counterattack was its near semblance to the one we'd delivered to them when we drove them eastward from our entrapped position on Central Point into the kill zone of our naval bombardment; only now, we were being forced slowly southward by their reorganized beachhead forces into a hail of artillery fire being lobbed from their batteries on the Argonne Point ridge opposite the waterway. Their mortar rounds flew over their soldiers' heads in the thick fog and inflicted heavy casualties on us, for the east-west line of their foot soldiers along the beach provided their artillerymen on Argonne Point a clear-cut distance they'd need to overshoot in order to successfully lob shells into our position without risking friendly fire on their own troops.

In the ensuing mayhem, Sergeant Malloy shouted down our faltering line to dig into the heathland and wait it out. Our grim alternative was to retreat back through the killing fields, which were far more difficult to traverse with speed due to the heavy cover of fog and endless mud-lined craters, especially now with Japanese artillery raining down.

As I took shelter within some rocky crevices alongside my unit, the terse words that passed beneath our steel pot helmets suggested a more bullish assessment: combat team 12-2 would stay to once and for all finish the job. The enemy's back was against the frigid waterway and their Argonne Point artillery had to be growing low on ammunition. It was rumored that once the fog cleared (or sooner), a combined US naval assault would target the well-defiladed Argonne Point batteries, nullifying that key asset in the enemy's counteroffensive.

The final battle for the North Arm beachhead, and Allied victory, could be imminent, if only we held in. We gritted our teeth and reloaded our weapons, passing a pack of cigarettes from ditch to ditch. Staying alert to our comrades was critical, as was remaining calm under fire.

ADAK COMBAT NARRATIVES, CONTINUED

ENTRENCHING OURSELVES in the rocks and muskeg of the heathland enabled us good sniping positions against the Japs, who were spilling in piecemeal over the shoreline hillocks. We picked them off one by one with our M1s, and still had a few machine gunners on hand to mow down scores more. In this manner we held off the advancing forces, who clearly outnumbered us in men.

Twenty-five minutes later, the cotton-thick fog rolled back once again, and when it did, it was not a naval bombardment that transpired, which may've been too tricky given the west-to-east nature of the target line and our close proximity to it. Instead, to our utter surprise and delight, the army air force roared in from the east with Colonel William O. Eareckson leading the charge in his B-24 bomber, his ensign discernible on the fuselage.

As sharp as they come: Colonel William O. Eareckson upon graduation from West Point (Photo by USN archives, August 9, 1924)

The celebrated colonel swooped down into the North Arm followed by several Allied P-40D fighter jets in a surprise bombing sortie and strafing attack against the enemy troops amassed on the waterway's southern beachhead.

The squadron soon disappeared into the receding fogbank to the west, only to reappear minutes later for a renewed attack, this time targeting the south-facing mountainsides of Argonne Point across the North Arm fjord. A few of Eareckson's 100 pound demolition bombs found home, taking out the enemy's radio station and some big Coast Defense guns on the opposite slope. It was a welcome sight to behold, allowing unit 12-2 a fighting chance against the Jap ground forces their artillery had been backing.

(Panel art from World War II comic strip, Kiska Surprise, 1946; no illustrator listed)

But there was no shortage of antiaircraft fire being thrown up from the Japs' heavy 20mm and 25mm shore guns, the flak of which grazed a bomber's wings and then rained down upon my pinned-down team in a hail of hot iron.

Eareckson and his fighter escorts continued east out of the North Arm fjord once again, heading toward Expedition Harbor. We watched in eager anticipation for their return to neutralize the remaining shore batteries. But as the minutes ticked by and there was neither sight nor sound of the Allied squadron from either side, we grew despondent. In all likelihood, they'd run out of ammo and/or an aircraft had been compromised, necessitating a return to A-2 to re-up, which we all knew would take some time.

B-24 Liberator Bombers of the 404th cycling through on bombing runs in the Aleutian Islands (Dept. of US Navy photo and caption, 1943)

We gnawed on our cigarette butts and spat them out, preparing for the final push against the south beach contention, shore batteries be damned. In the engagement thus far, unit 12-2 had lost approximately half our fighting force, being reduced to about thirty able-bodied men, and while we couldn't clearly ascertain the number of Jap troops still commanding the southern beachhead due to the hillocks separating us from them, Sgt. Malloy sent down "a working estimate of several hundred."

As incoming artillery from the remaining Jap shore batteries inched closer upon our heels, we kept gunning down enemy combatants as they appeared on the hillocks before us.

Awaiting the final order to advance "in a line" worried me to no end. While the single parallel line advance had worked well in mopping up Middle Arm, it was a highly undesirable mode of *combat* for US ground forces in World War II because it was too easy to target and left each man open with no secondary cover of fire. The preferred method in an infantry offensive was to advance in a staggered sequence as individuals or in small groups, gaining ten yards or so with each push, conveying the unit forward in successive stages. But with the enemy shore batteries about to blow us to Timbuktu, there'd be no time to constantly reorganize. Ours would be an all-out frontal assault, the surprise attack hopefully throwing the enemy off-guard and enabling us to inflict enough casualties to at least gain the beachside hillocks, from where we could fire down upon their beachhead from higher ground.

The sudden sound of approaching aircraft caused Sergeant Malloy to halt his hand about to signal our blitz, for even he was surprised by the rapid return of planes, forestalling his directive to advance. He slowly lowered his arm and we all watched the skies with dread. The aircraft sounded a northwest approach, so possibly could be deadly Jap Zeroes buzzing in from their Kiska airstrip. (Inconstant weather had prevented the deployment of carrier aircraft from Allies and Nipponese alike.)

The unknown squadron roared in around Argonne Point flying incredibly low, then hemmed up the North Arm, skip-bombing shore emplacements as they went. We beheld the bombs bouncing off the water before slamming into enemy cannon with such force that severed artillery barrels twirled sky-high like giant logs flung weightlessly up behind our bombers.

(War Gum #92 *insert, Gum, Inc., 1942*)

Unit 12-2 erupted in cheers up and down our entrenched line. We knew without a doubt that Colonel Eareckson had returned, for he was the one who'd recently invented skip-bombing—a method quite dangerous to the pilot, but extremely effective against his targets.

Eareckson and his squadron's excellent success in destroying numerous pesky shore and hillock batteries enabled composite group 12-2 to move forward in the preferred "leapfrog" manner, having renewed confidence that the Japs' heavy costal artillery had been pretty well subdued and would not create an imminent crises to our concentrated entrenchments.

No Japanese air counterattack eventuated, which was a blessing because their Mitsubishi Zeroes were far superior to the Curtiss P40-D Warhawks escorting Eareckson's B-24s.

This is the fabled "Aleutian Zero," which crash-landed on Akutan Island almost fully intact. Its pilot, 19-year-old Tadayoshi Koga, was part of the June 4 raid on Dutch Harbor when his plane was damaged by small arms fire, rupturing the return oil line. Making an emergency landing on nearby Akutan Island (where a Japanese sub was waiting to retrieve him), his landing gear struck the deep muskeg, flinging his plane upside down and breaking the young pilot's neck, killing him instantly. The airplane was found intact by the Americans in July of 1942, where it was brought in for test flying and reverse engineering, which enabled American tacticians to finally learn how to defeat the Zero, the Japanese Navy's most formidable fighter plane. Thus, "Koga's Zero" has been regarded as "probably one of the greatest prizes of the Pacific War," as described by historian Larry Dwyer. (Image by photographer's mate Arthur W. Bauman, from the U.S. National Archives; public domain)

We gained critical yardage against the hillocks, bringing our machine guns and grenades close enough to do some serious damage to the enemy commanding them.

As we advanced in small groups, the fog returned in puffy, broken-up sections, like little white clouds rolling over the ground. The Aleuts couldn't be blamed for disdaining talk of the weather, because the Aleutian weather was so changeable that any such discussion was fundamentally irrelevant.

With the help of our flamethrowers, unit 12-2 at last took the tundra-clad hillocks, losing one Canadian among us: a certain Tech/3 and booby-trap specialist named Bernard Stroyman.

But no sooner had we gained an area of high ground over-looking the shore did we find ourselves taking a surge of heavy gunfire from Japs hiding in craters left by our aircraft bombardments, their snipers and machine gunners almost impossible to find because they appeared to be using a special kind of shell that didn't discharge a report of smoke when fired. Two members of my group were killed as they stood to better ascertain enemy positions and numbers.

Regardless of such disheartening events, a general consensus was echoing along our defensive line that the Jap numbers had to have been dwindling, for the dozen-odd still smoldering beach craters before us appeared to be their final, desperate holdout after suffering a severe Middle Arm routing.

"We at last took the tundra-clad hillocks . . ." An American machine-gun nest dominates Japanese positions from a hilltop. (Department of U.S. Navy photo, ref#12096-N, 1943)

It was now nearing 19:00 and Sgt. Malloy was determined to wrap up operations before nightfall, lest the Japs gain the opportunity to escape under the cover of darkness. It was a bold but honorable determination to imminently crush the adversary, for with our garrison on Adak, we simply couldn't allow a continued enemy presence on-island.

In attempting to move down from the muskeg-covered hillocks to the deeply cratered sands, we commenced a standard forward advance procedure, the objective being to close the range of our grenades and flamethrowers—weapons that held great promise in a trench type battlefront.

Sergeant Malloy designated a certain tall but swift Specialist named Bob Mitchell as the first to advance.

Bob Mitchell replied that it was an honor, and then rushed down the embankment toward the first occupied crater as the rest of us covered him with a barrage of gunfire. He made it fifteen yards over the sand flats before the enemy gunned him down.

Several repeat attempts to get a soldier close enough to the occupied crater from where he might be able to lob a grenade into it also failed, and now each GI privately dreaded the curse of having his name called. In the slow, painstaking attrition, Combat Team 12-2 was whittled down to eighteen men. Progress in this sector remained negligible until the fog thickened, rolling in like a shadowy rainstorm over the ground.

In the increased cover of brume, a renewed essay was launched, finally winning us a string of craters with our grenades and flamethrowers.

There was nothing as terrible as seeing and hearing a man being burned alive, even if it was an enemy combatant. Our relative youthfulness—our bullheadedness, really—enabled us to absorb the shock to some extent, but it was this one horror above all others that haunted a soldier's memory of the war and caused him to remain silent among the general public long after putting his civilian's clothing back on. That being said, getting hammered on the battlefield as my team had, equated to a "no qualms about it" attitude at the time.

The reality was, kill or be killed by any means possible—which echoed the general mantra of World War II, right down to hand-to-hand combat.

Combat Team 12-2 now manned two successive, large forward crater positions. I was in the lead crater with six other specialists, while the blast trench to our rear was occupied by the remaining eight from our unit, including Sgt. Malloy.

We were growing low on ammo and Jap numbers remained hazy, but it appeared that only a few smaller craters remained to purge before we could call it a well-spent day.

Sgt. Malloy had just called up for an account of our munitions, when two enemy grenades were lobbed into his trench and exploded almost simultaneously, limbs and body parts ejecting from the ditch and littering the surrounding sands.

"Watch for grenades!" warned Private Second Class Michael Marks, not wishing to suffer the same fate in our ditch.

We shouted over to Sgt. Malloy's detachment, receiving only faintly audible moans in response.

Then suddenly, Sgt. Malloy crawled halfway out of his crater, rolled over and extended a hand toward us. A soldier from my ditch rushed over to assist him, but was shot in the chest before he could get there.

"Stay down!" ordered Private Marks, who had assumed de facto command of our unit.

"Chew on your sulfur tablets!" I called out to the sergeant. "And get the hell back down until we can get to you!"

The shell-shocked sergeant only had enough energy left to act upon the first half of my advice, pulling a small tin vial from his coat and dropping a few tablets into his mouth. He seemed to chew on the life-prolonging medicaments, but that was as far as he got. Either he had no water left in his canteen to wash the tablets down with, or his canteen had been compromised. It was also possible the sergeant had no waist left to speak of, which was the common result of a live grenade lobbed into a trench; his detachment had suffered two grenades. Whatever the case, my remaining group of six were too pinned down to further help our comrades, who most likely were already dead.

As the minutes dragged on, our desultory and bullet-prone glances toward the sergeant witnessed him opening his mouth to the mists, trying to placate his dying thirst with the thick Aleutian fog. He eventually froze in this eerie position: head cocked back, mouth wide open to the overshadowing skies. Then his brains were blown out by a Jap sniper.

The rear Allied crater having been silenced, the remainder of my unit became completely surrounded in our forward position crater. The sense of desperation was more than palpable. Over 90 percent of Combat Team 12-2 had been annihilated; we were the only ones left. We were low on ammo and under increasingly heavy retaliatory fire. Throwing incoming grenades back out of our ditch before they detonated became commonplace. The poor visibility meant the imminent air support we needed was unlikely, while our warships wouldn't be able to execute a fire support mission due to the narrow nature of the beach battlefield and the associated risk of friendly fire.

As for infantry reinforcements, this, too, was a dubious prayer at best, for the other Allied battalions likely had their own hands full on the adjacent promontories. We'd succeeded in silencing all of Middle Arm and backing the Japs against the North Arm fjord, but had pushed our luck too far and now had no radio from which to garner a fuller estimate of our situation, because our radioman was dead. At the end of men and ammunition, our destruction appeared both inevitable and imminent. Alas, if you push the edge, you eventually find the edge.

Japanese army soldiers fire a Type 92 heavy machine gun from a jerry-rigged anti-aircraft tripod emplacement constructed out of driftwood (Propaganda postcard issued by the Imperial Japanese Army during World War II)

Then shortly after 21:00, as the fog departed eastbound through the North Arm corridor, the impossible transpired.

RAINBOW WARRIORS

THE SUN broke through the westward horizon, and all along the hillocks overlooking the beach appeared a line of Aleut warriors with a great, luminous rainbow arching over them. They were wearing body armor made of rows of wooden rods lashed together, and carried harpoons, spears with throwing boards, stone and bone knives, and a mishmash of guns dating centuries back. Most strikingly, they were all going barefoot.

In short order, this seemingly magical battalion of three score Unangax̂ fighters made battle with 100-odd hardline Japs that'd been entrenched in blast craters up and down the beach. The indigenes began by launching lances from throwing boards, aiming at targets both near and far with uncanny accuracy. The Japs who didn't get pierced through the heart as they stood up in their shell holes got speared in the head as they attempted sniper action from the crater rims.

Some of the most adept native fighters wore fearsome wooden masks, and we witnessed with mouths agape as these elite warriors overran entire enemy entrenchments using only their stone and ivory knives. The speed and precision in which the Aleuts attacked was simply astounding.

But the battle was not entirely asymmetrical, for the native Adak army was taking on a hail of return fire from Japanese Type 100 submachine guns and Arisaka rifles.

I watched in shock as several Aleuts got shot and dropped, while the rest of my team looked on in awe as numerous other Adak warriors appeared to take on dozens of bullets without so much as flinching. I thought I knew what my Allied comrades didn't: that this strain of Aleut warrior was likely immortal, but that secret assumption didn't hold up in seeing some Unangax̂ bite the icy Aleutian shores.

The wooden-armored warriors returned the Japanese favor with their anachronistic guns, some of which appeared to be eighteenth-century pistols and M1891 Cossack rifles from World War I. The Japs likely would've laughed at such outdated weapons had they not presently been getting their asses kicked back to Shanghai, which isn't even in Japan.

Of the five other soldiers left in composite group 12-2 besides myself, some began asking if it was better to hold our position or retreat, now that the enemy was preoccupied with the native blitz. The reasoning was that we were too low on ammo to sustain a defense should the Japs or Aleuts refocus an attack on our crater. The logic made sense, but I was still trying to ascertain a definite identity of the newcomers. My answer was not long in coming.

In the mayhem around us, a warrior of smaller stature dashed by, and in passing we made eye contact as if in slow motion. The Aleut had facial piercings, tattoos, and black feather earrings, but wasn't wearing a mask. Smoky mascara created shadowy eye sockets from which coal black pupils stole my breath at a glance. *It was Igasix̂, the cave clan vampire!*

"Hold your fire!" I shouted instinctively to my men, just in case any of them were even thinking of firing upon the incomparable youngling. She dashed onward as if time were now moving at double-speed, so swift was her reentry into battle, then with the same skill and bravado displayed by the natives twice her size, she made mincemeat of a contingent of well-armed Japs hiding in a nearby ditch that my unit had previously missed. In very real terms, she was saving our six remaining lives.

"Is that a girl?" a specialist from my unit asked, for beneath the rows of wooden bars that composed her armor, she was naked save for a thin layer of sealskin top and breeches—all of which were quickly turning red as she slaughtered Nipponese with a double-ended spear.

"Come on fellas!" I said to the remainder of my team, rising to my knees and then to my feet. Waving my pistol forward, I spurred them on with the cry, "The Indians are on our side!" That was language I knew they'd get, and sure enough they followed me out of the sandy trench, their guns held forth in defiance of the enemy.

Once our ammo was spent, we fought on like our Aleutian brethren, skewering many a Jap with our combat knives and bayonets, the warriors of Adak all the while smiting the enemy alongside us as we went. The equipage of the whaler was the Aleutian warrior's friend, or so we discovered in seeing the cave clan vampires thrusting throwing-lances into the chests of our enemies, the bone ring at mid-shaft breaking after impact so that the spearhead could be used again for another kill on that same battlefield (after penetrating through the chest cavity and exiting out the victim's back, or otherwise being pulled out).

As Unangax̂ fighters began losing their vizards to the rigors of the combat, I recognized some of their faces. I saw Qagux̂ at last living up to the meaning of his name "Fierce" as he tore the head off a Jap with his bare hands. Then there was Tix̂lax̂, the young hunter whose name meant "Eagle," poking the eyes out of an enemy combatant with a bodkin-ended staff. There was the "big penis" Qatxamax, firing off an antique English, double-barreled shotgun, but the shells were only half good, fizzling apart before his sourpuss expression. Eye contact was also had with Olean, that experienced warrior among the undead, and finally there was Tayax̂ukichax̂, my true immortal enemy, who raised a captured bushido sword at me, but only in a cruel tease as he spun around to stop an attacking Jap, halving him above the waist in one fell swoop—and notably, before the Jap got to me.

"Where's your dad?" I asked, knowing my unit was out of earshot.

"Up your ass," was the prince's unsurprising response. He went off slicing up the Nipponese, and I was relieved he didn't kill me then, for he'd certainly had the chance. But then I looked upon the hillocks and the mystery deepened. Kuuyux the elder was there, taking in the battle's progression. And if the shaman wanted me alive, Tayax̂ukichax̂ would have to comply, because Tayax̂ukichax̂ was answerable to his father, Chief Aĝnakax̂, who in turn was answerable to the powerful tribal magician, or so I came to suspect in my prior dealings with them.

With a roar out of the eastern heavens, a Curtiss P-40 Warhawk descended with a 120 MM machine gun mounted to its starboard wing and sporting a fuselage painting of Betty Boop dropping bombs on Adolf Hitler. Some of the fellers from my group knew by the iconic, wrong-hemisphere hull rendering that the plane was the personal jet fighter of William Butler, commander of the US 11th Air Force. We took cover in some nearby craters and watched him run a low-flying strafing mission. As he attempted to dodge some pom-pom flak bursts emanating from a couple of remaining ack-ack guns that hadn't been neutralized, he flew into a hail of enemy machine gun fire.

(Panel art from World War II comic strip, Kiska Surprise, 1946; no illustrator listed)

Butler's fighter plane began to smoke from the fuselage, lose altitude, and roll. Conveying into a decelerated nose-down pivot, he crash-landed into a muskeg sinkhole along the shoreline, where a score of Japanese fighters rushed over to finish him off.

The leftover few from my unit exhorted to rally in the commander's defense.

"With what?" questioned Corporal Timothy Masters, a trooper among us, "our bayonets?" He was pointing out the fact that our ammo was entirely spent. We had, in fact, been fighting with our knives and bayonets, but taking on the scattering Japs one at a time. The 20-odd enemy fighters who were presently descending upon Commander Butler would clearly outnumber us.

As the beleaguered aircraft continued to smoke in a bad way, we decided to storm it anyway.

We had scarcely advanced three meters when Igasiẍ once again rushed forth to save the day. I shouted for my unit to fall back and let her handle it. They hesitated, doubting my sanguine assessment, so I reiterated they leave the commander-pilot's rescue to her and concentrate instead on mopping up the scattering Japs. She'd saved us once before, so they just kind of shrugged their shoulders and got on with the business of skewering retreating enemy Nipponese, all the while keeping a furtive eye on the heroine indigene. She had a manner of embarrassing us, but in a good way. It was 1943. More than 500 years had passed since Joan of Arc led legions of men into bloody battles for the Motherland, and now the likes of Igasiẍ reappeared to remind fighting men that the battlefield was not reserved exclusively for them.

This little Aleut encountered the distressed plane with such celerity in her bare feet that it looked as if she were using her staff as a flying broomstick. I knew this was entirely possible, so said, "Look at her run!" to obfuscate this from my mates.

The marauding Japs were already scrambling up the downed plane's wings, trying to get to Butler in the cockpit, when she all at once descended upon them like a bat out of hell, spearing them through with both ends of her staff before twirling them around and tossing them off dead.

"Holy smokes . . ." and "Good Lord" was all my team could utter, but amid Igasix̂'s uncanny, bloodstained acrobatics, she didn't reveal any movements that couldn't be said to be human—a soldier exquisitely trained in close combat.

And like my former *qaqmiiĝux̂* victor-in-*qayaq*, the other cave clan Aleuts likewise remained grounded, not revealing any of their *iidigidi* powers aside from great speed, strength, and alacrity to slaughter. Take wing, they didn't.

After having killed every invading Jap around Butler's plane, Igasix̂ tore off the damaged cockpit and wrenched the good airman out from the smoky wreckage. It was a good thing she acted thus quickly, because as she carried him in her arms back toward our position, the plane exploded behind her, its skeletal frame sinking deep into the mudflats shortly thereafter.

As the smoke cleared over the North Arm battlefield, the final tally was more than 230 Japanese dead, seven POWs taken, and the rescue of Commander Butler with two broken legs—but very much alive. Of composite group 12-2, another unfortunate soul had bought the farm in the final joint-offensive with the cave clan Aleuts. Of our original team of sixty, then, only five remained alive to see the sun setting upon that momentous day. Field Sergeant Terence Malloy wasn't among them. The memory and sacrifice of the many ranks of fallen must never be forgotten.

As for the Aleutian warriors, four, including my friend Sugangix̂ and Qihmux̂'s boyfriend, Qagux̂, had been killed by enemy fire, shocking the *iidigidi* to no end. Nothing remained of those deceased cave clan warriors, for when they were killed, their bodies turned into a white dust that shot up into the sky in a columnar line, disappearing from the face of the earth.

Members of composite group 12-2 photographed somewhere on Adak prior to the Three Arm Bay engagement, with Field Sergeant Terence Malloy in black fatigues at far left (Exclusive photo from the collection of Lt. Harper; identifications gleaned from his notes, 1943)

Enemy bullets captured by the Unangans proved to be silver, raising the intrigue about who these Japs really were and who had organized their Adak attack. While the survivors of my unit couldn't understand it, the insight the gleaming projectiles provided me was profound in its implications. The old legend held up under trial: silver bullets could kill a vampire.

As our joint militias continued to gather Allied casualties and pillage Japanese weapons and belongings, I was taken aside by yet another female warrior: a cave clan Aleut whom I'd never met before. She was dressed like the others in her battalion, replete with wooden armor, multiple labrets, and a bentwood visor. "Lieutenant Harper," she said, "I have something important to tell you. I must remind you to keep our true nature a sovereign secret from your men. You shouldn't pretend to know us or any of our names unless we publicly offer them. Do I make myself perfectly clear?"

"What is your name?" I asked.

"Do I make myself perfectly clear, Lieutenant Harper?" she repeated more adamantly.

"Yes, of course. I vow not to reveal your true identities to anyone."

"Excellent. Now you must radio your boats to pick us up and take us to A-2."

"That might not be such a good idea," I reproached.

"Why?"

"Our commander back at Longview will interrogate the lot of you."

"We'll manage."

"Why do you want to go to Longview? What are you trying to accomplish?"

"Look around you, lieutenant. Behold the aftermath of our intentions. We are exacting our revenge. The enemy of our enemy is our friend."

"What do you mean?"

"Japanese planes bombed our barabara, obliterating many of our clan."

"I'm terribly sorry to hear that. What about your chief? Where is he?"

"Chief Aĝnakax̂ was unhurt. He has stayed back at the barabara to oversee his domain. But our warriors have assembled. We will join with your frontline troops to put an end to the Japanese presence here, and after that, we expect your military to depart from our island."

"We could really use more of what you did here, but I'm warning you, General Buckner will likely treat you poorly."

"Given our powers, I think you are mistaken."

"The general is a man of procedure and prejudice. I don't think he'll be accepting of your incursion into this theater, even if it is to our advantage. You should depart and continue to fight by cunning and surprise, as you did here."

"Perhaps your Colonel Butler here can convince the general otherwise."

"Only if." I remained dubious.

"To the radio, lieutenant."

"We lost it with our radioman."

"Come, I'll show the way," she offered. We turned and began marching toward the hillocks overlooking the beach. "My name is Anĝix̂," she said as we went. "Thank you for asking." She led me over the hillocks to the downed radioman. Detritus from a grenade had ripped through his jugular vein, mortally bleeding him out. His radio pack was likewise torn with shrapnel, but still worked and radio contact with Longview was soon reestablished.

A subordinate to the general was on the other end. I told him to inform Buckner that the Middle Arm sector had been cleared, and to send transport crafts into the North Arm to extract about sixty persons.

I was told to stand by, and shortly General Buckner came on, asking me to repeat the message.

He appeared pleased by my cursory report. "After the softening up phase," he remarked, "I had a high degree of confidence that composite group twelve-two would pull through intact. The Three Arm Bay theater had received a total of two hundred and fifty-eight tons of explosives from our naval surface bombardments, thus I calculated the Japs would be mostly neutralized during preinvasion operations. Your troop numbers now affirm my estimation."

"There are only five of us remaining, sir," I relayed grimly.

"Repeat that, lieutenant."

"Composite group twelve-two incurred high casualties in the ground clearing of Middle Arm. The sixty persons here include POWs and another combat team that are awaiting transport to A-2."

Buckner's reply was warbled by atmospherics and apparent confusion on his end. "Please repeat, sir," I asked.

"I've just received word that some enemy fighters have retreated into the hills east of Three Arm Bay. Can you confirm this, lieutenant?"

When I pressed the receiver switch to reply, Anĝix̂ forced my thumb aside, then ordered over radio silence, "Tell the general that my detachment has already mopped up the stragglers in the eastern hinterlands. The Japs are now cleared from Adak, I can assure you."

I relayed the report to Buckner.

"What detachment is that, exactly?" he asked.

"We've been through hell here, general. I'm not even sure myself, sir."

After a long pause, he came back on, and amid heavy radio static said something to the effect of, "Thank you for a job well done, lieutenant. I'll send a pair of LC right away. You'll be transported with the task group back to Adak, where all able-bodied troops will be debriefed and reoutfitted for another engagement. The battle for the Aleutians has just begun and time is of the essence."

"Yes, sir. Thank you, sir."

That the general assessed the war in the North had barely gotten underway was striking to me. After almost a year of feverish garrisoning activity, heavy bombing runs, and joint air/naval/ground operations like the one I'd just narrowly survived, Simon Buckner held, in essence, that we hadn't seen nothing yet. Obviously, as army commander of the Alaska Defense Command, he knew things I didn't regarding the scope of this sodden engagement.

Chatting in a 20mm gun emplacement aboard a troop transport en route to Attu, these Yanks are rarin' to meet the Japs. In the distance, other ships of the convoy make their way across the Bering Sea to the Aleutian Island. (ACME war photo and caption, New York Bureau, 1943)

But how much did the cave clan know? My memory of my time spent with them was still filled with vast black holes. But one thing I now recalled for certain was that Chief Aĝnakax̂ had known about the Japanese occupation of Three Arm Bay early on, perhaps even before my government knew about it. I also recalled the manner in which I was poisoned by Chief Aĝnakax̂ and Kuuyux, and the disdain this latter shaman had shown for me.

I scanned the hillocks for Kuuyux, then asked Anĝix̂ where he was.

"I don't know," was her curt response. "We must return to the beach."

NO LOVE LOST

THAT NIGHT, in boating out to the destroyers, some captured Japs were terrified to be in such close proximity to the cave clan vampires, publicly calling them *iidigidi*—an Aleut word meaning, roughly, "boogeyman."

The Allies onboard my landing craft, who numbered three from my composite group and six navy sailors assisting with the extraction, didn't pay much attention to the Japs' mostly unintelligible gibberish. For all my Allied comrades knew, the Aleut unit we conveyed onboard were simply a band of indigene warriors whose vested interest in driving the Japs from their homeland spurred them to unilaterally join the battle and fight with uncommon resolve.

But how the Japs knew that these were *iidigidi* raised the intrigue for me and should've concerned the cave clan greatly. Some *iidigidi* had, in fact, interrogated several POWs on the beach, but it was conducted in broken Japanese, which native Aleuts ostensibly weren't supposed to speak, and so whatever information they gleaned was kept from my unit and me under the pretense of shrugged shoulders, i.e., communication uncertainty.

"See feet!" one Jap prisoner remarked in fair English, pointing below an *iidigidi*'s knees. "Feet no freeze!"

A surviving specialist from my team threatened to bash the POW's head in with the butt of his M-1, but this never eventuated and I couldn't let the question go unanswered, so obfuscated the truth with a historic explanation: "Over the generations, the Aleuts probably have become accustomed to going barefoot in the cold. But that's an aside, because as I recall it, Middle Arm was mostly free of snow."

Joint Unangax̂/Allied grumbles of approval backed my assessment.

"See teeth!" The POW kept at it, making a peace sign before pointing it at an *iidigidi* and then at his own canines in an attempt to show us that the Aleuts had fangs. I had, in fact, been watching that, concerned this one permanent physical abnormality of the *iidigidi* would be cause for alarm among my men, just as it was for the captured Jap. But ever since we'd encountered the cave clan Aleuts on the battlefield, they'd always kept their mouths shut or held a stiff upper lip when they spoke, making them appear like truly tough warriors, if anything.

The Japanese POW then claimed in very bad English that while he'd been playing dead in a blast crater, he saw an Aleut drinking the blood of one of his injured comrades.

"No more playing dead then!" exclaimed the unnamed (and undone) specialist from my team before bayonetting the POW through the chest and tossing him overboard. "See ocean floor!" he spat over the gunwales, having tired of hearing the Jap's screwy chatter.

From the adjacent landing craft, Corporal Timothy Masters shouted expletives over the dark sea, reprimanding the specialist severely.

"Sorry Corporal," the guilty soldier called back, "I didn't know hostilities were over!"

None from composite group 12-2, and not one Unanga had qualms about what the unscrupulous specialist had just done. The Imperial Japanese were invading North America and the Pacific in their quest to fulfill Phase Four of the Tanaka Memorial, murdering countless US servicemen and island natives in the process, and one thing became crystal clear in this frigid northern battlefront: if US conscripts were killed by the enemy or by the murderous Aleutian weather as they fought to drive the incursion back, the end result was nonetheless the same. Too many Allied conscripts had already lost a fellow soldier in direct combat, or otherwise had seen their planes, boats, and subs go sailing off into the Aleutian bleak, disappearing forever. As for the cave clan vampires, the Japs had recently blown their barabara off the map, and so there was no love lost on their behalf.

As the landing craft chugged forth o'er the briny deep, its POWs well guarded amidships, I gravitated toward Igasix̂, who was standing alone at the starboard bow, gazing ahead into the dark mist.

"That's quite a collection of guns you brought," was my opener. "Where'd you get them?"

She turned and our eyes met, her irises momentarily glowing red around her big black pupils. "Mostly from the *promuishlenniki*," she said. "We'd trade sea otter skins for the Russian's guns. But Kuuyux normally doesn't like us using them—it's not traditional enough." She rolled her eyes.

I was pleased to know that, in private at least, she could still speak to me openly.

"He didn't even want us bringing them on this mission," she continued, "but Chief Aĝnakax̂ thought otherwise. We couldn't exactly sink our teeth into the Japs without your kind noticing." She shot me a bandying wink.

"Do Chief Aĝnakax̂ and Kuuyux often disagree?"

"No, usually the chief does whatever the shaman asks, but once in a blue moon they'll bump heads hard enough for others to take notice. Theirs is a strange dynamic. Maybe one day I'll tell you the reason behind it."

"You can tell me now."

She gave me a playful push. "I hardly know you" *<pause>* "yet."

Olean, the bullish, thirty-something Aleut, approached the bow and warned tersely, "You must keep your voices down. It's best you separate."

I couldn't help but nod in agreement—voices have a way of carrying astern on a ship. I looked at Igasix̂: she was no longer smiling. As I turned to leave, three US destroyers loomed up through the swirling night mists.

PARTY AT COLONEL E'S REVETMENT

WE ARRIVED back at Longview at noontide on May 4. The POWs were taken for further interrogation while some of us fellers from unit 12-2 showed the Aleuts to a corner of the airstrip, as had been our "private directive" from Colonel William O. Eareckson.

Upon our arrival to the celebrated 11th Air Force pilot's revetment, we discovered the "classified" nature of his order. He was throwing a surprise party of sorts beside his bomber to congratulate us on our "mission accomplished" and to meet the tribe of indigenous warriors. Not one enamored to protocol, especially when it came from stiff-asses such as Buckner, Colonel "E" said he "didn't want to waste a golden opportunity to meet the mystery troupe before the general worked his people-moving wonders."

(Panel art from World War II comic strip, Kiska Surprise, *1946; no illustrator listed)*

The cave clan, for their part, had a fascination with airplanes and the pilots who flew them, so were not adverse to the diversion. It at first seemed peculiar to me that the *iidigidi,* who could procure wings and fly at will, would be so interested in flyboys and aircraft, but when I thought about it further, it sort of made sense: pilots were the closest thing to their mortal equivalent, and an actual mechanical airplane might help them make logical sense of their own flying dynamics. The *iidigidi* may've lived beneath a roof of grass, but their minds were extremely technical, calculating, and advanced.

Adak overview with bombers (Painting by Ogden Pleissner, 1944)

While sitting upon oil barrels and partaking of gin, rum, and cigarettes—rare provisions flown in personally by Colonel E—we listened to his tales of williwaw flying and highlights from the many bombing sorties he'd flown over Kiska, while the Allies present, who included some of my buddies from the nearby barracks, were held in equal marvel by the "barefoot army" seated around them, because the air remained ice-box crisp down there in Eareckson's revetment, nibbling at every inch of exposed skin. The revetment was cut directly into a muskeg bluff that encroached low upon the valley floor. The carved-out tundra half-encircling his airplane was constantly seeping with mud, and so sandbags and earth-filled gasoline drums were stacked against the walls to help shore them up. The totality of his entrenchment, as with all Adak revetments, helped to minimize the effects of flying bomb fragments in the event of an air raid, and, of course, served to keep the planes from blowing over in a williwaw. Even now, as a fresh gale went sweeping over his arcane trench, only the slipstreams came swirling in, and not the blunt force winds.

As for Eareckson the man, he may've been a thorn in the side of his superiors, but he was very well liked by the rest of us GIs. His debonair charisma was a huge inspiration to the support staff stuck on Adak, and while his operational conduct was often cavalier, he always got the job done, piloting aircraft like none other. "Wild Bill's" exploits in the unforgiving Aleutian theater were nothing short of miraculous. From wresting his bomber through williwaws to strike Jap installations on-target, to developing forward air control procedures that would soon be adopted throughout the Allied warfronts, the 42-year-old Don Juan of Viking descent commanded the 36th Bombardment Squadron with legendary flair.

Commander Butler and Colonel Eareckson prepare for Adak. "Brig. Gen. William O. Butler (left), head of the US Army Air Forces in Alaska, discusses future plans with Col. William O. Eareckson somewhere in Alaska. Col. Eareckson was recently awarded the Distinguished Service Cross for his work. As head of the bombing command he has flown on most flights against the Japs even serving as co-pilot, navigator and gunner on many occasions." (AP Photo dated September 15, 1942. Caption added later by US Army Signal Corps)

But it was more than valiance that made "Wild Bill" such a great squadron leader, more than his sharp, low-cut moustache that made him a man of casual precision. Born in 1901, William O. Eareckson had fought in World War I, graduated West Point in 1924, commanded the 28th Composite Group in Alaska with great acumen, earned a Purple Heart, Silver Star, Distinguished Service Cross, and was presented with a Navy Cross by CINCPAC Admiral Nimitz himself. Such accolades, coupled with his tendency to buck anachronistic directives, equated to Colonel Eareckson's revolutionary inventiveness, which the Allied high command desperately needed to counter the enemy's initial air superiority.

Thus, as another Aleutian dusk settled long and bittersweet upon Colonel E's revetment, a few cold-footed GIs began filtering back to their barracks. But most conscripts stayed, cooking up beans beneath his heavy bomber's wings as he waxed Alaskan flyboy philosophic—a subject that fascinated the ground crews to no end, and the "barefoot army" most especially.

Crewmen of heavy bombardment squadron, Aleutians (Painting by Ogden Pleissner, 1944)

THE INTERROGATION

THE INEVITABLE directive came from General Buckner, just as Colonel E was learning the finer details of whale hunting. (Apparently, the airmen who flew in the Aleutian theater saw whales frequently, giving Eareckson and the cave clan another unexpected common interest.)

The general's messenger, a Pfc from Adak Command, relayed to us revetment holdouts that Buckner wanted to see the "as yet unidentified unit" right away, and that they were answerable to him and not to Colonel Eareckson.

"Party's over, boys and girls," announced the jocular pilot. "The general's going to have a lot of questions for you Aleuts, but you've performed well in battle and hopefully can sell him on that. I'd hate to see you shipped out. I'd gladly attest to your skills in battle, but coming from me, well, let's just say the top brass aren't too fond of my mouthpiece."

As for myself, I knew it would be impolitic to attend the interrogation, because my very presence could easily place me in an awkward situation. But, of course, I was concerned for the cave clan's welfare and interested in their story, so I instead snuck up to Buckner's rear window to listen in.

I got there only a few minutes after the *iidigidi* had entered, and in peeking through the open window, I spied six or eight Aleuts standing in as representatives for the remainder of their battalion. Chief Aĝnakax̂ was there. He must've arrived at A-2 only recently. The other barefoots were presumably in a nearby room or structure, perhaps being held in containment.

Buckner began railing against the cave clan representatives, calling their fighters "non-conscripted natives who have shown up on Adak and meddled into my operations." He was particularly incensed that not only indigenes had entered the Battle of Three Arm Bay, but indigenous women to boot. He went on to call the group "warpath savages uncleared by the US military, and therefore a direct threat to my supreme authority here on Adak."

Chief Aĝnakax̂ replied, "Do you always act like Adolf Hitler, or only tonight?"

I found the chief's quip to be extremely disrespectful and unfair. True, Buckner could be a man of stubborn preconceptions, but he was spearheading a defensive in the harsh Aleutians with laudable resolve and acumen. A commander of quick-tempered decisiveness was exactly what the Allies needed if they stood any chance at driving the Japs out of their fogbound strongholds further west.

Buckner, always the effective strategist, responded with a direct order: "I shall now deliver you a joint directive signed by CINPAC and myself, which is for the immediate removal of all remaining Andreanof Islanders from Adak. You shall be flown to Ward Lake via Naval Air Station Kodiak."

"Fly, sir?" inquired a naval officer attending the meeting, as the usual procedure was to deport natives by boat.

"They will fly to Ward Lake rather than sail," Buckner mottled every syllable, "because Kinkaid needs all available ships for the amphibious operations on Attu, where there presently is no US airbase for Butler to use."

"Aye, general," replied the sailor.

Admiral T. C. Kinkaid, USN, who is in charge of the Aleutian operations, is shown looking over the Kuluk base from the shore of Adak Island. To Admiral Kinkaid falls the task of regaining and fortifying the Aleutian stepping stones to Japan. (Department of U.S. Navy photo and caption, cleared for release on June 7, 1943)

Buckner then grumbled something about working around
Butler to get a hold of one of his planes. "And I'll see to it," he
continued more coherently, "that you barefooted bastards ship
out before I do."

As he jawed this last sentence, he tapped sharply against a
piece of paper lying on a table just inside the window.

Alas, the prejudiced general continued to rail against
the Aleuts, gravitating toward them, and so I reached in and
grabbed the document. It was a wire copy of a joint directive issued on April 1 by CINCPAC and General DeWitt,
ordering Admiral Rockwell to draft an operational plan—
"Operation Landcrab"—to retake Attu. The stated objective
was as follows:

> *The objective of Operation Landcrab is the reduction and occupa-
> tion of Attu and the occupation of the most suitable airfield site
> in the Near Islands at the earliest practicable date. The purpose is
> to sever enemy lines of communication to the Western Aleutians,
> to deny the Near Islands to the enemy, and to construct an air-
> field thereon for air operations; to render Kiska untenable and
> to create a base of operations for possible future reduction and
> occupation of Kiska. The first task is to reduce and occupy the
> most suitable airfield site in the Near Islands and build an air-
> field thereon. Commander Task Force [KING] is in supreme com-
> mand. Commander Amphibious Force, Pacific Fleet, is to operate
> under Commander Task Force [KING] and command amphibi-
> ous operations until landing phase completed.*

A D-Day of May 7 had been penciled in beneath the official CINCPAC communiqué, the dispatch stamped in red:
"JACKBOOT."

Rendering Kiska untenable: 11th Army Air Force Preinvasion bombardment of Kiska. Notice Jap airstrip in construction in background, and circular anti-aircraft emplacement in foreground (Army air force strike attack photo, 1943)

A closer view of photo above, with 11th Army Air Force bombs seen falling on Jap installations

*American bombs take out Jap trench line, while the enemy
scrambles to respond from AA battery in foreground*

*Japanese soldiers are seen by their silver helmets as they move about within their
AA gun emplacement on Kiska, which is under bombardment by the 11th Army
Air Force as part of the Operation Landcrab offensive. Notice enemy trenches
connecting their defensive positions, along with stone walls and rudimentary
wooden boardwalks they've built from 2 × 4's around their laager*

Finally I understood. Buckner was hurrying to board a warship to Attu, where a major operation was pending. This helped to explain his curtness with the Aleuts. The natives may have saved the day at Three Arm Bay, but they were nevertheless imposters in his ranks. With a wider war on his hands, he just wanted them out of his hair. Overhauling strict protocol regarding the fate of indigenes was not to his nature, so the easiest and most official thing to do was to simply follow protocol and send them off to Ward Lake.

The general's directive to fly the Aleuts to an internment camp distressed me greatly, because I knew they'd never stand for it. Their "final option" to spread the *promuishlenniki* plague was the trump card they'd promised, but there was no way I could logically convince Buckner to stand down.

I hurriedly went to see General William Butler, commander of the 11th Air Force, whose life had been saved by Igasix̂ and whose planes were ostensibly to airlift the cave clan fighters out of Adak. I found him in the Naval Hospital, his legs bound in casts and raised above the level of his head.

I kneeled beside the balding general's bed and pleaded in private: "You must allow the 'barefoot army' to join Operation Landcrab. Buckner's got them on the carpet [i.e., he's scolding them for disciplinary reasons] and wants to fly them to Ward Lake, but as I'm sure you'd agree, they've displayed exceptional field knowledge and would be better served imbedded with an expeditionary unit at the front."

"*Fly* them to Ward Lake?"

"Yes, sir."

"With one of *my* planes?"

"I believe that is his intention, sir."

"Not on my watch," he grumbled, and then inquired directly: "How much do you know about Operation Landcrab?"

"I've seen the April one joint directive issued by CINCPAC and General DeWitt to Admiral Rockwell, ordering him to draft an operational plan to retake 'Jackboot,' with Admiral Kinkaid slated to command the assault's full implementation."

"When do they jump?"

"In three days."

"On May seventh, I know," the Eleventh Air Force commander tiredly replied. He'd been testing the depth of my knowledge regarding the pending covert action.

"Kinkaid may just work for Landcrab," he uttered despondently, "but I'm not too keen on how they stripped Fuzzy's COMNORPACFOR stripes."

"Yeah, it's a shame about Fuzzy."

"Admiral Robert A. Theobald was Kinkaid's predecessor as naval commander of the North Pacific Force, but when he ruffled the feathers of the army brass, they replaced him, just like that—goddamned poor Fuzzy. It's a screwy command structure around here, lieutenant. The branches are all crossed up. Be careful of who you piss off: even fellers from a different command tree can get you fired. My cooperation with them is not without great reluctance."

That Butler was irked did not surprise me, nor was I surprised that he was hyper-fixated on the local military power structure at present. While Butler was commanding general of the army air forces, he served under Alaska Defense Command Major General Simon Buckner Jr. (The Alaska Defense Command in turn served under Western Defense Command, Lt. General John L. De-Witt in charge.) With Buckner's army authority over Butler's air forces concerns, they for a long time had been bumping shoulders regarding operational prerogatives in the Aleutians theater.

Coincidentally, earlier on that same day of May 4, 1943, Major General Buckner was promoted to lieutenant general, further irking Butler in what he perceived as an unbalanced power structure.

"So you'll help me stop the relocation of the native battalion to Ward Lake?" I entreated.

Like a drunk pondering an unanticipated question, Butler raised his brows, causing his forehead to crease with furrows, his eyes glossing over with a blank stare. He eventually answered, "Well, they did save my life."

"They're the best fighters I've ever seen!" I countered energetically. "Yet Buckner wants to expel them from the theater! But with your planes, we can imbed them with an expeditionary unit at the front and teach the new lieutenant general a lesson or two about how to win a war."

Butler cracked a smile, barely noticeable, but without question I'd garnered his attention. This was his chance to get back at Buckner, for, while Butler was not supposed to meddle in the army side of US Army Air Force operations, Buckner, the commander of army field operations in the Aleutians, often tried to dictate to Butler about how his air forces were to be used. Now, even from his hospital bed, Butler could give Buckner a taste of his own medicine, and if we maintained absolute covertness, he could do so without Buckner's even knowing it. Finally, if the Aleut fighters prevailed in turning the tide of the Aleutian war, Butler could come out and take full credit for it, shaming Buckner's deportation decision in the process. It was Butler's perfect counterstrategy against Buckner, his unrelenting fellow West Point alumni.

"I have an idea," he said almost in a whisper, and thus began our secret alliance, after which we privately consulted Chief Aĝnakax̂. The Aleut did not take long to agree.

That night, Simon Buckner departed Adak, sailing westbound for Attu, and early the next morning, William Butler wired CINCPAC (commander in chief, US Pacific Command, who reported directly to the secretary of Defense) in Washington, copying the communiqué to Buckner, that the Aleuts had all been evacuated by transport plane, as ordered.

FLIGHT BY NIGHT

IN THE cobalt twilight, the entire cave clan detachment, including a recently arrived Kuuyux, had squeezed into a LB-30 Liberator bomber. The aircraft, stuffed with fifty-six passengers, begrudgingly lifted off the tarmac. Once airborne, she bore east, as ordered.

The crew of three who were operating the plane—Allies handpicked by Butler—knew they were taking part in a highly classified mission, but they didn't know, nor did Butler back at Longview, that the unit being transported was a small army of vampires. This latter, greater secret was almost exposed when Aĝnakax̂ and Kuuyux started going at it onboard . . .

"Going forward," the chief warned the shaman, "I intend to be more involved in the direct planning of operations concerning our warriors."

Many an Ununaga were overhearing them, and the flight navigator may also have been in earshot, so Kuuyux was slow to respond, answering carefully, "I choose our battles wisely. I shall seek your counsel at a more opportune time."

"I shall speak now," Chief Aĝnakax̂ surreptitiously growled. "I shall not, at all costs, permit Colonel Yamasaki and his tribe of moss-troopers to occupy Attu."

Colonel Yasuyo Yamasaki, commander of Imperial Forces in the Aleutians, flanked by high-ranking staff (Image from war postcard, dated 1945)

Kuuyux's eyes gleamed unwholesomely, his brows curled back and he stiffened his lips as if holding back a wicked curse, partaking of one exceedingly vexed by the chief's assertion.

"Attu," the chief proceeded against the shaman's silent censure, "is our penultimate fallback base, next to our final holdout of the Islands of Four Mountains. After that, we'd have no choice but to release the virus."

The navigator manning the rear of the cockpit half turned in his seat as if perhaps he'd overhead something concrete over the roar of engines.

"You need not state the obvious," rejoined the shaman in no kindly terms, "and especially not in public."

"Then I shall hold counsel with you shortly;" replied Chief Aĝnakax̂, "as soon as we get off this plane, for the final solution is too great an action to hold to any one shaman's account: I know it can be avoided."

Ultimately, I believe the chief was expressing his concern that, should the Japs prevail in holding Attu, and then succeed in annexing the remainder of the Aleutians on their eastward thrust into America proper, depriving the cave clan of their own fallback bases, the Aleutian vampires would be left with little alternative but to infect others with the plague in order to win back their territory; but by releasing the *promuishlenniki* virus into the formal military ranks on either side, it could proliferate the world over. The chief seemed eager to avoid such a scenario by stopping the Japs on Attu by more conventional means, but apparently, Kuuyux may have felt differently.

"What's going on between them?" I asked Igasix̂. She was sitting next to me and had mentioned something previously about their strange dynamic, while I was becoming concerned about how this might be affecting our current strategy.

"It's about the gen-cycle;" she revealed beneath the rumbling of the engines, "the chief's brainchild. It's why we're so selective about who we're allowed to transform. This war has brought to the fore the core reason Aĝnakax̂ instigated the law centuries ago: to avoid this doomsday scenario of the plague spreading out of control, transforming all of mankind into *iidigidi*. He just wants to make sure that Kuuyux makes the right decisions on this issue, and frankly, I don't blame him."

"Which issue is that?" I sought clarification.

"In winning this war militarily, so that we don't have to resort to the final solution." While her admission confirmed my suspicion, she had lost her levity in speaking, but ironically, the only one to overhear her was Chief Aĝnakax̂, who slid over in his seat to lament into my other ear, "If only the youngsters of today were more like Igasix̂ here, but they don't follow my wise counsel like she does. Outside influences have corrupted the ankle-biters of my tribe."

"It seems these fighters are on the same page as you," I replied.

"Perhaps, but I can no longer be certain. Bloodlust can be very difficult to resist, especially for the young ones who lack in experience. The battle before us worries me greatly—a battlefield spilling with human blood. If I can't control the lusts of homely girls such as Aniqdux̂six̂, what hope can I have for energetic young men at war? But we can no longer hide from this conflict, so have joined with the Allies to help expel a common enemy from our islands; this is our priority."

"Aniqdux̂six̂?" The name sounded strangely familiar.

The chief regarded me with deep curiosity, and then glanced concernedly toward the cockpit. "No more talk," he whispered close into my ear. "Your kind may overhear."

CHAPTER III
UMNAK BIVOUAC

AS THE sun rose over the Aleutian archipelago, the pilots in the cockpit had no shortage of visits from the Aleuts, nor did the bombardier's window and the various gunners' turrets, for almost everyone wanted a glimpse of the snowcapped volcanoes gleaming with fiery colors. I knew the *iidigidi* could fly on their own accord, but it seemed this was their first time in an airplane, which intrigued them immensely.

Consolidated Vultee Liberator—Army and Navy land based long range bomber over the Aleutian Islands (Dept. of US Navy photo and caption, 1943)

I took Igasix̂ up to the dorsal turret for a rooftop view. Fortunately, we weren't particularly big people so could both squeeze into the capsule. She was fascinated by the big machine gun there, so I made sure it was on safety, then let her grip the trigger handles and swing us around, with her sitting on my lap. Being this intimate brought back fond memories, perhaps for the both of us. I reached my arms around her belly and clasped my hands together, holding her firmly against me.

She had no qualms about this, but only used it as an excuse to swing us around more vigorously. We began laughing over the roar of wind and engines. I begged facetiously, "Please stop, you're making me seasick!"

We kept giggling long after we'd stopped spinning, and just before we vacated the turret, she planted a little kiss on my cheek and said, "*Taanga,* lieutenant," thanking me in Unangam Tunuu.

A US Naval Air Transport Service pilot-photographer made this remarkable view of Veniamenof Volcano in the Aleutians. The volcano is one of the oldest known, and is estimated to have reached a height of 20,000 feet before the top was blown off. (AP press photo and caption, undated)

After flying for about an hour more, we approached an airstrip situated atop the eastern bluff of a mysterious island. The runway was about 1,500 meters long and appeared to be constructed of Marsden matting, while several smaller runways lay beside it in poorer states of development. Numerous rutted tire tracks ran off from the airfield toward distant pyramidal tents, a few Quonset huts, and a large aircraft hangar.

The pilot carefully negotiated the mighty LB-30 Liberator down, and not long after her wheels released a puff of smoke upon the pierced steel planking, the copilot announced with a shout, "Welcome to Cape Field!"

"Where the heck is that?!" the young whaler-cum-warrior Algax̂ Malihnax̂ called forth.

The mission was so classified that we hadn't even been made aware of our destination, but Altixum Taĝaacha knew, or thought he did: "We're on Umnak!"

Fort Glenn, Umnak Island (11th U.S. Army Air Force photo, December 8, 1942)

"You got that right, soldier!" the navigator shouted affably back. "Welcome to our top-secret airbase on Otter Point, east Umnak! To get your bearings, the landmass you'll see beyond the pass is Konets Head, which lies on the west side of Unalaska Island!"

"We're that close to Dutch Harbor," I remarked under my breath.

"And the island in the middle of Umnak Pass that looks like a wrecked galleon is called Ship Rock!"

Looking out the bombardier's window, I spied about a dozen army jeeps pulling up alongside our plane. Condensation blowing from their exhaust pipes evinced we were still steeped in cold Aleutian air.

As the bomber powered down, the pilot announced with a laugh, "The boys outside will take you into town."

"Right, boss," chided the copilot. "Listen fellas," he told us, "there ain't no town here, and the dozen odd guys you see on the tarmac are about the only pongos left."

"The only pongos left?" I probed.

"That's right, sir. Just a few dozen American and Canadian muck-mites remaining from the ten thousand soldiers initially assigned here last year. But this being Butler's operation means you're in good hands: he's got your back on provisions. There may not be much out here, but it's a pretty little place for a vacation—and at least you'll have gin and cigarettes."

"A pretty little place for a vacation!" The pilot exclaimed, giving his copilot a hard shove in the shoulder. "Get lost!"

"Give me a break, boss!" replied the jokester. "These natives have got no shoes on. If they like the cold so much, they'll probably think it's paradise here compared to Adak."

"Open the doors of this sardine can already!" Qatxamax growled.

The copilot took one look at the fearsome, heavy-set Aleut with the sea lion whisker pieced through his forehead, and answered: "Sure thing, boss, sure thing—right away."

We were soon to make the acquaintance of all the "pongos" of "Fort Glenn," which was another moniker for the secret Cape Field airbase. As for the pongos—the two dozen or so hearty stragglers still running operations—they consisted mostly of fellers from the 28th Bombardment Group, the 21st Bombardment Squadron, and several Canadian soldiers.

Our first breakfast together was a little odd because I was the only one from my group to actually eat anything. Tuuyux and Chief Aĝnakax̂, who served as spokesmen for the cave clan battalion, politely stated that the Aleuts didn't care for "white man food" and would instead hunt and gather their meals from around the island. It was an ingenious response to the riddle of how the vampires would hide the fact they survived on blood and blood alone. Otter Point overlooked several sandy beaches and rocky outcrops, which were the sort of areas mammals such as seals liked to frequent, so I had no doubt the *iidigidi* would find the nourishment they needed locally without resorting to feeding on our hosts.

Thankfully, the Unangax̂ warriors didn't need to share pancakes and canned sausage links with the Allies in order for the two groups to coexist. The morning spent together in the primary Quonset hut saw some genuine intermingling, with questions asked from both sides about their respective cultures, while a smattering of laughter sounded from all quarters of the shelter. As far as the Allies knew of our purpose there, we were a detachment of the Alaska Territorial Guard undergoing special combat training. Word from Butler was that a plane carrying our training advisors and armaments would be arriving later that day or on the morrow, at which point a formal upgrade of our unit would begin.

For someone like me who knew the Aleuts better, the idea that these superhuman killers needed additional combat training was ludicrous; however, if they were to join the front lines covertly, it did make sense they'd need to be outfitted like US Army infantry, and likewise need to be taught how to enact similar troop motions.

Excited to get started, and still not knowing what our formal combat training entailed, the cave clan went outside after breakfast to engage in their own physical games and feats of daring, taking care to temper their abilities before us mortals. Their games included tossing a lance via a throwing board through a series of orca jaws propped up on spears, running races, and stone juggling. But the ultimate challenge was wrestling, which was done on a large rubberized mat that'd served as flooring in one of the now-abandoned subsidiary command centers. What the Aleuts lacked in height, they more than compensated for in girth and brawn, and invariably the winner of these matches was the heavier competitor. The *iidigidi* invited some Allies into their challenges, and the majority of the time it resulted in a draw or the Allies winning, or more accurately, the vampires occasionally allowing them to win.

When Tayaĝukichax̂ invited me for a tumble, I couldn't exactly back down without looking like a poor sport, or at the very worse a coward. The pongos at Fort Glenn, after all, didn't know my history with this brute. At first, the wicked prince allowed me to gain the upper hand, and just as I had him pinned down, he rolled me over and sat squat on my chest. This was cause for abundant hilarity among the camp in observation; little did they know that the deceiving bastard very nearly broke my ribs.

The Aleuts' version of "combat training" was not entirely useless however, because afterward, the base was for the better part convivial and any suspicion about the vampires' true nature had been negated by what amounted to good sportsmanship and indigenous hardiness.

After the games, I took the opportunity to shave within one of the pyramidal tents—lodgings I was invited to share with some of the Canadians. Using water heated from a stove, I used my upturned steel pot helmet as a washbasin. I left a low-profile moustache just over my lip like the dashing Colonel Eareckson, and a thin, high beard covering my facial tattoos, imparting me with the overall mien of a European Don. I put on my beanie cap to help moderate the appearance somewhat.

I spent the remainder of the day milling around the camp and doing nothing in particular. The Canadians had a dog named Stu that went ballistic every time one of the Aleuts came near the Allied camp, so we decided to chain the dog to a pole and bring the party to the Aleut camp instead. One of the fellers from the 28th Bombardment Group brought a big pouch of tobacco the size of a pillow that he shared with everyone, and I took great clandestine curiosity in watching the vampires smoke, because I knew they couldn't breathe. Their ruse was a superficial puff of the cheeks. Nevertheless, they took novel pleasure in smoking, so perhaps it was no ruse at all.

I procured a harmonica I'd found in one of the abandoned tents and proceeded to toot out classics like *Red River Valley* and *My Darling Clementine*. The Allies cajoled the *iidigidi* into singing, the natives making a noble attempt at our traditional ditties before sharing a few of their Unangax̂ songs.

There were now three women on base—a base without any nurses left. You'd think the Allies exiled to this isolated cape would've been drooling over the sight of women, but Igasix̂, Anĝix̂, and a third female warrior named Akuugax̂ looked too exotic even for the desperados of Otter Point. I'd become accustomed to, and had even learned to love the appearance of Unangax̂ women: their raven-black hair that evinced a subtle blue sheen in the moonlight, their wide almond eyes and coal-dark irises, their abundant facial tattoos and piercings—to me all this equated to uncommon beauty. I considered myself lucky the guys on base simply couldn't see it. Competition for Igasix̂ was not something I desired.

At 21:00, it became incumbent to haul the base's remaining squadron planes into a hangar, whose molding, wooden walls were kept intact thanks to heavy stanchions of steel too cold even for rust to take root upon. The stated purpose of the transfer was to prevent the aircrafts' exposure to sudden inclement weather or a surprise dawn patrol from the Japs. Apparently this arduous task was performed nightly—arduous because it was downright grueling pulling the aircraft in by hand. But when the cave clan arrived, the job was completed in no time. The Allies were amazed at the collective acumen of the fifty-two Aleuts, and pleased beyond measure to have a break from their nightly punishment. It was commented, what a battalion the Indians would make once they were trained as US infantry!

The following morning at 08:12, I was summoned to the defunct base's main Quonset hut, where General Butler was waiting to speak to me over secure radio. He privately told me via an earpiece that he'd just informed CINCPAC that his "transport plane" had gone missing en route to Naval Air Station Kodiak, with Adak Air Command receiving a sketchy mayday from the pilot (in whose name he invented one on air force rosters) indicating they were breaking up in a williwaw and had lost all bearing. Of course, Butler's cover-up was to remain our mortal secret. He then reported a jovial truth: the shipment of new uniforms and materiél, along with our training advisors, was presently en route, Umnak ETA 14:00.

Breakfast with the Allies—Chow time in the Aleutians (AP Wirephoto, 1942)

After a field camp breakfast with the Allies, I invited Igasix̂ to take a stroll down to the beach. The sunny weather was holding and there was time to burn before the shipment arrived, and so we walked to the bluffs overlooking Umnak Pass. The beach was a few hundred feet below, with no visible footpaths down the muskeg-laden escarpment. "I guess we'll just enjoy the view from here," I lamented.

"Who are you kidding, lieutenant?" she laughed, and then she took me in her arms, flared her wings and leapt over the cliff.

Before I could finish saying, "Holy shit!" our feet dug into the cold, soft sand. The *iidigidi* had a goddamn terrible way of surprising me like that. It took a minute or two for my heartbeat to return to normal, but then in realizing I was at last alone with Igasix̂, it increased again in lovelorn excitement.

We strolled along the beach, holding hands. The waves were every object of beauty. As they rolled up, the sun sparkled upon their crests and glowed green through their backs, and when they crashed, the whitewater rushed up the sand and expired into our ankles with a playful slap. We stopped and faced each another, hand in hand. "Did you miss me, Lieutenant Harper?" she asked.

"Yes, ma'am Igasix̂." I smiled back.

"Why do you call me ma'am?"

"I'm just joking, Igasix̂. You need not call me lieutenant in private, and I won't call you ma'am."

"Got it, Jake." She swung my hands playfully around in hers.

"But I did miss you, Igasix̂." I drew her close into my embrace, and in looking over her shoulder I saw a flock of harlequin ducks frolicking around a turbulent shoal. For some inexplicable reason, I suddenly became sad. I released my hands and stepped back.

"What's wrong?" she inquired.

"I don't know. I suddenly felt strangely haunted."

She turned and saw the ducks, then sighed.

"We can walk, ma'am," I teased, taking her hand once again.

"Yes, lieutenant," she smirked wryly, and we proceeded together along the stunning sunlit shore.

WARGAMES IN THE SNOW

AT 15:12, an aircraft, a C-43 Skytrooper, touched down on the Cape Field tarmac. The pilot and copilot deplaned, and these—the sum of the crew—were to be our military advisors. The plane's jumping bay was filled with supplies and materiél, which were summarily unloaded and transported by vehicle to a new training area, where it was placed into black pyramidal tents.

The advisors made my formal acquaintance at the camp, where I assisted in gathering the Aleuts before they announced their names and titles to the rest. The first was Senior Enlisted Advisor (SEA) Barretto Valens, an Italian American who spoke exactingly beneath a curling moustache, and the second was Master Gunnery Sergeant Frank White, a broad-shouldered yank with slightly bulldoggish features who didn't say much at all. SEA Barretto was from the army air forces, while Frank White, who could also be coined operation chief, had somehow been pulled from the marines, thanks to Butler's covert ingenuity.

SEA Barretto Valens and Master Gunnery Sergeant Frank White arrive at Fort Glenn, Umnak Island, early May, 1943 (Exclusive photo by Lt. Harper)

Barretto stated in his introduction the purpose of his and Frank's assignment, which was to further equip and train our "detachment of Alaska Territorial Guardsmen" for combat on Attu and/or Kiska. Butler had sold the situation well: the Alaska Territorial Guard were already serving in active combat roles in the Aleutians, and so their ostensible presence in an Umnak training camp wouldn't raise any red flags among the Western Defense Command, especially given the fact that the Fort Glenn airbase, once highly classified, was now all but decommissioned and thus a negligible focal point at best. The battlefront had moved to the far western Aleutians, with the massive Adak garrison serving as the main forward base, while smaller heavy-bomber airfields were being laid clandestinely even closer to Jackboot.

The cave clan warriors were ordered into a single-file line, where they proceeded into the first tent to "sign in" with Barretto and get fitted with uniforms. Due to my rank and the fact that I was the only member of the Alaskan battalion the specialists could readily identify with, I quickly became something of an intermediary in assisting with the training mission.

The uniforms distributed were standard summer fatigues, which I found perplexing, especially given the sight of a leaden storm front moving in from the west, rumbling like a swollen volcano. I was pleased, however, to see the Aleuts receiving gummies. Not that the barefoots needed them, but it showed that Butler had good intentions for our crack unit. If the Adak Naval Hospital served anything as an example, rubber boots proved extremely difficult to requisition for standard infantry, who suffered dearly in their lacking. I already had a pair that fit comfortably, courtesy of Simon Buckner, so declined new ones. Steel pot helmets were also distributed. Mine smelled like shaving cream, and so I helped myself to a new one of those.

From the fatigues tent, the Aleuts proceeded to an adjacent Quonset hut to receive army weapons from Operation Chief White. The standard issue was an M-1 rifle with bayonet attachment, set on safety with 500 rounds; six hand grenades; and a 10 inch combat knife with scabbard. In addition to these, each Unanga was given a steel Zippo lighter, an empty canteen, and a vial of sulfur tablets—all of which they had absolutely no use for because the accoutrements men needed in order to survive the battlefront were not necessitated by the immortals, not unless a canteen happened to deflect a silver bullet of unknown origin.

It was only with great reluctance that the Aleuts surrendered their own weapons, however: but it had to be done in order for them to blend in with the rest of the US Army—a directive that wisely came down from Butler. But the issuance of several machine guns more than made up for their loss. When tested by Chief White, the repetitive snap-rattle-roar begot by the German invention proved irresistible to all hands in training, including myself.

The formal training that began after our weapons were issued was blindsided, but not stopped, by the approaching storm. As Kuuyux and Chief Aĝnakax̂ looked on through the snowfall, Barretto Valens and Frank White had us march in columns and repeatedly hit the floor as we trained our weapons on pretended ambushes. For fear of friendly fire, the Aleuts wouldn't be taught how to actually fire their guns until visibility improved. This skill, however, I knew to be a foregone conclusion, as the Aleuts had abundantly proven their varied firearm skills at North Arm.

My summer fatigues weren't cutting it in the williwaw, so I repaired to the nearby Canadian base and bummed several extra layers of long johns, which I promptly donned beneath my paltry uniform.

I barely found my way back through the blizzard to the training area, where our two advisors were freezing their own butts off and amazed at the Aleuts' enduring fortitude against such weather. Barretto explained to me, shouting through the howling storm, that the uniforms were meant to match those issued to the infantry being deployed on Jackboot, to harden us to the situation ahead. I summarily followed the two advisors back to shelter while the cave clan continued playing wargames in the snow.

"We were issued standard summer fatigues to harden us to the situation ahead . . ."
American soldiers load a shell into a small mortar (foreground) on Chichagof Ridge
overlooking Chichagof Harbor on Attu. Other American soldiers in the background
send rifle bullets into Japanese positions. The men were so intent in their work that
they did not notice the US Navy combat photographer that took the picture. The
fur jacket worn by the man in the foreground belonged to a Japanese soldier. (Dept.
of U.S. Navy photo and caption, ref#1360-FN, May 1943) [*Editor's note: The dark
blotches appearing over the soldiers' heads are not scuff marks on the photograph,
but are massive, snowbound escarpments that typify the Attu topography.]

If there was one thing about Otter Point, Umnak, the weather proved even worse than at Kuluk Bay on Adak, which I wouldn't have imagined possible had I not made the transfer myself. The first two days after our arrival to Fort Glenn had been exceptionally staid, for since then, in addition to frequent, blinding snowstorms, aka williwaws, heavy fog and high winds were the norm. Unfortunately for me and every other Joe recruited to purge the enemy from this godforsaken archipelago, the spring of 1943 would go down as one of the coldest in recorded Aleutian Islands' meteorological history. Thank God for gummies and long johns.

This frozen-over Quonset hut on Umnak Island is so frostbitten that you can practically see a glacial blue sheen in this black and white photo of it (AP, 1943)

The two advisors, along with the two dozen Allies "imprisoned" at Fort Glenn, were astounded by the Aleuts' continued flippancy toward the perilous weather. The cave clan essentially ignored it, rarely even talking about it—a nonheroism for them, but a capacity that ultimately proved indispensable for the timely completion of our training curriculum. Their ability to perform so well militarily and to live off the land in such a hostile environment so much impressed our advisors that they wanted to inform Lt. General John L. De-Witt and the Joint Chiefs of Staff in Washington about "hands-down the best unit in the World War Two theater." It was only by great prodding on my part that I prevented such a breach of Butler's invented soldiers, warning the advisors that our operation was supposed to be highly classified among certain members of Western Defense

Command, and to contact the wrong person about it could risk sworn protocol regarding the communication of covert operational intelligence. I reminded them that they were to report directly to Butler only. He had been in daily contact with us, and would (presumably) disseminate any pertinent information further up the chain of command. To ostensibly save their own positions, Barretto and Frank thus reluctantly conceded to my arguments regarding maintaining operational secrecy.

Tireless reconnaissance efforts by Butler's Eleventh Air Force had enabled him to relay daily flyover reports and photos of enemy positions and activity on "Jackboot," but all we could really ascertain regarding our pending deployment to Attu was that it would probably be a cold, snowbound slog through difficult terrain.

Aerial view of Holtz Bay on Attu Island, six days prior to D-Day; remote, frozen-over, and well entrenched by Jap forces, "Jackboot" would be no walk in the park (11th Army Air Force photo, May 4, 1943)

The snowstorm over Otter Point continued unabated, with the collective base priority now being to keep the main runway free of powder buildup. Cat tractors fitted with snowplows were employed, as were most of the fifty-two Aleuts, who took to shovels to physically scrape the ice off the Pierced Steel Planking (PSP).

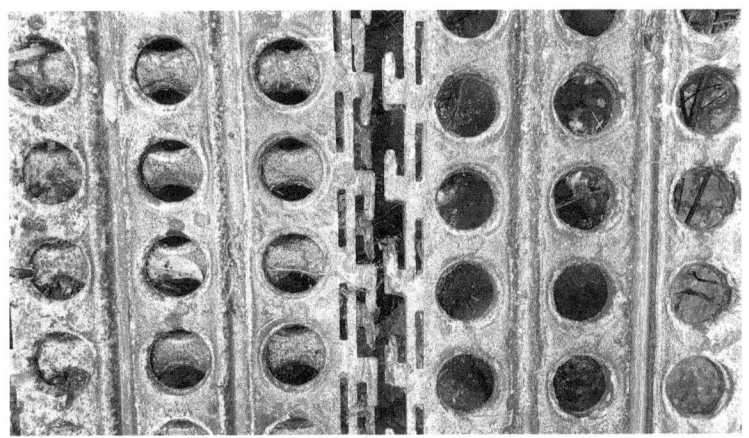

PSP aka Marsden matting (or Marston mat) showing hooks and slots where mats can be interlocked (Exclusive photo by the author)

They seemed to relish in the activity, primarily because for them it was easy. Working at lightning speed through near-zero visibility whiteouts, the natives continued to shock the advisors and Allies with their efficaciousness in performing outdoor tasks amid weather that left everyone else cowering down in their shelters.

The only question that Chief Aĝnakax̂ and Kuuyux had for Barretto and Frank was how much longer their warriors would have to tool around on base before they could be deployed. The answer, perhaps obvious, was that until the williwaw passed over nobody was going anywhere by plane, and with Attu being at least seven hundred miles away, nobody was eager to set sail to the front. Butler and the radiomen at Fort Glenn were doing their best to monitor the west-to-east moving train of storms, and at the next workable break, the general relayed, our deployment orders would come down. For now, we were advised to be on the ready and keep the runway open.

Radioing positions and searching for backup amid the Attu muskeg battlefront. "Private Kenneth Nelson (left) of Kelliher, Minn., is shown helping operate a switchboard in a dugout just behind the front lines during fighting on Attu. With Nelson is Corp. Gerald Twedell of Yuma, Colo." (AP photo and quoted caption, undated)

A PINCER MOVEMENT IN DIFFICULT RESTRAINT

IT WAS a snowbound evening when I awoke in the abandoned tent I'd commandeered for myself. All that illuminated the interior was the soft orange light emanating from my stove, which I kept always burning for warmth. An intruder of some bearing, sporting a steel pot helmet, was already standing before my cot. Perhaps Tayaĝukichax̂ had come to do me in once and for all.

I reached for my pistol.

"Jake!" the intruder said, and in hearing my one-syllable name, I recognized the voice of the forever-young Igasix̂. Like several other warriors in her tribe, she continued to wear her wooden-rod armor beneath her army fatigues, maybe for some manner of genuine protection, but probably just out of superstition. The end result was that it made her appear like a burly, barrel-chested man, especially from the lower vantage point of my bed.

"Igasix̂, is everything all right?" I besought.

"Sorry if I woke you, Jake. Everything's fine. I just came by to visit."

"Oh, I was already awake. I just didn't recognize you at first."

She removed her helmet and placed it on a rudimentary field table within the tent. "Do you recognize me now?" she continued seductively, undoing her hair bun. Her silken black tresses slid freely down the sides of her head, framing her cute face beneath her row of bangs in front. To me, Igasix̂ was a nineteen-year-old dream. I was but a few years her senior, and our mutual attraction had proven hard for the both of us to control. Was this our chance to finally lock in what we had going? Her visiting my quarters during a night blizzard was likely more than just a black tent tour. We'd gotten close on the beach and in an intervening moment in the cockpit of a fighter plane that'd been hauled into the hangar, but in both instances our chance at greater intimacy had been limited for one reason or another. "I like your hairstyle," I said as she kicked off her boots.

"Oh yeah? And what else do you like about me?" She continued slowly forward, unzipping her jacket all the while. "Will you still like me without my clothes?"

"Try me."

"Try you? Are you sure about that, Lieutenant Harper?"

Her fatigues hit the floor. All that remained on her body was a vest of wooden rods stretching from her neckline down to her waist like a naughty xylophone costume, and a pair of men's boxer shorts, sagging beneath her belly button. Her bare skin and breasts were visible through the cuts between the rods.

"I'm still not sure who you are," I remarked.

Her natural armor bounced off the ground with the report of wooden chimes. She was now completely nude, save for her briefs. She covered her breasts with her arms and slightly crossed her knees, pleading coyly, "I'm so cold, Lieutenant Harper. Won't you keep me warm?"

Operations chief Frank White stands before a black pyramidal tent at Ft. Glenn probably not unlike the one Jake was in when Igasix came to visit (seduce?) him (Exclusive photo by Lt. Harper, May 8, 1943)

I stood and embraced her. She *was* cold, *eerily* cold. I'd never pressed her naked body against mine before, but it haunted me with a strange memory I just couldn't place. Nevertheless, her seductive advance had gotten me excited down under, and before my mental lapse caused me to lose all steam, she started stroking my dingdong with one hand while guiding my palms over her supple breasts with her other hand.

I spun her around and laid her on my bed, and then with her assistance, I slid her shorts down over her knees and yanked them clear of her feet. "Ooh, Lieutenant Harper," she moaned as I explored every detail of her nakedness, first with my hands, then with my tongue.

Warmed by a woolen blanket I had pulled over us, we drew ever closer until I was pinning her down against the bed like I were a spider with a mighty abdominal stinger entering between her legs anchored spread-eagle. I pushed her knees further up beside her ears, flat against the springy mattress, practically turning her inside-out as I vigorously fucked her, while she pulled ever harder at my hips, driving me increasingly deeper into her wedging cave of wonders. "*Ooh lieutenant,*" she moaned. "*Please don't stop!*"

"Yes ma'am, I mean no, ma'am," I retorted with heavy breaths. We laughed together groaningly. But as our romping continued, it grew deadly serious. We were soon grunting, growling, and squealing unrestrainedly, the williwaw outside masking our lovemaking sounds. And then she arched her neck forward and sunk her teeth into my neck, or barely did— it was difficult to tell if she broke my skin in delivering the hickey, but as her fangs bounced off my jugular, I tempered the movement of my hips, changing from all-out pounding to a smoothly controlled gyration, being careful not to nudge her bite in further. As passionate as the moment was, I was reluctant to cross that threshold, and it seemed she was, as well. She withdrew her fangs and focused more on her hips, gyrating with me, milking my stinger tighter and tighter deep within the fold her leathery love glove. At last, the muscles of our groins contracted and released together, releasing over a pint of black and white cream in explosive repetitions.

I collapsed by her side and immediately reached for my neck. Checking my hand, there was no sign of blood. I was relieved, elated. There was no doubt she'd wanted to turn me, and easily could have, but for some reason she had held herself back. Lying beside her after our tryst was now all the more relaxing, for I could trust in her control over her own deepest desire. I lit a cigarette and expelled a puff of grey smoke toward the murky ceiling. "That was awesome." I handed the fag to Igasix̂.

"Yeah, totally." She took a superficial draw.

"Thanks for not holding back." I was hinting that it was her intimacy that mattered more to me than her viral immortality. But I should've been more careful with my words regarding our complex web of life, death, and the forever-after, for my remark only seemed to frustrate her. Her brows curled in critical thought and she puffed at the cigarette less gracefully and more like an addict. "What are you thinking?" I asked.

She leaned up on an elbow and handed me the coffin nail. "I don't want to hurt you, Jake. Quite the opposite, I think I'm falling in love with you. Ever since we went on *qaqmiiĝux̂* together I've had these feelings for you. But I sense something's holding you back, and I think I know what it is. It's time for you to know, Jake, that Aniqdux̂six̂ dumped you."

"Who?"

"Seriously, Jake? Are we going to play that game?"

I was perplexed and growing more distraught by the second, which probably showed all over my pained expression. "Who is Anak Dukix?" The name sounded vaguely familiar, and it deeply disturbed me that I couldn't place it with a face.

Igasix̂'s countenance became almost as concerned as mine. "You really don't remember, do you?"

"No." I got up on my shoulder and pushed her back down in loveplay fashion. "I have no idea who this person is, so maybe you can tell me."

"Amazing." She was shaking her head. "The potion really worked."

"What potion? You mean the one Aĝnakax̂ and Kuuyux tricked me into drinking before sending me back to Longview?"

Her lips were steeled.

"Was that the potion?"

"Never mind," she said, unfairly.

"You Aleuts with your bloody potions and superstitions. You know what, Igasix̂? I'm tired. I'm going to sleep." With that, I flicked the cigarette toward the stove, then rolled over, turning my back to her.

"Sorry, Lieutenant Harper."

I closed my eyes.

After a few minutes, she peeped, "Goodnight."

I fought back a smile. Whoever this Anak Dukix was didn't matter to me. I'd just made love to Igasix̂, a girl I'd had a crush on for quite some time.

In the wee hours, word spread through the darkness of camp like wildfire. Commander Butler had ordered the jump on Attu. The cave clan battalion was to meet at the airstrip at 06:00, armed and ready for deployment.

I pulled on my trousers and boots alongside Igasix̂, then hurriedly made some coffee and corned beef mulligan while she dolled herself up with makeup, using *spermaceti* wax dyed with salmonberry juice as lipstick. I had to admit, she looked hot in it. But in the urgency of our leaving, she forgot to take her helmet, or maybe had a bout of purposeful forgetfulness in the service of fashion and comfort. Instead, she grabbed a Soviet Army hat with a red star that must've been left in the tent by its former Canadian occupants.

The dark of the airstrip access road was broken only by the headlights of our impromptu convoy of jeeps, the array of double beams soon converging through the swirling snow upon a handsome C-43 Skytrooper idling over a sparkling clean runway. Obviously, some overeager vampires had been up early that morning, scraping down the Marsden matting, which was miraculously free of verglas. From the rear of a covered cat tractor, Operation Chief White blasted the volume on a radio amplifier, broadcasting a live directive that shortly came down from Commander Butler on Adak:

"Thank you for your patience and your fortitude in training while awaiting this deployment order. I understand the Aleut clan has showed exceptional discipline and acumen as infantry soldiers. Your voluntary service in this covert detachment of the US Armed Forces is both honorable and appreciated. With your assistance, I am confident the enemy will soon be swept from these islands we share as common territory.

"Every expeditionary group needs a field commander," continued Butler, his voice clear but tinny through the field speaker, "and for your unit I am appointing Igasix̂, the young female among you who showed exceptional skill and heroism in saving my life in the Three Arm Bay theater. Her forward command decisions should be heeded, and once you are victorious and return to your villages, your clan chiefs can resume their dictates in full confidence. The United States will have your back, as you now have ours. Thank you for your service, and Godspeed on the battlefront."

Girl General Leading the Army to War *(Illustration by Dusan Kostic)*

I could see neither Chief Aĝnakax̂ nor Kuuyux in the difficult light, but could safely assume their expressions had gone sour over the announcement that their authority had been temporarily stripped by the US military and placed squarely into the lap of one of their teenage subordinates, a girl no less.

That being said, I for one was both proud and confidant of Butler's decision, just as I was of my brave young lover in her momentous new role. And I had to chuckle: General Buckner would probably crack over the reality of an "Indian" woman leading a US combat unit, most likely to victory. This had to have been factored into Commander Butler's announcement as just another way to piss off his superior.

The cave clan boarded the C-43 Skytrooper in single file. Our training for Jackboot and covert embed would now be put to the ultimate test.

CHAPTER IV
ASSAULT ON ATTU

Troops in landing craft deploying in treadmill fashion about an attack transport before going ashore. Off Attu, Aleutian Islands, May 11, 1943. (AP photo and caption, 1943)

THE BATTLE for Attu had been raging. It was already D-Day+13 on that chilly dark morning of May 24, 1943, when the fifty-two cave clan vampires and I lifted off Umnak's classified airstrip in the C-43 Skytrooper. We were given a battalion name onboard: Unit 13, marking our belated jump days into the conflict. The weather over Umnak had been so horrendous that this was our first chance to fly out since our training had ended. SEA Valens also floated the joke that our unit number would bring bad luck to the Japs.

Valens was piloting the plane, with White copiloting. Neither advisor would be joining the ground phase of the mission. Not only did they have to control the plane, but I suspected that Butler didn't want to risk their careers should the Adak Aleuts be discovered in the field by Buckner or other high brass. Having a woman lead our unit now made this a real possibility. Butler may've surmised that Igasix̂, with her androgynous features and hair tucked away, would blend in sufficiently well with the men. Anĝix̂ and the other female warrior, Akuugax, had been issued steel pot helmets, khaki field scarves, and fatigues with high collars to evade overt detection. But Igasix̂ had left her helmet behind and given herself a conspicuous makeover with red lipstick. If Butler could see her now, I wonder if he would still designate her as field commander. But all that was a foregone conclusion—the women and men of Unit 13 would jump on Attu together, and a member of the former sex would lead them. The plane would not be touching down on-island, in any event, because Attu lacked a terrestrial landing strip.

Most of us didn't have the luxury of a field scarf, but then again, I was the only guy in our crack unit of fifty-three that actually needed one. The Aleuts were more than cozy in their summer fatigues, and with the addition of their gummies they even appeared a little overdressed. Their skin could not freeze because they were already dead, but for true mortals such as me, the subarctic climate was a constant threat. If our uniforms, already battle-worn in training, were supposed to mimic those being worn by the infantry currently engaged on Jackboot, I felt truly sorry for them. At least I had the benefit of three layers of long johns worn underneath, thanks to the convivial Canadians.

Circulating through the chilling mists off Attu, US forces in landing craft wait for the fog to clear so that preinvasion bombardment activities can commence. (Dept. of US Navy photo and caption, May 1943)

Pre-invasion naval bombardment explosion seen on shoreline (at foothill grassland, right center) as landing craft wait to deliver troops to the beachhead of Attu. (11th Army Air Force photo and caption, May 1943)

Alas, the push on Attu was strictly American, and given the problems of provisioning I'd already seen out west, it remained to be seen what the Yanks were actually contending with. But we could take a hint: I'd been told by my advisors to let my grooming go several days hence, while Unit 13 as a whole had been told to never clean their uniforms. Each one of us were now sufficiently sullied to appear as if we'd been in the field for a long, hard while; again—to replicate what the US infantry on Attu were ostensibly going through, poor bastards.

With the beachhead now softened up by naval bombardment, US ground forces are conveyed by landing craft to the snow-ridged Attu battle theater, not knowing exactly what to expect in this menacingly surreal warzone. (Dept. of US Navy photo, May 1943)

THE JUMP ON JACKBOOT

WE APPROACHED Attu from the south, and in the misty morning light could discern a massive backlog of equipment stacked up on Massacre Beach, where the southern landing force had made its beachhead. A mile-long, man-to-man chain of soldiers stretched from the pileup of materiél clear up into the foggy mountain passes, moving provisions forward by hand. They were having serious issues with the muck and muskeg, this much was certain.

(Dept. of US Navy photo showing 7th Infantry Division beach landing on Attu Island, May 1943)

Now it was our turn to enter the fog, but we didn't have to trudge through black taffy to reach the hinterlands. We leapt from the plane in blazing fast sequence, parachuting down behind a ridge lining the main valley of operations.

From Henderson Ridge, we consolidated our unit, then hiked single-file through the narrow Zwinge Pass, from where we surreptitiously filled in behind Company G of the 4th Infantry as they headed up the connecting Jarmin Pass.

The 4th Infantry looked cold, dirty, and haggard, and thanks to well-orchestrated planning, our soiled, standard uniforms made us fit right in. We only had to change our expressions from excited to grim. Perhaps serendipitously, many of the 4th Infantry appeared to have been of southwest Mainland and Native American descent, providing further anonymity to the Aleuts of Unit 13. The troops we'd embedded ourselves between were constantly scanning the fogbound ridges of Jarmin Pass and Black Mountain for enemy snipers, so we did the same in order to better blend in. Gunfire periodically snapped and rattled through the icy mists ahead.

Artillery was being hauled up by rope, and it looked like an extremely grueling task. The terrain and steep passes were clearly too rugged for trucks and cat tractors, so everything was being brought to the front via the sheer brawn of men.

An American soldier gets a free "buggy" ride up the steep side of a mountain on Attu as supplies are hauled up on a special "elevator." (ACME war photo and caption, New York Bureau, passed by censors in June 1943)

The slopes were icy and slick, while the leather boots worn by the infantrymen caused them to frequently slip back. Casualties, meanwhile, were being evacuated from the front, many with hands blackened by frostbite and/or feet made lame by trench foot, having been ill-equipped for the unrelentingly harsh environment. What they really needed were gummies and gloves, but due the secrecy surrounding their mission, they'd been issued leather boots and standard field jackets instead. Winter gear could've given away the location of their planned assault, and in World War II, secrecy, obfuscation, and misleads became paramount to gain the tactical edge against enemies tentacled with a long reach of international spies.

Panorama view from photo above, showing beach landing site in the background, with mucky access road leading to impossibly steep trailhead

In Attu, the result of this operational/environmental creep was a dearth of sufficient fatigues, food, water, and ammo for infantrymen—these latter indispensables of battle constantly delayed by the hand-to-hand supply lines necessary to their movement into the Attu hinterland. From what I could already see after serving only twenty minutes in the Jackboot theater frostbitten hands and feet were to cause a significant number of American casualties in the Battle for Attu.

This is the War Fought on Attu—Across this valley on Attu up above the fog line that obscures the tops of the mountains lie the passages that lead to Holtz Bay and Chichagof Bay, Jap Attu Island bases that must be captured. In the valley at right center leading back into the mountains are strong Jap positions. Those scattered dots on the valley floor are US troops advancing under fire to dislodge the Japs. At right is US gun position. (AP Wirephoto and Signal Corps caption, 1943)

We followed the *arrière* guard of Company G into the icy foothills of Buffalo Ridge, where a couple of GIs were resting on a medium artillery emplacement half-sunk into the snow and muck.

"What happened to the gun?" inquired a newly arrived trooper.

"The kickback from firing drove it back into the mud," answered a shivering GI. "Now it's stuck there out of aim, impossible to budge from the taffy."

A broad-shouldered feller who partook of a field commander went over to expound upon his problems with another bars-and-patches stalwart from the *arrière* guard, lamenting, "There've been mishaps caused by the terrain, while fog around the peaks has prevented major airstrikes. The enemy on high has barely been scratched."

The *arrière* guard officer answered: "That's just the quagmire here, ain't it? The goddamned howitzers didn't get more than fifty feet beyond the beachhead before they sunk into the muck. As for a preinvasion naval bombardment up here in the mountains, there was none, thanks to the fog."

"The howitzer problem,"—the heavier the machinery, the deeper it sinks into the muskeg. In this example from Adak Island, a howitzer equipped with steel tractor wheels sinks more than six feet into the muck before finding terra firma solid enough to support it. (Exclusive photo by Lt. Harper, 1942)

Stalwart #1 countered: "Lieutenant Murphy somehow wrested his mortar platoon up the ice floe and has secured a foothold against the Jap entrenchments on high, but the enemy still commands Buffalo Ridge in full force. Murphy needs our backup pronto!"

His dire report was punctuated by the whip-rattle of machine gun fire echoing down through the mists, and then suddenly, a body in a white uniform slid down out of the fog, gliding to a stop at the base of the mountain. A GI rushed out, looked the body over, then pulled off the dead soldier's boots and replaced his own with them, discarding his own to the icepack.

"Boy, could I use a pair of Jap gummies," lamented an infantryman sitting against the half-sunken artillery gun. To my surprise, the wishful GI was a black man. I eyed his badge: it signaled Company A of the 383rd Port Battalion. "My feet are so cold," the colored GI complained, "I can't even feel 'em no more." His leather boots were saturated and half-frozen over.

"How long have you been on-island?" I asked.

"Since May thirteen," he replied with chattering teeth. "Company A shipped out from Adak to support the Seventh Infantry. They jumped off first. We were doing stevedore duties when the Seventh needed us to join the human supply chain running up. As it turns out, some of us were handed the rifles of fallen infantrymen and got sucked up in the advance. The 383rd are now doing artillery and frontline combat up here. Imagine that."

"Under Buckner's directive?"

"No. Our orders come from Commander Task Force KING. But don't get me wrong, sir—we've had combat training. It's the cold that gets to me."

US soldiers dug into the ever-sinking muck of Attu fire off a mortar toward the mountain ranges, where Japanese forces are deeply entrenched (Dept. of US Navy photo, May 1943)

"Understood, solider," I privately sympathized, then raised my voice to him so that the surrounding infantrymen would overhear: "As field lieutenant under General Buckner, I'm ordering you to strip the boots off the next dead Jap that slides down that embankment!"

"Yes, sir!" he replied with a firm salute, then hobbled over and perched himself atop a rock at the foot of the slope.

Company G were soon ordered by their (legitimate) commanding officer to start making their way up the slope with their M-1
rifles and machine guns, at which point Igasix̂ gathered Unit
13 and directed us to follow in their footsteps. We moved up
behind them at a staggered distance, except for Kuuyux, who
remained at the base of the floe "to monitor our progress and
field any inquiries from the rear," he stated.

Igasix̂ took point, followed by the ballsy Tayaĝukichax̂ and
his father, Chief Aĝnakax̂. Behind the chief hiked Qatxamax,
then came me, followed by Anĝix̂, the woman who'd assisted
with radio communications at North Arm. Behind her marched
Olean the whaler, Tix̂lax̂ the teen, the female Akuugax, then
Altixum Taĝaacha—Igasix̂'s old hunting partner; then came
Algax̂ Malihnax̂, another young whaling initiate, and so on
and so forth on down the line. We may've been a mixed bunch,
but we'd been well-outfitted and regimented on Umnak, so by
all appearances were just another US infantry detachment carrying on with the requirements of our objective.

The ice floe steepened to a sixty degree angle, where further above, the rear of Company G disappeared into a wall of
clouds obscuring the summit. Suddenly, the Japs opened fire
on them.

Colonel Yamasaki had beefed up his ridgeline reinforcements, desperately pinning the 4th Infantry down about 200
yards from the top. Enemy machine guns, flanking fire, and
grenades being lobbed from well-defiladed positions caused
numerous wounded US soldiers to go sliding back down the
towering ice floe, trying to slow their glide by thrusting their
bayonets into the snow.

"A G.I. falls to his death amid the towering ice floes of Attu." (From Story of America Card #77-18 entitled The Aleutian Campaign—1942–1943—Battle under Bizarre Conditions)

We attempted to grab the hapless soldiers as they passed, but by the time they reached us, most were moving too fast over the icy, sixty degree decline for us to halt without inviting a disastrous domino effect upon our own line. The kicker came in the form of occasional outcroppings of rock, which claimed an untold number of additional casualties in gruesome collisions. Dead bodies began piling up at the base of the mountain—and they were mostly Americans. Within a few short minutes, the Battle for Buffalo Ridge had reached a critical state.

Unit 13 increased their pace up the slope. As we climbed, a ski-plane buzzed in from the south and landed upon the snowy valley floor between Fish Hook and Buffalo Ridge far below. Several men deplaned, apparently to watch the action above. This is precisely the reason the vampire battalion had placed a moratorium on flying: there were too many mortals around to clandestinely take wing like bats. The vigor with which they increased their climb on foot, however, took all my endurance to match.

We entered into the overhanging fog and saw the remnants of Company G struggling for cover within makeshift trenches they'd dug into the ice floe, while further up, Company C of the 32nd Infantry, who'd ascended earlier that morning, was pinned down bad beneath some rocky outcroppings high up on the left-flanking ridgeline. Another dawn patrol battalion—Company F—was meanwhile pinned down under the ridgeline to the right, with machine gun fire and bullets ricocheting wildly around their paltry rock shelters.

The Jap defenders were once again using smokeless shells, making them extremely difficult to spot along the toothy summit. What's worse, they were wearing white uniforms that camouflaged them in with the snow areas.

Igasix̂ brought Unit 13 up beneath a large rock outcropping on the right flank, well before we came into firing range. Six GIs had also taken cover there, and eagerly watched her reorganize our line. Their forward command structure seemed to be nonexistent, as if their leadership had literally slid away, while our crack unit, in comparison, was healthy and formulating bold, uncompromising plans.

On Igasix̂'s command, ten Aleuts (designated Company A) would rush across the floe to back up Company C trapped beneath the left ridgeline, employing a heavy discharge of machine gun fire and grenades. This left-flanking barrage would presumably draw the enemy to concentrate its forces there, and in their distraction, the remainder of Unit 13 (designated Company B) would rush the right and center flanks, purging any Japs still enfiladed there. This main assault force would then sweep left, connecting with Company A in a diagonal phalanx and forcing the enemy into a vise along the left-hand ridge.

"Jake?" a wily-eyed GI asked. "Lieutenant Jake Harper? I thought you were dead!"

"Miles? Holy shit it's you! I thought you were sent to Amchitka!"

"I was," replied Corporal Miles Perkins, my old Adak buddy from the 807th, "until I was shipped to Jackboot. The Amchitka airstrip is almost completed, so all able-bodied doughboys [infantry] have been redeployed here."

"Companies A and B!" ordered Igasix̂. "Ready your weapons and wait for my command!"

I checked to make sure my rifle's safety was released. I was in Company B, whose charge was pending in a handful of minutes or less.

"What outfit are you with?" Miles asked.

"Unit Thirteen."

"Army?"

"A Rangers composite group." I kept it vague.

"Company A, go, go, go!" Igasix̂ cried.

The ten *iidigidi* designated to draw the left-flank distraction went into high action, scampering across the slope with uncanny speed.

"Holy smokes!" Corporal Miles exclaimed. "They can practically fly!"

But Company A took fire during the transfer, and some appeared to get hit.

Miles knelt on the slope beside me, watching in astonishment as all ten troopers—with three machine guns—succeeded in making it across the ice floe in thirty seconds or less. "Army rangers?" he asked vacuously as crack Unit 13-A gave the pinned down 32nd Infantry, Company C soldiers a new lease on life.

The speed and precision in which Unit 13-A fought was almost enough to blow their cover. They emplaced their machine guns in no time, unleashing a wall of fire on high in conjunction with their M-1 rifles and hand grenades, thrown at distance and with accuracy.

Handfuls of dead Japs began tumbling over the escarpments and sliding down the ice floe, streaking it red as they zipped past. But of greatest curiosity to any objective party who might've been observing, was the deftness in which the cave clan Aleuts pulled knives from their belts and flung them at the enemy. The strikes that were not immediately fatal head or chest shots seemed to have a rapid poisoning effect upon their victims. Several enemy wounded by these projectiles were seen to grab their necks and gasp, even if they'd been struck in the shoulder, for example. A few of these luckless soldiers ended up sliding from the summit all the way down to the valley floor while choking to death. I could just make out, at the base of the slope where the dead bodies were piling up, a crew member from the ski-plane walking over and extracting a knife from a dead Jap. He apparently was studying the weapon.

Even as Unit 13-A kept up their onslaught against the left-flanking enemy, some *iidigidi* tended to injured soldiers of the 32nd. Luck was with these casualties, for help was otherwise a long way off. I'd yet to see a field hospital pitched on a sixty degree incline.

"Company 13-B!" shouted Igasix̂. "Ready your weapons and prepare to advance right and center!"

"Well then, Miles," I addressed my former Aviation Engineering Battalion cohort, "I guess it's good-bye again."

As he looked speechlessly on, Igasix̂ gave the command and I rushed up the slope alongside my Aleut brethren. I quickly fell behind, of course, for no mortal can run up an ice floe for any length of time. But this was more than serendipitous: I was fully cognizant of the fact that the cave clan warriors would rout the enemy before me. While it appeared I was an equal, albeit slow member of their team, I was really a mere mortal following in their flying footsteps.

Our Company 13-B took the right-flanking ridge with overwhelming numbers and speed, relieving Company F of the 32nd from a very dire predicament. These latter had been pinned down upon the ice floe for many hours. Frostbite to the hands and trench foot had started to set in for many, inhibiting not only the use their weapons, but also preventing them from making a controlled descent back down the floe, from where they could be evacuated through Jarmin Pass.

The Aleuts of 13-B who'd advanced up the center of the floe before me didn't do so without consequence, however. This deadly, unprotected middle was the easiest target for the Japs on high as they fled toward the left side of the ridgeline. The natives took a heavy barrage of bullets and grenades there, exploding the ice all around them and tearing into their flesh. But my and undoubtedly every fighting *iidigidi*'s greatest concern didn't come to pass: none of the bullets or shrapnel yet discharged from the enemy on Buffalo Ridge was made of silver, for after the Aleuts were hit, they were able to halt whatever backward slide the impacts incurred, then resume their march toward the ridgeline. Claims of "bullet-proof infantry" broached by the US soldiers in observance were answered with the explanation of "bulletproof vests." Many *iidigidi* had chosen to wear their wooden-rod armor beneath their army fatigues, so at least in image the excuse appeared legitimate.

As Units 13-A and -B connected into a flank running cross-wise up the slope toward the right-hand ridge, the Japs who'd retreated to their left-enfiladed crest began to feel the squeeze. We advanced our line there into a viselike grip, and as we did, scores of enemy casualties began cavorting over the rocky ridgeline and spilling down the floe once again. There were so many sliding past, and I was so slow in climbing up, that I was able to discern a pattern to the blades sticking out of the dead and dying Japs. While some of the throwing knives employed by Unit 13 were the steel ones issued by Butler, many partook of the native type I'd seen back at the barabara. Constructed of bone or walrus tusk ivory and causing their victims to suffer in a highly unusual manner, these aboriginal knives were undoubtedly laced with a naturally derived poison. It seems that, after the indigenous weapons possessed by the Aleut warriors had been confiscated upon their arrival to Umnak, they had merely constructed new ones from the local environment there, during our time in training. Whatever the case, the eclectic array of our armory, the deftness of our fighters, and the tactical plan of our leader, Igasix̂, enabled crack Unit 13 to take Buffalo Ridge in just under an hour.

In the aftermath of the battle, a distant rumble sounded from the heavens. As usual in the Aleutians theater, it was difficult to determine whether the noise emanated from planes, a volcano, or a storm. The surviving Americans became visibly frightened, perhaps believing a squadron of Japanese Zeroes was calling in to bomb the ridge—a fair possibility. As the roar increased, battle-worn US soldiers rolled beneath outcroppings of rock on high, while all about the surrounding summits, black ravens took to confused flight.

Suddenly, Colonel Eareckson's plane came buzzing over the summit from behind. He was employing forward air control procedures over Attu—another one of his strategic inventions, this time, to fly in through patches of cloud and fog that the naval guns couldn't fire through with any degree of accuracy.

The American and Aleut troops emitted a collective salvo of cheers and whistling as Colonel E proceeded to lay his eggs upon Jap enfiladed positions on Fishhook Ridge adjacent before continuing out over Chichagof Harbor, which in the breaking fog we could see was chock-full of US warships. The greater Rockwell/Kinkaid pincer movement offensive, after more than a dozen days of hard combat, was finally backing the Japs into an east Attu dead-end trap.

This view of the corner of Chicagof Harbor on the Island of Attu, with village of Attu nestling along the shore, shows general nature of territory where finale of offensive against Japs is taking place. Attu village, the Navy announced Saturday, has been wiped out by US Army bombers. Remaining Jap forces, Navy said, have been split into three isolated groups—one along shore of Chicagof Harbor, the others southeast and southwest of the village. (AP photo and caption, 1943)

General Simon Buckner sent up a radio call to Buffalo Ridge, demanding to meet the "unknown unit" that'd ascended behind Company G.

Igasix̂, Chief Aĝnakax̂, Tayaĝukichax̂, and I slid back down the ice floe in a controlled glide using two knives apiece, at the base of which we found Buckner already talking to Kuuyux, who had stayed behind. They were studying one of the Unangax̂ knives made of white ivory. Apparently, Buckner had been the person I'd seen deplane at the onset of our campaign. A pair of oversized binoculars hanging at his chest evinced he'd been watching the action firsthand. Looking up toward the ridge-line, I could just make out with the naked eye the ambiguous shape of semi-fogbound men.

Buckner, in examining the knife, appeared flabbergasted.

"Don't touch the tip," Tayaĝukichax̂ warned.

"Why?" Buckner asked.

"Because it's laced with aconite poison."

The general appeared both startled and impressed. "And where did you get that?"

"The monkshood root, of course," replied Tayaĝukichax̂ with a stiff upper lip, his manner of hiding his fangs while speaking giving him the appearance of a tough, hardened fighter. "Dig beneath the muskeg and maybe you'll find some," he added, almost mockingly.

Buckner, never having expected me there, was slow to recognize me. "Lieutenant Harper? What the hell are you doing up here?"

"I'm with this unit."

"What unit?"

"Unit Thirteen."

He scanned our faces and fatigues. Our collars were all turned up against the cold, while Igasix̂ had a scarf wrapped snugly beneath her chin, further masking her cover.

Unfortunately, with the fog lifting, the light of day was increasing in bearing.

"Unit Thirteen, huh?" the general was skeptical. He ordered Igasix̂ to lower her scarf. Her weathered, pockmarked cheeks didn't immediately give her away as female, but Buckner was still a little suspicious, so he ordered Tayaĝukichax̂ and Chief Aĝnakax̂ to lower their collars, as well. It seemed as if he might've recognized them, but in the now beating sunlight, they appeared fairer skinned than the Aleuts he'd met on Adak a fortnight ago. Such was the mysterious, photoactive trait of the *iidigidi* by day, and we were fortunate because of the sun's timely augmentation.

Chief Aĝnakax̂ wisely obfuscated, "Unit Thirteen are native Alaskans serving with the Alaska Territorial Guard. We hail from Skagway, Kenai, and environs."

"Why aren't you wearing dogtags?" Buckner probed further.

Several tense seconds passed before Tayaĝukichax̂ gambled at an answer: "We're special operations."

In light of how well crack Unit 13 had performed on the ridgeline, Buckner overcame his suspicion, congratulating me on a job well done. Apparently, he thought I was the unit leader. "From what I could make out through the obscuring mists," he went further, "that was the best fighting I've ever seen."

Had Buckner seen any real action beyond Jackboot, I would've been impressed by his assessment. But such was not the case.

"It was Eareckson's plane that helped complete the push," I remarked, knowing damn well Colonel E had nothing to do with it.

"Wild Bill, eh?" Buckner replied. "Not the most disciplined of flyboys, but apparently good enough to be promoted to Deputy Chief of Staff for the Coordination of Air and Naval Action for the Eleventh Air Force for this invasion. Perhaps

General Butler will be pleased, but I wouldn't float the idea to Admiral Kinkaid. As far as I'm concerned, it was the crack army boys of Unit Thirteen that finished the job on this ridge."

"General!" a radioman called over. "I think you should hear this, sir!"

We followed Buckner over to the radio box, where a desperate message, warbled by atmospherics, was being broadcast. From what I could make out, a detachment of army specialists from the North Force, 17th Infantry Regiment was stuck in a williwaw and was being attacked by Japs.

"What is your location?" Buckner grunted through the receiver.

Naught but horrific screams sounded back over radio static.

"North Force Seventeen!" Buckner shouted into the handset. "Where are you, over!?"

"Red Head!" the reply was unmistakable. "PLEASE SAVE US! *EEYAAAH!*"

"Who is your KO [commanding officer], over!?"

<more screaming, then only static>

"Come in, Seventeenth!"

<heavy atmospherics>

"This is General Simon Buckner. Please reply, over!"

<steady white noise>

Buckner stared critically at the receiver, then at the radioman. "Please save us?" he remarked. "What the fuck's going on at Red Head?"

"I don't know, sir," the radioman obliged a reply, "but it sounds like they're in trouble."

"No shit, soldier!" Buckner spat, then said to Chief Aĝnakax̂, Igasix̂, Kuuyux, Tayaĝukichax̂, and me, who were all gathered together, "You five, come with me! We're going to recon Red Head!" He marched toward his ski-plane.

"Sir!" said Igasix̂. "What about the rest of my unit still on the ridge?"

Buckner stopped and turned. "*Your* unit?" He glanced uneasily between her and me, then up at the peak. "Radioman!" he called over. "Radio up and give Unit Thirteen the following order from General Simon Buckner: They are to move forward with the Fourth and Thirty-Second Infantries to points three and four on Fishhook Ridge."

"Unit Thirteen to join the Fourth and Thirty-Second to points three and four on the Fishhook! Got it, sir!"

"Now come on, and that's an order!" he commanded the rest of us before marching determinedly on.

I was impressed by his and the radioman's swift retention of details—but then again, one didn't become lieutenant general or radioman without this essential ability. As for Igasix̂ and the cave clan vampires, they went along willingly with the general's plan. We followed him to the ski-plane, which was actually just a float plane equipped with skis instead of pontoons. Two grim-faced soldiers stood guarding the aircraft. Buckner told us to get onboard, and then he assumed the pilot's seat.

"I didn't know you could fly," I remarked over his shoulder, after having been packed in back with the others.

"Is that so, lieutenant?" he replied as his guards yanked at the propeller blades, firing up the engine. "You must've missed my flight training classes at West Point."

The sentries got onboard, one in the copilot seat, the other just squeezing in on the floor directly behind him, and soon the ski-plane lifted off willy-nilly into the broken fog carrying our ad hoc composite group of eight: General Buckner and his two attachés, Igasix̂, Kuuyux, Chief Aĝnakax̂, my good ole bud Tayaĝukichax̂, and me.

DON'T PISS ON ME

AFTER TEN minutes of weighted-down but stable enough flying, we entered into a thick, grey cloud. The aircraft vibrated
in the driving rain and shook at the controls, but Buckner was
able to fly her through, and when he did, he had to immediately bank hard to avoid the side of a mountain. Another few
seconds on course would've killed us (save for the vampires,
perhaps). Such was the perilous nature of flight in the Aleutian
Islands, and probably accounted for a good number of planes
lost with all hands.

"So much for your flight classes," Chief Aĝnakax̂ quipped.

Buckner glared sourly back at him and said, "I suppose you
think that's funny, mister . . . what was your name?"

"Chief Killisnoo," replied Aĝnakax̂, referring to one of the
Aleut internment camps set up by the US government.

"Chief Killisnoo, eh?" answered Buckner, and left it at that.
These two were still going at it, but for now, the general had
an overladen plane to land. He set us deftly down into a wide
snow bowl about a mile short of the Red Head location, which
was obstructed by a storm front and ridge escarpment, according to his copilot attaché holding a map. (In 1943, Attu Island
remained a topographic sketch, and as we'd just experienced
almost plowing into the side of a mountain, storm-hidden
ridges were better left to hiking.)

The Hazards of Aleutian Flying—the photo on top, showing the summertime skies over Kuluk Bay on Adak, presents a typical Aleutians meteorology, where layer upon layer of conflicting climatologic pockets spell dangerous unpredictability for even the most experienced of pilots. The picture at the bottom of Great Sitkin, also taken from Adak, reveals how even the greatest of mountains can be mostly hidden (sometimes entirely hidden) from a pilot's view until it's too late for evasive maneuvers, especially given the relatively sketchy flight technology that existed in 1943. (Exclusive photos by the author)

We deplaned and were about to hike into the frontier when Chief "Killisnoo" Aĝnakax̂ prodded Buckner: "Mister flight instructor, do you really intend to leave your plane out here on the ice? What happens if a williwaw comes?"

"The title is General Buckner!" Simon the Kentuckian was incensed. He ordered his two subordinates to anchor the plane.

The attachés retracted wing cables from the aircraft, but had no sledgehammers with which to drive the two stakes into the hardened icepack. They tried to jab them in by sheer brawn, but were quickly flummoxed. "What now, general?" one asked.

Befuddled, Buckner began scanning the icepack perimeter through his binoculars, probably looking for a boulder to anchor the plane to. The Aleuts were meanwhile having a laugh over the Americans' predicament.

"General flight instructor," offered Aĝnakax̂, "it's not that complicated."

Buckner dropped his binoculars, which bounced over his robust chest on their lanyard, while he took to warning with an upraised, shaking fist, "Call me that one more time and I'll wring your neck!"

"General, sir," continued the chief, "tell your men to piss on the ice beneath each wing: it will make holes to drop your lines into."

"Is this another one of your stupid Indian jokes?" Buckner quipped.

"Aleut talk straight—only white man joke," Kuuyux put in.

"It could work, sir," offered one of Buckner's attachés.

"So we piss out a few holes and drop the lines in," the general said, reconsidering. "What then? They're still not anchored down."

To which Aĝnakax̂ replied, "You, general flight instructor, along with Lieutenant Harper here, can piss in the holes again, freezing them over with quick-drying, yellow cement."

"It's General Buckner, you asshole!" The Kentuckian lunged at the chief.

I jumped between them. "Hey, hey, come on fellas! We've got a job to do!" The fact was, I knew Chief Aĝnakax̂ could rip off Buckner's head in the blink of an eye.

Buckner backed off and shook out his shoulders, trying to regain his trademark steely composure. Chief Aĝnakax̂, meanwhile, was smiling alongside his cave clan warriors. Kuuyux, however, held a grim countenance toward the northwestern ridgeline, where Red Head was situated.

"Well, I gotta go anyway," I mediated. "Let's give it a shot, boys."

Deflated, the general vaguely pointed to his two attachés, then signaled toward the ski-plane's wings, reluctantly conceding. These latter went over to their respective positions, unbuttoned their flies and proceeded to piss onto the ice.

"You *Americanchins* must plug the holes," Tayaĝukichax̂ teased the general and me.

Buckner got the message, instructing, "Lieutenant, just get over there beneath the starboard wing and I'll take the port side."

"Yes, sir."

The sentries' urine had bored two holes into the ice. The ends of the cables were dropped in, and then the general and I stood over the pitted ice and unbuttoned our flies, preparing to finish the job by filling them up with our own piss.

"Wait! Not yet!" warned Igasix̂, dashing in front of me.

I held my bladder just in time, as did the general when Chief Aĝnakax̂ went dashing likewise before him. As we stood there holding our yellow effluent in check, the two Aleuts proceeded to scrape at the surrounding icepack with their knives, filling the holes beneath us with shavings of snow.

"I know you want to, but please don't piss on me," the chief taunted Buckner politely.

As for me, I turned aside from Igasîx̂. She may've been my lover, but I felt awkward standing over her with my exposed dingdong dangling in my hand.

By the time the assisting Aleuts gave the signal, my wong was so cold that I had to concentrate hard to fight through the retention.

At last, the general and I released our loads into the holes. Our warm urine mixed with the shaven ice and began to coagulate as it rose up around the cable ends, freezing solid shortly thereafter.

"You really think that'll hold her?" Buckner put to Chief Aĝnakax̂ as he buttoned up his trousers.

"Rock solid," declared the chief.

The ice had been broken in more ways than one as we set off into the great unknown, together as one—more or less.

BLACK FINGERNAILS

EN ROUTE to the recon sector, a lone soldier stumbled forth from the storm line and collapsed before we could reach him. His fatigues were smoldering and his hands showed fresh burn marks. We were able to revive him with sips of cold water, and as we did, his eyes grew wide with terror. He grasped my and Buckner's sleeves, reporting with trembling, barely intelligible words: "I was with a covert company of the Seventeenth Infantry. We established a beachhead at Blonde Cove and were ambushed from behind. The enemy came ashore at night and threw their bodies at us in plumes of fire."

"Flamethrowers," Buckner said grimly.

"No, no," uttered the GI, curling his blistering hands, "with their bodies! Their bodies were on fire and they flew themselves at us sideways in the flames! We were burned horribly, then they tortured my guys with their long black fingernails. It was terrible . . . *just terrible*! My entire company, they're dying. Please, just get me the hell out of here! We're in grave danger here and must leave at once!"

"He's a little shell-shocked," Buckner told us privately. "He's talking crazy, but I think we can count on flamethrowers ahead. We shall advance under the cover of night."

"No, please, turn back! You must not go to Red Head!" the soldier implored.

What worried me most about the terrified infantryman's account was not so much his perplexing story, but the reaction it engendered in the cave clan vampires, who became visibly concerned.

"I'm with the general," Kuuyux put in, eliciting a look of surprise from Igasix̂ and Chief Aĝnakax̂. "We continue forward at dusk. Attu is presently falling, but we must make sure of that and finish the job at Red Head."

The burned GI rose to his feet and pushed back against the lot of us.

Disregarding the shell-shocked soldier's continued remonstrations about remaining in the area, Buckner ordered him to return to the anchored ski-plane and wait for us there. At the mention of an emergency box containing a First Aid kit, a wool blanket, and canned provisions, the infantryman prodded sullenly on toward the aircraft.

As our makeshift unit continued forward into the dusk, the Aleuts appeared troubled about following Buckner and Kuuyux into the target sector. But since neither Igasix̂ nor Aĝnakax̂— the de facto field leaders of Unit 13—waged a formal protest, we trekked onward beneath the ever-darkening sky.

RED HEAD

IN THE black of night, our composite group arrived on a ridge, from where in our nocturnal reconnoitering we observed a ship heaved to just offshore of Blonde Cove, its single tall sail set aflame. It was clearly not an American vessel, military or otherwise, but looked old and foreign, perhaps Russian or Siberian, with its one square, burning sail hoisted perpendicularly upon a massive crosstree over her main deck, while both the bow and stern were angled sharply upward like a leprechaun's boot. No movement, other than the flames, could be discerned anywhere onboard.

Ship with Burning Sail on Storm Sea *(Illustration by Dusan Kostic)*

Buckner suspected it was the work of the Japs, who were likely manning a beach defensive site in the dark, so he determined we hang back until daybreak to better ascertain the situation.

Hours passed in the freezing cold, but the burning of the sails did not dissipate.

Buckner and Chief Aĝnakax̂ did not get along well that night, continuing to take potshots at each other. At one point,

Kuuyux got drawn into the fray, siding with Buckner and publicly berating the chief for "lacking true authority."

Fortunately, late spring nights were short in the Aleutians.

In the twilight of dawn on May 25, as the ship's sail continued
to burn unabatedly some 400 feet beneath us, we got our first
view of the terrain in question, Buckner's field map naming
the prominent landmarks. The wide bay of Steller Cove splayed
out into the grey mist of morning, with Red Head denoting
its western promontory, barely visible in the distance through
the brume. A low-lying, tundra-clad point reached out into the
cove at center left, creating two smaller egressions on its either
side: Brunette Cove to the west, and Blonde Cove to the east,
while the flaming ship remained anchored below our present
position in a tighter, half-square cove with a seemingly deep
draft. Each cove had a dedicated creek running down from
the steep hinterland gullies. All in all, it was not dissimilar to
a scaled-down version of Holtz Bay, where the bulk of the US
Northern Force had landed closer to the primary battle theater
of Chichagof Harbor.

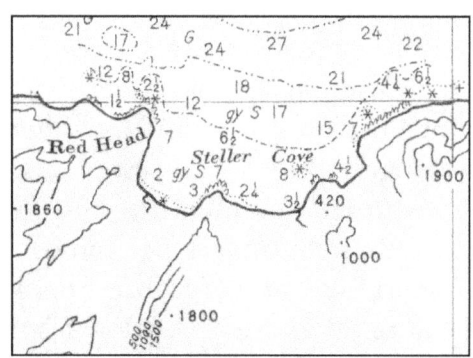

*Red Head and Steller Cove (From US Coast and Geodetic Survey
#9198—Attu [restricted], Washington DC, February 1945)*

At the tundra point at the center left of Steller Cove (that Buckner called "Central Tongue"), the enemy had indeed established, or overrun, a beachhead. An encampment of black tents was buffered by a landward-facing phalanx of lean-to structures apparently made from folds of muskeg that'd been cut from the tundra and bent upward on poles, creating a keen camouflage that at first was missed by General Buckner. Two score or more dark figures were seen moving about the well-defiladed encampment, making some sort of preparations, while others were apparently digging trenches.

Suddenly, four figures broke from the mysterious base and proceeded slowly up the gulch toward us, the apparent leader holding a hand up in a gesture of comity.

Buckner remained concerned. The approaching persons were carrying spears and swords.

Our unit of eight started cautiously down the muskeg-clad hillside to meet them. The terrain was half frozen and slippery, causing the uninitiated among us (the Americans) to walk awkwardly as our ankles twisted into the hardened vines. Finally, we came before Diehm Creek and stopped.

As the apparent leader approached the other side of the bubbling waterway, strange, iconic red markings could be seen on his chest and body, while his accompanying attachment looked equally bizarre, dressed up in primeval-looking garb.

Upon closer inspection, we could see that the mysterious party was carrying bushido swords and long, steel spears that I recognized as Unangax̂ throwing-lances.

Their leader, who commanded his men with odd, lanky movements, had only four fingers per hand, and big, black claws on each finger. Rows of ivory labrets bookended by fanglike bird beaks were set above and below his lips, appearing like an extra set of jaws framing his mouth. He wore bird skull earrings, and a sharp bone was pierced horizontally through his forehead, replete with sharks' teeth hanging from its either side, partially covering his coal-black pupils and crimson-red irises. In his bony, birdlike claws, he brandished a mighty sword, likewise embellished with indecipherable markings.

Fallen Angel of Death (*Illustration by Dusan Kostic*)

Buckner and his bodyguards appeared shocked, while the cave clan Aleuts held extremely wary expressions—except for Kuuyux, who calmly approached the freakish infantry leader and nodded in apparent recognition.

The four-fingered freak then repeated in four different languages—Unangam Tunuu, Russian, Japanese, and finally English—in quick succession, telling Kuuyux, "So we meet again." He then addressed the rest of us, speaking in all four languages at the same time, the English component I heard as: "Welcome to our summer fish camp."

My fellow Yanks and I were struck with mortal terror, while the freak's escorts just laughed.

"Who, or what, the hell are you?" Buckner demanded, aiming his pistol at the leader's chest. The rest of us followed suit, training our weapons on the three ghoulish escorts.

The demonic leader emitted a spurious laugh, and then responded, again in four languages concurrently: "I am Iĝanax̂, Iĝanax̂ the Terrible, and this coward,"—pointing his sword at Chief Aĝnakax̂—"the chief of the *iidigidi*, is the one who made me so terrible, terrible and terrific."

"What happened to my men?" Buckner pushed back. "The company of the Seventeenth Regiment—what have you done with them?"

This "Iĝanax̂ the Terrible" lifted a long, black claw before his mouth and licked it. "Do you really want to know what happened to your bony platoon?" he sniggered in English. "I'll show you, but you can blame Chief Aĝnakax̂ here for everything you see. *Tsk-tsk-tsk*, pathetic cave clan chief. You never should've abandoned me on the *Arkhangelsk*, forcing me to find my own way over the tumultuous sea. Surprise, surprise, I did not die, but was castaway on *Qax̂um tanangis*, where a rat-infested Japanese merchant vessel shipwrecked not long afterward. For two hundred years you left me to rot on Rat Island, where I drank the blood of brown rats to survive. Now behold your creation. Are you satisfied?"

Buckner, flabbergasted, replied, "Joke's over, Aleut freak. Surrender your weapons now!"

"Aleut freak? *Ha! Ha! Ha!* What a perfect coincidence, just as we, the *khoughkh*, have come out of the darkness to reign over the world, you have joined forces with the *iidigidi*—the weaker boogeymen, who I see have finally come out of hiding, into the sickly light."

As Iĝanax̂'s hideous attachments laughed derisively, their faces became flush with direct light from the sun, which was just peeking over the ridgeline behind us. Then suddenly their skin caught fire, along with the flesh of their terrible leader.

"What's happening to them?" a bodyguard of Buckner asked in horror, the cave clan vampires all the while backing away from the fearsome *khoughkh* creatures—all save for Kuuyux, who remained standing unperturbed.

"I am Chief Iĝanax̂," the black-clawed freak growled amid the flames of his burning body, "and vengeance is mine!"

"Welcome back, my son," Kuuyux said.

"*Nangaa!*" Chief Aĝnakax̂ cried *No!* in Unangam Tunuu.

Iĝanax̂ shape-shifted his body into an extension of flames that leapt over the creek and engulfed Chief Aĝnakax̂ in a flash, turning him to ash.

The column of white dust left from the chief's incinerated body shot up into the heavens as if it were being reclaimed by a powerful vacuum on high.

Buckner's terrified sentries took to their heels, but didn't get far before the deadly *khoughkh* threw fire at them, too, burning them alive.

Iĝanax̂ took a shot at Buckner, but in this instance, Tayaĝukichax̂ was swifter, grabbing the general and *flying* him out of the line of fire.

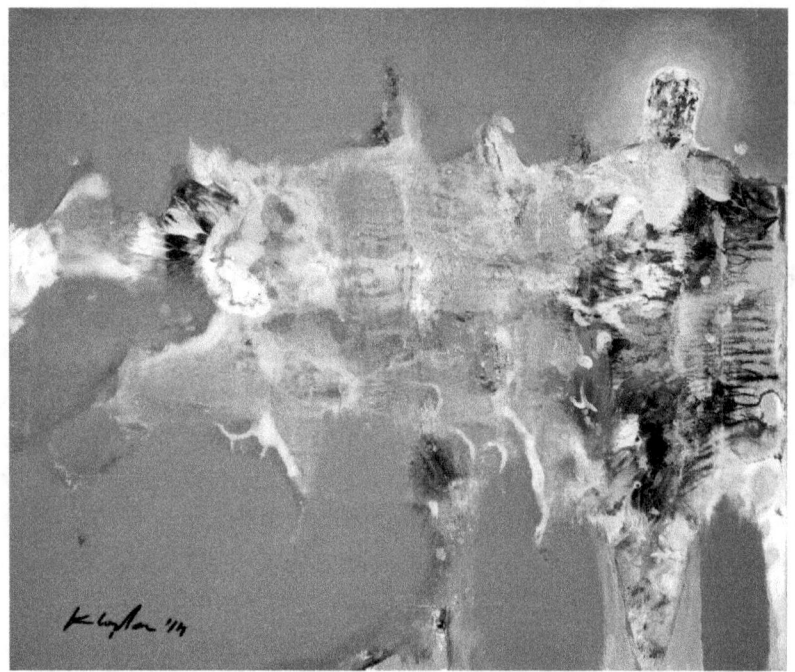

The fearsome, shape-shifting khoughkh creatures (Exclusive painting by Ovidiu Kloska, ref#12.03.2014)

Suddenly and without warning, the remainder of Unit 13, who numbered about two score cave clan fighters, flew up from holes in the muskeg of the surrounding hillsides and dive-bombed over us, waging a surprise counterattack against the *khoughkh*. Thus the *iidigidi* revealed their full powers to Simon Buckner.

There were thirty-nine *iidigidi* backup troops in all, but several were quickly incinerated by the bodily flares released by the *khoughkh*. In every instance I observed, the ashes of the deceased cave clan fighters shot up into the sky as if into a columnar vacuum tube.

As Igasiŝ did battle with the evil entities, protecting me all the while, the only weakness I could see with the *khoughkh* was an inability to fly more than a few meters at a time. When their wings appeared through their flaming bodies, I discerned feathers burned black and matted with muck, irrevocably damaged.

But even with over forty *iidigidi* against just four *khoughkh*, enemy resistance proved too strong, the rest of their ungodly battalion never even bothering to come up from the beach-head, so great were the powers being practiced by their leader Iĝanax̂ and his incendiary detachment of three. In addition to killing the cave clan vampires with fire, they smote them with unwieldy spears and swords. Apparently forged in silver, these mighty armaments melted the *iidigidi* on impact.

On seeing this, Igasix̂ called a wholesale retreat. As Unit 13 scrambled, she took me under her wing and flew me to a surrounding ridge, the remainder of our battalion arriving shortly thereafter.

Iĝanax̂ and his fighters did not pursue, but casually returned to their Steller Cove encampment with Kuuyux strolling beside them. The treasonous shaman proceeded to intermingle with dozens more *khoughkh* staked out there.

"Thank God you came," I told Olean, who'd landed beside us.

"Not God," he replied. "Thank Chief Aĝnakax̂, now permanently deceased: he's the one who covertly ordered us to follow Buckner's plane. He told us to hide at the recon sector and 'be ready for anything under the sun.' Alas, his prophetic insight spelled his own demise."

"I'll fly them to the gates of hell!" Tayaĝukichax̂ cried. "The gates of hell, I tell you!" he bawled aloud, then buried his tear-smeared face into his brawny hands. Some cave clan fighters went to console him, but he pushed them away and dropped to his knees, preferring to mourn privately.

"Iĝanax̂ had been friends with Tayaĝukichax̂," Igasix̂ revealed quietly. "Iĝanax̂ and Kuuyux betrayed Tayaĝukichax̂, by killing his father before him; Tayaĝukichax̂ will live to avenge Chief Aĝnakax̂."

Tayaĝukichax̂ had airlifted Buckner to our fallback site, where he stood watching the encampment below through his binoculars. He shook his head, then lifted the binocular strap clear from his head and handed me the oversized bifocals, saying, "Take a look, lieutenant. Maybe you or your unit here can help me make some sense out of this."

Iĝanax̂ and His Core Group of Fighters (*Illustration by Dusan Kostic*)

Through the general's powerful field glasses, I saw Iĝanax̂ and another flaming *khoughkh* put on large, iron, starburst helmets, which caused them to stop burning from head to toe. But what really shocked me was something else. I handed the binoculars back to Buckner and said, "Check the point of muskeg behind the tents."

He focused in and his mouth fell agog. "Lord have mercy," he uttered with dread.

"What is it?" Tayaĝukichax̂ inquired from his state of kneeling despondency. "What do you see?"

"Heads," I answered grimly, "human heads, impaled on stakes."

"In a circular formation," added Buckner, his hands starting to shake. "Those are my men, they must be: the ones we heard over radio, the unit that went missing. *The bastards!*"

Buckner, usually stalwart and circumspect—almost discreet—dropped his binoculars to his chest and with both hands pulled back his snowy thatch of hair, disturbed to no end.

Noticing the *khoughkh* still observing us from afar, Igasix̂ ordered us to fall back further.

We flocked out together, landing on a ridge about a mile from the ski-plane, which was visible on the ice field far below. In all, there were thirty-two *iidigidi* remaining from our unit. Buckner and I sheltered in a cave with them, licking our wounds.

The general was pained about having to retreat, remarking that retreat was not to his style, but in that same sentence, he was looking down at his feet in agony, and added that he might be getting trench foot—even with his gummies on.

I got a fire going with some dried shrubbery I'd found in the cave, and as I fanned the flames, Igasix̂ lamented to Buckner that Unit 13, of anybody, realized the importance of the battle at hand.

"The Battle for Attu?" the general asked.

"It's bigger than that," she said.

"Much bigger," added Tayaĝukichax̂, his once jocular expression now bleak and hardened over.

BAD BLOOD

AS I began pulling off Buckner's boots, Igasix̂ explained: "As you've just witnessed, the *khoughkh* are extremely powerful and dangerous to us *iidigidi*. The bad blood began in days bygone, when, during a raid by our clan, Kuuyux and his son Iĝanax̂ were kidnapped and made into slaves by Chief Aĝnakax̂ and Alix̂, Aniqdux̂six̂'s father.

"Then, four years prior to the *Arkhangelsk* shipwreck incident, Iĝanax̂, who had been Alix̂'s oarsman, stabbed Alix̂ in the back, killing him, but later claiming that his master had drowned. Kuuyux had witnessed the murder from an adjacent *baidarka*, but played alibi for his son. Alix̂'s body washed ashore three days later and was discovered by one of Chief Aĝnakax̂'s scouts.

"Chief Aĝnakax̂ told the rest of our clan that Alix̂'s body was in a real bad state, and quickly had it mummified and placed in the burial cave with the rest of Alix̂'s belongings.

"I'd witnessed the murder from shore when I was fifteen years old, but was too afraid to tell anyone at the time. Three years later, when I finally got the courage to tell Chief Aĝnakax̂ that Iĝanax̂ had killed Alix̂, he brushed it off as child's fancy, instead holding to the version of events as reported by Kuuyux and Iĝanax̂. Their explanation that Alix̂ had drowned continued to be the commonly accepted story as perceived by the clan.

"Aniqdux̂six̂ was incensed at me for waiting so long to tell anyone that Iĝanax̂ killed her father, and to this day she holds a grudge against me. She suspects that Chief Aĝnakax̂ was in collusion to knock off Alix̂, who was an increasingly popular tribal steward and thus a threat to his power. The fact that the chief rushed Alix̂'s body away and had it mummified so quickly lent credence to her theory.

"Meanwhile, Iganakuchax̂, Alix̂'s widowed wife and the mother of Aniqdux̂six̂, began giving away her possessions to the impressionable Chief Aĝnakax̂. She was mourning, you see, and this went on for thirty days until she hit rock bottom. It was then, when Iganakuchax̂ was poor, lonely, and desperate for a mate, that Chief Aĝnakax̂ took her as his own wife.

In this manner Iganakuchax̂ found a new home, her possessions returned, and a new man—a chief, moreover—to take orders from";—she rolled her eyes—"all this did not sit well with Aniqdux̂six̂, of course, but I digress."

In her remarkable revelation of past events, Igasix̂ several times had mentioned Aniqdux̂six̂. Finally I knew who this person was. But it bothered me that I could spend so much time in intimate quarters with the likes of Iganakuchax̂, Aniqdux̂six̂'s mother, and Chief Aĝnakax̂, her stepfather, yet they never spoke a word about her. I was also peeved at Igasix̂—and a little nonplussed—that she should also shield me from the story of this poor girl Aniqdux̂six̂ for so long.

"After the cave clan was turned into *iidigidi*," Tayaĝukichax̂ interposed, "we were all deemed equal and Kuuyux was no longer our slave. My father realized the importance of keeping our disease quarantined from other tribes, thus he knew that holding infected slaves wouldn't work well for us in the long run: they would eventually try to defect, which could spread the plague. His only choice was to co-opt Kuuyux and grant him concessions of power.

"Over the decades," Tayaĝukichax̂ continued, "Kuuyux's influence grew until he became the real decision-maker for the tribe, superseding Chief Aĝnakax̂. I don't know why my father started doing Kuuyux's bidding. Somehow, after we were changed, Kuuyux gained the upper hand in affairs of the clan, but always worked in the background, using my father as the leader only in appearance. Perhaps he had blackmailed my father by threatening to spread the plague outside; or perhaps . . ." Tayaĝukichax̂ paused, hanging his head deep in regret, "perhaps my father was in collusion to murder Alix̂ in order to take Iganakuchax̂ as his own. He'd always had an eye for her, but Alix̂ wouldn't let him near her. But by having Iĝanax̂ kill Alix̂ in order to take his wife, if such was the case, Aĝnakax̂ was mistakenly relinquishing his supreme authority to Kuuyux, Iĝanax̂'s father and alibi, who could then blackmail my dad, promising not to confess to others what had really transpired, so long as concessions of power were granted."

Only a mind like Tayaĝukichax̂'s could intuit such webs of deceit—I of all people knew that. But as blood of Chief Aĝnakax̂, perhaps his complex assessment of his father was accurate. Alas, that great and ruthless trickster had laid bare his tender soul, even if it were damned.

Igasix̂ patted him on the back, and this time he didn't resist the consolation.

I'd gotten to thinking during their exposé of things past, and after they'd finished speaking, I said: "This might explain why, once your clan was changed into *iidigidi*, Chief Aĝnakax̂ instigated the gen-cycle, thereby banning polygamy and ensuring Iganakuchax̂ would always be his."

"And his alone," Igasix̂ agreed with my cursory assessment.

"Once Iĝanax̂ was infected," Tayaĝukichax̂ continued, gathering himself to posit, "he never returned from the *Arkhangelsk*, but got lost at sea and shipwrecked on Rat Island. Since then, it seems he'd somehow gotten back into contact with his father on Adak, conspiring with him from afar. Perhaps they'd been meeting at the Red Head fish camp for years, from where they now seek to launch their campaign of revenge."

Igasix̂ interposed: "I believe they regained contact with one another only recently, perhaps when the Imperial Japanese started occupying our islands. The Japs probably landed on Rat Island, where Iĝanax̂ and his homebred army of *khoughkh* would've turned them. In my estimation, this war is what brought Igasix̂ and Kuuyux back together. It wouldn't be beyond Kuuyux to give away the location of our barabara for the Japs to bomb, which must've gone up through Japanese high command. Can't you see? This is Iĝanax̂'s and Kuuyux's chance to seize more than just clan power or even power over an island. With the Japanese military at their command, thanks to the *promuishlenniki* plague, their putsch for world domination begins."

Buckner, visibly disturbed, inquired, "How high up the Imperial chain of command do you think the *khoughkh* have infiltrated and infected the Japs? Do you think that Kuuyux and Iĝanax̂ are in on the Tanaka Plan? Are the Japanese high command also these *khoughkh* entities you speak of?"

Nobody could answer, but Buckner's concern was legitimate: was infecting North America, starting with the Aleutians where the *khoughkh* could gain a foothold and spread their disease to American forces on US soil, the core strategy behind Phase Four of the Tanaka Memorial?

"I don't know," Igasix̂ answered in time, "but the plague threat posed by the *khoughkh* is real. We remaining Unit Thirteen warriors must stop them at all costs, and you, General Buckner, must leave the area at once, along with the soldier currently sheltering in your plane. You are easy targets for the *khoughkh*, and we might not be able to protect you again. The risk of Iĝanax̂ infecting your army with the *promuishlenniki* plague is too great."

Buckner took a deep breath, nodding subtly. He began pulling his gummies back on, relaying in low, slow tones, "I shall contact Commander Butler about quarantining the area as a no-fly zone to prevent Jap reinforcements, while you, Igasix̂, lead your remaining force of thirty-two *iidigidi* on a counterattack against the *khoughkh* at Red Head. Do you think you've got what it takes?"

"Yes, sir," Igasix̂ answered with full confidence. "We have our ways."

It seemed to me that, whatever the truth to Igasix̂'s assurances (given Unit 13's recent routing by just four enemy vampires), she at all costs was seeking to keep Buckner's troops away from the *khoughkh* and the associated risk posed by the *promuishlenniki* plague.

"And you, sir?" I inquired of the American general.

"I shall return to Holtz and Massacre Bays to assist in commanding our fronts there."

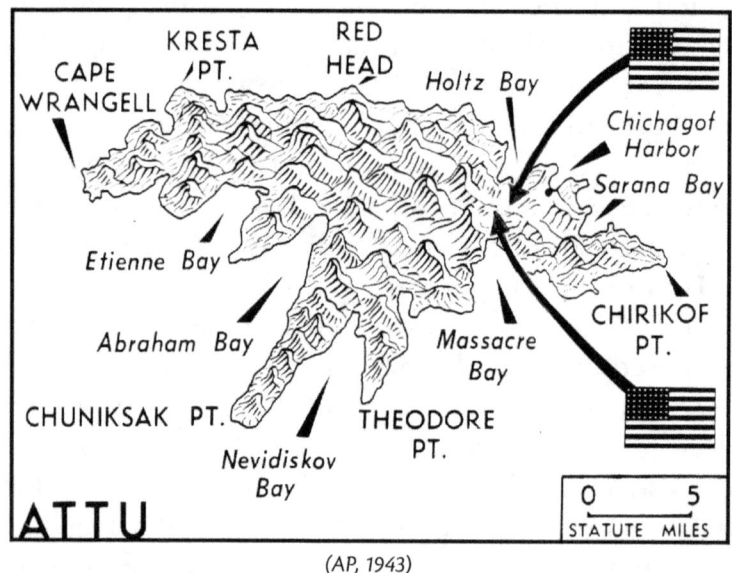

(AP, 1943)

He stood to test his feet. His trench foot had been much alleviated by the fire. "Thank you for your service!" he barked, saluting us like the stalwart general he was. "All this madness should serve as a reminder of the true evil of Fascism."

"Yes, sir!" I returned a firm salute.

"Yes, sir!" and, "Thank you, sir!" were added by many an Aleut.

Buckner dropped his salute. "I've seen some screwy jazz in my time," he said, "but this takes the cake."

With that, he did an about-face and marched out of the cave, from where he jumped onto the ice floe and effected a controlled slide toward his ski-plane. Come hell or high water, Alaska would still be his playground, if he had his druthers.

DIVIDE AND CONQUER

I'D BEEN warming my feet in the same manner as Buckner, trying to defrost them. Most of the *iidigidi* had gone out to further recon the area and make preparations, when suddenly Igasix̂ returned, trying to hold back another Unanga in whom I vaguely recalled having had met in the barabara on Adak.

"Get out of here! You don't belong here!" Igasix̂ scathed, trying to keep the woman from advancing.

"Don't try to stop me, Igasix̂!" the visiting native shot back. "He has a right to know!"

They began clawing at each other and pulling each other's hair, so I intervened before things really got serious: "Hey, hey cool it you two! What's this all about?"

"Oh, there you are, Lieutenant Jake Harper!" the mysterious Unanga said. "Remember me? I'm Ayagaadax̂, Aniqdux̂six̂'s best friend."

"I do faintly recall you, actually," I replied as Igasix̂ kept trying to wedge herself between us, "and I've only recently learned of Aniqdux̂six̂. Where is she now?"

"So you do remember her!" Ayagaadax̂'s irises flared red. "She's still at the barabara, or what's left of it. She's hurt and awaiting your return."

"Waiting for me? Why?"

"See!" Igasix̂ reproached Ayagaadax̂. "Jake doesn't care about her! He dumped her cold! Get it?"

"Now wait just a second," I interjected. "Like I said, I've heard about Aniqdux̂six̂, but what am I missing here? How am I supposed to know her?"

"Mister Harper! She was your lover!" admonished Ayagaadax̂. "And now you've gone off with this, this little wench? This is a travesty!"

"A travesty?" I still didn't understand.

"Like I said," riposted Igasix̂, "Jake dumped her cold! End of story! Now get the hell out of here!"

My young companion drove Ayagaadax̂ clear out of the cave, where the snubbed Unanga unfurled her wings and took flight into the rumbling skies.

"Igasix̂?" I called out as I returned to the fire to warm by bare feet. "Are you going to tell me what this all about now?"

She marched in, wrapping her disheveled hair back up into a bun. "That bitch Ayagaadax̂!" she cursed. "Pay no mind to her. She's probably a spy working for the *khoughkh*, trying to seed your brain with lies. The classic divide and conquer."

"Working for the *khoughkh*? Really, Igasix̂? Then why'd you tell her I dumped this Aniqdux̂six̂ girl? What's that all about?"

"It's complicated."

I lifted a brow. "Try me."

"I think some in my clan are trying to hook you up with Aniqdux̂six̂," she conceded.

"Why?"

"Because she's the chief's stepdaughter, and as you've seen, the chief was subordinate to Kuuyux, who turned out to be *khoughkh*. I don't know who else in my clan are working for the enemy, but especially now that Chief Aĝnakax̂ is dead, they'll continue to try to woo you over, if not outright infect you! As I said, it's the classic divide and conquer: and their first step is to try to separate us, but I won't let that happen—ever!"

Now I was really confused, but I sort of got what she was saying. In the end, Igasix̂ had proven to be more than just my friend and lover—she'd become a trusted protector, so I decided to just drop it and not dwell on this Aniqdux̂six̂ madness anymore.

A serious war was at hand, and if spies abounded among the cave clan, I trusted that Igasix̂ would, in fact, shield me from them.

"A tactic not unlike Innokenty's book," she continued, perhaps ignorantly, "which sought to divide and conquer Aleuts by discouraging us from practicing our traditional ways—ways that could've helped us unite against the colonial occupiers . . ."

She ranted on, bemoaning, "His Majesty the Emperor, the Imperial Family, the Right Reverend Mikhail, Bishop of Irkutsk, Yakutsk, and Nerchinsk," calling them all, "imperialist toions."

"Imperialist what?"

"Imperialist toions: Russian feudal nobility, otherwise known as *promuishlenniki* bourgeois scum . . ."

As Igasix̂ continued her diatribe, a few Unit 13 sentries remained on guard just the outside the cave, but for the most part, she and I were alone. Perhaps for this reason, she got the gumption to draw close to me and privately try to persuade me that the Shield of Repentance should be used to fight "the Siberian threat," aka the *khoughkh*. "It must be destroyed," she deemed, "melted down and made into weapons powerful enough to combat the enemy at Red Head. Without such spiritual armaments, we don't stand a chance."

I became haunted by uncertain feelings again, but ultimately put my trust in my protectress, who'd already abundantly proven herself as a smart and able unit commander.

As *iidigidi* fighters began filtering back into the cave, Igasix̂ ordered them to stay put, and when enough had gathered, she announced: "Our only present advantage over the *khoughkh* is our air superiority. Iĝanax̂ and his Rat Island battalion, for whatever reason, have lost the ability to fly. Therefore, you must try to blockade them from advancing further east while Lieutenant Harper and I repair to Adak to forge the proper weaponry from iconostases, which only he can access."

I was a little confused about this last assertion, but the *iidigidi* seemed to understand, and agreed with her directive. Several of them surrendered their fatigues to me, and after dressing in layers, I was taken under Igasixˆ's wing for the long, cold flight back to Adak.

THE CRUCIBLE

WE ARRIVED at Boot Bay in dawn's early light. I'd slept part of the way back, thanks to my seven layers of clothes and Igasixˆ's further cocooning me beneath her wing like a bomb latched to a Flying Fortress. But make no mistake about it: it was still bitterly cold in the Aleutians, and if it weren't for numerous jackets, hats, and scarves, our open-air flight at just 500 feet wouldn't have been survivable for a mortal such as me.

Even closed-cockpit aircraft had a terrible time in the Aleutian climate, such as this Catalina "Splash Landing" at Longview, where "a crash ambulance comes racing up to the runway as the lumbering patrol bomber comes to a halt. Pontoons would have been more useful than wheels on that kind of landing field—but the pachyderm of the air fleet will be out there again the next day, wheeling through foggy Aleutian skies in search of the foe." (Official US Navy photo and caption, 1943, cleared Army censor and filed March 28, 1944, ref#TR-3713)

The barabara had essentially been leveled, but a nearby blast crater provided a scant opening into the tunnel between the boathouse and the Shield of Repentance chamber. We were lucky that the armor's chamber remained accessible, because the way back to the boathouse was sealed shut by collapsed rock and soil.

Once inside the chamber, Igasix̂ removed a large, crimson slate slab from near the center of the red adakite floor, revealing a hot lava crucible beneath, which she said had long been diverted there in the event of the drastic purpose we were presently there to undertake: to maintain a quick destruct option against the holy armor, should it prove to be somehow damaging to the *iidigidi*. It was the surrounding "slab melt rock," she relayed, that had kept the armor in safe keeping for more than a century.

We removed the armor from its stand and placed it beside the molten crucible, apparently preparing to drop it in. All that remained was for Igasix̂ to retrieve some wrought-iron bowls from the collapsed barabara, which we needed in order to recapture the silver once it melted.

While Igasix̂ was away, I took Priest Veniaminov's book, *The Way to the Kingdom of Heaven*, from its stand and began thumbing through the pages. As it was written in Unalaskan Aleut, I couldn't understand a word of it.

Igasix̂ returned about ten minutes later, carrying two huge iron bowls and some hefty bullet molds. The heavy, dull *THUD!* that sounded as she placed the iron caissons on the adakite floor evinced serious tonnage that only an immortal could've lifted.

She was about to rip the helmet off the armor and place it into one of the bowls, when suddenly Ayagaadax̂ flew in with another Unanga and tried to force her off the suit of silver armor. I tried to intercede, but was shoved away as the two intruders vehemently tried to stop us from melting down the Shield of Repentance.

The Unanga who held me down was a taller woman, perhaps in her mid-twenties. Her right shoulder showed signs of recent trauma, being outwardly crushed and charred, thus I could fight back against her—an undead one—with a mite more leverage than I would've been able to otherwise. "Please, Jake!" she cried, tears streaming from her eyes. "Don't do this!"

"Why not? Who are you?" I besought as we wrestled upon the red floor, Igasix̂ and Ayagaadax̂ tumbling in like manner perilously close to the lava pit.

"It's me, Aniqdux̂six̂! Jake, what hast come over thou!? Please stop! I beg of thee!"

I was able to momentarily prevail over her, rolling on top of her and pinning her down. While her voice sounded vaguely familiar, I still had no recollection of her, but was pained at having to struggle against her, for she was pretty and her watery eyes maintained a look of deep concern, perhaps even compassion.

"Jake!" she pleaded. "Don't let Igasix̂ do this! Thou knowest what the shield means to me, to us! Don't abandon me to this living death, this eternal damnation!"

In our tussle, her hand slammed into Innokenty's book. She pressed the tome against my chest and opened it, apparently to the beginning, which she read aloud, even as we fought:

"Humans were not made by God to exist like animals that disappear once they die, but to live with God and in God, not for a hundred or even a thousand years, but to live forever in His light. But only Christians can live with God. Only those who believe in Jesus Christ will find everlasting life, even after they die."

"Don't you see, Jake?" she entreated, tossing the book aside. "I choose to be mortal again! I want to die in Christ! Without the shield I'm doomed! I would rather live one lifetime with you than all of eternity as I am now!"

"Jake!" Igasix̂ cried out for help. Ayagaadax̂ was on top of her, pushing her head back into the pit of molten lava.

I leapt over and grabbed Ayagaadax̂'s shoulders, trying to pry her off my lover, and as I did, I caught sight of Aniqdux̂six̂ watching me in astonishment. As Igasix̂'s hair drew near to the magma, I pried at Ayagaadax̂'s shoulders with a superhuman strength, causing her to scream in distress.

Aniqdux̂six̂, shaken from her momentary stupor by the cry of her friend, rushed forth and pulled me off of Ayagaadax̂, and when she did, Igasix̂ used the opposing shift of leverage to throw Ayagaadax̂ over her own head and into the pit of lava.

"*YAAAAAH!*" Ayagaadax̂ shrieked in bloodcurdling horror, trying to climb free of the pit, but Igasix̂ delivered a sharp kick to her forehead, causing her to go splashing back into its center, where her hair and face quickly caught on fire. Moaning and screeching like some terrific, witchlike demon, Ayagaadax̂ tried to fly free with half-melting wings; she found little success.

Aniqdux̂six̂ flew over and grabbed Ayagaadax̂'s head, freeing her only partially from the pit, for Ayagaadax̂'s body had melted away completely below the chest.

Igasix̂ darted headlong into Aniqdux̂six̂, who dropped what was left of Ayagaadax̂ back into the magma, where it was quickly subsumed by lava. The adversaries crash-landed on the floor opposite the crucible and continued with their death-defying struggle, trying to throw one another into the hellfire pit.

"Jake!" Igasix̂ cried "The *caelum divinatorius!* Strike her with it!"

I pried the fire witching rod from the right hand of the repentance armor. It was long and unwieldy; I could barely keep it balanced when lifting. As I struggled to aim it toward the dueling women, Aniqdux̂six̂ told Igasix̂: "And now thou seekest to kill me here just as you let my father die so ignominiously centuries agone, hiding the facts from the light of day. But it wasn't enough for you to shame me thus: now thee must also take my Kayuu!"

At that, Igasix̂, who was nigh forcing Aniqdux̂six̂'s head back into the lava, eased her grip; I, too, was shaken by Aniqdux̂six̂'s words, just as I let fly the *caelum divinatorius*. The mention of "Kayuu" struck a deep, mysterious chord in me, causing my aim to go off just a twinge, which was enough for the staff to miss Aniqdux̂six̂'s head and pierce her previously charred shoulder instead. She pealed in excruciating pain, the point of impact becoming electrified with some sort of web of blue static that quickly spread out over the greater extent of her shoulder.

Igasix̂ extracted the rod, short-circuiting the charge before it could do any further damage, and then she moved Aniqdux̂six̂ away from the pit, saying, "I won't kill you, but you shall suffer dearly for meddling here. I know how you seek to become mortal again, using the Shield of Repentance to be with Kayuu. But there's a far greater cause that requires the immediate destruction of the armor, and now you shall watch as we proceed."

"No, please, *Igasix̂* . . ." Aniqdux̂six̂ was slurring, barely able to move, let alone speak, "*please, Kayuu, don't do it.*"

"What's happening to her?" I asked.

"It's the silver from the witching rod," Igasix̂ explained. "It's highly toxic to *iidigidi*, even fatal. She's taken on some residue, but you hit her where she was already burned and I think I removed the rod in time. She'll probably just remain incapacitated for a while."

"I'm sorry."

"Don't be, Jake—it was the perfect shot. It was never my intention to kill her, and now she won't bother us further while we melt down the armor."

The internecine fight I'd just witnessed and played a hand in, I found very regrettable. And I was deeply troubled by this Aniqdux̂six̂ girl and some of the things she and Igasix̂ had said. Alas, I'd have to wait until later to probe further, for Igasix̂ and I were on a mission of dire time and consequence. I thus compartmentalized what had just transpired, and as Aniqdux̂six̂ sat propped up against the opposite side of the crucible watching us deliriously, Igasix̂ and I began breaking apart the silver armor and melting it down within the iron caissons.

"Aniqdux̂six̂'s got it all backward, anyway," Igasix̂ kept up the intrigue, as we poured the molten silver into the bullet molds rummaged from the barabara. "If you want to live forever with someone, you don't do it by becoming a mortal. I mean, *duh*! How stupid can you get? I'll show you later, Jake, how to make a forever-after mate."

"I'll show you later . . . how to make a forever-after mate."
(Exclusive acrylic painting by J. Crow Smith, 2019)

"Why wait?" Aniqdux̂six̂ managed to say.

"Oh, you're still awake?" Igasix̂ quipped. "Well then, I know how much you hated your stepfather, so I can't expect you to understand the wisdom of his teachings. His gen-cycle philosophy may've helped him lock in your mother once he had her, but it was also a way to make sure we conduct ourselves appropriately when securing our forever-after mates. You never got that—you never cared to understand the value of our ways, but I do. My gen-cycle will soon be up, and then Kayuu and I shall become inseparable according to our time-honored laws and traditions. Try to stop me, dear, and I'll finish the job I've suspended with you here."

As we worked, in addition to silver bullets, we forged some swords and throwing-lances from the Shield of Repentance and its *caelum divinatorius*, using obsidian and iron materials that Igasix̂ scavenged from the barabara to complete the process.

Finally, using an upturned iron caisson as an anvil, I forged a mighty Rommel stake from purely smelted silver. Several layers of my own clothes were sacrificed in wiping the spike clean, the blackened and torn fatigues giving witness to a gleaming rod, which I had a deep mastery with. Even my rubber gummies were tattooed with permanent melt marks. In seeing this, Igasix̂ invited me to the bombed-out barabara to salvage some new Unangax̂ wear.

We were leaving Aniqdux̂six̂ slumped up against the opposite wall, where she appeared unconscious or dead. When I mentioned this to Igasix̂, she just shrugged her shoulders and said, "So what? Let's get moving."

Thus Aniqdux̂six̂ remained an enigma to me, but the bottom line was that she'd tried to seriously compromise our mission, so I really didn't care too much about her or what her story was. For all I knew, Aniqdux̂six̂ may've been working for the enemy, trying to deceive me with her sweet talk. This conviction was backed by the present action of Igasîx, who took care to load our freshly made armaments into the caissons to take with us so that Aniqduxsix, if she should awaken, wouldn't have access to them.

Once aboveground, we took the weapons to a nearby hillock, where we stashed them in a cave, and then we proceeded to the barabara, whose collapsed roof effected a pitiable sight. Upon descending to the floor of the ruined structure, we began sifting through the mess of detritus, searching for some Unangax̂ habits for me to wear.

Discouraged by the dearth of whole materials, Igasîx took me to the boathouse, where we found some twenty-six Unangax̂ hiding out. Most were women and children who had survived the Japanese bombing raid. Some I recognized, and they were surprised to see me again, believing I was never going to return. Datuu was there, and after a jocular reunion of sorts, she asked if I'd seen "Auntie Aniqduxsix."

Igasîx beat me to an answer, saying that Aniqduxsix had flown off somewhere.

Datuu was puzzled to the extent that she probed no further.

"Where's Iganakuchax̂?" I inquired about her godmother. "Is she around?"

The little Unanga's face went sour.

Igasîx pulled me aside and said, "She didn't make it."

"What?" I was shocked.

"Silver bomb fragments. The Japs knew the brood of Aleuts living here: they knew we were *iidigidi*."

"Kuuyux!" I uttered crossly, snarling between clenched teeth.

"Perhaps."

I shook my head disappointedly. Iganakuchax̂ had treated me with exceptional courtesy and care. She'd been a perfect Unangax̂ ambassador, exemplifying all that was good and honorable of her people, not to mention she'd simply been a really sweet lady. I was saddened by her passing, and none too pleased that Igasix̂ had continued to keep such major occurrences from my knowledge until I found about them by happenstance.

"Where's my daddy?" Datuu asked, pulling at my last layer of summer fatigues.

"Tayaĝukichax̂ is fine," answered Igasix̂. "He's with the other warriors."

"I want to fight, too," the little vampire said.

"Maybe next time, Datuu. For now, you can help us find some new clothes for Lieutenant Harper."

Datuu ran off, soon returning with a new *kamleika* parka, a pair of knee-high boots with thick, seal esophageal skin leggings and a double layer of sea lions' flippers for the soles. An abundance of dried heath grass had been embedded throughout the costume for additional warmth. Datuu, it turns out, was responsible for the entire outfit. Being among the rare few that believed I would return one day, she'd crafted the entire uniform with her own hands, ostensibly even making Aniqdux̂six̂ jealous, according to some of the others present.

Igasix̂ took me aside and, fearing spies, she flared out her wings and advised me in private to remain mute about Aniqdux̂six̂.

I nodded in agreement, and there behind the cover of her wingspan, I stripped off my Buckner-issue boots and military fatigues, tossing them aside in favor of my new Aleut garb, which I knew would camouflage me better against our new nemesis, and which, I knew from experience, proved entirely capable in the harsh Aleutian environment—more functional even than my Attu regimentals, Buckner's boots notwithstanding.

HOLY MATERIEL FOR AN UNHOLY WAR

NEEDING MORE weapons to arm Unit 13 back on Attu, we recruited most of the barabara survivors and flocked to Saint Ephraim of the Caves Church on Adak, bringing with us several rifles the cave clan warriors had left behind, plus the silver bullets, swords, lances, and Rommel spike that Igasix̂ and I had forged from the fire witching accoutrements. The ponderous iron caissons were also airlifted in.

Only I could enter the church, for it physically repulsed the vampires. Inside the sanctum were many iconostases and holy icons, some forged in silver—and all of which were harmful for the *iidigidi* to merely behold. Without question, we'd hit the jackpot of holy materiél from which to wage a most unholy war.

As I gathered the iconography and ecclesiastical objects onto the church floor, Igasix̂ and the barabara survivors worked quickly outside to set up an ad hoc workshop. Weaving plaited mats from the local reeds, the vampires constructed a tent-like shelter with blurring speed. Into this "praetorium" they delivered the iron caissons and other tools for me to work with. Because the iconostases could burn the vampires' eyes on sight, the *iidigidi* had to evacuate the praetorium before I could transfer the holy artifacts to the field crucible that Igasix̂ had set up for me there.

Once resituated inside the praetorium, I worked feverishly to melt down the silver crucifixes, silver plates, the goblets, wall decorations, and candelabra, and only after all these ecclesiastical objects had been liquefied did I invite the *iidigidi* back in to forge new weapons from the sacred quicksilver now flowing high within the iron caissons.

As the natives set to work building their new armaments, I proceeded back into the church and commenced to break apart the chapel's pulpit. Constructed of solid silver, this podium alone would provide approximately 400 pounds of holy materiél for our coming war. The Aleuts went into high production with this windfall, forging a virtual mountain of silver bullets, swords, and lances.

And then, after using my silver Rommel spike to pry the wooden panels from the very chapel walls, we sawed and reshaped them into stakes, which, once stacked into orderly piles outside the praetorium, evinced such a great consolidation of pickets so as to smite an entire legion of vampires, which is precisely what was needed. And thus, with the bold and courageous help of the barabara survivors, by 20:30 the entire church had been leveled, and in its place were neat stockpiles of holy throwing-lances, wooden and silver Rommel stakes, bullets, spikes, and bayonets—these last being affixed to a myriad assortment of rifles.

Probably the most inventive weapon we devised on Adak was a flamethrower-like contraption made from capsular bentwood bowls worn over the warrior's back in conjunction with a sea lion bladder sack that hung beneath his or her arm as a fuel injection system. But instead of flaming petrol, the damaging substance was Holy Water wrought from Ephraim's Lake, which I personally loaded into the enclosable bentwood bowl tanks. The soldier would simply aim an attached seal intestine tube at an enemy vampire, then squeeze the connecting sea lion bladder sack beneath his arm, shooting out Holy Water from the dual reserve of tanks worn over his back. Like a real flamethrower, it was a little dangerous to work with, but could burn an opposing vampire just as badly. Its intended use was to purge the *khoughkh* from defiladed positions such as muskeg holes, or to ward off scores of enemy in a single pass. However, the Holy Water-throwers were not expected to inflict any *khoughkh* fatalities, for it was rare that a vampire ever died from consecrated water. It was the silver armaments that would instantly kill a vampire, as well as the wooden stakes and bayonets in the event a close-combat situation enabled a direct strike to the heart.

Meanwhile, back on Attu . . . "Major General E. M. Landrum, U.S.A., Commander of the Aleutian Island Forces, is seen going over the side of a transport into a ramp boat for a point in the Massacre Bay area for the attack against the Japanese Imperial Forces." (US Navy photo and caption from ACME, May 1943)

In addition to the holy wooden armaments, wooden armor was forged from stacks of driftwood flown in from the remnants of the barabara. It seemed an antiquated form of protection to me, given the high-caliber weapons encountered on the modern-day battlefront, yet there was something the *iidigidi* regarded as mystical about the wood-rod armor—an intangible facet not yet revealed to me; or perhaps it was beyond a mortal's capacity to logically understand. Rainbows had a similarly auspicious regard, especially when appearing behind the warrior; but again, my capacity to expound upon such things was still very limited.

New bentwood hats were also constructed on-site, and these, I knew from personal experience, lent special powers to the hunters wearing them—but I couldn't be pressed on exactly how.

As Igasix̂ and the others were splitting, sawing, sanding, soaking, bending, and piercing driftwood, Datuu flew into our Ephraim's Lake cantonment, coming to see me expressly. Her eyes were teary, and even before she could say a word, Igasix̂ darted between us, reprimanding her, "You shouldn't be here: there are dangerous materials about. Return to the boathouse at once, and remain there like I told you!"

"But I wish to speak with Kayuu," the fanged bairn pleaded.

"*Nangaa!*" Igasix̂ admonished, meaning *no!* in Unangam Tunuu, and then she pointed a finger sharply skyward and ordered, "Go home!"

"What hast thou done to Ayagaadax̂?" Datuu stood defiant.

"Go now!"

"*Hmphf!*" huffed my ostensible protector, at last stepping aside, where she stood impatiently crossing her arms and frowning upon the little *iidigidi* to no end.

I shot her a glance of disapproval, starting to seriously tire of Igasix̂'s bossy overprotectiveness.

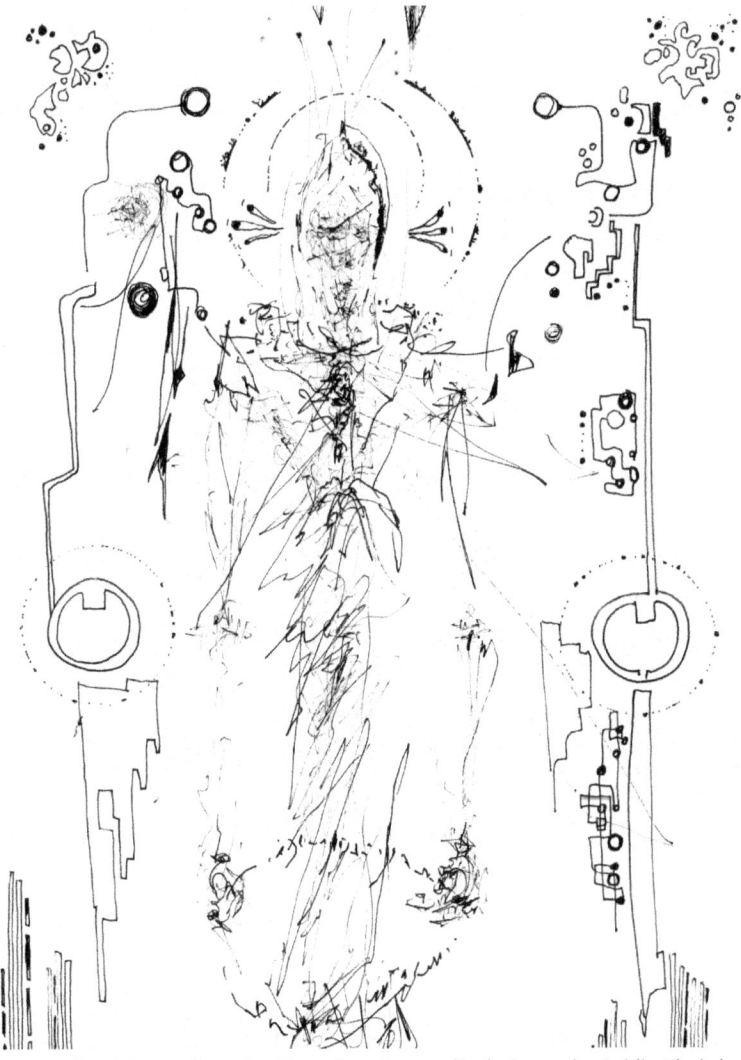

Wood-rod Armor Contains Mysterious Powers (*Exclusive art by Ovidiu Kloska*)

"And Aniqdux̂six̂?"

"Go!"

"Mister Harper!" Datuu begged for my intercession.

"Igasix̂," I reproached, touching her shoulder, "you must allow Datuu to speak. I'd like to hear what she has to say."

Getting to a knee, I gently pulled Datuu before me and asked, "Yes, Datuu, what seems to be the trouble?"

"Thou!" she fired back, "and Aniqdux̂six̂. How come thou dost not love her anymore?"

"I beg your pardon?" Her antiquated English vernacular sounded odd for a child, but somehow quaintly familiar, and it piqued me with untold curiosity.

"She's really hurt by thee, Kayuu. Whatever thou hast done to her back at the barabara was all she could bear. I'm afraid of what she might do next."

"What do you mean?"

"She asked me to deliver a message to you, and then she told me she was going to her father's *umqan* to mourn over thee; but I'm worried she intends to kill herself. Oh Kayuu, is this really the end? Why won't you go back to her?"

"Datuu!" exclaimed Igasix̂. "We're busy now! You must—"

"No Igasix̂!" I reproached, grabbing her hand and cutting her off midsentence. "Leave us alone, just this once!" And then I supplicated Datuu thus, "What is Aniqdux̂six̂'s message, my little one?"

"A passage from William Shakespeare," she relayed:

*"In winter with warm tears I'll melt the snow
And keep eternal spring-time on thy face."*

My expression pruned in consternation as I struggled to understand the meaning of Aniqdux̂six̂'s message.

"Don't let her brainwash you," Igasix̂ warned.

"So Datuu's a spy now, too? Is that what you're getting at?!" I snapped.

"Fine, Jake Harper, but don't say I didn't warn you!" With that, she stormed off in a temper.

But Igasix̂ wasn't the only female that had issues with me, for when I went to address Datuu again, the little waif pushed me hard over. "If thou art done with Aniqdux̂six̂," she cried, all puffed up and red, "then I am done with you!"

She took wing before I could post a defense. The fact was, I was certain now that I was being misled about Aniqdux̂six̂, not by the likes of Datuu—whom I knew would never conspire against me, but by Igasix̂ and some of the other warriors from Unit 13. I clearly remembered having been in an Unangax̂ burial cave known as an *umqan,* and I distinctly remembered a woman there with me, showing me her mummified father. The face of this woman had escaped me, but her voice, and her accent—like that of Datuu—had not, and if my memory served me correctly, the voice did match that of Aniqdux̂six̂. I was deeply disturbed by all this. There was something significant about my life, something involving Aniqdux̂six̂ that I was, in fact, forgetting.

I marched around camp asking for Igasix̂, but nobody knew where she had gone. I was advised by Qihmux̂, who claimed she was Aniqdux̂six̂'s sister, that in the meantime I should be fitted with the protections of an Aleut warrior, so I took her advice and followed her into a corner of the praetorium.

Now Qihmux̂ is someone whom I remembered clearly from before: after all, I'd saved one of her kids, Maguun. And I did recall her once mentioning she had a sister, although I didn't recall ever having met her. At any rate, Qihmux̂ had suffered the recent loss of her mate, Qagux̂, and only that day had learned of the passing of her stepfather, Chief Aĝnakax̂, and in light of all this, she remained strikingly stoic while attending to my outfitting.

"The ones who killed Chief Aĝnakax̂," she said, tightening a vest of wooden rods over my chest like a corset, "—this bastard

Iĝanax̂ and his two-timing father—will quickly turn to dust, I trust, once we strike them with all this powerful weaponry."

"That is precisely our mission, Qihmux̂. Chief Aĝnakax̂ will be avenged, as will Qagux̂, who you should know died protecting the rest of us at Three Arm Bay. The *khoughkh* scum, starting with their leadership on down through the Jap parasites, shall soon be wiped off the face of the earth. The final battle is imminent, madam, and speaking on behalf of the US Air Force, I thank you for your service at this critical hour. The efforts we presently undertake shall not be in vain."

"There," she said, tightening the last cord of my body armor, "that should protect you from some of their devices."

"Such as?"

"Such as projectiles seen or unseen, which the wooden armor can deflect before making contact with your flesh."

"Really?"

"Yes, but we must do more. It goes without saying, as a wight you'll be targeted right off by the *khoughkh*. We must disguise you better."

"What'd you have in mind?"

"One of these, for starters." She procured a bentwood hat of the *chagudax̂* visor type and fitted it atop my head. "We have a belief about these, too. A shipment will be sent to our warriors on Attu, along with the new armaments."

"*Qaĝaasakung*," I thanked her in Aleut.

"Don't mention it." She managed an unhappy smile. "But you might want to hold your applause until I'm finished with you. We also must apply these." She unrolled a satchel containing several ivory labrets, bird bone pins, a sharp, black sea lion whisker, and a lengthy bodkin to pierce me with.

"Ah, I see," I reluctantly conceded. "No pain, no gain, as it were."

"That's a funny way of putting it," she chuckled with a heavy heart, already removing my new *chagudax̂*, making way for another bloody makeover at my expense.

Minutes later, I had three fresh piercings beneath my lower lip, the pain of which was worse than before because this time she had punctured the holes directly through the old scars that remained from our antecedent piercing session. Well, at least now I was resplendent with white ivory labrets, that is, when they were not reddened with my blood.

Qihmux̂ slightly tongued her lips, but resisted a bloody French kiss in favor of dabbing my face with a rag, which she periodically dipped into a bowl of seawater that she'd supplied to clean and disinfect my wounds with.

"*Qaĝaasakung,*" I mumbled.

"Wait, I'm not finished yet." She was twirling the sea lion whisker between her thumb and forefinger. "This was given to you by Igasix̂: she won it in battle. You should be honored." She tilted my head sideways and thrust it through my ear. I vocalized a low growl.

"I think Igasix̂ is good for you," she continued, her cross eyes now sizing up my forehead. She removed the two bone pins from her unrolled satchel and said, "This might hurt a little, but I need to be honest with you: I never thought my sister was right for you. I mean, to begin with, she's not very bright. She knows her gen-cycle is far off, but thinks she can make it work out between you two anyway. It's ridiculous! I mean, at least Igasix̂ can change you soon, under our laws. So go for her, all the way, and forget about Aniqdux̂six̂, which I hear you've done anyway. Okay, hold still."

She grabbed my face with one hand, holding my head steady, then with her other hand she thrust one sharp bird bone vertically up through the skin of my forehead, then one horizontally not long in following. The blood of my front flowed down over my eyes in little rivulets, mixing in with my salty tears.

Qihmux̂ had turned away as soon as she thrust the second bone in, and then while still avoiding looking at me, she asked me to clean my face. Once I'd done so, she handed me the bentwood visor in the blind, telling me to wear it.

Finally, she regarded me and said, "You now have a bone crucifix on your forehead, hidden beneath the visor of your bentwood cap. You must keep your *chagudax̂* on in the presence of the *iidigidi,* for the sign of the cross will burn their eyes. But when you come into contact with the *khoughkh,* remove your visor and you have a very strong repellent that only you, a mortal, can have. Bear in mind, however, that wearing the sign of Christ will give you away for who you really are: a wight. Therefore, display it only when absolutely necessary, and you can't go wrong. You can thank me now. I like the English, please."

Again, her stoicism and banter amid such a tumultuous time for her family was laudable, if not a little bittersweet for her to maintain.

"Thank you, Qihmux̂."

"Don't mention it. I like the look of a fierce Aleut man, just like Qagux̂. Now I want you to go and kick some *khoughkh* ass."

"Will do, my friend."

"Just look out for those silver bullets, or any kind of bullet, for your sake. Like I said, I want to see you and Igasix̂ pull through this intact. You're much better off with her, believe me. One thing Aniqdux̂six̂ never got about the *promuishlenniki* plague is that immortality is sweet! The only thing that sucks about it is if you lose your forever-after mate and have to wait for another one. But it's worth it, if you're patient. Aniqdux̂six̂'s never had a real *iidigidi* partner and has never had any patience, either, so she's always bitter—even toward the elders. But what does she know? Look at Igasix̂. She's been patient and soon can claim her reward. Enjoy it, and don't blow it between you two. She's much hotter than my sister anyway. Consider yourself lucky."

"Thanks, I guess." Qihmux̂, in helping me, was also only confusing me once again regarding the true allegiances of her female kin.

Night was falling and I was tired, if not a little traumatized from all the rigors I'd been through that day. I couldn't even begin to ponder if I really wanted to become immortal or not, but I found the concept a little spooky and needed to sleep on it for the night, or so my body was telling me.

"Goodnight, Mister Harper," Qihmux̂ said, leaning me back onto a wild rye mat. I closed my eyes, utterly spent.

"Sweet dreams, Kayuu," she whispered.

Igasix̂ woke me up. It was morning.

"Igasix̂, we need to talk," I said.

"About what?"

"About us, and Aniqdux̂six̂."

"Not now. It's late, Jake. The tribe is ready to flock."

"Ten-thirty?" (—checking my watch—) "Jesus Christ! Why didn't you wake me sooner?"

"Don't invoke that name! Well anyway, obviously you needed more sleep. Now come on, let's go. I'll help you up."

I offered my hand, and in true *iidigidi* fashion, she expended not a mite of perceptible effort in lifting my 165 pounds.

Save for my Rommel spike, the praetorium had been cleared of our newly crafted weapons, and when I stumbled out into the fresh morning air, I was instantly embarrassed. There at the Ephraim's Lake encampment, dozens of *iidigidi* women and children were standing around and on top of the stores of materiél, the entirety of which was neatly bound in seaweed cables and woven mats, ready to airlift. If it wasn't enough that I had overslept, I presently had to take one hell of a piss, and so after excusing myself from Igasix̂, I sprung behind the praetorium to relieve myself while the entire weapons-making party looked on at my late-morning antics.

Upon my return, Igasix̂ teased, "Humans, *tsk-tsk-tsk*. How can you still stand being one? I suppose you'll now require something for breakfast."

"As a matter of fact, I do, *madame*," I bandied back, "but at this late hour, that would be brunch, not blood, I'm afraid. Look, I'm sorry to keep everybody waiting, Igasix̂, but I really will need to get some food in me before the long flight out. After all, I'm only human." I shot her a wry wink.

"I anticipated that," she replied, handing me a bound satchel.

I undid the pouch's reed tie and discovered several smoked fish inside, plus a miniature woven basket filled with dried berries.

"Thanks, Igasix̂. This looks nice."

"Don't forget your canteen," she advised, shoving it hard against my chest. "I refilled it for you. Now let's get flocking, lieutenant. You can eat while airborne—just don't drop your so-called brunch over Kiska: we wouldn't want to feed any Japs."

That was the most I'd be hearing from Igasix̂ for the rest of the daylight hours, for we were soon lifting at altitude, bearing west against a stubborn headwind. Flocking together with so many winged Aleuts carrying bundled materiél was a sight I'd never forget. A special delivery was coming to our enemy, this much was certain.

Alas, Igasix̂ had been right about my in-flight supping: half my store of water ended up splashing into my face, and I even dropped a fish—hopefully not on Boodle.

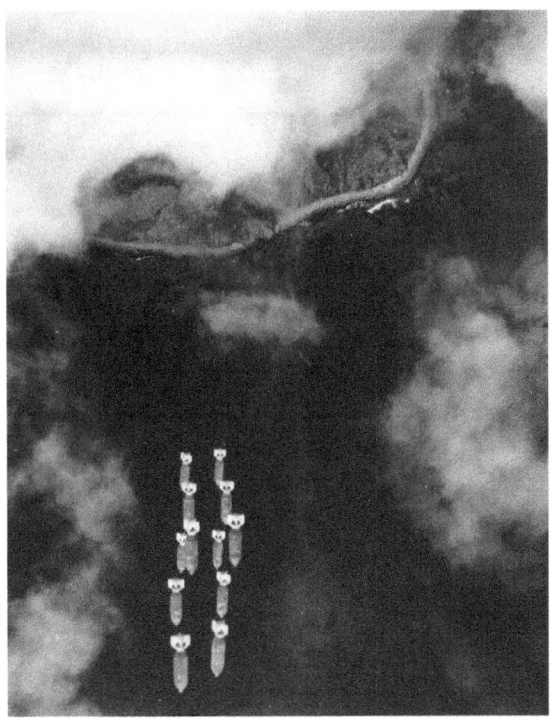

The 11th US Army Air Force bombs North Head Japanese Camp on Kiska Island, aka "Boodle," USA (Exclusive 1943 photo as part of the "magnetic album" [photo #11] attributed to Clyde Royden sample, Rank: PHOM c/3, Photographers Mate 3rd Class)

At dusk on May 30, the skies rumbled from on high, and in the waning light, scores of women and children vampires winged down, delivering a powerful cargo to Unit 13 on the ground. Igasix̂ and I, adorned in full Aleut warrior vestments, were received gladly by the infantry-in-waiting. Olean whistled at the sight of my war regalia, and then gawked alongside the others at the sheer volume of inventive new armaments we were delivering.

As the weaponry was being unpacked, Tayaĝukichax̂ told Igasix̂ that the *khoughkh* were up to something strange at Red

Head. On the muskeg ness below, he said, in their well-defiladed encampment, they were working some unknown black magic.

On hearing this, Commander Igasix̂ ordered the immediate return of all women and children noncombatants back to Adak Island.

DAWN OF THE UNDEAD

MAY 31, 1943, dawn. Distant Chuginadak Volcano, on the Island of Four Mountains, was raining ash on the battleground when we jumped. The Battle of Red Head had begun. Thirty-two *iidigidi* and the mortal I swarmed down upon two score *khoughkh* camped on Central Tongue.

Iĝanax̂ the Terrible met Igasix̂, Tayaĝukichax̂, Olean, and me head-on, ranting amid the clash of arms: "It wasn't enough to make slaves of me and my father! Petty oarsman to do your bidding on raids! Nay! Once infected, you abandoned me to two hundred years of misery, to eating brown rats on *Qax̂um tanangis!*"

"You were lost at sea, Iĝanax̂," replied Olean, momentarily holding back. "Don't blame the tribe for that. Your father made it back and became *de facto* chief. Your fate was not our making."

"Ha!" replied he, taking a swing at the great whaler, which Olean narrowly deflected. "Tell that to Tayaĝukichax̂ here, whose father enslaved us personally. But the chief is no more, I have seen to that!"

A building roar rumbled from deep within Tayaĝukichax̂'s chest, exploding out with a shout as he lunged forth in counterattack: "The gates of hell await you, scum! I shall personally usher you back!"

"You, prince of Adak!" rejoined Iĝanax̂, their mystical swords releasing fire as they clashed. "Kuuyux has informed me you're not fit to rule over your own shit, but what would you know of that? Can you see my wings? These are the wings of a *Qax̂um tanangis* king, destined to rule the sodden earth and all its dirty little beings. A king borne on rats," raged he, "whose varmint shit poisons the muck everywhere on *Qax̂um tanangis*, dirtying my wings. And do you know just how I'm afflicted? The rat shit in the muck eats at the waxy substance of my feathers like an acid, causing them to wither and break."

"You don't have to do this, Iĝanax̂!" responded Igasix̂ in a rare reconciliatory flash. "Soiled plumage can be cleaned and fixed!"

Iĝanax̂ cried insanely back, "But the rats can never be eliminated! They just keep breeding! I tried to burn them out with a spell my father once taught me, but made the wrong mixture or spoke the wrong words, and *lo!*—the fire came onto us instead, a fire that never burns out, not without our iron *qayaatx̂ux̂* helmets, forged from the same quicksilver used to make the Shield of Repentance. Where is the unholy armor?"

This prince of darkness leapt lamely over Igasix̂, driving his sword before her face, but she held him back with her lance, together forming an electrified blue cross as sanctified silver and leaden metal clashed. "You must surrender the saint's armor now!" demanded the terrible king of rats.

But the sword of Igasix̂ proved more powerful, driving a blue bolt of such force into Iĝanax̂'s arm that he flew back, landing on his ass; and so, too, did the holy materiél being levied against the army of *khoughkh* find wide success. Employing impressive air superiority, the *iidigidi* struck at the enemy with Holy Water, consecrated wood, and silver, exhibiting laudable aim. When pierced anywhere by blest silver or staked through the heart with our chapel wood, the afflicted *khoughkh* would flare up into black fire and then swiftly turn to dust.

All around me, columns of dark ash marking the recent destruction of *khoughkh* lingered only momentarily before being sucked down into the muskeg, never to return again. Verily, old tales of hell had laid bare their locus: the damned were doomed to the infernal regions beneath.

A different kind of battle; a singular brand of soldier: Lieutenant Harper knows how to get himself into hotspots, such as in this June 4, 1942, snapshot he took of Dutch Harbor burning in the aftermath of the two-day blitz there. (Exclusive photo by Lt. Harper, 1942)

The battle, however, was not purely asymmetrical, for the shape-shifters' fires claimed several Unit 13 fighters. Our only defenses against it were our Holy Water-throwers, which could momentarily douse a *khoughkh*'s flames, and our wood-rod armor, which deflected the advent of fire like an invisible glass barrier a few inches preceding the wearer's body. Alas, some *iidigidi* warriors, abandoning their own superstitions, had chosen not to wear them, and it was these who were incinerated. Whenever an *iidigidi* died, his or her ash remnants were white and shot up into the sky, not down into the earth as with the *khoughkh*.

Iĝanax̂ the Terrible, meanwhile, had been helped up by a formidable *comrade-aux-armes*—a burly, lumbering, hunchbacked

Caucasian whose massive frame and Cossack fur cape made him appear more like a Kodiak grizzly.

As we went to encounter the formidable duo, a line of lesser *khoughkh* rushed between us to make battle. It was then that I saw the enemy infantry close up. Some appeared to be Japanese, with Nipponese features and the steel pot helmets worn by the Imperial Army, while others seemed a strange Siberian anachronism, dressed like Russian fur hunters of bygone times, replete with hidebound hats and old powder-cap pistols. And in every instance I could see, the standard *khoughkh* infantry had bluish, sucked-in features, resembling horrific, reanimated mummies. Verily, these were vampires that truly *looked* like the living dead. Their behavior was equally atrocious: like true fascists, they sought only to kill (or enslave, apparently) anyone they couldn't "convert." I was the only mortal around, and when they got a whiff of me, they came at me with biting mouths.

But I wasn't about to become a fascist *khoughkh* zombie, so I drew my pistol—armed with silver bullets—and succeeded against them where we'd failed against Iĝanax̂ the Terrible. While this last had been able to shape-shift around any bullet we discharged, his infantry was neither as quick nor as agile, and I prevailed in shooting some in the flesh. The black dust begot from three freshly extinguished undead lingered momentarily in our midst before being sucked down through cracks in the earth as if from a powerful underground vacuum machine.

Iĝanax̂ and his Cossack henchman appeared where the black dust had just been, the former announcing: "Behold my commander-in-arms, Ivan Solov'iev, 'Destroyer of Aleuts.' So that you know how deep is my hatred for you Unangax̂ foxes and the way in which you treated me and my father, I shall relay to you how Ivan came into my charge, and then together we shall destroy you insipid cowards once and for all!"

The young warrior Tix̂lax̂ suddenly rushed forth with a rifle, charging its wooden bayonet headlong at Iĝanax̂.

But Ivan Solov'iev was quicker, driving his long-sword through Tix̂lax̂'s chest, turning him to dust, the boy's rifle bounding off the muskeg and stopping at Iĝanax̂'s feet.

In a fit of rage, Igasix̂ launched a counterattack.

"No Igasix̂!" Tayaĝukichax̂ warned, holding her back, for Iĝanax̂'s skin was starting to flare.

Iĝanax̂ laughed derisively through the flames now dancing around his partially exposed skull: "Smart move, son-of-a-dumb chief. I see now you recognize our superior 'fire' power. Hee-hee-hee . . . let's see, where was I? Oh yes, the Destroyer of the Aleuts. When Ivan came upon my island in 1792, he was so impressed by our powers that he offered his neck to me willingly, and so began our reign of revenge, beginning with Umnak the following year. The sixty Unangax̂ warriors amassed in their *baidarkas* there were the first Aleuts to feel our wrath, and once we destroyed them, we destroyed their boats and weapons. The many secondary fighters we caught in retreat made fitting slaves for Ivan's sea otter and fur seal harvesting camps in the Pribilofs. But what I enjoyed most was the bloodfeast on land. How many hapless Aleuts did we torture and kill as we grew drunk on their blood?"

Ivan held up three black-clawed fingers.

"Just three?" Iĝanax̂ laughed. "Come now, comrade, you must still be intoxicated from the pogrom."

"Thousand," Ivan said, grunting.

"Ah, there we have it, my good rat-man. Three thousand Aleuts tasted our wrath, and after we tasted their blood, we destroyed their homes, boats, and weapons—every trace of them. But Ivan has a heart, don't you, my bear-clawed friend? He made some of the Umnak villagers into slaves, shipping them off to work his otter grounds along the Pacific Northwest coast of America, including far-off California. You always had such good business sense, Ivan—if only your brain didn't succumb to the 1920 disease of sickened rats."

"*Humpf,*" sounded the lumbering Cossack.

"But no matter," continued his terrible leader, "you still have the killing sense in you. Shall we, then? Attack, Ivan, *attack!*"

At this command, Iĝanax̂ fell back, and the formidable bear of a man struck forth, slashing his long sword out like a whip, so swift was his hirsute hand.

Igasix̂ pushed me aside, my face feeling the wind of Ivan's passing blade, then she and Olean took on the demented Cossack while Tayaĝukichax̂ went after Iĝanax̂. Their being preoccupied and the bullets in my pistol running low, I grabbed Tix̂lax̂'s rifle with the intention of killing Kuuyux for precipitating the death of Iganakuchax̂ and Chief Aĝnakax̂, amongst others. I'd been stealing glances at the betraying shaman ever since we'd jumped on Red Head. Indeed, he was up to some dark, funny business on Central Tongue.

With my pistol snug within my thigh holster and my Rommel spike slung over my back, I crept into one of the enemy's black pyramidal tents and silently killed a sentry there with Tix̂lax̂'s wooden bayonet. Even before the *khoughkh*'s dirty ash remnants were sucked down to hell, I proceeded through the unholy dust cloud and found a vantage point through a tent flap, from where I trained Tix̂lax̂'s rifle on the nefarious shaman.

Kuuyux, stealthy bastard that he was, had completely avoided engaging in the battle at hand in order to work some more of his mumbo jumbo bullshit upon the killing fields behind the laager of tents.

"Killing fields"—alas, how else to describe that tract of muskeg where Buckner's covert 17th Infantry detachment had been ambushed, their heads ripped off and impaled upon stakes in a circular formation, the center of which now hosted Kuuyux, kneeling and reciting some wicked incantation.

As the blood of the decapitated GIs seeped down the poles and into the sod surrounding the dark shaman, the muskeg before him stirred, stretched, and then began snapping vine by vine as some terrible creature forced its way up through the heath.

Vampire God 2 (*Exclusive art by Mike Dubisch*)

From what I could see, the emerging monster had horns, arms, eyes, and teeth, and continued to grow and metamorphose under the shaman's spell until at last it stood firmly upon clawed hindquarters as a formidable, fire-breathing dragon (for want of a more intelligible description).

Having become entranced by the uncanny spectacle, I finally came to my senses and fired a shot at Kuuyux's head.

The shaman calmly turned toward me. My bullet, if it'd been sure, had gone right through him.

The dragon took wing over my tent, the shaman's shape-shifting body flying at me in a spray of fire shortly thereafter.

I ducked behind the tent flap, which, with a weighty impact from the outside, began to incinerate.

I took to my heels, but all too late, for no sooner had I exited the tent did fire surround me, the heat of which felt like an instantly blistering sunburn. Miraculously, my wood-rod armor shielded me from direct contact with the conflagration, creating a buffer of empty space just inches between.

But as the shaman's inferno swarmed ever more feverishly around me, his laughing face appeared through the flames in nightmarish relief, his eyes, ears, nose, and fangs mere sharp, molten pinnacles. Alas, the heat was too much for me to bear: I dropped Tix̂lax̂'s rifle and fell to my knees, at last rolling onto my side and curling this way and that in the initial throes of an excruciating death.

Suddenly, I was lifted skyward out of the fire and beheld the underside of Igasix̂'s wings fluttering desperately as she retreated over the battlefield, carrying me firmly in her grasp. Not far behind us, I witnessed the terrible dragon darting this way and that, incinerating *iidigidi* as it went. It quickly came upon our heels and released a barrage of fire from its jaws, Igasix̂ winging up and athwart in impossible acrobatics, just avoiding the incendiary discharge. She continued to beat her wings and cavort around the dragon, which in turn continued to burn Unit 13 fighters or outright eat them as it advanced.

With each *iidigidi* consumed, the monster grew in might and bearing, while the cave clan fighters it burned—regardless of their wooden armor and supposed cloak of immortality—were all turned to ash.

The battle against the *khoughkh* had suddenly reached a critical state, the retreating *iidigidi* down to twenty-three and dwindling fast, until finally the dragon abandoned the pursuit, winging back toward the Red Head encampment.

We sought refuge on the side of a steep promontory, the sea barely visible through a steady fall of volcanic ash. Some of our unit had been inexplicably injured and so winged back to Adak, or otherwise were flown home by others if their injuries prevented their controlled piloting.

Down to sixteen, the remaining cave clan fighters (including myself) took stock of our weapons and argued our abilities against the *khoughkh* shape-shifters and their fire-shooting dragon. A periodic roar from the monster in the distance evinced its continued presence at Red Head, and with volcanic fallout mixing with a billowing Aleutian fog, day quickly darkened upon Unit 13.

FIRE ON THE MOUNTAIN

THE DECISION was made to stay and fight the dragon. The creature was mostly black, so we would wait until dawn on the following day to attack. Even though the shape-shifting *khoughkh* drew their fiery powers from the sunlight, to try to fight their fast-moving dragon at night would put us at too great a disadvantage. It had already been proven that our wooden armor could protect us against the incendiary magic of the *khoughkh* leadership, but not against the white-hot fire that blasted forth from the monster's mouth. The creature had been resistant to silver bullets, but it was believed by some of us surviving warriors (myself included) that a silver harpoon shot to the head might kill it. After all, the same tactic with a standard throwing-lance had been used to great effect against whales of the same approximate size as the beast we were now facing.

We tightened the seal-gut laces around our wooden armor and took stock of our silver harpoons. We had three of the full-length type remaining, replete with hallowed wood shafts and blest silver tips. A further inventory tallied two throwing-lances of similar construction, four silver swords, and my burly Rommel spike, forged of solid silver. After hemming out a plan of attack, we concealed ourselves within crevices along the bluff to wait out the night.

Tayaĝukichax̂ and I took third watch on the ridgeline above, and by then it was pitch black out, with the full moon and stars completely obscured by the volcanic brume that had drifted over Attu. Frequent, distant rumbles kept us on high alert, as did a recurring trembling of the earth. It would've been preferable to assume that such phenomena was the result of a volcano going off, but the terrifying reality was, it was equally as possible that the great dragon was making its presence known on Jackboot.

Tayaĝukichax̂ had brought a silver-tipped harpoon to the top, and I held tight to my Rommel spike as we peered west toward Red Head. (Our present location may've been closer to Red Beach, another US infantry landing site to our east.)

Suddenly, the promontory to our west flickered orange in fogbound relief, almost like a wildfire was creeping up from behind the mountain. Fixated on this inauspicious sight, Tayaĝukichax̂ and I didn't see Iĝanax̂ and Ivan emerging upon our ridgeline until they were standing before us, their unmistakable frames silhouetted against the conflagration behind.

Iĝanax̂, the Fallen Angel (*Illustration by Dusan Kostic*)

"Intruders!" Tayaĝukichax̂ cried, alerting the others as the pernicious duo made swift battle against us. Iĝanax̂ lunged at

Tayaĝukichax̂, while Ivan struck at me. I'd barely raised my Rommel stake when his blow hit it like a box of bricks, driving me back against the ground, our lances rudely crossing with an effusion of feral blue sparks. The power wrought by my holy silver picket was all that'd saved me, its static discharge swiftly spreading from Ivan's sword far up into his arm. He groaned and decreased his weight over me, and as he did, I delivered a firm kick into his chest, sending him tumbling back over the ridge.

Tayaĝukichax̂ had likewise barely had time to react to the surprise attack, but was succeeding in pushing Iĝanax̂ back with the sides of his holy harpoon, knocking the sickening *khoughkh* leader left and right with his silver-pointed staff. However, Tayaĝukichax̂ could not clear enough distance to engage his silver tip, nor could he grab any of his other weapons, so preoccupied were his hands.

Iĝanax̂, for his part, was striking back with his sword while flaring his body in fits and starts, trying to summon his fiery powers by night.

Igasix̂ landed before me and helped me to my feet, and as I stood, the shape of a Kodiak grizzly bear rose up menacingly behind her.

"Behind you!" I cried, but all too late as Ivan thrust his sword up into Igasix̂'s back, causing her to arch her shoulders and stand awkwardly erect.

"*Igasix̂!*"

She stumbled forth into my arms, her wooden armor breaking away from her chest and dangling upon Ivan's sword behind. She was trembling in fright, but had not been turned to dust—the Destroyer of Aleuts had missed her flesh, snagging only her armor.

"Get out of here!" warned Tayaĝukichax̂, who had just pushed his nemesis back with his harpoon-cum-staff. He tore

Igasix̂ from my arms and threw her back toward the relative safety of our hiding place beneath the ridgeline, for Iĝanax̂ was once again flaring his shoulders, and without the protection of her wood-rod armor, Igasix̂ would be easy prey for his fiery powers, should he at last succeed in evoking them.

The rest of Unit 13 had rallied, but before they could surround our enemies and enfilade the ridgeline, the black dragon came swooping down from the night sky, incinerating them left and right.

I charged at Ivan with my Rommel spike. He grabbed its side and flung me over his back. Alas, he and Iĝanax̂ came sauntering over my either side with their swords raised high.

The dragon had forced Tayaĝukichax̂ to take cover beneath the razorback, leaving me alone before the formidable *khoughkh* duo. Facing certain doom, I tore off my *chagudax̂* visor, exposing the bone crucifix worked into my forehead by Qihmux̂.

The eyes of my enemies flared red, smoked, and then bled black, causing them to turn away in unprecedented pain, at which point Tayaĝukichax̂ returned and we regained the edge, fighting our half-blinded opponents back up along the ridgeline.

As this was transpiring, scores more *khoughkh* infantry appeared out of the night to do battle, further harrying the remainder of our cave clan warriors, who were struggling enow to evade the crafty dragon. Thus we fought the collective *khoughkh* forces as best we could, eventually succumbing to our own constant retreat and attrition along the ridgeline. Whenever one of our *iidigidi* tried to fly off the razorback, the dragon swooped down and, by threat of fire or feasting, kept him running.

As we were being driven back along the promontory's lofty edge, I caught sight of Kuuyux watching from atop a rock pinnacle situated safely offshore, as was his cowardly nature in times of combat.

MOURNING OF THE EARTH

MORNING DAWNED ashen grey, Tayaĝukichax̂ and I backed to the end of the cape in critical combat against the varied *khoughkh* forces, the remainder of our unit likewise embroiled in monumental showdowns on our flanks. Here came a Jap vampire, there a shape-shifting flame, while from above and below blazed the dragon, harassing and killing us as it came. We'd only been able to *deflect* it with our harpoons: a clean shot to the head had yet to be obtained.

Kuuyux suddenly appeared amid the anarchy upon the cape, exhibiting a bold air of invincibility as he walked before Tayaĝukichax̂, reciting some black incantation. Or perhaps he wasn't suspecting the "son-of-a-dumb chief" to act so quickly, for before he could speak his seventh word, he was pierced through the heart by Tayaĝukichax̂'s throwing knife, forged in blest silver.

The shaman emitted a shriek both high enough to shatter glass and low enough to shake the earth, his body all the while dissolving into thousands of burning rats and flying bats.

I scampered around, trying to stomp the flaming pests, but it was a foregone conclusion: they soon turned to black ash at my feet, as did the burning bats flying over me, their unholy dust puff aftermaths summarily succumbing to hell's suctioning effect, *and down they went!*

In beholding his father's final death at the knife of the chief's son, Iĝanax̂ went berserk, wrapping around Tayaĝukichax̂ in a whirlwind of fire while slashing and chopping at him with lighting speed, driving him down against the ridgeline shale and succeeding in breaching his wooden armor, which flew apart in pieces.

Tayaĝukichax̂'s skin began to sizzle and smoke at the first exposure to Iĝanax̂'s unblocked power and, unable to hold him back, he screamed aloud, "Kayuu!"

Iĝanax̂'s back to me at last, I leapt over him with my Rommel spike and drove it down into his fiery mass. His body turned to black dust in Tayaĝukichax̂'s hands, then got sucked down between the crags of shale that had been supporting my stubborn old friend; next stop: hell. Tayaĝukichax̂ smiled up at me, even as his own flesh continued to sizzle. Then, suddenly, he frowned.

A sharp pain tore through my back as the tip of Ivan's iconic blade erected out from my chest beneath my right collarbone.

The murderous Cossack withdrew his blade. I looked blankly down at Tayaĝukichax̂, gasped, and then collapsed. Ivan had skewered me through the right side of my torso, opposite my heart, but still, bleeding out as I was and with one lung collapsed, I knew if I didn't get medical help fast, my death was *fait accompli.*

Avenging me, Tayaĝukichax̂ grabbed his harpoon off the ground and launched it up at Ivan. But his strength was diminished and the crags further hindered his aim: the mighty lance barely lopped over the Cossack's shoulder before disappearing over the ridge.

Ivan laughed with abandon, then approached Tayaĝukichax̂, who was just sitting up, and then the Cossack delivered a strong kick to the befuddled prince's chest, causing him to go tumbling over the opposite side of the ridge.

Now my death was certain, for even as I struggled to remain conscious, the Cossack raised his weighty sword with both hands, preparing to guillotine me upon the rocky razorback.

As the blade came down, I held up a hand, preparing to lose both it and my head; when suddenly Ivan was blindsided by a flying vamp, his sword sparking off the rocks at my ear with a loud *CHING!* as the battlers crash-landed next to me.

I glanced over to see Aniqdux̂six̂, already kneeling over Ivan with his head in her hands. A second later, she twisted his head in a full rotation, breaking his neck, then turned it again, tearing his skull free from his spine and connective flesh.

Ivan's body turned to black dust, as did his head in Aniqdux̂six̂'s hands. She dropped the chaff into the vacuum force already sucking between the shale, and as the remnants of the unholy Cossack were drawn down to hell, Aniqdux̂six̂ came over me and pleaded, "Kayuu! Please stay with me, Kayuu!"

She was squeezing my palms, grabbing my chin and slapping my cheeks, trying to keep me awake, but while dying in her hands, I hadn't even the energy left to warn her of the dragon appearing over the crest behind her. Furthermore, she kept looking to my side, because the crucifix in my forehead burned her eyes.

I tried to speak, but could only mumble, the monster all the while extending its scaly head and neck silently over the ridgeline like a cobra readying to strike.

"Jake, what is it?" Aniqdux̂six̂ was still rubbing my hands and looking beside me like a blind person, crying black blood all the while. "Please Kayuu—I don't want to lose thee!"

The dragon's eyes glistened like green emeralds, its black diamond pupils constricting as it honed in for the kill. It cocked its head back and opened its flaming jaws, revealing a white-hot furnace, readying to fire.

Whoever this Aniqdux̂six̂ was, I pained more over her pending passing than I did mine, for from what I could gather, her life had been one of continual strife.

I was about to close my eyes for the last time, when from out of the grey, Igasix̂ landed between us and the cocksure monster. She wrested my Rommel spike off the ground and pointed it at the rearing beast. "Wing it!" she cried back.

Knight Fighting Dragon (*Illustration by Dusan Kostic*)

Aniqdux̂six̂ turned, and we both watched Igasix̂ thrust my Rommel spike into the dragon's lower jaw.

The creature counterattacked with a blast of hellfire, but Aniqdux̂six̂ had already taken wing, narrowly evacuating me from its infernal stream.

"Igasix̂!" I forced a final cry. Alas, my young lover had been incinerated by the dragon, her white ashes rushing toward the heavens.

The fire-breathing behemoth began stumbling dizzily about, trying to extricate the silver spike from its lower jaw with its smallish arms and hands. It soon stumbled over the ridge-line, falling out of sight amid the swirling vog (an admixture of fog and volcanic ash).

Aniqdux̂six̂, while suffering excruciating pain from her injured shoulder, carefully set me down upon the rocks as the remaining Unit 13 fighters continued to smite lesser *khoughkh* on our peripheries.

I could barely keep my eyes open, and she could barely look at me without severely afflicting her own eyes. This unten-able situation on her part was resolved by her removing the horizontal bird bone transept from my forehead, at which point she looked at me with her eyes bleeding black and said, "All I wanted was to grow old and die with thee; but if I cannot die with thee, by the storm's cradle I pray thou shall forever live with me!"

She bore her fangs, and then lowered her head beside mine.

I exhaled a final breath.

A two-pronged pang struck deep into my neck.

All was blackness. I was dead.

TWILIGHT OF THE IMMORTALS

A DISTANT birdsong echoed into the dark recesses of my unconsciousness, become louder and more familiar as my awareness returned. It was the call of the Aleutian sparrow, trilling over a rumble of heavy surf emanating from somewhere below.

I was not breathing, yet I was cognizant of my surroundings; and by this I knew I had entered the afterlife. I opened my eyes slowly, for the light that filtered in was difficult to behold.

An angel appeared before me in the light, or so I assumed as I gazed blurrily at a winged hominid figure whose skin was white and scintillating.

My focus slowly returned and, as it did, I found myself staring into the golden eyes of Aniqdux̂six̂, who was smiling back at me with dripping red fangs, while her wings, dove white, were partially extended over us. She tenderly pushed my upper lip back on both sides, observing my mouth all the while.

I reached up and felt her hand, then followed it to my teeth. A pair of prominent canines now extruded from my upper palate.

My eyes widened in shock, glowing molten red in the reflection of hers, which flared likewise, subsuming the reflection of mine.

(Exclusive art by Ovidiu Kloska)

I gripped her hands and held on tight, overcome by a wave of emotion that no mortal words could describe. But a cursory attempt would be, "my life passed before my eyes," only it was the lifetime I'd spent with Aniqdux̂six̂ in the few short months I'd known her that I was reliving in one timeless moment. Kuuyux had erased my memory of her, and Chief Aĝnakax̂ had sent me away, but Aniqdux̂six̂ had somehow broken the spell, and now I remembered everything in one unbroken train...

I saw her taking me in from the storm, felt her making me warm and tending to my leg...

I saw us together in her father's burial cave, from where we repaired to her fumarole garden and shared our first kiss...

Aniqdux̂six̂'s fumarole garden, abundant with greenery and lavender even in the heart of winter (Exclusive photo by the author)

I was bathed in the warmth of her presence at the hot springs, where we first made *passionate* love...

I heard her speaking to me so regally, with a voice full of honor and sweetness...

I was with her every step of the way as we evolved together, falling in love, and in our slow dance following the whale hunt...

And I knew now what I'd for so long forgotten: I knew who Aniqdux̂six̂ was, intimately, as she'd known me in flesh and blood.

My hands, as pale as I'd ever seen them, trembled, while black tears flowed from the sides of my eyes: I was home again, in the arms of the only girl I'd ever truly loved, and we were very much alive. *Or were we...?*

"I'm so sorry, Kayuu," she sniffled, sharing my tears, "but I love thee too much to let you perish without me."

"The Shield of Repentance," I remembered; "it's gone. It is I who am sorry, Aniqdux̂six̂ —we had our promise."

"It wasn't thy fault: Igasix̂ put you up to it. But in the end, she sacrificed her immortality so that we could be together, forever-after."

"For that, Aniqdux̂six̂, we owe her an eternal debt of gratitude."

"I could not have spoken it better, Kayuu. Are you pleased by what I have done?"

"Saving my life?"

"*Umm*, Kayuu, just to be clear…" She fanged her lower lip worriedly, "thou hast died, but not ere I turned you into one of us: an *iidigidi.*"

"I sort of figured that out already."

"Oh, Kayuu, thou art my forever-after now. I wish that I shall satisfy thee."

"Remember the words you taught me, '*Txin yaktakug*'?" I inquired.

"Dost thou believe what I said?"

"More than believe: I know your heart, Aniqdux̂six̂, and it is good. And now, please listen closely as I return those words to you, knowing that I've always loved you, and shall forever-after. *Txin yaktakug*, Aniqdux̂six̂ —I love you."

She took me into her embrace and fluttered her wings, spinning us 'round and 'round, lifting us off the ridge interlocked, circling up as one, our wings beating in unison as we broke through the vog, shooting toward the sun.

ORIGINS OF POWER

LANDING AGAIN on the ridgeline, the dozen-odd remaining warriors, led by Tayaĝukichax̂, came over to congratulate us on becoming forever-after mates.

Aniqdux̂six̂ curtsied some, replying, "And I congratulate thee, brave fighters of Unit Thirteen, for winning the battle against the *khoughkh*. I see none are left in the vicinity, while I've recently reconnoitered Red Head and found the camp abandoned. You have prevailed on this momentous day for the *iidigidi* and all of mankind, while Igasix̂ has smote the dragon. May the ashes of our fallen return swiftly to the sun."

As the cave clan warriors raised their arms high in approbation, General Buckner appeared through the vog on the ridgeline, saying he'd flown in on his ski-plane. "It took me bloody three hours to climb up here," he growled. "What's going on in this sector? Where's the enemy now?"

All the *khoughkh* had turned to dust, and their dust had been sucked down to hell, so there was naught left for the general to see save for the surviving Unangax̂ infantry, Aniqduxsix̂, and me.

"What the hell happened to you?" he inquired. "Gone native, lieutenant?"

I lowered my eyes and kept a stiff upper lip over my fangs. "Collateral damage," I replied vaguely. "The Red Head sector has been cleared, sir. You're looking at the last of Unit Thirteen, who fought admirably in your service. How did you find us and what is the situation at Chichagof Harbor?"

"How'd I find you?" he scoffed. "For a while there, I thought this whole bloody ridge was on fire. What the hell happened up here, anyway, and why is your skin so white? It looks like you've seen a ghost!"

"We fought in Butler's service," grumbled Olean to no one in particular, but motioning toward Buckner, "not his."

"Speak up, soldier!" the general ordered. "What was that you said?"

"*Yaaa!*" Aniqduxsix̂ screamed.

Buckner turned; "Holy shit…"

The dragon lifted its head over the ridgeline behind the general and struck down with incredible force, taking Anĝix̂ into its jaws.

Buckner wasted no time in drawing his pistol and firing several rounds into the monster's head as it chewed on the female warrior.

Alas, Anĝix̂ quickly turned into ash, her white dust remnants funneling out between the dragon's teeth and zooming heavenward.

With my Rommel spike still dangling from the monster's maw, the creature's continued faculty for destruction remained unquestioned. Its black diamond pupils honed in on the general and then it cocked its head back, preparing to subsume the ruddy Kentuckian in a hellfire blast.

"Incoming!" Buckner cried, diving over the opposite side of the ridge.

The rest of us did likewise, and none too soon, for from over the ridgeline above, dragon's fire blasted forth as if from some ungodly flamethrower, shooting this way and that, forming a roiling red ceiling that all were loath to penetrate.

"Look there!" shouted Qatxamax, pointing toward the dead-end side of the razorback ridge.

A figure was approaching along the ridgeline as if out of nowhere, and paying no mind to the dragon's fire, kept walking directly into the inferno.

"Holy smokes!" exclaimed Tayaĝukichax̂, while the rest of us could only watch and gasp.

"*Father!*" Aniqdux̂six̂ cried. "You've come back!"

"*But how...?*" I wondered aloud at how a mummified man could return to life, for if it truly were Aniqdux̂six̂'s father, Alix̂ had been dead, like truly dead, for a very long time.

The lanky figure marched forth into the conflagration with jolting, robotic movements, probably because, for the most part, his body was a skeleton, with no flesh, muscles, or internal organs to help modulate his locomotion. He wore a spiked iron helmet, a seal-gut cape that fluttered in the fire without burning, and he carried a mighty, serrated sword. His chest, hands, and legs—the sum of the anatomy visible beneath his cape—were naught but bone, while black eye sockets, a skeletal ridgeline nose, and teeth without cheeks to hide them completed his living skull.

"Please explain!" Buckner demanded of Aniqdux̂six̂ as the fire blasted clear through the marching warrior's frame, blowing his cape hither and yon without incinerating it.

"By the power of Agugux," she shouted over the roaring inferno, "Alix̂ has risen! I mourned over my father in his *umqan*, evoking our sun god's name, Agugux! My cries have been answered, general! *Look!*"

The diabolical mummy stopped and turned, and while facing us from within the conflagration, he raised his mighty sword high over his head and emitted a terrible scream.

We cowered back in fright—all save for Aniqdux̂six̂, who remained watching in steadfast jubilation.

"But are you *sure* that's your dad?!" questioned Algax̂ Malihnax̂, the youngest remaining warrior among us.

Indeed, he wasn't the only one concerned that yet another eldritch being had been summoned from the gates of hell. The thing's continued posturing from within the firestorm appeared ever more malefic, and if the dragon was parcel to the mummy's inciting us, we didn't stand a chance.

"Yes!" Aniqdux̂six̂ exclaimed. "I'm sure! He's wearing the armor from his mummy sack!"

"This can't be happening!" the general deemed, shaking his head in dread, but he was quickly proved wrong by the mummy as it grabbed a horn on the dragon's head and flung its skeletal legs up over the behemoth's back, straddling it. And then, lifting its sword high with both hands, the mummy impaled the dragon through the top of the head.

The reptilian monster arched back, emitting a final, yawning moan while spraying fire this way and that, at last expiring, head to tail like spilling sand, into a heap of black ash. The black dust disappeared into the crags of the rocky razorback, and in the smoky aftermath stood Aniqdux̂six̂ father, conqueror of dragons.

Aniqdux̂six̂ started on foot after him, but the shale lining the ridge was so hot from the conflagration that she ended by taking wing. As she hovered before her otherworldly father, they shared words none could hear, and then he touched his sword to her injured shoulder, causing her burnt flesh to effervesce with violet sparkles before instantly healing over.

"Remarkable," breathed Buckner, getting to his feet, while the cave clan likewise rose in awe, beholding the mummy's great powers.

Alix̂ proceeded before us, and standing upon the ridgeline not ten meters away, addressed our unit thus:

"*Taanga*, Kayuu, for killing Iĝanax̂. The backstabber deserved to die. You have by right and honor earned my daughter's forever-lasting alliance."

He then thanked the young prince in Unangam Tunuu, saying, "*Taanga*, Tayaĝukichax̂, for disposing of the traitorous Kuuyux. You by right and honor have earned your place as chief."

As the sun broke through the clouds over Alix̂'s shoulder, he continued with booming voice: "And my beloved daughter, Aniqdux̂six̂, who by her own power has spurred the will of Aguguax to enable me to fight another day! Let it be known throughout all time and history that it was she who smote Solov'iev, Destroyer of Aleuts!

"Your deeds here today are worthy of your great ancestors, the first cave-dwelling immortals! I shall now return to reside with them on the Island of Four Mountains, where we will forever watch over and protect our original place of power!"

With that, Alix̂ turned and continued marching east among the snowcapped peaks.

Skeleton Knight in Winter (*Illustration by Dusan Kostic*)

In all, only seven *iidigidi* warriors were left from our initial battalion of fifty-two, and the lot of them remained speechless by the mummy's visitation.

Buckner, after likewise gawking at the departing being, uttered to the remaining unit: "I'm sorry for underestimating your powers. I have misunderstood."

"Look there, general!" announced Aguuĝax̂, the only remaining female in Unit 13. "A submarine!"

Buckner donned his binoculars and followed her pointed finger to the eastern cape of Red Head. "An *RO-Thirteen*," he murmured through clenched teeth. "Those blasted Japs are escaping!"

He procured a radiophone from beneath his parka and radioed for Colonel Eareckson to deliver a 250 pound bomb to the sub posthaste, but as the boat moved offshore and submerged, chances of that became ever more dubious. (Eareckson was already en route from Amchitka, but not yet over Attu waters.)

Colonel Eareckson poses before a Martin B-26 Marauder medium bomber, which could reach a top speed of 315 miles per hour and required a well-experienced pilot to safely fly, especially in Aleutian airspace. His other preferred aircraft at the time were the Consolidated B-24 Liberator heavy bomber, the P-40 Warhawk, and the B-17 Flying Fortress. Colonel Eareckson served in World War I, World War II, and the Korean War. (Exclusive photo by Lt. Harper, Adak Island, 1943)

As we awaited Colonel E's B-24 Liberator, Buckner posed the question, "Were those operatives of Baron Tanaka?"

Baron Tanaka was supposed to have died in 1929, and nobody could answer. But it begged the question: Was Tanaka still alive as a vampire, or behind the secretive *khoughkh* army?

"What's the situation on the east side of the island?" I inquired.

"We succeeded in backing the Japs onto Fishhook Ridge overlooking Chichagof Harbor," Buckner said, "but then on May twenty-ninth, Colonel Yasuyo Yamasaki launched a massive Banzai charge of a thousand men in a counterattack. They ambushed our infantry, our command posts and medical stations, slaughtering us by all means, while yelling, 'Japanese drink blood like wine!'"

"...Drink blood like wine," he repeated in soliloquy, his brows crunching in critical thought, "*hmmm...*"

"So have they been stopped?" Tayaĝukichax̂ asked outright.

"Yes, sir," replied Buckner, at last speaking respectfully to an indigene, "by a detachment of army engineers, who ultimately resorted to their bare hands in combating the surprise counteroffensive."

"Then your soldiers probably weren't batting *khoughkh* forces," Tayaĝukichax̂ remarked. "But I congratulate you and your men, nevertheless. We all must fight with the hands, or wings, we've been given." The new chief winked at the old general, who smiled stiffly in return.

Finally, Eareckson's plane arrived. He circled around a mile offshore of Red Head, searching for the enemy sub. His bomb bay doors never opened, his eggs remaining in cold incubation within the hull of his humming Liberator.

"Well," Buckner reluctantly conceded, "we're still mopping up. Next comes Boodle."

軍神山崎部隊長像

松田文雄筆

Colonel Yasuyo Yamasaki, the commander of the Japanese defenders on Attu Island during the Battle of Attu. Although the Japanese defenders were greatly outnumbered (2,900 Japanese vs. 15,000 Americans), Colonel Yamasaki showed noteworthy leadership throughout the battle, fighting off American attacks for nearly three weeks. On the last day of battle, Yamasaki, with sword in hand, led a massive Banzai-charge against several American positions. His attack penetrated deep across the American lines and inflicted heavy casualties on US troops in a furious hand-to-hand combat that lasted for hours, until almost all the Japanese soldiers, including Yamasaki, were killed. After his death, Yamasaki became a national hero, and was widely admired for his bravery in battle. (Propaganda postcard issued by the Imperial Japanese Army during World War II. Artwork by Fumio Matsuda. Note Colonel Yamasaki's holding a stake to his heart, and his webbed feet, which some believe symbolize the death of a great khoughkh leader in the Imperial Japanese Army)

"Where?" queried Tayaĝukichax̂.

Buckner returned a wink and replied, "You'll find out soon enough. For now, I'll see you all back on Adak." With that, the general marched down into a lingering patch of fog and into Aleutian Campaign history.

More Japanese midget submarines found on Kiska, along with an entire operational sub base that was left abandoned during the enemy's hasty retreat (Dept. of US Navy photo, 1943)

AFTERMATH

IN CHIEF Aĝnakax̂'s passing, Tayaĝukichax̂, his surviving son, became the new clan leader by default. The jocular young prince would have to reconsolidate the remaining tribe and rebuild their lives from the blown-out barabara up. But none, not even I, questioned his potential to lead the *iidigidi* of Adak, given his brave and selfless actions in battle, while Alix̂ himself, that immortal of Immortal ancestors, had openly praised Tayaĝukichax̂ for disposing Kuuyux, the shaman imposter who'd hurt the clan the most.

Whether I should stay on or not was already a foregone conclusion in my heart as much as it was in my mind. I had flocked with my remaining Unit 13 comrades back to Boot

Bay, where TayaĝukichaX̂ called me "brother" and "second-in-command," Datuu was on good terms with me once again, and where AniqduX̂siX̂'s clan fully accepted me in, based upon her love for me and tales already circulating of my reputed heroism in combat. Only QihmuX̂ appeared displeased by my return, probably because I'd come back holding her envied sister's hand. QihmuX̂'s boyfriend QaguX̂ had died at the Battle of Three Arm Bay, while she had tried to get me to be IgasiX̂'s forever-after mate while I was under Kuuyux's amnesiac spell. In short, she'd always been jealous of what AniqduX̂siX̂ and I had going, because it was true love, unbound by culture, authority, circumstances, and time itself. All I could offer QihmuX̂ was my remorse at QaguX̂'s passing, and to remind her that he died protecting the rest of us, adding, "Don't wait for your gen-cycle to be up, or you'll remain bitter for a very long time."

"Japanese base at Holtz Bay, Attu, after it was captured by the Allied troops in May, 1943." In the background are several USN landing craft, along with a Daihatsu landing barge approximately fourteen meters in length. (Dept. of US Navy photo, with original caption in quotation marks, 1943)

Traditionally, Aleuts had no marriage ceremony. But AniqduX̂siX̂ had for decades dreamed of having a modern ceremony, like the kind she'd seen contemporary Aleuts entering Russian Orthodox chapels to experience.

Now, for obvious reasons, a church marriage was out of the question for us. We'd never get past the front door without smoking like dressed salmon. So we improvised, holding our marriage on the dunes overlooking Boot Bay, where, as summer beach fleabane wobbled like sunflowers amid the windblown wild rye, Olean, that august old whaler and friend, wedded us with a reading selected by Aniqdux̂six̂, a poem by William Shakespeare entitled *Hymen of the Forest*—

> *You and you no cross shall part;*
> *You and you are heart in heart;*
> *You to his love must accord,*
> *Or have a woman to your lord;*
> *You and you are sure together,*
> *As the winter to foul weather*

Whereupon we vowed, "Till death do us part," which would probably be forever.

Close-up of Natives of Oonalashka, and their Habitations, *showing women emerging from a traditional barabara, as drawn by HMS* Resolution's *artist John Webber*

As for Simon Buckner and William Butler, they soon met in private about the Red Head incident and agreed to keep the whole operation there, and the Adak cave clan, Code 1 Classified. The dossier of evidence was locked into a vault at Foggy Bottom, from where it was eventually transferred to the Pentagon.

EPILOGUE

IN THE spring of 1945, after the Aleutian campaign was officially over, the Aleuts who'd been displaced by the war returned to their homes but, by then, one in every four native evacuees had died from diseases and hardships associated with Alaska's internment camps, which, given this high casualty figure, was what the evacuation centers basically amounted to. The refugees simply were not acclimated to the sudden change in environment, where they were exposed to numerous new diseases.

Then came the 1960s' nuclear bomb tests in the Aleutians, primarily on Amchitka Island in the Rat Island group. The largest underground nuclear test ever conducted by the United States happened there, and, to this day, radioactive materials leak from Amchitka's shores. So while the war against the Japanese was concluded and the remaining Aleuts repatriated, the ravages to their race and homeland that started during wartime and continued well into the second half of the twentieth century have not been remediated so easily.

Adak Island's 50+ year status as a multiuse military facility has left a buildup of infrastructure, housing, materiél, and toxic wastes, including unexploded ordnance, landfills, spill sites, pits, and drum disposal areas containing an uncanny gallimaufry of hazardous substances. The northern half of Adak is especially infamous for its ghost town barracks and abandoned military assets in various stages of decomposition and disposal, such as in the photo at the bottom of the previous page, which shows discarded barrels near Finger Cove, and in the photo at top, which looks out from a shattered barracks window upon the massive military housing enclave of Bering Hill. (Both pictures are exclusives and were taken by the author in 2015)

While the Adak U.S. Naval Air Facility was decommissioned by the Pentagon in 1992, and the base operationally closed on September 31, 2000, the island has been left with a military legacy of toxic debris and UXO (unexploded ordnance), with many areas remaining off-limits because of it. Even the occasional Rommel stake can still be found rusting above the muskeg, but the most critical hazards, aside from UXO, are in the recently cleaned disposal areas for substances such as transformer oils containing polychlorinated biphenyls (PCBs), chlorinated solvents, batteries, petroleum, and other releases, all of which were contaminating the groundwater, sediments, and soil.

The navy began remedy construction in 1996 by capping old landfills, excavating contaminated soils, treating infected groundwater, and clearing UXO. While most of the contaminant cleanup has been finished, unexploded ordnance removal remains ongoing, and in some of these areas access has been restricted, preventing the wider removal of toxic contaminants. A tract identified as OU B-2, for example, has so much UXO that the navy refuses to place a timeline on when exactly the removal action will be completed. This is unsurprising, given the isolated nature of the island and the magnitude of the job in those highly volatile tracts, which have anyway been well fenced off from public use. In fact, it is a federal offense to trespass in these well-marked areas, not to mention a mortally risky endeavor.

But the navy has clearly not abandoned ship on Adak, where its remediation efforts continue in the form of long-term maintenance and monitoring of hazards, as well as short-term cleanups that address "immediate threats to human health and the environment." More than twenty such urgent removal actions have occurred since year 2000, usually addressing the cleanup of PCB-contaminated soils, buried drums, UXO, and other releases.

The view at the bottom of the previous page is of the eerie "Parcel 4" on Adak's north shore. This stretch along Andrew Bay was used by the U.S. military for target practice and as a hazardous wastes dumpsite from World War II onward. Because of that, it is rife with UXO and leaking toxins, and remains strictly off-limits to the general public. The photo above displays a formidable Panama gun mount, one of several 155 mm coastal artillery pads slowly rusting away in plain sight along the Zeto Point area just east of Adak town proper. (Both photos are exclusives and were taken by the author in 2015)

But Adak Island is big, sprawling, and for the most part pristine and untouched, having been recertified in 1980 as part of the Alaska Maritime National Wildlife Refuge, while Aleut culture is also on the comeback, with their own seafood processing plants begun on Adak, Atka, and beyond, and language and cultural revival movements happening from Dutch Harbor, to islands north, east, and west.

"Most of Adak Island remains pristine and untouched," with the waterfall at the top, spilling down through lush tundra from Lake Betty, serving as a prime example, while below is a picture of the equally gorgeous natural setting of Nurses Beach closer to downtown Adak. (Exclusive photos by the author)

Lieutenant Harper, on his own accord, chose to return with the cave clan to their bombed-out barabara, where he helped rebuild their Adak home and lifestyle, ultimately settling down on that special emerald isle with his new wife and tribe.

Onetime Chief Aĝnakax̂'s gen-cycle was abandoned by the new chief—his son Tayaĝukichax̂—who, in overseeing Jake and Aniqdux̂six̂'s formal union, decided he wanted a new wife of his own and didn't care to wait a total of two hundred and seventy years to remarry. But many of his father's other dictates remained strong and effective, having been deemed as indispensable by his only surviving son.

To this day, Lieutenant Harper and the cave clan are always preparing, training, and watching for the return of the *khoughkh*. The next war will be different, they believe. It could start tomorrow, or it could start centuries in the future, but make no mistake about it: the *iidigidi* will be ready and waiting, for they will *never* be driven from their homeland.

The Unangans share an ancestry of unbroken Aleutian Islands habitation of 9,000 years, and over those many millennia they've successfully warded off a plethora of incursions and attacks. Now, thanks to the power and resolve of the Aleutian vampires and the love they share for their homeland, that tradition will continue. After all, Aniqdux̂six̂ had just showed the world, or at least the glittering emerald isles draped across its neck, that love conquers all—even death itself.

AFTERWORD

Seabees Raise a Tent City on Attu—Their tents spreading over a wide area,
Navy Seabees rush work on establishing an American Base on Attu Island,
recently captured from the Japs. Landing boats are bringing supplies ashore.
(Dept. of US Navy Wirephoto, AP caption, 1943 [ref# c31524])

IN 1987, the Japanese government placed a prodigious star-burst monument on Attu Island. The official line from Tokyo was that the memorial, made of solid steel titanium, intended to recognize the sacrifice, in lives, of soldiers who served on "Jackboot," both Imperial and Allied.

But in truth, the Attu Monument is constructed of silver titanium and covertly symbolizes *khoughkh* defiance against the *iidigidi*. Moreover, it's a six ton reserve of silver that the imperial *khoughkh* intend to melt down into weapons when they resume their attack on American/Aleut soil, and worldwide. Eleven of these silver titanium starburst monuments have already been strategically placed throughout the Pacific, and each one is structurally identical. Thus the *khoughkh* have marked their territory, their future "ground zeroes" from where they will one day restart their war against the *iidigidi* and its Western Allies.

Japanese Monument, Engineer Hill, Attu Island (Photo by Jan Kocian)

The Pentagon is well aware of the Imperial Japanese *khoughkh* ascendancy, thanks to a classified monitoring program started by General Buckner before he was killed in action on Okinawa. Yes, Simon Buckner Jr. proved himself a frontlines man in the end, tragically taking a stray enemy projectile in his chest late in Pacific combat operations, on June 18, 1945. He died in Okinawa a three-star general, which equated to the highest-ranking US military officer to be killed by enemy fire during World War II. In 1954, his astute service and heroic deeds were formally recognized by a special act of Congress that posthumously promoted him to the rank of full four-star general.

Buckner's covert World War II dossier kept on the *khoughkh* had been started none too soon, enabling the United States to track the enemy vampires as they infiltrated the Korean leadership during the Korean War to follow. The *khoughkh* established, and still maintain, a major base of operations in North Korea, where there can be less scrutiny of their activities. The North Korean labor camps are believed to supply the *khoughkh* overlords with human blood as they attempt to weaponize the *promuishlenniki* plague via their clandestine "nuclear" program.

Recent CIA documents show the North Korean leadership working out of a secret base beneath the Ryugyong Hotel in Pyongyang, a building in itself composed of silver titanium. This promiscuous superstructure could supply enough core materiél to equip a massive *khoughkh* army with anti-*iidigidi*-grade weaponry in short order.

Ryugyong Hotel, Pyongyang, North Korea (Photo by classified source)

Thus the covert war against the *khoughkh* continues, the Allies dealing with them like a terrorist organization and preferring to whittle away their leadership from the top down and bottom up, while constantly trying to reassess their potentialities. However, given the near seamless stranglehold the North Korean leadership has on its country and borders, it has proven very difficult to send in moles or to recruit them from the local populace. Reconnaissance is ongoing.

Aleutian War Summary

The following brief summary of the Aleutian Campaign comes from the collectible *Story of America Card #77-18* [© 1981, Panarizon Publishing Corp, USA, used by permission], offering a realistic snapshot of the conflict and some intriguing background information.

The Aleutian Campaign—1942–1943—Battle under Bizarre Conditions
"During World War II the men who were sent to fight on Alaska's Aleutian Islands faced one of the war's toughest assignments in terms of weather. Stretching more than 1,000 miles (1,610 km) west from the mainland in a long string, the Aleutians mark the line where the weather of the Pacific Ocean meets that of the Bering Sea. Constantly shrouded in icy fogs and rain and torn by terrible snow-choked winds called 'williwaws,' the Aleutians are barren, treeless, muck-covered volcanic islands. Additionally, the area was then poorly mapped and was so close to the pole that magnetic compasses gave distorted readings.

"The Aleutian campaign began in June 1942 as part of the battle of Midway. When Lt. Col. Jimmy Doolittle's bombers, flying from a US carrier, bombed Tokyo in April, the Japanese mistakenly believed they had come from bases in the western Aleutians. Thus, in June, when Adm. Yamamoto launched the Midway Operation, Japanese warships were sent to strike at the US base at Dutch Harbor, close to the mainland, and Japanese troops were landed on the western islands of Attu and Kiska."

Oil tanks burn at Dutch Harbor during a nighttime bombing raid by the Japanese on June 3–4, 1942. The fires glow on the water across the bay. (Exclusive photo by Lt. Harper, whose cursive on the back reads: "Japanese bombing Dutch Harbor. Oil tanks burning.")

"Japan wanted to secure the flank of her conquests in the Pacific and to protect her home from further bombing. But the Aleutian conquest was played up in Japan's propaganda. This, together with the islands' proximity to the United States, quickly led to an American counteroffensive. But the problems of bringing men and equipment into the remote and inhospitable area were enormous, and bases had to be built from scratch."

These early May 1943 photos of the first U.S. landing on Attu illustrate the enormity of the task in transporting enough men and matériel to oust the Japanese from the rugged, remote, and inhospitable island, whose shores were fringed with jagged reefs, whose lowlands were muck-covered and slippery, and whose mountains were steep, icy, and fogbound. Complicating matters even more was typically terrible flying weather, and the fact that the spring of 1943 would go down as one of the coldest in recorded Aleutian Islands meteorological history. (11th Army Air Force photo, including sector zoom for detail, 1943)

"By November 1942 the Alcan Highway somehow was built. Stretching from the United States to Alaska, it served to bring an increasing flow of men and supplies to the war zone.

"Finally, in May 1943, Attu was retaken after a bloody battle. (Ironically, it could have been taken at little cost not long before, because the enemy had temporarily evacuated it.) In August 1943, weeks after the Japanese had left it, the island of Kiska was occupied by US forces. Overall, both sides lost more men and materiél to the weather than in the warfare.

"The Aleutians were an impossible battle zone—a trap into which both sides were drawn by mistaken estimates of enemy intentions. But, in winning the campaign, the United States secured her northern Pacific flank, assured a flow of supplies from the United States to the Soviets in Asia, and opened Alaska to postwar development.'

The new Adak runway with beautiful Great Sitkin in the background (AP, undated)

Adak Island in 1961, showing the Bering Barracks and Chapel, with
Mt. Sitkin in the background (Photo by Paul B. Lowrey)

Graphics Data

Use rights and/or full ownership rights have been properly obtained for all images, photographs, graphics, and maps found in this book that are not already in the public domain. Images marked "exclusive" indicate they are one-of-a-kind originals found only in this book. No text or images shall be reproduced outside of this book for any reason, except for the quoting of limited sections of text for review, advertisement, or marketing purposes.

The patches displayed in a cross design on the book cover are, from top to bottom:

Air Traffic Control Facility Adak Alaska #2 (1960s);

Attu Blood and Ice Wargames (1980s);

U.S. Army Alaska Defense Command (ADC) polar bear patch, original issue from 1940 to 1943 when commanded under Colonel Simon B. Buckner;

Original, red borderless patch of the 7th Infantry Division of the U.S. Army during World War II, who fought intensely on Attu beginning on May 12, 1943 (in the 19 days that followed, 549 of their soldiers were killed on Attu, and more than 1,200 injured);

U.S. 11th Army Air Forces (AAF) Alaska original shoulder patch as worn by Task Force "X" and the Air Striking Group as commanded by General William O. Butler (1942).

The patches from left to right are:

Late-period World War II Alaska Air Command Army Air Force uniform patch (1945);

Attu Blood and Ice Wargames patch (again);

U.S. Army Northwest Service Command shoulder sleeve field patch (authorized to wear on March 23, 1943)—this unit was largely responsible for the construction of the 1,700-mile Alcan Highway, which connects the contiguous United States to Alaska across Canada, and which was completed in 1942 in just under eight months of round-the-clock construction time.

Disclaimer

This is a work of historical fiction. All dialogue and incidents, with the exception of some well-known historical and public incidents, and all characters, with the exception of some well-known historical and public figures, are products of the authors' imagination and are not to be construed as real. Where real-life historical or public figures appear, the events and dialogue concerning those persons are not intended to depict actual incidents or to change the fictional nature of this work. Any semblance to similar events or characters extraneous to this work is entirely coincidental and purely unintentional by the authors.

This book does not realistically attempt to displace or replace Aleut culture and history, or World War II history as it relates to the Aleutian campaign. The authors share the deepest respect for the Unangax̂ people, and for the hearty and heroic Allied troops who served in the "Forgotten War."

"Historical fiction"? This was the coauthor's tough call when considering a report from settings that are both "stranger than fiction." The photo at the bottom of the previous page, for example, is purportedly the gravesite of Lieutenant Jake Harper, while the picture above reveals a defunct nuclear missile facility, both of which he photographed on Adak Island during his research there, and both of which aren't supposed to exist. Thus, for his own peace of mind regarding oxymorons such as these, he chose the label of "historical fiction" to err on the side of commonly accepted history, even as contrary evidence slowly creeps into the public sphere.

Qaĝaasakung!

Janice, Ocean, and Asia Haber, in whom I find my home; Bill Haber, Imelda Cleary (Adak), Michael Rainey (thank you for your service), Debra Sharrah (Adak), Keith Hamilton (Unalaska), Susie Silook (Paallengetaq), Darren Bereskin (Akun), Nancy Zaochnee (Atka), Cynthia Galaktionoff, Elaine Smiloff (Adak), Brenda Baker (Unalaska), Di T. Tran, Doanh Thi Tran, Cory Herendeen (of Aleutian Outfitters on Adak, probably one of the most knowledgeable outdoorsmen out there today), Ovidiu Kloska, Sharmaine Santiago-Butac (Laoag, Philippines), Amnet Systems (India), Randy Lum, Paul Diamond, Ed Gregor, Sean Stratton, Eric Holland, Ari Marsh, James Senechal, my grandfather Norman Haber (a navy pilot [enlisted 1940–1946] who was flying reconnaissance near the Japanese squadron as they approached Pearl Harbor on that fateful day in 1941—he was just twenty miles athwart of changing the course of history; he earned the Distinguished Flying Cross for his actions at Pearl, Elsie, and Midway), and to all the courageous Allies who served during World War II, your sacrifice is the Free World's greatest legacy.

Little Falls Cemetery, Attu, Aleutian Islands, Alaska, 1944. The cemetery was a temporary location for deceased soldiers during the Aleutian Campaign of World War II. In 1946, the Americans' remains were removed and buried at Ft. Richardson near Anchorage, AK, or in other locations as designated by their relatives. Since then, the ground on Attu known as "Little Falls Cemetery" has been recaptured by the tundra... with no visible signs of it today. (Photo by unnamed U.S. Army Air Force soldier belonging to the 77th Bombardment Squadron assigned to the Alexai Point Airfield)

Finally, I offer my heartfelt thanks and gratitude to the Unangan race for inspiring me to write this book. You are truly original people that the world can learn much from.

Quinn Robert Haber, coauthor and editor-in-chief on assignment in Adak Island

Other Great Titles from Phantasea Books

Tonkin
The Somali Pirate Trilogy
Old Lanai: A True Ghost Story from Hawaii
The Volcano Trilogy: A Philippines Surfing Odyssey
Islands on the Fringe: A Year of Micronesian Waves and Wanderers
The Heart of a Traveler: Reflections from the Fathomless Edge of the World

Promotional flyer posted in Adak's only grocery mart, "The 100 Knot Stop," broadcasting the original Aleutian Vampire Book Tour Signing Event to all 150 of the island's remaining residents in 2015. It was a smash hit!

PHANTASEA BOOKS
HONOLULU, HI